Dear Reader,

This month we [...] ces for you which we hope will help chase away those winter blues.

Share *That Cinderella Feeling* with Anne Styles's heroine and find out if 'Cinderella' Casey really does live happily ever after . . . When the lawyer meets the dancer, sparks are bound to fly – and they do in *The Marriage Dance*, as author Jillian James brings us a new slant on the old problem of reluctance to commit. We are delighted, too, to bring you *A Darker Shadow*, the latest long novel by Patricia Wilson, in which Luc Martell is forced to remain in England with computer buff Amy Scott – the bane of his life. And finally, *Slow Dancing* by Elizabeth Smith shows us that life in Hollywood isn't always the stuff of dreams.

As always, it has been a pleasure *and* a challenge for me to select these latest *Scarlet* titles for you and I hope that you enjoy reading these books as much as I did.

Keep those letters and questionnaires flooding in, won't you? We are always happy to hear from you. And don't forget, if you want to write to a favourite *Scarlet* author, I'll be glad to pass on your letter.

Till next month,
Best wishes,

Sally Cooper

SALLY COOPER,
Editor-in-Chief – *Scarlet*

About the Author

Patricia Wilson was born in Yorkshire and is married to her childhood sweetheart. Her husband's work took them to live in Singapore and Africa and Patricia now lives most of the time in the South of France or Spain.

She gave up her career as a teacher in order to write and has become so popular that over eighteen million copies of her books have been sold throughout the world.

Patricia first started writing when she was in her teens. She tried her hand at children's stories, detective novels and historical romances before realizing that she should focus her efforts on becoming a romantic fiction writer. Her books always reflect Patricia's deep interest in people and her sensitive understanding of personal relationships.

Scarlet is delighted to offer readers the latest long novel by this best-selling author of more than forty romances.

Other *Scarlet* titles available this month:

THE MARRIAGE DANCE – Jillian James
THAT CINDERELLA FEELING – Anne Styles
SLOW DANCING – Elizabeth Smith

PATRICIA WILSON

A DARKER SHADOW

SCARLET

Enquiries to:
Robinson Publishing Ltd
7 Kensington Church Court
London W8 4SP

First published in the UK by Scarlet, 1998

A copy of the British Library Cataloguing in
Publication data is available from the British Library

ISBN 1-85487-871-9

Printed and bound in the EC

10 9 8 7 6 5 4 3 2 1

CHAPTER 1

It was a beautiful day and Amy tried to think of the lines that people quoted about a funeral, but all she could remember was 'Happy the bride the sun shines on today.'

Most inappropriate – not only because it was a funeral but also because Aunt Celia had never married. She had scorned the idea of matrimony, declaring acidly that no man was worth the sacrifice of complete liberty and the control of one's own destiny.

Amy wondered if Aunt Celia had died a virgin. It was something she had never considered before, and the fact that the question had drifted into her mind now positively shocked her. It was a very improper thought, here in this place with all the solemnity, but it was something to do with the purpose of life, she mused, something to do with what it was all about anyway.

She tried to listen to the vicar but it was difficult. He was behaving as if he was addressing a vast multitude, turning his head from side to side to include everybody. When he turned his head away she couldn't quite hear him. His voice drifted into the distance.

He was boring now at this stage of the funeral, in any case, because he was simply repeating things he had said so often. In the church it had been different, but his words by the grave were very monotonous and rather mechanical as far as she could make out. Amy had the feeling that his mind wasn't quite on it.

It was a lovely old churchyard with very ancient headstones, many of them moss-covered, some of them as old as the church itself. The church was Saxon, one of the very few remaining examples, and Amy wondered how it had survived with a busy, thriving town not more than ten miles away. The church was also quite close to the rather splendid house where Aunt Celia had spent most of her adult life.

The fact that her aunt had wanted to be buried here had greatly surprised Amy. Knowing Celia better than anyone else had done, Amy would quite have expected that any orders would have been in keeping with her aunt's general attitude to life and other people.

Something like, 'Put me under that big tree in the garden and see that a powerful electric fence is put round the whole area. See that it's tasteful.' But Aunt Celia had specified this place, this church, and now she was gone.

There were not many people at the funeral and Amy thought that was sad, even though she knew her aunt had discouraged most people while she was alive. Aunt Celia's imperious nature and her acid tongue had not been an incitement towards friendship.

Over the years, most people had drifted away, avoiding her wherever possible. There really were not hordes of friends to come and mourn her passing, but Amy had expected a few more than the mere handful who had turned up.

Surprisingly enough there was a neighbour, a fact which astonished Amy, considering that her aunt had issued writs against the poor woman when her dog had made frequent forays into the garden which had been Aunt Celia's pride and joy. The disquieting thought came into Amy's head that the neighbour was perhaps here to make quite sure that Celia was finally gone, and couldn't pop back to harass her ever again.

Mr Hetherington, Senior, was there, looking suitably saddened. He had been her aunt's solicitor for years, and had battled with her endlessly and skilfully, but he had been quite fond of her and even though he was now retired he had come to pay his last respects.

'Respect' was a word that suited her aunt very well, because although most people had either avoided her or quarrelled with her – when they had dared – the respect had always been there. Amy had really loved her even if nobody else had, and she was going to miss her badly.

She assumed that respect was the only thing that had brought Uncle Peter here today too, because certainly there had been no affection for his stepsister. During the past few years he had never once mentioned her to Amy and Aunt Celia had refused to even breathe his name.

Of course he was probably here just to give

support, and Amy was glad of it. It was good to have her hand tucked under his arm as the vicar intoned the final, doleful words.

And Peter Jensen knew how to deal with most things. He knew, for example, when to urge Amy away and turn her from the grave and out into the sunlight along the path to the gate. He knew exactly what to say to the vicar as they left. He knew what words to utter to Mr Hetherington, Senior, and how to nod in a sad and kindly manner to the neighbour who was, in fact, now crying openly.

Amy stared at her in astonishment and then sighed as Peter guided her away and onwards towards the gate. Some people came to funerals just for a good cry; she'd heard about that. They read the obituary columns in the newspapers for the same reason, weeping over people they had never even met. It was really a terrible shame, inexplicable to Amy. Maybe it was their only way to grasp emotion?

'The saddest thing, though,' Amy said aloud, looking round in a mournful way, 'is that life goes on.'

'Of course it does,' Peter Jensen muttered a trifle impatiently. 'Now remember, you have to face this sensibly, Amy. Just because Celia's died there's no reason for the world to stop turning.'

'Well, it wouldn't, would it?' Amy countered, giving him a swift reproachful glance. 'I'm just saying it's sad that Aunt Celia died, sadder still that things go on as if she'd never existed.'

'It's this place, love,' Peter assured her, dropping his words of stern caution and becoming avuncular. 'The atmosphere is getting to you. A funeral is enough to upset anyone. I'm glad I came with you.'

'So am I, Uncle Peter.'

Amy tucked her hand back under his arm and tried to throw off the feeling of vague insecurity that the loss of her aunt had brought. She knew that Aunt Celia had been seventy, but that was no age at all nowadays and it had all been so unexpected. A sudden heart attack, astonishing in such a vigorous woman.

'I thought she would live for ever,' she murmured, and Peter covered her hand with his, giving her fingers a little squeeze of sympathy.

'It was quick,' he reminded her in a soothing voice.

'Too damned quick!' Amy snapped, not really appreciating his attitude. 'I never got the chance to say goodbye. She brought me up and I just let her slip quietly out of my life. I feel as if I've carelessly lost her, as if I've misplaced a valuable possession through lack of attention to detail. I feel thoroughly selfish.'

'Now just stop that, Amy!' He planted his feet firmly and turned to her with equal sharpness. 'People die. It happens. You're clever, successful and grown up. Pull yourself out of this before it gets a grip on you. If you're going to start shouldering the blame for the fact that Celia neglected her health . . .'

'She didn't! Nobody knew she had a bad heart. She didn't even know herself.'

'She must have had some symptoms, and in any case she should have had regular check-ups at her age. I do.'

5

'You're only fifty,' Amy reminded him.

'Then all the more reason for Celia to have check-ups at seventy.'

'Maybe she didn't want to know,' Amy mused gloomily, and Peter Jensen frowned at her, letting his exasperation surface.

'You're simply being morbid, Amy. You've got to stop this right now. Let's get out of this place and back amongst living people. It's all over.'

He turned for the gate again, quickening his pace and drawing Amy along with him, but her eyes still lingered on the green of the trees in the churchyard, the green of the grass, the bright flowers. She couldn't get it out of her head that there should have been some sign, some small acknowledgement from nature that Aunt Celia was gone. The hot sun of late summer still shone, though, the sky was blue, the clouds white and fluffy. Things just went on. It was the same when anyone died.

'I think I'm depressed,' Amy pronounced bleakly as they reached the gate and went towards their cars, which were parked one behind the other a short way up the quiet lane that led to the church.

'Funerals are depressing events,' Peter murmured. 'That's why I avoid them. I'm only here today because I knew how you'd be, and how right I was.'

'Aunt Celia was your stepsister,' Amy reminded him quietly. 'I'm glad you came with me but you would have come anyway, I expect.'

'Believe me, I would not have come. Celia hated me in a very comprehensive manner. She wouldn't

6

have wanted me to go to her funeral. In fact, if she'd known beforehand, she would have forbidden it. If she's up there looking down at this moment I can guarantee that she's tapping her foot and tutting loudly, glaring at the top of my head.'

Amy grinned to herself. She could well imagine it, and the idea of Aunt Celia looking down, vastly irritated, took away a lot of her gloom. Aunt Celia had shown displeasure whenever she thought it necessary.

'She was iron-clad,' Peter observed, unable to prevent himself from glancing skywards when Amy did.

'She was scrupulously fair,' Amy pointed out in her aunt's defence.

'And mean as a weasel.'

'Not to me.'

'That's why you'll inherit her considerable wealth, my dear child. There's not much chance that Celia left anything undone. Pretty soon you're going to be a very rich young lady. She only had you.'

'No, she didn't. She had you too.'

'I don't need her money. I've got plenty of my own. She brought you up from the age of thirteen so who else would she leave it to? In any case, she did *not* have me. Celia wouldn't have touched me with a long, pointed stick. She hated me whether you like to believe that or not.'

'Oh, she never breathed a word about you, Uncle Peter,' Amy protested.

'Which in itself goes to show something. The last time I saw her she was talking quite nastily about everyone else. The fact that she left me out of her caustically declared beliefs is significant. To Celia, I was beneath contempt, too low to even be censured. And don't call me Uncle. It's aging. I'm too young to be your uncle and not really one of the family.'

'Bosh!' Amy retorted. 'You are now my only living relative. There's just the two of us. We stand back to back against adversity.'

'Speaking of adversity,' Peter said as they reached their cars, 'how are you getting on with your new boss now?'

'He's not new. He's been here for six months and he hasn't changed at all. Nobody could possibly get on with him. He's not human.'

'What's his name again?'

'Martell,' Amy snapped irritably.

'Ah! Good!'

'What's good about it?'

'Sounds French. Doesn't he call you *chérie*?' Peter asked with a slyly amused glance at her exasperated expression.

'He's only half-French. I believe his mother is English, but it's only a rumour and probably untrue. He can't possibly have a mother. The chances are he's straight off some production line – "Model 176, perfect specimen, store packed in ice". He calls me Miss Scott in an imperious voice. He looks over my shoulder at the computer screen, narrows his eyes and points a long, powerful finger at my work before making comments.'

'He doesn't like your work?'

'I said comments, not complaints,' Amy reminded him with a suddenly satisfied smile. 'He can't complain; I'm too good at what I do. If I left there'd be a panic and he's well aware of it. I'm the only one who knows all the systems. I control too much to be cast aside. All the same,' she added with a return to gloom, 'working close to him is extremely stressful. It's not nice to have the Ice Man watching you.'

'I'll take you to lunch and cheer you up,' Peter offered, but Amy shook her head.

'Thanks, but I've got to nip home and change and then I'm having lunch with Jill. And there's another thing. Jill leaves for America tomorrow night. She's going for a whole year. That's someone else out of my life in a flash.'

'She's not out of your life, you goose. Didn't you tell me it was only an exchange visit? A year is no time at all. You'll be able to visit her in any case. Now cheer up, get off to lunch and stop being so damned depressed.'

'I'll try. Do take care, Uncle Peter.'

Amy looked at him sadly, as if he too was about to disappear from her life, and Peter gave her a gentle push in the direction of her car.

'Get along with you, girl. I'm here until I'm at least a hundred – and think about this: if I should suddenly be sent to join Celia, you'll get all my money too. After that you could tell this icy boss where to go.'

Amy managed a smile and watched Peter walk briskly to his car. Nobody would ever suspect that he was fifty, or even close to it. He looked like a vigorous younger man. Only the streaks of silver in his brown hair gave any hint of his age. He was a handsome man, quite tall, well built, with amused eyes and a rather sceptical smile.

She was close to Peter in spite of her aunt's dislike of him. The fact that he objected to being called Uncle in case it aged him didn't matter very much. He'd told her several times in the past to simply call him Peter, but old habits were difficult to cast off. She had always called him Uncle.

He had a very easy-going life, and that was what accounted for his youthful appearance in many ways – an appearance he wanted to cling to. Amy couldn't remember a time when he hadn't been wealthy, and he usually had some woman on his arm – many of them much younger than he was. But he had always been wonderful to get on with. Peter Jensen had a lot of charm.

All the same, she thought as she got into her car, he might have been a little more gentle about Aunt Celia, even though they'd had some sort of long-standing feud that had never been explained to her. It wasn't just the idea of speaking ill of the dead, somehow Peter's sarcastic comments had increased the rawness of the sudden gap in her life where Aunt Celia had always been. Now there was going to be another gap, when Jill left for America.

'How did it go?' Jill Davis asked, and then made a wry face. 'Sorry. That was a particularly stupid thing to say.'

'I know what you mean.' Amy sighed as she sat down and picked up the menu. 'I suppose it went as well as any funeral goes. It was terribly depressing, though. Not many people were there, but, as you know, Aunt Celia was a bit tart with most people.'

'I can vouch for that,' Jill remarked drily. 'She invariably gave me one of her cold, autocratic inspections. I only ever called at the house to see you or to do her some medical favour. She felt it was beneath her dignity to see the doctor for minor problems, so I could deal with them. At all other times I got that suspicious glance. I was never quite sure what she suspected I would do wrong – or *could* do wrong.'

'Nothing, in all probability. She was just like that. But she was good to me and I got on well with her. I liked her sense of humour, her taste in clothes, her choice of food and the way she spoke her mind.'

'Well, she brought you up and it shows,' Jill pointed out as her eyes scanned Amy's immaculate appearance. 'Did you go to the funeral in that?'

'Heavens, no. I went in black. I've just nipped home to change.' Amy glanced down at her clothes, a silky flowered skirt and matching top. 'Even though she couldn't see me, I would never have gone to Aunt Celia's funeral improperly dressed. I would have expected some sort of message, some reprimand, even a thunderbolt.'

'No doubt you would have answered back,' Jill laughed. 'You have the habit of speaking your mind too.'

'I know.' Amy glanced up ruefully. 'It has its drawbacks. I'm not exactly Personality of the Year

11

with the boss. He never says anything but he looks at me dangerously.'

'You know, I've never actually seen this ogre,' Jill reminded her. 'Is he young, old, what?'

'About thirty-six, at a guess. He's a top-flight architect and business genius, extremely good at his job, and expects perfection. He's utterly cold-blooded, though. In fact, he might just be an alien with a slight French accent.'

Jill burst into peals of laughter and Amy tried to look a little less gloomy. It would be a long time before she heard that ready laughter again. She seemed to have known Jill Davis all her life, and their friendship was quite astonishing when you considered that Amy was only just twenty-five and Jill was thirty-nine.

They were quite opposite in looks. Jill was naturally fair, her dark eyes a lovely contrast to her pale skin and blonde good looks. Amy was darker, her hair a deep, shining brown and her eyes the same purple-blue that seemed to run in the family.

Jill had already been an experienced nurse when Amy's father was dying. She had nursed him at home in his last days and she had been very good to Amy. After that she'd always sent cards and presents for birthdays and Christmas. She'd never lost touch with the young girl who had been so devastated at her father's death. As Amy got older the friendship had deepened. Now Jill was going away and it was such a blow. Another blow.

'I wish you weren't going off to America,' Amy muttered, with a return to depression.

'Only for a year, and you can visit if you like,' Jill pointed out cheerfully. 'It's going to make a good excuse to travel.'

'That's what Uncle Peter told me not more than thirty minutes ago.'

'Was he at the funeral? I was praying he'd be there with you. He's a staunch ally for you, Amy. Don't ever lose touch with him.'

'As if I would! I must remember not to call him Uncle, though. He objects. He says it's aging.'

'Aging? Peter Jensen? I just can't imagine it. He's the most attractive man I've ever known.'

'He's a womanizer, Jill,' Amy warned when she heard the usual romantic interest that was always in Jill's voice when Peter was mentioned.

'I know. If I was younger, though . . .'

'You're a good ten years younger than Peter.'

'Eleven, actually,' Jill corrected wryly. 'I know all his specifications – not that it does me a lot of good.'

'You're beautiful,' Amy pointed out, giving Jill the benefit of a close inspection.

'Thank you. But I'm well over thirty. That seems to be his stopping point, some invisible line he draws. Anyway,' she added, 'I would never have met him if I hadn't been nursing your father. I'm merely a nurse. Peter Jensen is a wealthy playboy.'

'Don't remind me,' Amy ordered woefully. 'His last remark this morning was that I would finally get all his money too. *That* was supposed to cheer me up.'

'He'll never die,' Jill pronounced firmly. 'People

like Peter Jensen just go on and on, getting more attractive with age.' She glanced at her watch. 'Got to go, Amy. I've loads of things to do and I'm out of here tomorrow night.'

'And I'm supposed to be back at the grindstone in a few minutes,' Amy muttered, rising and collecting her bag. 'If I'm not on time, the boss will freeze me with a glance.'

'I'd love to meet him.'

'Oh, no, you wouldn't, believe me. Don't even think about it,' Amy warned.

'Take the afternoon off,' Jill advised brightly. 'Make up an excuse.'

'Nobody makes excuses to Luc Martell. The clocks would stop and a chill would settle on the world. I'd be sent to France for re-programming.'

'Look, I'll pop round tonight. I'll not be seeing you for a while so how about a pizza or something as a farewell meal?'

Amy brightened slightly at the suggestion. It would at least take a bit of the sting out of a terrible day.

'No pizza. I'll cook a goodbye meal,' she offered, and Jill beamed at her.

'I knew you'd say that. I'm quite cunning. One last good meal. I don't know how long it will be before I get another.'

'They do eat in America,' Amy reminded her somewhat glumly. It would be bright and busy in America, fast-paced, everyone filled with boundless energy and the capacity to enjoy themselves to the point of exhaustion. The whole idea of it made Amy feel oppressed and indecisive.

14

'Cheer up,' Jill ordered. 'Follow my advice. Take the rest of the day off, unwind and enjoy yourself.'

'I daren't,' Amy assured her. 'I'm not going to America. Skipping work is fine except for the fact that on Monday I'll have to face the cold eyes of the boss.'

All the same, Amy thought mutinously as Jill said goodbye and leapt into a taxi, why not? If she didn't go back to work this afternoon, what could he do? He would never dismiss her, he never raised that cold voice and if he glared at her she would ignore him; she usually did. It didn't leave him with a lot of options.

She had been quite happy in her job until the firm had merged with Martell International, a giant French construction company. It hadn't been a merger so much as the big firm swallowing the small English firm whole, like a predator – one great gulp and they were gone. Normally it wouldn't have bothered Amy one little bit. She was brilliant at her job and happy with her computers but along with the great change had come Luc Martell, the son of the new French owner.

Luc Martell had come in like a rush of cold air, resentment in his dark eyes. Rumour had it that he had wanted to stay in France, but then, rumour was rife about a lot of things. He hated the climate, the town, England, the English and almost everything his eye fell on that wasn't work, or so they said.

'They' also said that he had an English mother, but as Amy found it difficult to imagine any sort of background for him other than a shining production line that turned out perfectly formed humanoids, it made the other rumours open to doubt.

Amy watched Jill until the last minute, thinking again about how they were almost opposites. Jill wasn't slender and graceful, but she was very sophisticated. She was tall for a woman, and you never noticed that she was quite big. The blonde hair was smooth and well groomed, fashionably short. There was glowing health on the attractive face. Maybe it was because she was a nurse – an experienced sister, in fact.

Amy set her lips firmly as the taxi pulled away out of sight. She glanced in her bag to make sure she had her cheque book and made up her mind. As she was about to be reasonably well off soon, she could give herself a treat this afternoon. Self-indulgence would probably lift the gloom, dispel the depression, and it would also strike a defiant note for Luc Martell to notice. She walked off down the street, determined to enjoy this afternoon of freedom, and was soon deeply engrossed in window shopping.

It was astonishing how uplifting the feeling of playing truant could be, Amy thought a little later. It cleared the mind of a great deal of nonsense. It was even better than an official holiday, because everyone else was at work and she was out, roaming around, utterly free. It gave her an almost buoyant feeling, as if she was enjoying something seriously wicked.

She caught sight of a dress in the window of an exclusive department store and stopped to have a good look at it. The dress was expensive, black and white, and it looked very impressive in the wide, imposing window.

She was speculating on the possibility of buying it when a tall, powerful reflection quite eclipsed her own.

'How astonishing to see you, Miss Scott. And how fortunate.' The voice was cold, sardonic, very well known to her, and Amy felt the strange mixture of sensations that always seemed to grip her when she heard that curiously sensual accent. She spun round and looked up a long way to meet the cool, dark eyes of authority as Luc Martell stared down at her like a prosecuting judge.

The boss! She couldn't think of a thing to say. All her defiant bravado vanished and she had the definite feeling of a small mouse in a large trap, caught and about to be tormented.

His dark gaze swept briefly over her and then settled momentarily on the dress in the window.

'The dress is not at all suitable. It is designed for a much more dynamic woman. You are too softly feminine to wear such garments. It is called "power dressing", I believe. You would need a much more forceful personality.'

'Er – I – yes,' Amy managed as her tongue refused to accommodate her mind. Not that her mind was doing anything in particular. It seemed to be searching frantically, and she assumed it was looking for an excuse all by itself.

The impassive face in front of her was no help at all, and it was only as the long, mobile lips showed signs of twisting in coldly satisfied amusement that she made any further attempt to speak.

'Er – I never expected to see you – er – out here.'

The dark eyebrows rose slowly, his expression mockingly surprised, and Amy had the nasty impression that the near-black eyes were laughing at her predicament.

'Out here? Do you mean in the normal atmosphere? I'm capable of breathing the same air that you breathe. I don't need special apparatus to enable me to leave the office. Like you, I'm shopping.'

'Oh? What for?'

Amy was furious with herself for behaving in this stunned manner. She was normally a match for anyone and here she was, tongue-tied. He had also, with few words, pointed out that he was well aware of her truancy. She was shopping on Martell International's time without permission. And she seemed to be trapped against the big, plate glass window with no hope of escape unless she pushed him out of the way forcefully.

'You really want to know what I intend to buy?' he asked with a further raising of his eyebrows. She hadn't been wrong about the tormenting. He was going to keep her trapped here and goad her endlessly before he really attacked. Amy felt her cheeks begin to burn with embarrassment.

'No,' she assured him quickly. She made a little nervous movement and he stepped aside to allow her to escape – or so she thought until he moved forward as she did.

'You seem to be confused.' He looked down at her in his normal superior manner, his voice still taunting. 'However, it doesn't matter. Meeting you here is, as I said, very fortunate. You can help me.'

'How?' Amy asked anxiously. She wanted to turn round and walk off with some speed, but this was the boss and orders came naturally to him. He hadn't asked her to help him; he had told her.

'I need to buy a birthday present for a lady. Your assistance will be invaluable. A woman instantly knows what another woman would like.'

Amy had Technicolor visions of a glamorous woman in France who had been born with dress-sense and exuded confidence with every breath she took. It made her own predicament seem worse. She suddenly felt unkempt, unsophisticated and, at the moment, terribly unintelligent.

That last thought brought her to her senses. He was walking along beside her like a large, lazy, very dangerous cat. Even the way he moved seemed to be menacing, as if he had just strolled in from some jungle and was looking around idly for a victim.

He was goading her, taunting her, lulling her into a feeling of false security before he pounced and asked why she was still out of the office when she had only been given the morning off. She could deal with that. Arguments were absolutely painless to Amy. She took a firm grip on the situation.

'I'm willing to help,' she informed him breezily, 'although I'm not quite sure what a woman in France would like.'

'Exactly the same thing that women in England like,' he muttered sardonically, leading her into the store. 'Something expensive.'

'Then follow me.' Amy gave him a flashing look with violet-blue eyes. His opinion of women was obvious, regardless of nationality. She smiled grimly to herself and led the way purposefully to the jewellery department. This store really knew how to charge for things, and some of the jewellery was so expensive that it was under tight security.

Luc Martell hid his satisfaction. He had never expected to see Miss Amy Scott, but he had recognized her instantly from across the road. The slender, graceful figure, the shining shoulder-length brown hair, the softly feminine way she dressed made her stand out at once in any sort of crowd.

For a moment he had been quite taken aback. She had been needed urgently this morning but she had been given the time off to attend her aunt's funeral. It had dawned on him rapidly that she was taking the rest of the day off with her usual defiance, and that Martell International could come to a standstill as far as she was concerned.

They *had* almost come to a standstill this morning too, and he had not been pleased about it. Amy Scott was the Systems Manager. She made sure that all the computers in the offices could talk to each other. This morning a couple of them had ground to a puzzled halt and she had not been there. He had also wanted information from her office, computerized information. He had found that the file was password-protected. *She* was the only one with the password.

He felt extremely pleased with himself at having captured his irritating little employee. She got away with far too much in the normal day-to-day running of the offices because of her expertise, but this time she had overstepped the mark and he could punish her with the very smug feeling that she deserved it.

'What sort of colouring does this lady have?' Amy asked as they arrived at the appropriate counter and stood gazing at glittering stones that quite dazzled her. 'What colour hair?'

'Grey.'

Amy looked up at him in astonishment, her eyes wide and startled.

'Grey? You mean she's dyed her hair *grey*?'

She was filled with awe, wondering what sort of fashion that would turn out to be and hoping it didn't catch on over here. Imagine anybody dying their hair grey!

'It grew like that all by itself,' Luc Martell informed her, looking quite entertained by her obvious stupidity. 'The lady is my mother. In three days it will be her birthday. I've left things rather late. It has to be posted.'

'What colour eyes does she have?' Having to make such a rapid adjustment was a bit tricky, and Amy had to turn her glamorous Frenchwoman into a little old mother with some alacrity.

'Her eyes are hazel, a sort of grey-green. She's very fair-skinned, like you. She is also still very beautiful, very smart, very sophisticated.'

The little old mother vanished in a flash, and Amy concentrated on the brooches with rather sketchy impressions of a duchess in her head. At any rate, she now knew he had a mother, which probably meant that the other rumours were true also. He hated everything, particularly her.

'That one,' she suggested, pointing to an emerald brooch that looked sufficiently expensive to satisfy his idea of what women wanted. It was set in small diamonds and glittered enough to be real and costly.

'You have very good taste,' Luc Martell murmured, glancing down at her as if it really surprised him. 'I'll go with your judgement.'

'You haven't learned the price yet,' Amy cautioned, unexpectedly filled with Christian forbearance.

He shrugged in that elegantly masculine way he had. She had noticed it before and been rather intimidated by it.

'It doesn't matter. This is for my mother.' He looked up into the expectant face of the assistant. 'We will take it.'

When Amy heard the price she was glad that the 'we' was merely a figure of speech. It took her breath away.

A lot of strangely shaped keys were produced and the assistant selected two and then glanced up at a guard who was leaning with apparent nonchalance against a nearby pillar. He gave what Amy took to be a very sinister nod of his head and the showcase was opened. Amy watched in fascination.

The assistant produced a black velvet box and placed the brooch inside with admiring, loving care as Luc Martell wrote out a cheque that would have appalled even Aunt Celia. It seemed to be so much money for so very little.

'We'd like it gift-wrapped,' Amy said firmly, contriving for extra value for money spent. 'It's for a birthday and it's going to Paris so it has to look exceptionally good. They do very chic wrapping there with just about everything.'

The assistant gave her a rather condescending glance, and Amy was about to assert herself by adding that they even wrapped vegetables beautifully when she noticed Luc glancing down at her in a startled way. She stared up at him a little anxiously, quite surprised by her own daring.

'Well you *did* say you'd left things rather late,' she pointed out defensively. 'Having it wrapped here will save you time – unless you wanted to take it home and sit gazing at it for hours.'

'I don't want to gaze at it,' he assured her quietly. 'I was merely wondering why I hadn't thought of the gift-wrapping myself.'

'You're a man,' Amy murmured in an off-hand voice, as if it excused very little but accounted for a total lack of common sense.

Luc smiled slightly, enough to assure her that he knew better, and she began to think of escape and looked round longingly at the other shoppers who were able to walk off whenever they chose. They had freedom. She was trapped. She wanted to browse through things even if she decided not to spend any money, but she couldn't really say goodbye and walk off briskly. She *had* been shirking her duty.

'I'm very grateful for your assistance,' Luc said when he had the box in his hand and the guard had relaxed from his intent vigil.

'Good,' Amy stated in a firm enough voice to indicate that it was all over and she was about to leave.

'We will buy a scarf now,' Luc decided, and even took her arm in a firm grip in case she tried to make a run for it.

Amy sighed quietly and gave up her free afternoon. Truancy was not so great after all – not when you were caught. She settled to her role of mouse in trap and tried to look at things philosophically. He wouldn't be likely to insist on explanations now, although she would much rather have had a battle than this very unsubtle captivity.

She wasn't fooled at all. He was making quite sure that she did not enjoy herself when she should have been at work – a change of tactics for him, but obvious and clever. She could not just walk off. She glanced at him secretly and suspiciously. If he was pleased with himself he didn't look it. He was probably laughing inside, but he had his normal enigmatic look that was totally impenetrable.

'Scarves, second floor,' she advised with gloomy resignation, stepping on to the escalator and glancing downwards at the things she might have bought if she hadn't been in captivity. Luc stepped on behind her and they were swept inexorably upwards to the scarves. The handbags were up there too. Maybe he would prolong this by buying his mother a bag?

Amy scowled. This was such an obvious ploy to punish her, but there was nothing at all she could do. It was a bit like shopping with God. She didn't have one doubt at the moment that God was a Frenchman. Luc Martell probably didn't have any doubt either, at any time. He was the most aloof, imperious man she had ever known.

She tripped on the top step but a hand like a steel glove caught her arm and swept her forward out of danger.

'You are daydreaming,' Luc murmured reprovingly, and that really irritated her, especially as she felt extremely foolish about stumbling off the escalator.

'I'm dazed!' she snapped, and he slanted a dark-eyed look of amusement at her as he walked forward with Amy firmly clamped at his side.

'Probably because you're not accustomed to being out of the office on Friday afternoon. Unexpected holidays tend to be disorientating. An escape into the great outdoors while everyone else works can leave one feeling very odd.' His voice was softly taunting and Amy felt ready to explode into violence.

'Now look . . .!' she began, stopping in her tracks and turning on him.

He never even glanced at her.

'The scarves,' he murmured smugly. 'You were quite right. I notice that there are handbags on this floor too.' He took her arm again, sweeping her along, and Amy set her lips in irritation. Quite obviously he was going to keep her from enjoying herself even if he had to buy up the whole store item by item and ship it off to France.

'Blast!' Amy muttered, but he seemed to have become conveniently deaf. When she glanced at him with acute dislike he was looking straight ahead, steering them purposefully towards the scarves, but the long, mobile lips were quirking as if he was holding in a good deal of amusement.

He knew exactly what he was doing and so did Amy. She wondered what he would choose next. If it was undies she would insist that red would go very nicely with grey hair. She would make a small scene and embarrass him.

He only wanted coffee. When the scarf was purchased he made his way purposefully to the escalator and pointed to the board.

'There is a restaurant on the top floor,' he confirmed in a very satisfied voice. 'We will have coffee.'

CHAPTER 2

'I've only just had lunch,' Amy protested, but by that time she was already on her way up, like it or not.

'Coffee can be drunk at any time,' he admonished, as if she'd made some foolish social gaffe.

'I'm not French,' Amy snapped.

'Coffee is a universal drink. France has not cornered the market. If you would prefer tea, I imagine they will have that too.'

Amy was disgusted with everything. She just gave up. Quite clearly he was not about to let her escape unless she made a big scene. He was diabolical. There was one good result, though. All this had completely dispelled her depression. She wasn't even a little unhappy. She was just quietly fuming, but even that seemed to be a complete waste of time and energy.

She gave a long, audible sigh and Luc Martell's dark eyes glittered with satisfaction. He had been wondering how many more presents he would have to buy for his mother before Amy Scott accepted the inevitable.

He had every intention of showing her who was in charge of the firm. She usually gave the appearance of imagining that she was. Prickly as a little hedgehog and the most defiant female he had ever known, she was fast becoming a daily irritant and impossible to ignore.

She was the most beautiful woman he knew too, although he rarely had the chance to appreciate that. More often than not her head was firmly turned towards one of her beloved computers. He didn't need to study the back of her head; he knew it off by heart. He knew every wave in the shining nut-brown hair.

Even when he was talking to her at work, which he had to do frequently, she somehow managed to turn her head away. Some computer or other always needed her attention and she was extremely skilled at addressing him over her shoulder.

Well, she couldn't do that now, he thought with satisfaction. She could just face him head-on and notice who ran the damned firm.

He manoeuvred them into a small corner table and ordered coffee while Amy glanced round in some surprise. She made a definite decision to relax and accept things, changing her previous attitude with no difficulty at all. It even changed the expression on her face, and Luc glanced at her warily, wondering what her next trick would be.

'It's quite nice here,' she murmured. 'I've never been in the restaurant before. It's certainly worth a visit.'

'I thought you lived in town?'

'I do. That's why I don't eat out much – well, not now anyway,' she added with a small frown.

Before she'd split up with Eric they used to eat out a lot. Now, though, she usually ate at home, in case she met Eric at one of their old haunts. It had not been an amicable parting and she knew that Eric would not hesitate to throw a semi-violent scene if the mood took him. It was unlikely that he would actually attack her physically, but she was not absolutely sure on that point.

'Where did you have lunch?' Luc asked, trying to keep the frown from his own face. Her parting from Eric Somerfield, three months ago, had been the talk of the office and Luc had a pretty good idea of the way her thoughts were going at the moment. For some unfathomable reason he didn't like it either. He didn't like it one little bit.

'I had lunch at the Majestic with a friend.' Amy glanced up at him and then looked away quickly, the gloomy expression back on her face. 'She's going to America tomorrow night. She's a nurse, on exchange for a whole year. I won't see her.'

'You are going to miss her?' he asked quietly, finding himself unusually fascinated now that she was facing him. She had the most beautiful skin he had ever seen, and those eyes were glorious. He had never noticed eyes quite that colour before. They were purple-blue, edged with thick lashes, astounding. She might be vastly irritating, but there was a sort of fragile grace to her that he had observed the very first time he had seen her. It normally drew his eyes in her direction even when his expression was irritated.

Amy nodded.

'Yes, I'm going to miss her. Jill is older than me but we've been friends for years. I'll be pretty much lost without her now that Aunt Celia's gone.'

'Ah! The funeral today. This has been a bad day for you.' His expression softened considerably but Amy didn't notice.

'It has,' she agreed with a small, heartfelt sigh. 'My aunt brought me up. I lived with her until I was twenty-one.'

'You have no parents?' Luc asked quietly. He was probing carefully and so far she hadn't noticed. She seemed to him to be wrapped in a sort of dreamy cloud of grey gloom.

'My mother died when I was a baby. I was thirteen when my father died. So, in a way, Aunt Celia was like both parents to me. I'd always lived with her but we decided jointly that it was time to spread my wings, so when I came out of university I got my present job and took a small house in town. Aunt Celia's house is in the district but it's ten miles away – a little too far out for daily travel. I actually bought a house here last year, just before you came.' She looked up and gave a sudden, astonishingly brilliant smile. 'It's small but it's mine.'

Luc found himself staring at her intently. When she smiled her whole face lit up, became even more beautiful, and her eyes looked like blue stars. He'd never noticed that before because this was the first time she had ever smiled at him. He now knew everyone in the offices quite well, but Amy Scott was still a distant figure who irritated him almost daily.

He wasn't quite sure why she irritated him so much. However he felt though, he could have watched that smile all day. It turned her beauty into something much more potent. He wanted her to keep on smiling, because if she did he knew he could keep on looking.

'Have you bought a house here?' Amy asked, suddenly aware of the silence and wondering if she was talking too much as usual.

'No. I have a flat on the edge of town. Buying a house seemed to me to be an irrevocable step. I'm always hoping to go back to Paris.'

Amy nodded. It was pretty much as she had suspected. He hated the English, the climate, the office, and it must be costing him a great effort to be pleasant to her. It just showed how determined he was to punish her for her temerity in taking the afternoon off.

'I know,' she murmured, nodding sympathetically. 'You hate England.'

Luc's mouth tilted with surprised amusement.

'I sincerely hope I do not go around giving that impression.'

'Oh, no,' Amy assured him earnestly. 'I don't think anyone else knows.' She lowered her voice to conspirator level and leaned forward. 'I just happen to know because you give off vibes, and I'm particularly good at picking up vibes. They sort of float in the air and I catch them.'

He grinned in sudden delight, white teeth flashing in his dark face. He hoped he was not giving off vibes of any kind at this particular moment. He was supposed to be here to get the better of her but

31

he seemed to have lost interest in punishment. She was very entertaining, fascinating.

It was surprising to discover that she was imaginative and inclined to be fluffy-headed – surprising considering her brilliance at her job. Still, he had always known she was unusual. He had often heard her talking to her bank of computers as she whizzed about between them on her little red chair, like a modern witch casting electronic spells.

With her skills she should have been an upbeat, forceful woman, in thick-rimmed spectacles – a woman with a chilling frown. Instead she was enchanting in some way that he couldn't quite grasp. He felt as if he was being edged into a different sort of world.

His grin widened and Amy glanced at him seriously over the rim of her coffee cup.

'You do, you know,' she insisted, nodding her head sagely.

'What do I do?'

Suddenly he felt very patient with her, almost lazily indulgent, and he assumed it was because he was enjoying looking at her. In fact, he was enjoying himself altogether.

'You give off vibes – vibes of dislike, displeasure . . .'

'But not disinterest, I hope? I'm supposed to be running the English side of the firm,' Luc interrupted quietly.

'Oh, no!' Amy exclaimed with the earnest look still on her face. 'You really don't need to worry about that. Everyone knows how clever you are. You've certainly pulled the place together.'

'In a nasty sort of way?' he enquired wryly, and Amy nodded, seeing no need for subterfuge as they seemed to be having some sort of genuine heart-to-heart talk.

'Mmm,' she agreed, nodding again and putting her head on one side as she looked across at him seriously. 'You're not at all easy to get on with, are you?'

Luc stared at her in astonishment. She was not diplomatic, apparently. She just came straight out with the truth with a total disregard for the consequences.

'Few men are easy to get on with,' he pointed out softly, remembering all he had heard about her ex-boyfriend and quite enjoying the little dig at her.

'Not true,' Amy insisted firmly. 'I spent most of the morning with a man who is wonderfully easy to get on with.'

'I imagined you had spent the morning at your aunt's funeral.' Luc's voice was faintly threatening, the indulgence vanishing swiftly.

'I did, but Peter went with me to give me moral support.'

'And who is Peter?' Luc asked with the beginnings of annoyance gathering on his face. So there was someone else besides the ex-boyfriend – another one, no doubt. He might have guessed that she wouldn't be alone for long, not with those looks.

'He's my uncle.' Amy paused and frowned. 'Well, to be strictly truthful, he's not really my uncle, but I've always called him that – except that I'm not allowed to say it now because it ages him, apparently. But, as I said, Peter is wonderfully easy to get on with, so you can't make generalizations as you just did about men. Mind you,' she added, when Luc sat looking at her fixedly as he tried to work out exactly what she was talking about now, 'Peter is very rich. He always has been, so I expect that helps a lot with an easygoing attitude. But then again,' she continued with an interested and deeply assessing glance at him, 'you're probably rich too, and it hasn't made you easy to get on with, has it? So actually, my theory isn't proved after all.'

'You are considering things in a scientific manner?' Luc enquired, wondering how she managed all those computers, maintained an unrivalled position as Systems Manager for a huge firm and yet was able to be so astonishingly guileless, as if she looked at the whole world with wonder. Apparently she said anything that came into her head the moment it arrived there.

'It's impossible to be scientific unless you have all the facts,' Amy stated briskly in a new voice, a firm, practical voice. She put her coffee cup down and sat up very straight. 'I know all about Peter, you see. I've known him all my life. He was my father's stepbrother. I know nothing at all about you, apart from the fact that you want to go back to Paris.'

'What would you like to know?' Luc asked, feeling slightly dazed. He was supposed to be putting her in her place, but she seemed to have talked him into a corner and he appeared to be enjoying it.

Instantly Amy's prickly shield went up. She didn't want to know anything about him. She was as close now as she wanted to be; in fact she didn't want to be even this close. You didn't have cosy chats with a dangerous hunting creature who had tracked you down cunningly. He was probably storing up this little talk to use it against her later.

'Nothing,' she assured him brightly. 'I know all I need to know. You're the boss. You say jump; I ask, "How high?" Do you want to buy that handbag now?'

'I think not,' Luc stated with a quick return to coolness as the dreamy look left her face. She had taken him for a swift ride on a pink cloud and now she had abandoned the cloud with such speed that he felt disorientated. He had not had the chance to float back to earth. His return to reality had been a crash landing. It annoyed him considerably. 'I would imagine that my mother has quite enough handbags,' he finished coldly.

He signalled for the bill and Amy gathered her belongings. She felt as if she had had a very narrow escape somehow, and she wasn't quite sure why. No doubt it came from the fact that her tongue very often had a mind of its own and for a minute she had felt quite comfortable with him.

It would be as well to remember why he'd brought her here in the first place. She glanced at her watch. It was almost three-thirty. He'd kept her occupied for a long time and she hoped he would let her escape now.

'Shall we go?' he asked in a stiffly polite voice, and Amy nodded her agreement. She hoped he meant it. There wasn't much chance of doing anything but returning to work now that he knew she was wandering around free. He might even grasp her by the back of the neck and march her to the office.

Outside the main doors she found it difficult to look at him. He seemed to have suddenly become himself again, a man she worried about. She was tongue-tied once more because he had iced over.

'My car's still parked at the Majestic,' she muttered. 'I'll have to get it before I go to the office.'

'Don't bother coming back in today. It's hardly worth the effort now. Continue to do what you were doing when I saw you.' He looked decidedly frosty and Amy tightened up even more.

'There's still two hours left,' she began guiltily.

'Then do your shopping, Miss Scott. You were all set to do that before I met you. I'll see you on Monday morning.'

He nodded to her and walked off and Amy stared after him resentfully. Before he met her? He meant before he had tracked her down. Why had he gone back to being icy? After all, he had succeeded in wasting a lot of her stolen time. He should have been quite pleased with himself.

Maybe he objected to having his aloof faults pointed out to him, but on the plus side she had helped him with his wretched shopping. It could probably all be put down to the fact that he was half-French.

Amy walked defiantly back into the store before he was even out of sight. She wasn't going to trot back to the office like a guilty slave and he had made the mistake of telling her to get on with her shopping. Well, she would!

Luc strode off to get his own car and he was frowning irritably. He wasn't going back to the office either, because he was too unsettled to work now. He had not managed her very well at all. She had run rings round him. He had been too fascinated by her beauty and her character to put her severely in her place.

She still looked as if she thought she was in charge of things. She was not at all subdued. He was not one step further forward except for the fact that he now knew that she didn't want to know anything about him. He also knew that he was not at all easy to get on with.

He muttered angrily. She was probably right. He had never been particularly easy to get on with anyway, and he had not wanted to leave Paris to come to this big northern town with its lack of glitter. He missed dining out, seeing friends. He missed the speed and excitement of Paris. He spoke English like an Englishman, with hardly any accent, but he preferred his father's language.

He slammed into his car and drove off to his flat across the town, glancing at his watch as he went. It was a long time until Monday, a lot of hours when he would be bored out of his mind. What did one do in this godforsaken place?

He noticed the things on the seat beside him and brightened considerably. He would go home. It was near enough to his mother's birthday and the presents were already gift-wrapped, thanks to his irritating little employee.

He would go home – take the presents himself instead of posting them. Paris would cheer him up and he could give his mother a birthday meal early. Maybe he wouldn't come back until after her birthday.

His lips twisted ruefully when he realized that he certainly would. There was a big project on at the moment and Amy Scott was deeply into it already. She would expect to be able to consult him.

He frowned as he stared through the windscreen. He was letting her annoy him when normally he would have put her in her place with a few well-chosen words. His idea of making her tow the line this afternoon didn't seem to have been too bright now. For a while he had forgotten where he was and who he was. He had simply enjoyed it all and that had not been the point of the exercise.

He wasn't at all sure who had won either. As she was probably shopping at this instant, he suspected that she had won. In future he would be much more firm with her. There were other computer geniuses. It was time to make her realize that she was not indispensable.

The trouble was that he didn't really like the thought of looking up and seeing someone else in her office. He had grown accustomed to watching her, so much so that he wouldn't have been able to stay on in Paris even if there had not been a big project on at the moment.

He thought rather guiltily of Veronique. He hadn't been in touch with her for ages and she was not going to be pleased when she saw him.

They had a sort of unofficial understanding. Although he sometimes wasn't at all sure what their understanding was.

In a way, Veronique Dubois was powerful herself. She ran her own fashion business in Paris and they had known each other for years. He had always thought she would make a good wife when he finally got around to it. He had never been in any rush about getting married, although his mother dropped plenty of hints. He had always assumed, though, that when he did marry it would be Veronique.

Lately, however, he seemed to have become reluctant to even think about her at all. Life with Veronique would be smooth, glossy, sophisticated. Since he had come to England he had been swept into work with a vengeance, and he had also become irritatingly fascinated by Amy Scott, and at the back of his mind he knew it, even though it annoyed him. He seemed to be watching her every spare minute he had. Capturing her this afternoon had been an act of sheer fascination too, no matter what he told himself about discipline.

It would probably bring him to his senses to see Veronique again. He would have to think of a good excuse, however, because he had not written too often. He wondered if Veronique had missed him at all. Somehow he was sure that she would not have. Veronique was very self-sufficient. Veronique would never sit talking nonsense, gazing at him with purple-blue eyes and speculating on his state of mind.

Damn! He glared through the windscreen and gave himself a mental shake. It certainly was time he went home. This place was damaging his brain.

When Jill came for a meal later that evening, Amy had managed to throw off her feeling of annoyance with her imperious boss. She wouldn't see him until Monday so she placed him at the back of her mind to wait. He was usually at the back of her mind waiting nowadays. It was nothing unusual.

'Superb!' Jill pronounced when the meal was over. 'The moment I get back home we'll do this again.'

'That gives me a whole year to practise,' Amy reminded her gloomily.

'It's going to pass very quickly. These things always do. You've got to face it, Amy. It's not just my going and you know it. Your aunt Celia dying has thrown you back to the past. It was terrible for you when your father died. I haven't forgotten.'

Amy nodded as she poured coffee and led the way to the sitting room with the tray carefully balanced.

'I know. Things just fell apart. It was difficult. I don't know what I would have done without you and Aunt Celia, especially as there was no money then.'

'It was the business agreement, love. I know your father worried about it in the end, but he and Peter Jensen were tied into it. It was Jensen and Scott. Whoever died first, the other took over. In any case, he knew your uncle Peter would look after you.'

'He didn't get the chance,' Amy reminded her. 'Aunt Celia was in there like a battalion of shock-troops. No man was bringing me up, especially not Uncle Peter.'

'I remember,' Jill said with a wry grimace. 'Your uncle Peter just let it go, and she would have won in court anyway. She was a blood relative; Peter wasn't.'

'You know, I never did discover why Aunt Celia and Uncle Peter disliked each other so much,' Amy murmured. 'I once heard them quarrelling violently. It was soon after I went to live with Aunt Celia. I came down to get a drink of water one night and they were in the little room that Aunt Celia called her den.'

'What was the quarrel about?' Jill asked with a quick glance at Amy's thoughtful face.

'I don't know. The door to the den was closed tightly. I heard her say something about my father but I really didn't want to hear.'

'Maybe one day it will all come back to you,' Jill mused. 'The mind is a funny thing. It conceals things, imagines things. If something was said that you didn't want to hear, something you couldn't bear, the mind is quite capable of protecting you. Sometimes, later, it just reopens that particular chapter and you remember.'

'I can remember the scene quite vividly,' Amy assured her. 'I didn't hear properly because the door was shut, and I was too upset by everything to linger and eavesdrop.'

'I'm surprised you ever got over all the pain of losing your father, your home and all the things you'd been so used to,' Jill said quietly.

'I didn't have a lot of choice. All the same, one would have thought that my father would have made provision for me, whatever the business agreement said. We were not at all poor. I know there was personal money.'

Amy sat thinking deeply for a moment and Jill cut into her thoughts.

'I was there at the time, Amy. You know that. I thought it was awful the way you seemed to have been ignored and I told Peter in no uncertain terms, although strictly speaking it was nothing to do with me. He was really upset himself, and I suppose I didn't make things any better by raging about it. He said he would always take care of you and in any case you would finally get everything – his own money as well as your father's. Of course when your Aunt Celia descended like the Wicked Witch of the West, Peter had no alternative but to back off. She wouldn't even let him take you for a little while.' Jill looked thoughtful for a minute. 'It was cruel of her, you know. You were too grief-stricken and too young to notice but she really surprised me by her attitude. Peter Jensen was her stepbrother too, but she treated him like an enemy.'

Jill suddenly brightened and pulled herself out of the past. 'No more speculation. It's all past. Let me tell you about this great new job of mine.'

'I don't want to know. I fully expect to get a letter from you saying you're never coming back.'

'No chance. I live here. I have plans.'

'So long as they don't include Uncle Peter,' Amy warned.

'I don't intend to spend my time dreaming about Peter Jensen. There are other fish in the sea.'

'I'm glad to hear it,' Amy said firmly. 'I expect in the course of his life he's broken a few hearts.'

'I'm no simple-minded female,' Jill reminded her with a laugh. 'You take care of yourself while I'm away.'

When Jill had gone, Amy thought back over the evening. It had been pleasant but Jill had been a little on edge – not surprising, really, when she was flying off to a new life tomorrow. Anyway, she had been on edge herself. It had not been a good day but, surprisingly enough, the best part of it had been her unwanted meeting with Luc Martell. She admitted to a degree of worried fascination in that direction. She wondered if by any chance he was in Paris for the weekend, presenting the brooch to the duchess. Amy went to bed feeling quite worn out by events. Delving into the past was never a good idea, and being uneasily fascinated by the boss was even worse.

On Monday morning the post came before Amy left for work and she recognized the long envelope that lay on the mat at the front door the moment she saw it. Hetherington's, her Aunt Celia's solicitors. It would be about her aunt's will. Bryan Hetherington, who now headed the firm, had been at the funeral with his father and he had warned her before they went into church that the letter about the will was already being prepared.

Amy felt a certain amount of dread as she opened it. Somehow or other it emphasized the fact that her aunt was no longer alive, and Amy sat in the kitchen to read the short letter before she went out to work.

It was brief and to the point. Could she be present at the office at five-thirty today? Bryan Hetherington realized that she might be a few minutes late but he was quite prepared to wait for her until six. He would tell her the contents of the will.

Amy stuffed the letter into her bag and picked up her car keys. It was all very inevitable, not something she could slide out of. Right at that moment she hoped her aunt had left her money to some obscure charity. And she would certainly be late.

After Friday's little fiasco there was no way she could leave the office before five-thirty, and there was no way either that she would be willing to ask Luc Martell for permission to leave early. She intended to keep her head down today. She didn't want any unnecessary eye contact with the boss.

Being with him on Friday had somehow altered her feelings. She had the uneasy conviction that he had carefully prowled one step closer and she had no idea why. The only thing she could think of was that he was preparing to get rid of her and had used the unexpected opportunity to study her more closely. She had talked too much too, because she had suddenly felt very confident in his company. And she hadn't missed the amusement on his face. Maybe today he would have made his mind up to dismiss her. Maybe that was what he had been amused about.

He was already there when she arrived, and Amy walked through the main building, well aware, as usual, that he could see her. Martell International had taken over the original building, altered and expanded it. The large office that had always housed the director was still there and Luc Martell occupied it.

Previously, the glass-fronted room had been concealed by bright pictures. It had been possible to approach the room or pass it without the watchful eye of anyone glancing up to enquire. The pictures had gone. Luc Martell had got rid of them as soon as he had taken over. And he did not 'enquire'; as far as she was concerned, he stared balefully.

Amy was very much aware of him as she crossed the main room and made her way to her own office. She was surrounded by glass too, but once safely in front of her computers she never noticed because her back was to his office.

Amy refused to quicken her steps and scurry into her own little hole. She walked gracefully forward before turning to her own door. Once in there she was on her own ground and, as far as she knew, Luc Martell was computer illiterate.

She closed her door behind her and breathed a sigh of relief greatly tempered by annoyance. It was ridiculous, a daily trial, like running the gauntlet. Amy got down to work at once, taking off her jacket and sitting on her little red chair – safe.

Luc frowned after her through the glass, greatly disgruntled. He hadn't really enjoyed his weekend at home. He had been thinking about the irritating Miss Scott for most of the time, even when he had had dinner with Veronique. He hated to admit that anyone could get under his skin. He had been here early too, telling himself that he wanted to make quite sure she was on time but knowing deep inside that he wanted to watch her walk across the office before she buried herself in front of her wretched machines.

She had come in like a dream, as usual, her silky corn-coloured dress swirling around her legs, her shining hair swinging round her shoulders, and she had ignored the fact that he was sitting there watching her. She hadn't even looked slightly embarrassed that he had caught her skipping work on Friday.

She was cool, at least on the outside, and he could scarcely believe that she had talked in that fluffy-headed manner at the restaurant. Today she was back to normal, Miss Computer. He gave an irritated grunt and rang for his secretary, another person who annoyed him beyond words.

Meanwhile, Amy settled to her work, seeing that two computers were down and dealing with them at once. Then she was back to normal.

'Right! Here we go, Jim,' she muttered to her main machine. 'Back to the wire-works.' She started and the wire frame for the latest building came up on the screen.

Today she had to face Luc Martell close up and she knew it. He would be in here with his plans and she had to turn them into reality in front of his eyes. It didn't really matter. She didn't actually have to look at him at all. She had managed like that since he came here. She watched her machines and pretended he wasn't there.

He gave her time to settle in and then he was there, right behind her, a great sheaf of papers in his hand, a roll of blueprints under his arm. Even the way he came into the room was predatory and alarming to Amy, although she didn't turn round. She didn't dare, really.

'I assume we are ready, Miss Scott?' he enquired coldly, and Amy was quite surprised at the way she tightened up even further, considering that arguments never bothered her one little bit.

She didn't actually want to argue with Luc Martell, though. He was altogether too powerful. Apart from being the boss, he was cold, unapproachable and unsympathetic, and she couldn't quite reckon how she had relaxed with him in that restaurant on Friday.

It had been his second-in-command, Gordon Sheen, who had given her time off for the funeral. And she *had* noticed that two of the computers had been down. Luc Martell had probably been furious that she wasn't there.

Amy felt a slight twinge of conscience. If she had come back immediately after lunch, she could have seen to that on Friday. In all fairness she couldn't really blame him for being annoyed.

She did blame him for alarming her, though. He hadn't alarmed her at the restaurant. He hadn't been cold, unapproachable and unsympathetic there. All she could conclude was that he was strange and it was probably because he was half-French.

'Ready as far as I know.' Amy didn't look round and Luc deposited his things on the corner of one of her desks and drew up a chair. She gave him a small mark for intelligence when he put the chair at her left-hand side, otherwise she would have been bowling him over each time she wanted to scoot across to another screen. She indicated the wire frame.

In computer-aided design, the bare bones of a building were always like this. They had to be exact, drawn from the architect's specifications, and this was Luc's own project, plans for a building in London. He stared at it until she began to imagine she had done it all wrong.

'A forty-five-degree turn, please,' he ordered in an aloof voice, and Amy's fingers flew over the keyboard. The whole skeleton of the building turned and he did some more staring.

'What does it look like from behind?' he asked in the same robot-like tones, and she turned the whole thing around.

She realized that she was back to being a mouse again, and at the moment it didn't even irritate her. He was so *close*, sitting on that chair beside her. He always did that, but it was beginning to get to her more each time. It was something the other architects in the firm did too, but she never paid much attention. She noticed it when the person beside her was Luc Martell.

Besides, she could smell his aftershave, and out of the corners of her eyes she could see his hands. They were strong, long-fingered, strangely exciting, very masculine hands. Amy quickly looked away when she felt her cheeks begin to get hot.

He was usually too busy to do much designing. There was the whole firm to run – a money-making giant – but this building was very important. The best architect had to do it and that was the boss. It dawned on her that in some strange way she was just a little scared of him, but it was definitely in an excited sort of way, as if she was waiting for something momentous to happen.

'Have you done the surrounding buildings?' he enquired, after studying it for a while.

'They're on Alfie,' Amy muttered, skimming across to another computer.

'What?' When she looked at him he was staring at her with a puzzled frown on his face and he hadn't made a move to join her . . .

'Er – this computer,' she told him with a slight look of embarrassment. She brought the surrounding buildings up on screen, the new one set in place, but Luc still stayed where he was, staring at her with dark-eyed interest.

'You have given names to these machines?' he asked, as if it confirmed her insanity.

He realized that she astonished him all the time. She intrigued him too. There was something perky about her, like an elf about to make mischief. But she was far too beautiful to be classed as an elf, too elegant. She was a curious creature all the same.

'Why not?' Amy enquired defiantly. 'I'm with them all day. I talk to them.'

'They reply?' he asked scathingly, trying to keep the amusement and fascination out of his voice.

'They would if I wanted them to,' Amy assured

49

him tersely, 'and they wouldn't say one thing I objected to either.'

She turned back to the screen and he got up to have a viewing. Her cheeks were slightly pink, he noted. Was it because she was embarrassed about calling her computer by a name? He decided that it must be, because as far as he knew she never reacted at all to his own presence.

This time he stood behind her chair and bent over close to her, watching the screen, and Amy felt quite trapped, a flutter of excited panic rising in her throat. She wanted to slide out of her chair and run. It was stupid but he had that effect on her.

'Good,' Luc pronounced softly after what seemed like ages. 'Given that the measurements are exact . . .'

'They are!' Amy assured him testily, leaping towards anger to steady her nerves.

'Then we have room for manoeuvre,' he concluded. He went back to his chair. 'We can now render the building, stone on concrete.'

Amy whizzed back and he watched her for a minute as she turned the framework into an actual building, colour-perfect, realistic, and she managed it – smooth as silk. He watched her fingers fly over the keys. The nails were short, oval, no nail varnish. She had delicate hands, like a fairytale princess in a book, some book that had been beautifully drawn.

He suddenly had a tremendous urge to reach forward and take one of those slender hands in his. His own hand would swallow it up, enclose it completely. Her perfume was teasing his nostrils, faintly, tantalizingly. He had another urge – to lean much closer to her.

'What is the name of this machine?' he asked, to take his mind off her very feminine presence and the odd effect it was having on him.

'Jim,' Amy told him, feeling her cheeks flush at his wry tone. 'It's my main computer.'

'And your dearest friend,' he surmised quietly.

'At least it likes me,' Amy found herself muttering.

'Merely because you control it,' he murmured drily. 'It would give its allegiance to anyone else with the same skill.'

It seemed a bit cruel and it made Amy feel quite sad, more so because it was quite true, and she concluded that he was telling her that she was nothing special really. He was probably going to get rid of her because she annoyed him. She had known for ages that she annoyed him. She considered sabotaging the whole office network and resigning, but decided against it when she imagined his fury.

'Make me a garden,' he ordered softly, extremely softly when she considered her own turbulent thoughts. 'Let's see how artistic you are. Remember the drawbacks to a garden in the city, nothing lush, just something pleasing to the eye.'

He got up and walked out, pausing at the door to tell her he would be back. She didn't doubt it. He was inevitable, ruthless, efficient and icy cold. Amy frowned at Jim, almost jumping when Luc spoke again . . .

'You are called Scott because your family originally came from Scotland?' he asked unexpectedly, when she was quite sure he had already gone. He sounded quite intrigued, interested, and it startled her into turning to look at him.

'My family came from Ireland originally,' she informed him blankly, puzzled by his interest.

'Peculiar,' he muttered, frowning at her thoughtfully.

'I can't see why,' Amy began defensively. 'I was asked a pointless question about you on Friday. It's just the same when you come to think about it.'

CHAPTER 3

His frown deepened.

'I was a subject for discussion at this lunchtime date you had?'

'At the funeral, actually,' Amy told him airily. 'Peter wanted to know about you. And don't ask me why. I have no idea why a stranger should be at all interested in you.'

She knew she was skirting on the very edge of insubordination, if not actually stepping right into it, but all she got was a long look from narrowed dark eyes and then he walked out and left her in peace – for now.

Luc walked back to his office feeling vaguely thunderous. He felt as if he had been bandying words with an impertinent witch and it annoyed him. For one thing he was on the very best of terms with the rest of the staff, first-name terms with the other architects. Amy Scott was a thorn in the flesh and he always had this urge to goad her.

It would have been better to ignore her, but that was impossible; he had to work with her and he knew she was the very best. His father was more than impressed with her work. Besides, he was becoming more fascinated each day and he knew it. He also knew it had to stop.

He walked into his office and only just controlled the urge to slam the door. When he had come here there had been double-sided posters on the windows that looked out into the interior of the building. His side had shown gardens, the other side had shown buildings of an imposing nature; offices, bridges, huge modern factories. Everything they did on a worldwide scale.

He had ordered their removal to give the staff more access to him. He had failed to take into account that the staff were English and liked to be private – in Amy Scott's case liked to be secretive. Unless she was there, nobody in the whole building could get access to those machines. She had built herself a small empire in one long office.

Jim and Alfie! Obviously she preferred machines to people. He wondered what the boyfriend had been like. A turbulent relationship, according to office gossip. How did they know? She never seemed to bother with anyone at all here. Everyone showed her a good deal of respect, though.

He had seen her joking with the other architects when they were working with her. Apparently he was the only one to get the edgy reception. She might be scared of him but he doubted it. Prickly little witch! And he had to go back in there before too long. He relied on her and those blasted machines.

* * *

Amy was glad to see the end of the day. She had been involved with Luc Martell for far too long, not that she hadn't expected it. They were well on the way now, though, and she knew he was pleased with the work – although he was obviously disgruntled with her on a personal basis. She had actually been close to trembling for some of the time and it worried her considerably.

She left the office at the stroke of five-thirty and couldn't help glancing into Luc's office as she passed. He deliberately looked at his watch and she glared at him defiantly. It was closing time and she was going. She had an appointment that she didn't really want but she had to keep it. In any case, she wasn't hanging about round here. She wasn't even sure if she liked her job any more. And it was all Luc Martell's fault.

They seemed to be constantly circling each other like deadly enemies, each reluctant to make the first strike. Anyway, whatever happened he would win, because he was the boss; he held all the cards. Besides, she had almost decided that she was scared of him in an odd sort of way, because she never liked it if she was off work for any reason. She didn't see him if she was off work and she was always quite desperate to get back, ridiculously relieved to see that nobody had come from France to take his place. Amy thought of her great urge to look up and see him as a sort of addiction. People were addicted to all sorts of things. She wondered if she was addicted to anxious excitement.

'Not bad, Amy,' Bryan Hetherington said, glancing at his watch as she was shown into his office.

'You made it in just over ten minutes. Hope you didn't go through any red lights.'

'I'm in enough trouble at work without taking on the police,' Amy muttered.

'Ah! The new boss,' Bryan assumed. He had been to her aunt's house several times when she was there because her aunt Celia had frequently considered suing people for minor infringements of her rights. Bryan had inherited her when his father retired and he had usually been able to sidetrack Celia's irritation with the world at large. He knew Amy very well.

He was nice, she concluded as she sat by his desk. He looked just like a nice man should look. He was about the same age as Luc Martell but there the comparisons ended. Bryan was gentle, easy-going, fair and pleasant, everyone's idea of an Englishman.

She looked him over as he sorted out his papers. Bryan was afternoon tea on the lawn, a boat ride on the river, cheerful smiles and ready laughter. Luc Martell was a lethal weapon.

She frowned when she realized that she was thinking about him again, as usual.

'It's nothing to look furious about,' Bryan grinned as he glanced up and saw her forbidding expression. 'Celia left you the lot.'

'I was thinking about my boss,' Amy muttered, and his grin widened.

'Oh, him again. Work is over for the day, Amy. Concentrate on this.'

She didn't have a lot of choice. Aunt Celia had left a very neat, tight will. The gist of it was that everything was for her niece, Amy. Nothing was left to another soul. Amy got the money, the house and its contents, her aunt's car, which had not left the garage for years, and all other assets.

'She had quite a lot of shares in a variety of things,' Bryan Hetherington told Amy as he glanced through the papers. 'I'm seeing you today just to let you know the overall picture. We'll have to sort out where all the money is and get to grips with things. It will take some time. Then you have to consider whether or not to sell the house and contents.' He glanced up at her seriously. 'What I can tell you for sure, Amy, is that you'll be very well off indeed. Your aunt checked the will with me quite recently. I've never known her to be so anxious. She wanted to be quite sure that you had everything down to the last candlestick. I had to go through it twice with her. She was quite jubilant when she was certain that everything was water-tight. She actually gave me a bottle of brandy.' He grinned reminiscently and then adopted his solicitor expression. 'You should now make a will yourself.'

'I'm only twenty-five,' Amy reminded him with an indignant look. 'Are you suggesting that I might get knocked over by a bus?'

'Perish the thought, but you never know,' he laughed. 'Seriously, though, there'll be a wait for this to be processed. In the meantime you should make a will, however short.'

'OK,' Amy muttered resignedly. 'I'd like you to know, though, that you're depressing me – and lately I depress very easily.'

'Right. I'll take you out to dinner tonight, then,' he suggested, and Amy gave it a moment's thought. Why not? He was good company and if by any dreadful chance they met Eric, Bryan was sufficiently large to act as a cover.

'OK. You're on,' she agreed brightly.

'I'll pick you up at seven-thirty,' Bryan told her, looking very pleased with himself and somewhat surprised.

'I'll give you directions.'

'I know where you live,' he grinned. 'It's my business to know everything.'

Amy smiled and left, musing that she had assumed it was only Luc Martell's business to know everything. She gave herself an irritated mental shake. She was allowing that man to take on enormous proportions in her mind. He was the boss and nothing but the boss and she was indispensable. Maybe she wasn't, though? Maybe he just couldn't stand her any more? Anyway, she was about to be rich. She could laugh in his face and leave.

She thought about her computers and looked grim. She didn't want anyone else messing about with her machines. Imagine another person sitting in front of Jim or Alfie! It wasn't even possible to imagine it. Nobody but her had ever touched them and she kept all their secrets hidden, password-protected, firewalled so that nobody could gain access.

She wasn't about to leave. Luc Martell could leave. He could go back to his beloved Paris and his glamorous ladies with their deep sophistication and overwhelming self-assurance. He could go back to his mother with her emerald brooch and expensive silk scarf. He could just go!

She wasn't quite sure that she wanted him to go, however. Amy had a vivid imagination and already she could see somebody else in his office, looking up as she came in each morning. She was used to seeing Luc Martell's dark, handsome face. She couldn't imagine the new face but she knew she didn't like it.

Amy drove home, feeling vaguely uneasy and not at all sure why. It was a lovely evening. Now that the summer was drawing to a close it wasn't light for quite as long at night but it was still quite warm. She started to wonder what she should wear for the evening with Bryan and decided to really dress up.

Besides, she hadn't been out in the evening for ages, not since her break-up with Eric, actually. She hadn't liked to chance going out with Jill and meeting him because at the very least he would make a scene, if he felt that way inclined. She wondered why she had got mixed up with him in the first place and then made a wry face. Inexperience.

School, university, computers. She hadn't had much time for a social life and she had always been too enthralled with her work, almost addicted. The men at college had pored over computers with her for hours, admiring her skills, treating her as more than equal and then taking some lesser mortal out in the evening. She put most men off with her intelligence.

Amy frowned even more. Luc Martell thought she was a halfwit. It showed on his face. In any case, she usually managed to say something pretty stupid when he was there because he scared her and she wasn't quite sure why. He made her feel fluttery inside. In some way he was a threat.

He needed watching, but she didn't feel like being the one to do it. Let somebody else watch him. Her own inclination was to lie low, to conceal herself with Jim, Alfie and their brothers. She usually followed her instincts, and as far as Luc Martell was concerned she would follow her instincts slavishly and hide.

She wondered if he would object if she got some big pictures and pasted them on the windows of her office? Yes, he would. He had taken down the pictures on *his* windows so that he could spy on people – most likely so that he could spy on her. He knew everything. God was definitely a Frenchman. Maybe she ought to let other people know that astonishing fact.

Amy's house was in a short, modern terrace. Her aunt Celia had despised it but Amy had stuck to her decision. It was big enough for her, in a safe area and small enough to be able to manage when she was working all day. She had persuaded her aunt that it was ideal for the modern businesswoman and Celia had liked the sound of that. It had the ring of independence and, once won over, Celia had used her influence, her taste and her money to furnish it, whether Amy liked the idea or not.

In consequence, Amy had a small but luxuriously appointed place of her own, a place filled with treasures that had been her aunt's and other luxurious pieces that they had bought on shopping expeditions. Amy always had a feeling of satisfaction when she stopped her car outside her little refuge. She thought of it as a bijou residence, and going in through the door always relaxed her.

Her clothes, too, were the result of many sorties to London with her aunt, and she had plenty to choose from when she prepared for her unexpected date with Bryan.

Finally, she chose blue, her aunt's favourite colour. The dress brought out the unusual violet shade of her eyes and Amy inspected her appearance critically as she stood before the mirror later. She always felt critical of herself now, ever since Eric had informed her of her failings – which, she had discovered, were many.

He had lectured her scathingly on the subject of her nut-brown hair. Neither straight nor curly, it hung in shining waves around her face and curled under at the ends with no help from her. According to Eric Somerfield it was nondescript. He had wanted her to dye it blonde.

Her figure, too, had come in for radical criticism. She was too slender, no voluptuous curves in the right places. He had called her skin and bone and she had believed him. Not that she had done anything about it. It was not her nature to be in any way voluptuous, and she was far too brisk and energetic to put on weight – not that he would have liked that either. He was a bully, a controller, and although Amy had finally seen that, she was still a little unsure of her appearance.

By the time she was ready, though, her natural independence had reasserted itself, and when Bryan called to collect her she was further relaxed as she noted the gleam of admiration in his eyes. It was all that staying in every evening, she decided, no jaunts out after work. Since the very upsetting end of her relationship with Eric, Amy had done far too much staying in. In future this hermit-like existence would cease. She settled down to enjoy herself. Bryan would take her somewhere expensive and Eric was not likely to saunter in there.

It was a place where Amy had never been before, a smart new restaurant on the very edge of town. Even the entrance was glossy, and the discreet lighting was enhanced by candles on each table. Bryan had reserved a table for them and Amy was sorry that it was almost in the centre of the dining room. She would have preferred to sit at the side and watch the other diners. As it was, the other diners would be able to watch her.

She gave herself a quick mental shake. What was wrong with her? Hadn't she decided not half an hour ago that she was now sure of herself, indifferent to her public image? She just had this feeling of being scrutinized thoroughly, but it was all nervous reaction to staying indoors so long.

Amy smiled at Bryan and made a determined effort to relax, telling herself that imagining that eyes were on her was quite arrogant and definitely self-satisfied. It was not. She looked around with a show of polite interest and her eyes met the dark, intense gaze of Luc Martell.

'Damn! Damn, damn, damn!' Amy muttered as she looked away rapidly. He was like her nemesis. She only had to see him and she started searching her mind for faults, always sure she had done something very wrong. She had the uneasy feeling that somehow he had known she would be here and had arranged to sit where he could spoil her evening and control her behaviour.

Her hands were tingling, as if she was close to some source of electricity, and she knew she usually felt like that when Luc Martell was near. This was why she had been sure she was under observation. Well, she had been right. She *was* under observation. She felt trapped.

'What's the problem?' Bryan asked with his usual grin.

'It's *him*, the boss – Luc Martell, the bane of my life. He's actually come to spoil my evening.'

'I never told a soul,' Bryan assured her with an even wider grin. 'It's sheer coincidence, Amy. Relax. The poor chap has to eat – forget him.'

The trouble was, she couldn't. She hadn't been able to forget him since she had first set eyes on him six months ago. And he wasn't a poor chap either. Bryan was alarmingly naïve. You only had to look at Luc Martell to know he was dangerous, and it wasn't just because he was the boss either.

Her earlier thoughts of Bryan being comfortably big faded into insignificance. Luc Martell was big – athletic, tall, full of lean energy, every ounce of him smoothly co-ordinated. He was big like a dangerous wild animal in prime condition, intelligent, watchful, capable and silkily silent. She could imagine him coming soundlessly out of the dark, to punish. Every time she saw him she was on edge. He was assuming enormous proportions in her mind.

It would take someone imperious to deal with him, someone like Aunt Celia. The trouble was, Amy was not Aunt Celia. Even though every action necessary to survive elegantly had been drilled into her from an early age, how to deal with dark-eyed danger had been sadly neglected. Now Amy didn't want to stay, but she was too embarrassed to point this out to Bryan.

He had told her to relax and he appeared to have assumed that she had. Little did he know. She would much rather have stayed in and worked on her own personal computer than sit here all dressed up, with Luc Martell staring at her with stony-eyed disapproval and a great deal of potent concentration.

'When are you coming in to make the will?' Bryan asked as they ate their first course, with Amy trying not to choke on it from sheer nervous reaction.

'Any time you care to specify,' Amy muttered. Making a will didn't seem such a bad idea at this moment. She might not survive the evening. 'Just say the word.'

'So what are you going to do with all this cash?'

'I haven't seen it yet,' Amy pointed out wryly.

'Soon enough. Probate should be swift. It's all laid down smoothly and there's nobody to contest it as far as we know.'

'Not a single person,' Amy assured him. 'There's just me and Uncle Peter now.'

'What about him?' Bryan asked with a quick frown of legal unease.

'Forget him. Peter is rolling in money and always has been. In any case, he's not strictly family, not really. He was my father's stepbrother. Aunt Celia was my father's older sister, so Peter was her stepbrother too. He's not a blood relation.'

'One would have thought, though, that . . .'

'That she'd leave some to him? Not a chance. There was some sort of quarrel that neither of them ever spoke about. It was probably not much. Aunt Celia could be very quietly vindictive if she chose. She never mentioned his name – in fact she behaved as if he didn't exist. He felt the same. If she'd left him anything he would have refused it. And, as I told you, he's wealthy. He runs two racehorses out of the petty cash.'

'That lets him out, then. So who are you going to leave your money to when you make this will?'

'Assuming the existence of a carelessly driven bus? Peter, of course – who else?'

'And if he dies?'

'We'll cross that bridge when we come to it,' Amy told him firmly. 'Anyway, according to Jill, Peter will never die.'

'She's already gone to America, then?' Bryan enquired, adding with a sort of vague warning, 'Your aunt only tolerated Jill Davis, you know. She never actually liked her.'

Amy gave him a slyly amused glance.

'She wasn't too fussy about you either. Off hand, I can't think of anyone she actually *liked*. She used to tell me that all the good people were dead now and the rest were incredibly vulgar.'

'Well, she liked you, Amy. That's why you'll soon be comfortably off. Will you sell her house?'

'I'm not sure,' Amy mused. 'It's a lovely place, and perfect inside. It seems a shame to sell all the things she collected, to have them scattered around with strangers. She didn't care for people much.'

'She's dead, Amy,' Bryan pronounced in a very final voice. 'Everything is yours and you must decide.'

'Peter and I sort of imagined her looking down at us, disapprovingly.'

'That's too foolish, and he shouldn't encourage you in such thoughts. You're supposed to be a very practical computer-orientated person.'

'I am,' Amy protested, thinking uneasily about the way she called her computers Jim and Alfie. She called the other two 'the boys'. Luc Martell didn't know that. She glanced up, but he was getting on with his meal and she was no longer caught by the dark vibrance of his eyes. While she had been talking to Bryan she had almost forgotten about Luc.

Amy congratulated herself. Maybe he didn't scare her all that much anyway. It was just that she seemed to have acquired a wild imagination.

She concentrated on her meal and on Bryan. He was a nice man. His blond good looks and his quiet smile made him seem so trustworthy and unthreatening. Luc Martell looked threatening even when he wasn't. She cast a secret glance at him and her eyes just lingered.

He was drinking his coffee and reading a book at the same time. He was probably lonely. Still, as far as she knew he hadn't tried to get to know anyone. He just shot off to Paris whenever he had the chance. There was always a lot of conferring to do with Head Office, and it was always Luc who went. He probably didn't know anyone here, except on passing terms.

It was unusual to be able to study him, and Amy took the opportunity without even knowing why she was doing it. He was very dark – continental dark. She improvised the description and felt quite pleased with it because it covered a lot of things, like the darker skin that wasn't just tan but showed his ancestry. His hair was a true, total black and so were his eyes, as far as she knew. She had never quite had the nerve to look into them for more than a second – well, not at close quarters anyway.

He looked what he was: wealthy, aloof, irritated by his surroundings. It was almost impossible to imagine him being warm and gentle, to imagine him laughing easily. He must do, though. After all, he had a mother. He probably had a woman of some sort in Paris, Amy mused. He looked far too much the male animal to be a loner of any sort. He managed to make her shiver most of the time. She wondered why he didn't bring the woman here. She might have a job of her own, though. No wonder he hated being here in this town.

Her rather dreamy musings were interrupted when she heard Bryan murmur under his breath, and she glanced across to find him looking over her shoulder.

'What is it?' she asked, but she didn't really have time to get any reply. She knew what it was the moment a familiar voice sounded almost in her ear.

'Venturing out into the world again, are we? Does this mean you're getting over our parting or is this just your usual play-acting at being happy without me?'

There was a nasty, biting edge to the voice and, as usual, Eric Somerfield was making no attempt to keep his voice low. Amy's face flushed with embarrassment. The fear of a scene had kept her out of circulation for almost three months. During that time she had not seen Eric and now he was here, behaving exactly as she would have expected. Amy took a steadying breath.

'I'm having dinner with a friend,' she said quietly. 'Please go away, Eric, and leave me alone.'

'What sort of friend have you got this time?' Eric Somerfield asked in an even louder voice. 'Is he going home with you? Is he taking my place?'

'I think you'd better go about your own business,' Bryan suggested, standing and looking at the other man furiously. 'Amy can do without any sordid scenes. If you're eating here, then go and eat. If not, then leave the restaurant.'

Eric Somerfield did not answer. He leaned across and pushed Bryan hard in the chest, all his considerable weight behind the action, and Bryan went over. His legs had been against the chair as he stood and he had no chance at all to save himself from the unexpected attack. He fell back against the chair, which tipped over, taking him with it.

There was a crash, and all eyes that had not been looking at them already were now turned in their direction. Amy saw the waiter hurrying forward, but he was a small man and she knew he would not be able to control Eric in his present mood. She moved to help Bryan, who was having difficulty in disentangling himself from the chair, but hard hands grabbed her and Eric spun her round.

'I told you it was me or nobody,' he snarled into her white face. 'You can leave with me now, unless you want a bigger scene.'

Suddenly his face twisted with what Amy recognized as pain. He gasped, and it was only then that she became aware that Luc was standing behind him with one hand on his shoulder. She wondered how one hand could make Eric gasp. Eric was strong. She saw one of his arms disappear behind his back and the gasp became even louder.

'I think we've all had more scene than we require. You may walk out of here, *m'sieur*, or I will throw you out.' Luc's voice was frighteningly soft, dangerous. Amy could hear that even if nobody else could.

'It's got damn all to do with you – !' Eric blustered, his voice suddenly cut off again as more pain crossed his face.

'I was drinking my coffee in tranquillity. I was also reading a book. You irritate me. Make your choice quickly. For myself, I would prefer to throw you out with considerable force. I do not like to have my evening meal interrupted.'

'I'll go,' Eric muttered, shaking his arm free as Luc let him go. 'But she's not heard the end of this!'

'You're threatening this lady?' Luc Martell asked in a quietly menacing voice, and Eric turned and left without looking back.

Amy's face was still unnaturally pale, and Luc turned to look at her as Bryan Hetherington managed to get to his feet with help from the waiter, who was casting grateful glances in Luc's direction.

'Are you all right?' Luc asked, his dark eyes taking in Amy's distress.

'Yes, thank you,' she whispered, biting at her lip. 'I'm sorry you had to be involved with that.'

'I involved myself,' he assured her. 'There is no reason to be sorry. You did not cause that unpleasant little interlude.'

'Thanks for helping. He took me by surprise.' Bryan stood, looking embarrassed but holding out his hand to Luc.

'It is not important,' Luc pronounced coolly. 'Perhaps it would be better if you took Miss Scott home. I cannot think that your intruding acquaintance will be too pleased when his wits finally settle back into place.' He nodded in a stiffly polite way at both of them and then went back to his coffee.

'He's right,' Bryan agreed. 'Let's get out of here, Amy. I assume that Somerfield wouldn't hesitate to wait outside for you?'

'He wouldn't hesitate normally,' Amy muttered, trying hard not to meet the eyes of any other diners as she went with Bryan to the door. 'He might think twice about it now, though.'

She felt devastated, shaken. Apart from the terrible embarrassment, she couldn't get over the fact that Eric's threats when she had broken up with him were all too real. And she couldn't shake off the feeling of real danger that had been in the air as Luc Martell intervened.

He was everything she had thought he was: swift, dark and dangerous. She managed one last quick glance at him and he was finishing his coffee as if nothing at all had happened. He was even reading the book again. He had quelled a disturbance without any effort and the staff were looking at him with grateful expressions on their faces. Amy was grateful too, but now he scared her more than ever. She ought to be feeling warmly pleased with him but she wasn't.

'I wonder who our guardian angel was?' Bryan murmured as they drove through the town towards Amy's house.

'It was my boss,' Amy said quietly. 'I told you he was there in the restaurant.'

'I see. He's French, then?' Bryan asked, glancing sharply at her. 'I never knew that.'

'Half-French,' she corrected automatically. 'I think that distasteful little episode brought out the worst in him, the French side.'

'Well, I'm glad he was there,' Bryan assured her. 'That lunatic caught me off guard. I never expect people to behave like that in civilized surroundings. Whatever drove you to going out with him in the first place, Amy?'

'Stupidity,' she told him shortly.

It must have been that. Eric had hidden his real character initially, but she had known deep down before very long and she had let it continue when she should have sent him packing right from the first.

Maybe her aunt had been right. Maybe she was too involved with machines to be able to recognize people for what they were. And what they were was a nuisance, according to Aunt Celia.

Amy just couldn't believe that. It was true, though, that every time she lifted her head from her machines and tried to be with people trouble loomed up very speedily. She suddenly felt quite helpless, because there was a sort of foreboding in the air. Her life didn't seem to be her own, what with one thing and another.

Amy was more than pleased to see her own little house as Bryan drew up outside her front door. She had no garden at the front but it didn't bother her too much. She accepted that this was a town-house, with only street parking. It suited her fine, and even though it was quite dark now she was greatly relieved to get out of the bright lights and the embarrassment of the evening.

'I'm sorry about all the fuss tonight,' Bryan began earnestly as she turned to thank him.

'You didn't make the fuss, Bryan,' Amy assured him quietly. 'Perhaps I should have stayed in my own little nest and not ventured out. I knew that sooner or later I was bound to encounter Eric in one of his moods.'

'You can't just hide indoors,' Bryan told her forcefully. 'Somerfield has no right to accost you. If he does it again we'll report him to the police.'

'Heavens, no!' Amy gasped. 'It would only make matters worse. I expect it will all blow over in time.'

'Maybe,' Bryan muttered angrily. 'I'm irritated that he attacked me so quickly and caught me off guard. It was left to your boss to protect you. I suppose I'm feeling inadequate.'

'Oh, Bryan, for goodness' sake! You're a very civilized person. I'm not sure that Luc Martell is civilized at all. He could deal with that sort of thing while eating his breakfast.'

'He certainly rose to the occasion, didn't he?' Bryan mused thoughtfully. 'I wonder if he's been in one of those élite French army groups?'

'You mean like the Foreign Legion?' Amy laughed. 'No. I think he was just born ferocious.'

'Well, he put paid to Somerfield expertly enough,' Bryan muttered. 'It makes you think.'

'Thank you, but I'd rather not,' Amy informed him, making a move to get out of the car. 'It's bad enough facing him at work. It will be worse now and I don't really like to dwell on his possible training. He makes me shiver as it is. Thanks for the evening anyway.'

She smiled her brilliant smile and Bryan reached across to kiss her cheek.

'Next time,' he promised, 'we'll dine right out of town.'

'That's a good idea. We should have thought of it earlier.'

Amy waved him off and then went into the house. She wasn't sure if she wanted a 'next time'. This time had been traumatic enough. It had left her very shaken and she had to face the boss tomorrow. She hoped he wouldn't want to ask any awkward questions about tonight. It would put her that one step dangerously closer to him.

She couldn't help thinking that things seemed to have taken a turn for the worse, though. Aunt Celia was dead, Jill had left for America and Eric had come out of the woodwork with scenes and threats. Everything had happened so suddenly too.

Also, there was Luc Martell, and the scary, excited danger she felt whenever he was there. Worse than that, though, he was always on her mind. It was beginning to drive her frantic.

Further up the street, Luc's black Porsche was parked in the shadows. He had left as soon as they had been out of sight of the restaurant and he had followed them skilfully to Amy's house. He had the feeling that the man in the restaurant was by no means finished, and he wasn't at all convinced that her escort for the night would be any more capable of tackling an assailant in the street than he had been in the lights of the dining room.

He assumed that the noisy and violent intruder had been her ex-boyfriend. He felt irritably astonished. How had she ever got mixed up with anyone like that? She was a delicate sort of woman, beautiful, obviously fastidious, vulnerable in spite of her tongue and her irritating ways. If that had been the notorious Eric Somerfield, he was bordering on the uncouth.

Luc's mouth twisted disgustedly. The man was handsome enough in an uncultivated sort of way, but Amy Scott was clever, very clever. Maybe when she was away from her beloved machines she was naïve and defenceless as a child? A ready tongue wouldn't help with someone like Somerfield. And anyway, she had been another character when she had been talking to him in that store, telling him he was not easy to get on with.

Luc moved exasperatedly in his car as they sat talking. He wanted to see her safely indoors and then he could leave. Hadn't it dawned on the man with her that at any moment Somerfield might put in an unwelcome appearance? She wouldn't be safe until that front door was locked behind her.

He saw her escort lean across and kiss her and he was surprised at the swift wave of annoyance that flooded through him. If they were just going to sit there kissing and cuddling, he was leaving!

She got out, though, and even then she didn't have the sense to rush into her house immediately. Luc had the great urge to get out of his car and shout at her. He was fuming by the time she finally had herself locked in. Normally he was imperturbable, but he only had to see her and he was either intrigued or vastly irritated.

He pulled out of the shadows and let the car ease forward closer to her house as the other vehicle left. One look round and he would go too. He felt quite awkward and vaguely guilty about being here, and his temper was rising by the second.

To his surprise he could see Amy inside the house. She was walking around closing curtains and he could almost guarantee that she was only doing that because she had had a scare tonight. It was more than likely that she wandered around with the curtains wide open in the normal course of events, even though there was a violent ex-boyfriend somewhere in the town. She was as naïve as he had assumed. It was easy to mistake intelligence for worldly wisdom.

He saw the lights go off downstairs and then she was drawing curtains upstairs. She was going to bed, thank goodness. He looked up and down the street slowly and carefully. If that lunatic was coming at all, he would in all probability have come by now. Luc had simply been wasting his time, trying to protect somebody who really got on his nerves. And he was quite certain that she did just that in spite of his constant desire to watch her face.

Luc started the car and it purred quietly into life. He glanced in the mirror before pulling out and then automatically looked up at Amy's window once more, his expression definitely disgruntled. If he couldn't glare at her personally he could glare at her window.

A wave of shock hit him as his eyes found the lighted room. She was silhouetted against the curtains with the light behind her and she was getting ready for bed.

He saw her slip out of her dress, her shadow as graceful as a ballerina, and the muscles in his jaw tightened as his imagination took hold and left him very far behind. Another few seconds and she would be silkily naked up there, a slender figure waiting for warm hands to skim slowly over her, sweet ripe breasts waiting to be touched, to be kissed.

He wondered how she would be in a man's arms. Was she experienced, or as innocent as she looked?

Would she be passionate, eager, reaching out to participate? Or would she be bewildered, defenceless, melting, softly warm and beguiled?

He saw her slender arms lift to smooth her hair. The action outlined her figure even more and his manhood was suddenly hot, heavy and painful. He swallowed hard as he tore his gaze away. He felt like a scoundrel, as if he had been spying on her, but good God, didn't she know that those curtains were too flimsy? She had no common sense at all! Anybody could be parked or standing here, watching her.

He drove off without looking again and he was angry, angry with himself and with her. She was just an irritating employee and she was asking for trouble in a big way. She must have known that Somerfield was likely to come prowling round, even without this evening's display of violence. What effect did she think that delicate, erotic, shadow-dance would have had on *him*?

Luc glared into the darkness. Maybe that was exactly what she wanted? Only Somerfield had not been prowling round tonight, *he* had! His lips were set in one tight, furious line, his dark face darker still with annoyance. His quixotic efforts to protect her had been a waste of his time and he was left with a hot aching inside that he could well have done without.

He was also left with the feeling that he was some sort of Peeping Tom. In future, she was on her own. He would ignore her, and she could face her own battles or go to the devil in her own peculiar way. Because there was one thing that was absolutely certain: she was the most peculiar person he knew.

CHAPTER 4

Amy had a strange dream. She was dancing in the air among wisps of cloud, light as a feather and free. It was exotic, wonderful, and a man was close by watching her, moving in the same free way. She couldn't see him clearly. She could only see his size, his strength and power. He could lift her up and allow her to float weightlessly in the clouds. The thought excited her and she turned to him as she saw him reach for her.

It was only then that she understood it was Luc. His dark eyes flared over her and she felt no shame at all when she realized she was naked, with just the thin strands of cloud drifting around her like gossamer. She closed her eyes as his hands touched her possessively, and the shock of his embrace brought her back into reality as she awoke with a start.

Amy jumped straight out of bed, gasping for breath, glad to see that it was morning. Her heart was pounding from the effects of the dream, and although there was nobody to know, she was shaken, excited and hot with embarrassment. She couldn't get into the shower fast enough, and it was some considerable time before her heartbeats returned to normal and the guilt died down to bearable proportions.

Even then she had to tell herself very forcefully that it had only been a dream and probably had some obscure meaning that had nothing at all to do with sexual fantasies. The peculiar aching warmth inside was very slow to go, however, and she didn't want to go to work at all. Luc would be there and she knew she would have trouble facing him. The idea of seeing him had been bad enough after last night's episode at the restaurant, but after that strange, erotic dream she felt ridiculously vulnerable. She had the alarming feeling that by some mystical means he would know.

Later, as she walked down the main office and knew that Luc was in his own vast room, Amy felt her legs start to tremble. She bit at her lower lip and told herself quite ferociously that this was ridiculous, but she was so nervous that she felt close to tears.

And *he* didn't know about her dream after all. She told herself that quite forcefully but it didn't do a lot of good. She had to face him and pull herself together and there was only one way to do that. She clenched her hands on her bag and marched straight towards his office.

Luc had heard her come in. She was the only one who ever used that particular door but he had every intention of ignoring her today so he didn't look up from his desk. In fact, he had every intention of ignoring her in the future unless work forced him to speak to her. She was a menace.

He had not had a good night's sleep and he blamed Amy for that. At the moment he felt like blaming her for everything that annoyed him. If he had seen anyone else getting undressed behind flimsy curtains as she had done last night, he would not have suffered instant heated arousal. He would have laughed and driven off.

He was perfectly normal, but he didn't go around filled with lust. He glanced up in extreme irritation, but instead of being able to ignore her, his dark eyes opened in surprise. This, apparently, was a very different Amy Scott.

He was accustomed to seeing her in beautiful, entrancing clothes, feminine and graceful. It always seemed to him that she had an uncanny ability to float rather than walk. It was something to do with the type of clothes she wore and her own graceful way of moving.

This morning she was very much down to earth with a thud. She was wearing a skirt and blouse, and the way she was dressed made Luc wonder if she was about to enter some fancy dress contest that he didn't know about. It seemed that she would be going as the office frump. He was intrigued.

He was even more intrigued when she changed direction and came towards his office with a look of determination on her face that proved she was making herself do something she dreaded. She carefully avoided looking up at him but, knowing that she would finally have to look if she really intended to come in here, Luc simply waited.

He suddenly had a slight pang of misgiving. Did she intend to resign just because she had been embarrassed at the restaurant? He hoped not. He wasn't sufficiently annoyed to want to lose her. In fact, he found the idea of not seeing her at all extremely alarming.

Luc sat back in his seat and regarded her coolly, leaving it up to her to take the initiative. The skirt was dark navy blue and clearly too thick for the warmth of the day. The blouse was drab and plain, looking like some leftover from her university days. It dawned on him that she was hiding behind the drab clothes and he almost smiled. She would have had to wear a sack over her head to achieve that.

He stopped the smile in time because he couldn't get last night out of his head; he hadn't been able to get it out of his head all night. He realized suddenly that he was staring at her intently, imagining her beneath the clothes, the unlikely garments making the thought of her slender shape more tantalizing than ever. The palms of his hands grew warm and he frowned icily as heat began to pool inside, and Amy looked up as she reached his door, her face going quite pale as she met the furious dark eyes and the equally dark frown.

All the same, she had to go in, and she opened the door as if she was going to her own destruction. And telling herself that this was ridiculous no longer seemed like a good idea. Her hands were shaking and he was looking at her with so much dislike that she half expected him to shout at her.

Luc leaned further back in his seat, stretching his long legs out under his desk.

'What can I do for you, Miss Scott?' he asked quietly.

The quietness of his voice almost made Amy jump. He had looked so ferocious a second before that the quiet voice was really alarming, but she knew what it was all about. He was a big, dangerous jungle cat disguising his savage growl. In all probability he would pounce on her at any moment.

'Miss Scott?' he prompted softly when she just stood there.

'It's about last night,' she began, as firmly as nervous tension allowed. 'I wanted to thank you for dealing with everything. I couldn't thank you properly last night because I was too upset. It was kind of you to help.'

Luc stared at her in a very cool manner.

'I am not kind, Miss Scott. I was vastly irritated. I intervened on my own behalf as well as on yours.'

'Yes, well, I'm grateful,' Amy muttered, looking away from the dark, glittering eyes. 'I'm sorry you had to face the embarrassment.'

'I was not embarrassed,' Luc informed her in the same cool, detached voice. 'I have already explained that I was irritated. You were the one subjected to the upset and the embarrassment.'

'It won't happen again,' Amy assured him determinedly.

'You are about to employ a bodyguard?'

She looked up quickly at the sound of cold irony in his voice, but he didn't give her the chance to speak.

'I imagine that the intruder was the ex-boyfriend we have all been hearing about?' he queried. 'Assuming that it was, what makes you imagine he will be any less offensive when you encounter him again?'

Amy's face flushed softly at his sceptical tone.

'I'll just stay in, then I'll not "encounter" him. He can't keep it up for ever. He can never sustain any effort.' She glanced up sharply. 'How do you know about him anyway?'

'A little while ago the whole place was ringing with the intrigue,' Luc assured her drily.

'I would never have thought you would listen to gossip,' Amy pointed out in a stiffly accusing voice. She sounded deeply disappointed in him, let down, and Luc's annoyance grew.

'It was not a question of listening, Miss Scott. Sometimes I was not quite quick enough to duck when the barrage of information hit me.' He frowned and the derision left his voice. 'What is this nonsense about staying in until he gives up?' he asked testily. 'As he was your boyfriend you probably know him well enough to realize that he will not give up until he has had enough cruel amusement out of the situation.'

'He didn't look too amused last night as he left,' Amy muttered unwisely, and the dark eyebrows shot up in surprise.

'Regrettably, I cannot always guarantee to be on hand in case you should require my expertise.'

'Bryan thinks you were probably trained in some élite army force in France.'

Amy studied him with very assessing interest and Luc stared at her in renewed astonishment. She was off again. She simply slid into another character with smooth dexterity and with no warning whatsoever. Apparently she was back on that pink fluffy cloud of hers now. It had drifted by and she had leapt on to it with casual ease. He could never understand her and he decided that the best thing to do was completely ignore remarks like that, as they were impossible to cope with.

'If this man accosts you again,' he advised sternly, 'you should inform the police.'

'That's what Bryan thinks,' Amy muttered.

'Then, whoever he is, Bryan has given you good advice,' Luc snapped.

'He's my solicitor,' Amy told him seriously, and he only just stopped himself in time as he was about to enquire if she normally allowed her solicitor to kiss her goodnight. She would have known at once that he had followed both of them to her house. He didn't even want to think about that himself.

'Why are you wearing those clothes?' he suddenly asked harshly when he found his eyes running over her and his imagination beginning to trouble him again. Far from putting him off, the clothes seemed to sharpen his erotic thoughts about her. His mind was pondering on what she was wearing underneath.

'I'm trying to look invisible,' Amy assured him as her face flushed a rosy pink. He stared at her in amazement for a few seconds and then his glance flashed over her once more.

'You do not look invisible,' he informed her stiffly. 'On the contrary, those clothes draw the attention. You will be the focus of all eyes. You look like a schoolgirl who has wandered in amongst grown-ups by mistake.'

Amy's blush deepened and she bit anxiously at her lip.

'Oh,' she murmured. 'I wanted to look dowdy.'

'At first glance I assumed there was to be a contest to discover the office frump,' Luc informed her sarcastically. 'I naturally concluded that you had entered the competition with every intention of winning. However, having had the chance to study your efforts in some detail, I have changed my mind. People will assume that we are allowing sixth-form students in here on a training scheme. As a disguise, it has some merit, but as there is bound to be speculation, invisibility is out of the question. Perhaps you should consider hiding behind your computers instead?'

'It's too late to go back and change,' Amy muttered with a panic-stricken glance at her skirt and blouse.

'*D'accord*,' Luc agreed, slipping into his favourite language with derisive satisfaction. 'You are stuck with the image for the day, Miss Scott.'

Amy looked thoroughly miserable and definitely chastised he noticed as she dived out of his office and into her own. He felt a wave of self-satisfied pleasure. That should keep her in her place for the day. Apparently her brain stopped the moment she left her computers behind. Unless she was seated in front of her mechanical companions, she had all the makings of a first-class pest and madwoman. Her naïvety was phenomenal.

The telephone rang and Luc was soon holding a rapid conversation with the Paris office, relaxing into his preferred language and pushing Amy Scott from his mind. But he couldn't quite manage it. She kept drifting back into his thoughts, especially as he could see her if he turned his head slightly to the right.

He turned his head back immediately, with the ease of long practice. It was a miracle that he ever got anything done round here. Even now his mind was not completely on what he was saying, and twice he dropped unthinkingly into English.

He was annoyed to discover that he felt guilty about his behaviour. She had come into his office because she had wanted to apologize and because she had felt embarrassed. He had embarrassed her further. He was not quite as self-satisfied as he had thought. He wondered if he should do a little apologizing himself.

Luc never had the chance in any case. He was very busy until lunchtime, and when lunchtime came around Amy had disappeared from the office without his noticing her departure. He assumed she had gone to the staff canteen, where she usually ate, but when he arrived, she was not there.

He felt unaccountably worried, and that annoyed him more than ever. He would definitely not take up some role as guardian for his irritating Systems Manager. She could take care of her astonishing problems herself.

Meanwhile, Amy had shot out of the office as soon as lunchtime came around and sped home to change. By now the erotic dream had faded from her mind; a few hours in front of Jim, Alfie and their brothers had wiped such nonsense out of her head. She did not find it so easy, however, to dismiss Luc Martell's sarcastic comments about her clothes, and she hadn't at all liked the way he had been looking at her, as if she had dressed up for some unspecified sexual adventure that he disapproved off.

When she walked back into the office, exactly on time, she was once again dressed in her silky, feminine clothes. She avoided looking at Luc's office and drifted serenely into her own little den to take up the work where she had left off. She wasn't even sure if he was in the building anyway.

He was, and when he came back to his office Luc glanced into hers, irritated at the relief he felt to see her sitting in front of her machines as if nothing had happened at all. He glared in her direction even though she was presenting the back of her head, as usual. He had been fighting anxiety all lunchtime and where had she been? She had been home to change her clothes. He gritted his teeth and slammed his door, throwing himself into work in a very bad mood indeed.

Amy ate at home that night and she also drew the curtains closely the moment it was necessary to put on any lights. She had realized that Eric might come round, and there had been no need whatever for Luc Martell to point out this fact in his nasty way. She washed the dishes and then decided to settle in front of the television for a while before going to bed. All in all, it had been a trying day.

By the time she started for bed it was almost eleven o'clock, and she made herself a hot drink and put off the kitchen light. She was almost at the kitchen door when some irresistible impulse had her going back to peer through the closed curtains. Afterwards she had no real idea as to why she had done that, but she seemed to be drawn to staring surreptitiously out into the night, almost against her will.

Across the road and slightly to the left was a streetlight. Its height did not give a very good view of anyone close up to it but there was plenty of illumination even so, enough for Amy to see that a man was standing there, leaning against the upright support and gazing steadfastly at her house.

She let the curtain fall back into place as the shock of it hit her and she stood in the darkened kitchen thinking rapidly. The surrounding shadows made it impossible to make any sort of identification but her mind had instantly flashed to Eric. The man was the same height and roughly the same shape. She carefully moved the curtain again and looked across the road.

He was still there, and her heart began to beat painfully as she forced herself to study him. He wasn't dressed like Eric. He was wearing a sort of raincoat, for one thing, even though the evening was mild. The coat was some dark colour, possibly black. His trousers were dark too and he had a hat on. Everything seemed to be black.

Eric never wore a hat, and he didn't wear dark clothes, but all the same she was utterly convinced that it *was* Eric. Who else could it be anyway? It would certainly pander to Eric's cruel streak to appear like the dark avenger and scare her, because he must still be smarting from humiliation at the easy way Luc had dispatched him at the restaurant.

Amy took one last look and let the curtain drop, quite secure in the knowledge that the watcher had not seen her. She went to bed, but she put the light out immediately and undressed in the bathroom, where there was no window overlooking the street. Then she sat on the edge of the bed in the reflected light from the bathroom and drank her hot drink as she thought things over.

Nothing like this had ever happened to her before. She hadn't been afraid when Eric had come to the restaurant, she had just been very embarrassed – he had been doing the sort of thing she had half expected. This was quite different. It was sinister – if it was him!

Amy got up and peered through the curtains with great care and the man was still there, only now he had shifted his gaze to her bedroom window. She instantly dismissed all hopeful thoughts that he was merely waiting for somebody. There was no doubt about it, he was watching her house with the particular emphasis on *her*. She studied him intently, trying to make her mind up, trying to see if it really was Eric, and the more she looked, the more she was sure.

She let the curtain fall back into place and sat on the edge of the bed again. What did he intend to do? Was he simply amusing himself in his cruel way or did he intend to try and get into the house? When she had split up with him, she had changed all the locks in case he had taken a key on one of his visits. Peter had wanted her to put locks on the windows too, but she had not thought it necessary. This was a new house, with good solid window-frames. Anyone trying to break in would have to break the glass and she would hear it.

But would she? Would the sound of breaking glass wake her if she was deeply asleep? She pulled herself up sharply when she remembered the alarm system. That, too, had been Peter's idea and she was thankful she had proceeded with that. If anyone broke in the alarm would ring loud and clear, loud enough to wake everyone on the road, bells would ring and lights would flash outside. Nobody would risk that.

All the same, Amy went to the door and crept down the stairs in the near darkness. She was definitely anxious, her nerves stretched like thin wire. Now she wasn't even sure if she had set the alarm. She did it automatically each night but she had no recollection of doing it tonight.

She had. The little red light was staring cheerfully at her as she went to the box and Amy felt a slight relief. All the same, it seemed to her to be a very flimsy line of defence. When it had been installed she had thought it looked powerful and businesslike. Now it looked like a toy. She switched it off and went into the kitchen to look through the curtains again.

The man was still there, still staring up at her bedroom window, and there was definitely something familiar about him. It could well be Eric. If he broke in, could he get into the room without the sensor catching him? If he broke the kitchen window, could he slither over the sink and avoid the beam that looked across the room like a mechanical Cyclops?

Amy climbed on to the sink and tried it, but as far as she could make out the beam would have had her instantly. It did little to reassure her, though, until she remembered that Eric didn't know about the new alarm system. Maybe he wouldn't notice the bright yellow box outside on the wall? Maybe he would just blunder right into it? It would serve him right and give him a fright. He would have to retreat ignominiously.

Amy went back to bed after switching the alarm on again, hurrying up the stairs before the warning bleep stopped and it caught her too. She felt a little more safe, but she noticed as she walked into the darkened room that the light from the streetlamp outside lit up the bedroom very well.

It could only mean that the curtains were too thin. She had never noticed that before. She needed some new ones immediately and it was something she would have to deal with tomorrow. Once again she would have to miss lunch, but it was necessary.

Going to sleep was difficult, and although she finally managed it, Amy awoke several times in the night. The man was still there at one o'clock and at three. She peered out through the crack in the curtain and saw that he was walking about, but he hadn't gone, even so.

She didn't know when he went, but by five he had disappeared, a fact which brought renewed anxiety. Now she didn't know where he was at all. He might be trying to break in round the back but she dared not go down to investigate. Finally she fell into a deep sleep at about six o'clock, and then only because she was exhausted.

Gordon Sheen was in Luc's office when Amy arrived next morning. She was half an hour late and he glanced up as he heard her come in through the door. She was hurrying to her own office and both Gordon and Luc watched her with matching frowns on their faces.

'Amy looks wiped out,' Gordon muttered. 'I wonder if she's ill?'

Luc said nothing immediately but he agreed with his second-in-command. Whatever it was, Amy was not herself today, and she was late. She might defiantly decide not to return to the office, as she had done after her aunt's funeral, but she was invariably on time each day.

'Maybe I should nip into her office and see what's wrong,' Gordon muttered.

'No, leave her,' Luc ordered quietly. 'I have to be in there in a few minutes. I'll try and find out what's bothering her.'

He had seen her too pale face and the circles under her eyes as if she'd been up all night. His mind had not turned to ill health; it had turned to Somerfield. If she had been troubled by him, she would not want news of it spread around the office. In any case, she wouldn't tell Gordon Sheen.

Luc's lips twisted wryly. She wouldn't tell him either. He had put her in her place quite savagely yesterday. Now he was sorry, because she certainly looked as if she had trouble. Of course, she might just have had a late night with her solicitor, he thought disgruntledly. Whatever it was, he would be lucky to find out and Sheen wouldn't fare any better.

For some obscure reason he wanted to see to her himself anyway. He was the boss, she was *his* Systems Manager, and her little glass-sided den was next to his own. Apparently he had acquired a responsibility, which was amusing in an annoying sort of way.

She practically had control of the damned place, and this morning she looked like a waif. Perhaps she would improve after a few minutes with Jim and Alfie? Luc glared at the papers on his desk when he realized that he too was calling those computers by their idiotic names.

As it turned out, Luc didn't get in to see Amy until it was almost lunchtime. By then she looked as if she could hardly keep her eyes open.

'Can I see the latest work on the Eaton Point building?' he asked as he strode into her room. She didn't even look up at him, and Luc noticed that she moved across to her main computer with less zest than usual. A lot of the life seemed to have gone out of her.

The work came up and he moved forward to take a close look, but he had to admit that his mind was on Amy and not on the splendidly depicted projection on the screen. There was the same light perfume about her, and her fingers were agile and delicate as ever, but there was definitely something wrong.

'That's fine.' Luc leaned over her chair, his hands on the arms, effectively trapping her, and he decided that the game of cat and mouse was definitely not to his liking.

He spun her round in her chair and looked down into her startled blue eyes.

'Straight out, no evasion,' he ordered. 'What's wrong with you this morning.'

'You mean because I was late?' Amy asked, manoeuvring for time.

'I do not.' Luc regarded her with narrow-eyed concentration. She looked tired, uneasy, and he was fairly sure that it was not because he was towering over her. She usually had plenty to say for herself, even if a lot of it didn't quite make sense to him. 'I asked what was wrong. I did not ask why you were late.'

'There's nothing wrong,' she muttered evasively. She refused to meet his eyes and he therefore concluded that she was lying. It annoyed him. She resisted everything, even assistance.

'Look,' he said quietly, reining in his unruly temper, 'I realize that you are uneasy with me, that we do not exactly see eye to eye on some matters. Nevertheless, if you need help, I am willing to offer you any assistance that you need.'

Amy looked at him nervously, as if she was trying to make her mind up about telling him her problems. Evidently she decided that it was better to have unspecified troubles than to take him into her confidence.

'Thank you,' she said quietly, 'but there really is nothing, I – I'm just a little tired for some reason or other. I didn't sleep very well, that's all.'

Luc stared at her with a good deal of speculation in his dark eyes, and the effort to meet his gaze made her tremble. He'd noticed that. He hadn't slept too well himself, for the second night running. He knew why *he* wasn't sleeping. He wanted a woman – this one! He wondered why she was having the same difficulty. Whatever the reason, it was clear that she wasn't about to enlighten him, even if he shook her – and the temptation was very great.

He straightened up and looked down at her. All he could see was the top of her head, the shining nut-brown hair. It didn't do anything to ease his temper.

'*Eh bien!*' he rasped. 'I have offered assistance and you have refused it. No doubt we are both agreed on that, Miss Scott. Let us hope that your tired condition does not lead to errors.'

He walked out and Amy winced as he slammed the door. He was very annoyed, because he only lapsed into French when he was angry. She felt quite forlorn. She really needed help and advice, but after all, how could she tell the boss? He expected high standards from her. She was the Systems Manager, not some simpering, scared creature who ran to the biggest man present when she was in trouble.

She didn't really know why she was so scared. When she had broken up with Eric she had dispatched him neatly all by herself. She hadn't run to anyone. So what was so different now?

Amy knew really. The man watching her last night had looked sinister and determined, as if he

95

had dreadful plans for her and wanted her to know well in advance that she was marked for destruction. Could that be Eric? Was he so dangerous? Actually, she knew deep inside that he was. She had been lucky to get rid of him so smoothly. He was violent.

If, on the other hand, it was a stranger then that idea was more frightening than ever. If Jill had still been in England she would have rung her up and talked the whole thing over with her. But Jill was in America and the only person left was Peter. Did she really want all the fuss that would ensue when Peter heard about this?

Amy decided to wait and see. Perhaps the man would not come tonight, because if it was Eric, then he wasn't capable of keeping something up unless it actually fell into his lap – like seeing her in that restaurant. He was an opportunist but he couldn't sustain any effort. To stand each night outside her house would take a lot of effort, and Eric was not too good on that score.

The man, whoever he was, had waited for most of the night. He would have been tired, stiff and finally cold. She could imagine Eric doing that spitefully once, could imagine him laughing to himself. But keeping it up? She thought not. Amy brightened considerably and made her mind up. Yes, she would wait and see.

A week later, Amy awoke in the night with the same old feeling of anxiety. She lay in bed and stared at the light coming in through the closed curtains. She had forgotten to replace the rather flimsy coverings at her bedroom window even though she was very much aware of their inadequacy. It was because she was so tired.

She dreaded getting out of bed to look through the window because she knew what she would see; she knew the dark figure would be there, leaning against the upright of the streetlamp, watching, always watching. He had been doing that for the whole week.

He hadn't come every night, but that fact had been little consolation. It was a sort of mental torture because she had told herself firmly that if this continued she would do something about it – she would tell Peter, she would go to the police, she would make a definite move to put a stop to it.

But the watcher had not been there each evening. Sometimes she went to bed feeling that it was all finished and that he would not come again. She spent hours each night getting up to see if he was there, only to find that it was almost morning and he had not come.

Sometimes he came early, just after dark, and stayed all night. Sometimes he came in the middle of the night and stayed for just a short time. She could never be certain, and if she reported it the police would perhaps not believe her. They might drive past and, seeing nothing, think that she was either imagining it or that she was seeking attention.

Jill would have known what to do and Jill would have been with her at the police station, laying down the law firmly.

These past few days Amy had been anything but firm. She was so tired that she felt quite ill.

Sometimes the figures on the computer screen swam before her eyes and she knew she looked absolutely awful.

Luc was giving her some odd looks, and so were plenty of other people, but since she had refused to tell Luc what was wrong he had never mentioned it again. In fact, now that the project that had taken his attention was finished, he rarely needed to speak to her. Other architects were needing her skills, though she wondered just how long her skills would last if she didn't get more sleep.

She slid from the bed and made her way tiredly to the window. It was two in the morning and there had been no watcher when she had gone to bed. This was all wasting her sleep but she had to look.

The man was there, staring up at her window, silent, dark and still, the hat pulled well down over his eyes, and Amy sprang back as soon as she saw him. Her heart took on the familiar tempo and she moved away, feeling for the bed behind her, sitting down and trying to stop the trembling. She knew she could not go on like this.

She dared not phone the police now, not tonight. It would mean putting off the alarm, putting lights on, letting the watcher know that she was aware of his presence and frightened by it. Tomorrow. Tomorrow she would get the police. She would make them believe her. She went back to the window and took another look.

He was gone. How long had he been there while she slept? Where had he gone now? Why had he gone? Amy sat back on the edge of the bed and was shocked to discover that she was crying quietly, crying from total fear.

Luc watched her as she came into the office the next day. A week had changed her so much that he was seriously worried. She no longer drifted across the floor in that enchanting way she had. She looked ill.

He scowled, his hands clenching on top of his desk. What the hell was wrong and why wouldn't she tell him? Had that bastard come back to live with her? The thought filled him with fury and he could do nothing about it.

He could, of course, throw his weight about, figuratively speaking. He could go into her office and demand an explanation. He could break her down to such a point that she would be only too glad to tell him, but he hesitated to do that. He did not like the idea at all. He didn't know if he could bear to see those violet eyes filled with tears.

Dieu! She looked terrible. There were dark rings under her eyes. She looked as if she never slept at all. She looked as if she could hardly move. He wanted to help her, in fact the desire to help was tearing away at him daily, but he could only watch her disintegrate and keep silent.

The hell with it! He could do a damned sight more than that. He slammed his hand on the desktop, stood and walked out of his office and into Amy's.

'The boardroom, now!' he snapped as she looked up anxiously.

He turned and walked off, knowing she would follow. She would be worried too. The boardroom was the fear of all the staff, as he knew full well.

Those he had been forced to get rid of initially when he had first come here had been told their fate in the boardroom. They all dreaded it.

But it was one of the few places in this modern, glass-walled building where there was privacy. The door was solid oak; the walls were panelled. Nobody ventured there unless invited. It was the lair of the tiger.

Luc's mouth twisted ruefully. She would be feeling scared, having been summoned to the dreaded place. She would certainly be following him. He didn't need to look round.

When he got to the door he opened it and stood aside as she came up to him. She was white-faced, pitifully changed from her old, defiant image, and he was perfectly aware of the glances that had come in their direction as they had walked through the building. He even knew what they were thinking. Amy Scott was about to be dismissed. He had also noted their resentment of the fact.

Dismiss her? It was the last thing on his mind. The idea of anyone else sitting in front of her computers appalled him. He seemed to be consumed with the need to protect her, not get rid of her. He motioned her into the room and closed the door.

'Sit down,' he ordered harshly, indicating a chair, but he made no move to sit down himself. Instead he began to pace about, determined to get this out into the open but wary of saying anything to upset her more. She already looked as if the whole world sat on her slender shoulders.

He spun round to face her and she was sitting with her head bowed, her slender hands clenched in her lap. She looked as if she was waiting for a blow with no hope of coping. He had the idiotic urge to pull her to her feet and hold her fast, to rock her against him and murmur words of comfort. Instead, he leaned against the edge of the huge shining table that stretched halfway across the room.

'This time,' he informed her grimly, 'you will tell me. You will tell me why you are looking so ill, so tired. You will enlighten me, Miss Scott, and you will do it now. If any of my staff are ill I wish to know. It is my duty to know.'

'I'm not ill.' She was speaking in little more than a whisper and Luc's ready temper rose instantly at her prevarication. *Dieu!* She was about to react to his attempts to help exactly as she had reacted before. She was going to plead insomnia, or some such damned thing. She didn't trust him one inch. He cut that off at once.

'You are not ill?' he enquired coldly. 'We are back to this lack of sleep story? Very well, you have serious insomnia. The firm's doctor will see you immediately. I will ring for him.'

'No!' Amy looked up, a panic-stricken expression on her face. 'I don't want to see a doctor. I really don't.'

'Why?' Luc rasped, glaring at her furiously. 'You are afraid he will notice the bruises all over you?'

'What bruises?' Amy stared up at him in bewilderment, her eyes enormous in her pale face, and Luc frowned blackly.

'The bruises you have been given by Somerfield. I assume he is back with you and that this is the reason for your present pitiful condition?'

CHAPTER 5

'He – he's not back with me,' Amy stammered. 'I'm not bruised either.'

'Then what the hell is wrong with you?' Luc roared savagely, forgetting where they were and giving vent to his own frustrations. She jumped as if he had hit her. She actually cringed and he was instantly contrite. 'I'm sorry,' he muttered, turning away and beginning to pace about again. 'I didn't mean to frighten you but you're so damned irritating.' He swung round to face her, glaring at her in exasperation. 'Every day I expect to look into your office and find you in a state of total collapse, lying on the floor, unconscious.'

'Do I look that bad?' Amy asked, glancing at him worriedly, and he stood still to scowl down at her.

'Yes,' he said tightly. 'You do.'

'It's just shortage of sleep,' she told him in a low voice.

'I know. Insomnia.' Back to annoyance at once, he glared at her again. 'You have suddenly become an insomniac but you refuse to see a doctor. It is just one of those things that happen to healthy people with no reason at all. Do not imagine you can play me for a fool,' he grated. 'You have problems and you refuse to tell me what they are. Very well. I will pretend that I believe you and we will class this insomnia as an illness. As you cannot sleep when normal people sleep, you will sleep during the daytime. You will take two weeks' sick leave from this moment. I will find a replacement for you this very day.'

He was gambling on her attachment to the computers, almost holding his breath, and he was not disappointed.

'Oh, please!' Instantly she jumped to her feet, clasping her hands in front of her, staring up at him in a horrified manner. 'Please don't do that. I can manage, really I can.'

'I don't think so.' Luc kept his voice deliberately hard, seeing her panic and pressing further while he had the chance. 'You will make costly mistakes eventually, and in any case, you are ill.'

'I can't be off work,' Amy pleaded shakily. 'Don't send me away.'

'You are afraid that your beloved computers will miss you?' he derided deliberately. 'Believe me, they will not even know that you're gone. You can come back to them when you are well again.'

'It's not the computers,' Amy whispered, standing with her hands clenched more tightly together.

'Then what is it?' Luc demanded in an exasperated voice. He was glaring down at her and she had no choice at all. She had to tell him.

'This is the only place where I feel safe.'

Luc's face went quite still. Suddenly he could tell that she was terrified, and not of him either. When he bent his head to look at her more closely he could see tears on her cheeks.

'You are afraid?' he asked softly, coming towards her.

'All the time.'

She looked up at him. There were tears streaming down her face now and Luc felt everything inside him contract. His anger turned outwards, soaring, skimming through the air, searching for an enemy like a hunting missile as a deep wave of protectiveness swept over him.

He reached out and pulled her close, folding her against him as if he could shield her even from her own thoughts, and Amy just gave in. There was no fight left in her. The week of fear, the lack of sleep had left her completely defenceless.

For a few seconds he held her fast, his hands moving comfortingly over her back, and then he tilted her face and looked at her closely. She looked defeated. This little pest with her mechanical friends, her pink cloud and her peculiar ways was crushed by fear.

He led her back to her chair.

'Now,' he ordered quietly when she was seated again, 'you will tell me everything. You will explain to me how a woman with so much spirit can become a frightened girl in such a short time.'

Amy took a deep breath and surrendered to the inevitable.

'There's a man watching me,' she began shakily. 'He appears outside the house and stares up at the window. He's there almost every night but he comes at different times so I never know when it's safe to sleep. And if he's not there,' she added, her voice rising, 'I can't sleep for wondering where he is and what he's doing. Sometimes he doesn't come until the early hours of the morning, but I seem to know. I wake up and tell myself it's all imagination but I just have to get up and look and then he's there. Sometimes, like last night, I look again a minute or two later and he's gone. Then I start wondering how long he was there when I was asleep. I wonder if I would have woken up if he'd tried to get into the house.'

She was shaking almost uncontrollably and Luc drew her to her feet.

'Come with me,' he ordered quietly. He sounded calm but his face was like thunder and Amy glanced at him anxiously.

'Where? What are you going to do?'

'I am going to deal with this menace,' he informed her tightly. 'And don't ever be afraid in future, because I am angry enough to tackle any amount of men who watch you in the night.'

'Y – you're very kind,' Amy whispered, and he glanced down at her imperiously.

'I am not kind,' he snapped, from sheer force of habit. 'I have explained that to you before. I am merely angry.'

She nodded silently and walked along with him as he went to collect his jacket and wait for her while she gathered up her bag and various belongings.

'There's a call from Paris for you, Mr Martell,' his secretary gasped hurriedly as she met them on their way though the big office. She was almost rushing at them, a fussy, big-bosomed, self-important woman. Amy had never liked her, and now it looked as if she was about to insist that Luc couldn't leave his own office.

'I'm out,' Luc informed her sharply, giving her a potent glare. 'I'll call Paris later. If you can deal with it yourself, then do so.'

'But they're speaking in French, sir.'

'Then shout back in English. I believe that is normal,' Luc advised pithily.

Amy felt a smile touching her lips for the first time in days. No, he didn't like the English. The rumours must be true. All the same she was glad he'd forced her to tell him her problem. If it *was* Eric who was watching her, a good sight of Luc Martell might just send him scurrying.

Not that the watcher would be there in broad daylight, but Amy had become so nervous lately that she often thought she was under observation even during the day, even in town. What she had told Luc had been perfectly true. She only felt safe in the office.

Luc almost bundled her into her car. His face was quite thunderous and Amy was hard pressed to decide whether he was angry at her problem or merely annoyed with her on the regular, personal basis.

'Drive to your house. I will follow.' He turned and walked to his own car and Amy gave a deep sigh and pulled out of the car park. She had a suspicious feeling that she should not really be driving at all, because she felt so tired that she had some doubts about her ability to react quickly in any sort of crisis.

She drove slowly, well aware that Luc's expensive car was growling away behind her like an angry tiger. Even if he was impatient, though, she couldn't go fast. Her greatest inclination was to stop and put her head down for a quick nap, and that was only because she felt safe each time she glanced in the mirror and saw Luc's Porsche trailing her relentlessly.

It was astonishing that such a short while ago she had felt both excited, irritated and scared by him all at the same time. Right now he seemed like a golden lifeline, her unexpected protector. He was, of course, as he had told her, merely angry, and after that altercation in the restaurant he seemed to have developed a great dislike for Eric.

Amy was not surprised at that. She had developed a great dislike for Eric herself. She wondered what plans Luc had made. She hoped he understood that Eric would not be there now, watching the house. It wasn't even lunchtime. She couldn't quite grasp what Luc intended to do but it didn't really matter. Just the fact that he was there, furious as usual, was enough to settle her nerves.

When she pulled up outside her house, Luc came striding along to her. His car was tucked in behind her own and as she got out Amy felt again that she was playing truant, coming back home in the middle of the morning when everyone else was at work. Once again, she felt guilty.

'What's wrong?' Luc asked quickly, bending

over to look at her suspiciously when he saw her anxious face.

'Nothing, except I feel guilty about not being at work.'

'I'm not at work either,' Luc muttered

'You're the boss, though.'

'I know. When I say jump, you ask, "How high?"' he reminded her caustically. 'Let's go inside and you can show me what you see from your windows.'

Amy didn't really have a lot of choice, but she couldn't think how it would help. She opened the front door and Luc came in with her, scaring her a little. He was so tall, so powerful that he made her bijou residence seem quite tiny. She walked to the kitchen when she had put her things down and Luc stalked behind her, not saying a word.

'I first saw him from this window,' Amy said, pointing out across the road. 'He was standing under that streetlight. As you can see, the light's fairly high. It casts a lot of shadow so it wasn't possible to really tell who the man was. All I know is that he was dressed in dark clothes – black, I think. He was wearing a raincoat, dark trousers and some sort of hat with a fairly big brim. It shaded his face.'

'Stay here,' Luc ordered. 'I'm going to stand by the lamp and you will get some idea of his height when you compare it with mine.'

'What a good idea!' Amy exclaimed in a sudden, shaky burst of enthusiasm.

It earned her a sardonic glance as Luc walked out of the kitchen and she watched him leave the house and cross the road to the lamp. It set her mind straight on one thing at least. Luc was taller than the watcher, quite a bit taller.

When he came back in she told him somewhat gloomily.

'It's no use. He wasn't like you at all,' she confessed in a dejected voice.

'I'm pleased to hear it,' Luc murmured, giving her another derisively exasperated glance. 'I don't particularly want to have to account for my movements for the last week or so.'

'Oh, I wouldn't ask you,' Amy assured him solemnly.

'But perhaps the police would. Now, let us get down to this seriously. How tall would you say this man is? You have seen me over there and I'm six feet two.'

'You seem taller,' Amy mused.

'Taller than the man?'

'No. Taller than six feet two. I always think of you as being very big.'

'That is probably because you are very small.' He gave her another wry look and pointed to the kettle. 'You also seem to be more light-headed than usual. Make some coffee and think carefully. How does your villain compare with me?'

'He's awful, frightening. He's not a bit like you,' Amy pronounced gloomily. He was implying that she was normally light-headed, which just wasn't true. She was efficient, computer-orientated.

'Amy!' Luc looked down at her, slightly amused but very frustrated. 'I do not want compliments from you. Try to be logical. I know you're tired but you must try to think clearly. How tall is this man?'

'About five feet eight.' She cheered up because she felt quite pleased that Luc had called her Amy. He'd never done that before.

'And his appearance?'

'Frightening.'

'Describe him. Do not describe your own feelings.' To her surprise, Luc sat her down at the small table in the kitchen and proceeded to make the coffee himself. She was quite glad. She felt utterly worn out.

'He's tall, but actually, when I come to think of it, he's not all that big. I mean he doesn't look like you. I shouldn't think he has powerful muscles and things like that. He looks – bulky.'

'Bulky because of his weight or because of his clothes?' Luc asked, spinning round to look at her sharply.

'Impossible to tell,' Amy assured him, yawning and letting her eyes close for a minute.

'Don't go to sleep. I haven't finished with you yet,' Luc ordered. He handed her a very hot coffee. 'You can sleep when I've got more information.'

'Not likely,' Amy muttered. 'I'm not sleeping. He might come back.'

'I surely hope he does,' Luc breathed savagely. 'He will find me waiting for him.'

'Now? You mean if he comes back now? He won't. It's daylight. He only comes when it's dark.'

'We will deal with him.'

Luc sat at the table too, looking across at her in a very determined manner, and Amy stifled her yawns and regarded him solemnly as he proceeded to question her about the man who was making her life one long nightmare. Luc seemed to be willing her to stay awake, but finally she folded her arms on the table and fell asleep with her head on her arms while he was still speaking.

Luc watched her for a few seconds and then shook his head resignedly. He wasn't going to get another thing from her for a while. She was too tired to think straight. When he stood and went round to wake her, she simply murmured plaintively and shrugged his hand off like a petulant, sleepy child. How different she was from his original Miss Computer.

He sighed, picked her up and carried her upstairs into the quite lovely bedroom with the flimsy curtains. He knew where it was because of his little spying expedition a week ago. But, oddly enough, he didn't feel at all guilty about that now. He felt definitely uneasy about the effect of the memory of it on his senses, but the guilt had gone. He was too involved with this to waste time on guilt.

She was light to carry and she snuggled her face against his shoulder, giving a small sigh and making herself comfortable. He glanced down at her, his lips twisting ruefully. He wanted to keep her there. He wanted to let her sleep on his lap, hold her close and stroke her hair.

His self-discipline was too strong for that, though. He put her on the bed, covered her with the quilt and walked across to look out of the window, trying to imagine the man who watched her.

Was it Somerfield? He suddenly knew that he hoped it was. Any other idea was extremely sinister to imagine. Amy looked quite fragile, in spite of her normally sparky tongue. The idea of a man, a bulky man, watching her house at night was alarming. He was greatly relieved that she had finally told him about it.

Luc glanced at his watch and then went downstairs to the telephone. It was no use pretending that he could go back to work and leave Amy alone. Work would have to wait and so would his call to Paris.

He rang his secretary, being quite harshly firm with her when she fussed as usual, and then he telephoned the police. Whoever the man was, he had to be stopped, and although Luc would have preferred to stay here and deal with the man tonight, he had to acknowledge that in a civilized society the police should be called first. It was unfortunate because he didn't feel very civilized at the moment.

It was late in the afternoon when Luc woke Amy by shaking her arm gently. She had been so deeply asleep that calling to her had had no effect. He had been obliged to come upstairs and wake her because the police would be here in a short while.

'Amy,' he said softly. 'You have to get up now.'

'No,' Amy muttered plaintively, and snuggled more deeply into the bed, frowning in her sleepy state.

Luc found himself grinning. She sounded like a spoiled child. Her shining hair was tousled, spread out over the pillow, and her cheeks were flushed with sleep. She was only partly awake and had no idea where she was. He shook her again and insisted quietly, 'Amy. You must get up now.'

'Why?' She reluctantly opened her eyes and peered up at him, and then looked absolutely appalled when she realized where she was and who he was.

Luc felt quite disgruntled. He had been downstairs for ages, making coffee, wandering about and inspecting her lovely little house, sitting thinking and generally wasting his time. He had grown quite accustomed to being here by now, and her shock at seeing him was something of a blow. For some reason he had expected her to smile and be glad he was there. He had half expected her to reach out her arms to him.

'Very soon the police will be here.' He returned to his old, stiff attitude, firmly squashing foolish thoughts. 'They will wish to speak to you.'

'I'll get up at once.'

Even though she had been lying under the quilt, completely dressed, she made no move to get up while Luc was standing there and that only added to his irritation. One would have imagined that she knew him well enough by now to risk putting her feet on the floor. He walked out of the room and left her to it, his lips set in one grim line.

Amy was down in another few minutes. She had taken the time to change her dress and tidy her hair but there was still something warm and sleepy about her. She looked delightfully vulnerable and it suddenly struck him that he wanted to pull her close, to see how she felt when she wasn't stiff and anxious. He would have liked to cuddle her. The sight of her aroused him quite unexpectedly, and the unreasonable twinge of desire infuriated him. He glared at her in silence.

'When did you get back?' Amy asked uneasily, giving him her usual wary look.

'Back from where? I've been here all the time.'

Amy nibbled at her lower lip.

'I just can't remember going to bed,' she mused with a slight frown on her forehead.

'You were asleep,' Luc informed her impatiently. 'You went to sleep while I was speaking to you. I carried you upstairs.'

'Oh!' Amy breathed anxiously, and Luc's glare became more pronounced.

'I did not undress you, Miss Scott!' he rasped.

'I – I never said you did.'

'Then stop looking at me as if I'm a potential sex maniac. I stayed because it was neither wise nor practical to leave you alone and go back to the office.'

He stood and walked across the kitchen to put the kettle on. He had taken over the kitchen by the look of it, and Amy stood there like a visitor while he made coffee and handed it to her.

'The police have promised to come as soon as possible. They gave their latest time as four-thirty. It's that time now,' he informed her, eyeing her over the rim of his cup. 'You had better decide exactly what you're going to tell them.'

'That's no problem. I know what I'm going to tell them,' Amy assured him firmly as she sat down with her drink. 'I'm going to tell them about the man watching the house and I'm going to tell them that I think it's Eric.'

'Good.' Luc looked much more human for a minute. She wasn't going to try and shield that bastard, then. It gave him a great deal of satisfaction. He let the subject drop for the time being.

'There was a delivery of mail while you were asleep,' he murmured. 'I put it on the table in the hall.'

Amy got up and went to fetch it and Luc paid no further attention. He knew it was a postcard. He assumed it was from her friend who had just lately gone to America.

'It's from Jill,' Amy told him as she came back in, reading the card. 'She's having a good time, it seems.'

Luc merely grunted. It didn't interest him in the slightest. He had never met this Jill person and had no desire to hear about her. All he wanted was to see the police and then get back to his own place. For once in his life he was being troubled by turbulent emotions and it didn't please him at all.

He stood and went to watch for the police. He knew it was a pretty pointless thing to do but it released him from the necessity of watching Amy. He glared out of the window into the street when he admitted that watching Amy was fast becoming just that – a necessity.

'If I'd gone to America with Jill,' Amy sighed as she sat drinking her coffee and glancing again at the card, 'none of this would have happened.'

'You were thinking of going?' He turned his head and shot a swift look at her.

'No, not really. I was sorry to see Jill go but I wouldn't have wanted to go with her. I've just got myself set up here – at least, I *had* until this happened. Anyway, I like this town.'

Luc just grunted and resumed his watch on the street.

'Oh, I know you don't like it,' Amy assured him, as if she was capable of reading his mind. 'And when you come to think of it, it's pretty much impossible to really like a place and settle in well when you're wanting to leave it all the time. I can understand that perfectly. I'm not really surprised that you don't like it in England. I don't expect I would like Paris.'

'Of course you would,' Luc grated without looking round. 'Paris is a beautiful city, exciting, colourful.'

'I bet it's not colourful all over Paris,' Amy surmised in a vaguely assessing sort of way. 'I bet there are some really tatty parts. There always are tatty parts in any city, and Paris will be no exception. I mean it's just the same in London, isn't it? Lovely old buildings, lots of history, and then, suddenly, tat.'

Luc gritted his teeth and glared through the window. Once she had her mind on a subject, however pointlessly, she never let it go. She would look good in Paris, right for the place. He could just imagine her walking down some boulevard in one of those silky dresses, her lovely shining hair drifting around her shoulders.

'You're not going to tell me,' Amy persisted more firmly, pursuing her argument vigorously when he made no comment, 'that you can go all over a city as large as Paris and not encounter places that fail to come up to scratch. I can actually guarantee that there will be high-rise flats, run-down dirty areas, traffic fumes . . .'

'You,' Luc stated forcefully with his back to her, 'are irritating me.'

'I'm not surprised,' Amy assured him with another long sigh. 'I seem to be irritating Eric too, or he wouldn't be doing this to me.'

'Do not class me in the same breath as that lunatic!' Luc ordered irately, turning to glower at her.

'I wasn't going to,' Amy said mildly, looking up at him in some surprise. 'It's just that – '

'It's just that when you start talking you allow your tongue to lead you almost anywhere it will,' Luc snapped. 'For the most part, it leads you into trouble, Miss Scott.'

'You called me Amy before.'

'An unthinking course of action taken by my own unruly tongue,' Luc said sarcastically. 'Please forgive the oversight.'

'You're not very nice, are you?' Amy murmured dejectedly.

'We were already agreed on that some time ago, if you recall.'

Amy sat looking very downcast. She couldn't remember actually saying he wasn't nice. Of course, he wasn't, but she hadn't actually told him so outright. She sat with her cup cradled in her hands and said nothing else, and after a second Luc glanced at her.

117

She looked miserable. He'd done it again – glaring at her, snarling at her, simply because she got under his skin and made him act out of character. He should apologize but he wasn't going to. It was best to keep away from her because he didn't like the effect she had on him. This idea of wanting to hug her close and protect her was crazy. He couldn't imagine any sort of situation where he would have to rescue Veronique. Veronique was a Parisienne.

He turned back to the window, scowling at it and through it. Amy Scott was a weird mixture of all sorts of things. *Dieu*! Sometimes she was little more than a girl, for all her twenty-five years. If the wind blew strongly she would laugh and drift off over the rooftops, and her conversation was absolutely *ridiculous*!

He felt quite pleased with himself when he thought of that. She was enough to drive anyone mad with her friendly computers, her electronic brain and her inability to even think straight when she was out of the office. He wanted nothing to do with her at all. This trip here was merely a kindness. Anyone in his place would have done it.

Amy got up with another of those irritating sighs and went to search in one of the cupboards.

'What are you doing?' he snapped.

'I'm trying to think what to have tonight for a meal,' she muttered, totally ignoring his abrupt tone of voice. 'I seem to have missed lunch. By the time it gets to be later I'll be starving.'

'Make a sandwich,' Luc advised tersely. 'When the police have been, I'll take you out for an early dinner.'

118

'All right,' Amy agreed. She gave another sigh and Luc's jaw tightened as he turned back to his obsessive watching for the police. Why had he *said* that? What did he want to take her out for? He didn't want to take her out!

He clenched his teeth together and scowled like thunder. He was not going to get mixed up with this girl. He was going to Paris on every conceivable occasion. He *never* got mixed up with anyone. His relationship with Veronique was comfortable, mutually acceptable, almost businesslike, and in any case, the only Englishwoman he liked was his mother.

When the police finally came, Amy and Luc were both eating ham sandwiches. Amy had made enough for both of them but Luc had at first stoically and stiffly refused. When Amy simply ate and ignored him, however, he'd made more coffee and helped himself to the sandwiches without a word.

And that was another thing, Amy thought darkly. He seemed to think that only the French could make coffee. As far as she was concerned, she could make it a whole lot better but he simply took over. He had a very bad attitude as far as she could see.

Two policemen came in when the patrol car arrived and they asked pretty much the same questions that Luc had asked so Amy was quite ready for them.

'Can you describe this man who watches you?' one of the policemen asked, and Amy wasn't quite sure whether or not she liked his attitude any better than Luc's. There was a sort of tone to the question as if she was imagining this whole thing. Of course she might be mistaken in her assessment, she conceded, but, even so, she wasn't about to be fobbed off by attitude.

'He's approximately five feet eight,' she informed them briskly. 'I know that for sure because Mr Martell has been outside to the streetlight and I estimated the height from that.'

'Mr Martell?' the policeman asked, pen poised for notes.

'My employer,' Amy stated in a superior tone, indicating Luc with an airy wave of her hand. Luc nodded. The policeman wrote it down and Luc tried to suppress a wave of annoyance and a deep black frown. Why had she said that? Was that how she thought of him? As her employer? Didn't she recognize him as a person, a man?

'What kind of footwear?' The question quite startled Amy and she glanced at the policeman who had asked it.

'Black, I think. At any rate, something dark.'

'I wasn't meaning that, Miss Scott,' the policeman said patiently. 'Did you notice if he was wearing boots or anything like that. If he was in anything other than flat shoes it could alter the estimation of his height.'

'I never noticed,' Amy stated firmly. Were they mad? Did they expect to see a man in high-heeled shoes? This was serious, not some cause for idiotic speculation. She told them what he was wearing and they wrote it all down, but it only added to the

impression she had that they were merely humour-
ing her.

And she didn't like the thought, either, that they
might have humoured her even less if Luc hadn't
been there. He was standing with one broad
shoulder propped against the wall, He looked
important, powerful and very watchful. He had
his usual 'about to pounce' attitude about him.
Both policemen had given him wary looks when
they came in.

'I have a pretty good idea who it was too,' she
said, asserting herself sharply, and that certainly
gained their attention.

'You know the man, Miss Scott?'

'I believe so. His name is Eric Somerfield. I used
to go out with him. He lives at the other end of
town – that lane down by the edge of the wood.
There are some modern houses there and he lives
at number seven.'

'Parville Road, isn't it?' the policeman muttered
to his colleague, but it was Amy who answered.

'Yes. That's it. He lives there. I know because,
as I said before, I used to go out with him.'

In the background Luc was keeping quiet, but
his face was set hard. Used to go out with him! As
far as he knew, she used to do a whole lot more
than go out with him. Gossip had it that they'd
lived together. He had a vision he didn't want of
her living in this house with Somerfield, sleeping
in the same bed. She knew his house too. Maybe
they used to sleep there sometimes.

He put his hands in his pockets and stared out of
the window. What the hell was he doing here? She

had an uncle who wasn't in his dotage. Why hadn't she gone to him? It should have been quite natural to go to her uncle.

Well, he was stuck with taking her to dinner tonight and then he was out of this. She didn't need him. *Dieu*! She didn't even like him. And she was vastly irritating anyway. She was not the sort of woman he was used to.

'We'll have a look around outside and then we'll make it a priority to have a patrol car round here every couple of hours during the night. Don't worry, Miss Scott.'

The police were very polite, but they left, and Amy couldn't really think of anything they could have done other than leave. She was going to be worried whether they came round or not. This whole thing had devastated her.

'What about Somerfield?' Luc asked sharply as the police got to the door.

'We'll call round and see what he has to say for himself. Don't worry, sir.'

Luc's lips set grimly. That seemed to be their answer to everything. Don't worry. He wasn't worrying. He was interfering, and it was nothing at all to do with him.

'It's not much use them coming every two hours,' Amy muttered glumly after they had gone, 'if the man comes in the middle of their patrol and breaks in before they pass. He could do anything in two hours. He could hide until they passed and then rush in and – '

'He doesn't even know they'll be passing,' Luc interrupted quickly. She was scared. How could he have forgotten how terrified she had been before, how tired and pale?

'How do you know he won't be expecting it?' Amy asked tremulously. 'How do you know he isn't watching all day in some place where he can't be seen?'

'Now, Amy,' Luc cautioned seriously, 'you must try not to let this thing get out of proportion.'

As an attempt to soothe it failed magnificently. Amy did some furious glaring of her own.

'I've never heard such a patronizing statement in my life!' she snapped angrily. 'This isn't some wild twist of my imagination. A man comes almost every night and he watches this house. He dresses in black, he pulls his hat down over his forehead and he stands right across there and stares at the window.' She pointed out of the window and then raised her voice. 'Do you realize that I have to get ready for bed in the dark? Do you realize that I spend my evenings creeping around my own house like a thief, in case he sees me? Do you realize that I daren't let him know that *I* know he's watching in case it gives him some diabolical advantage? How dare you tell me that I'm getting things out of proportion?'

She stormed off to the other end of the kitchen, folded her arms and turned her back on him, and Luc stood looking at her, feeling in a state of near shock. The little witch was in a rage. Apparently he would have to take care with words in future. He had never imagined she was capable of losing her temper. He discovered that he was secretly amused that she had a temper to lose.

'I apologize,' he murmured quietly, trying to keep the laughter out of his voice. 'I did not mean to suggest that you had things out of proportion. I realise that this is very frightening for a woman.'

'It wouldn't be too nice for a man either,' Amy sniffed angrily, throwing him an irritated glance over her shoulder. 'If you saw this person you'd realize that even a man would be scared – unless the man was somebody like you with your special training.'

He was about to point out that this business of his special training was a figment of her solicitor's imagination. He thought better of it. If her solicitor wanted to think that he was a commando then let him. For himself, Luc wanted no further outburst. She constantly stunned him, and when she did he wanted to either shake her or hold her. At the moment he was wavering between the two things with a definite bias towards holding.

'We could drive out of town for dinner,' he suggested soothingly. 'That way it would take a while and we would not be too early for the meal.'

'All right,' Amy agreed, back to quiet submission. She gave him a curious glance. 'You called me Amy again, right out of the blue. Sometimes you're very strange.'

'I realize that,' Luc murmured. A little while longer with her and he would be more than strange. When she had been upset just then he had wanted to hold her and kiss her. He had never before felt this inclination to cuddle a small, irritating madwoman.

His eyes slid over her slender hips as she reached across to get a coat when they went into the hall, and he admitted that he wanted to do more than cuddle her. But he would not get involved. She was eroding his common sense. Anyway, she was English, and staying here in this town was something he would most definitely not do. He had told his father that very firmly when he had gone home for the weekend.

Amy turned at the door and gave him one of her sudden brilliant smiles. It almost stopped him in his tracks. He forgot that Paris even existed.

'I'm sorry I yelled at you,' she said softly. 'You've been very kind to me.'

'My pleasure.' Luc was deliberately formal and got another of those astonishing smiles – probably for good manners, he decided. Her eyes were shining just like blue stars again. He couldn't stop looking at her. He found himself smiling just because she was smiling.

'You'll probably be back to being ice-cold tomorrow,' Amy mused as she locked the door while he waited on the step for her. 'Don't worry. I'll not expect you to put on this wonderful rescuing performance again.'

Luc's dark brows rose sceptically and the long, mobile lips twisted in amusement.

'And how are you going to stop me, Miss Scott?' he enquired softly. 'You said not long ago that I didn't fit in here. Obviously I need a hobby. Protecting you would be a good hobby to take up, don't you think?'

Amy looked quite startled. She stared at him for a second and went delightfully pink. Luc just looked back at her with his dark, unfathomable eyes until she looked away. The small smile she gave him then was confused and embarrassed. She didn't try to talk him out of it with her usual complicated logic. He felt quite pleased with himself.

CHAPTER 6

When Amy arrived at work the following day, Luc had already left for Paris, and she was surprised at the disappointment she felt.

'Well, I expected it because I knew he would have to go,' his secretary told Amy in a righteous manner. 'He went off with you yesterday and never came back, but that phone call he ignored was important. He had to leave for Paris first thing this morning. I've no idea when he'll be back.'

'It doesn't matter,' Amy said hurriedly. 'It's just that I wanted to talk to him but it will wait.'

'Well, there's Gordon Sheen,' the secretary began importantly. 'He takes over when Mr Martell isn't here, you know.'

'Yes, I know, but – er – no. It's personal.'

Amy shot off into her own office, glad to escape the interested speculation in the other woman's eyes. She wondered why Luc didn't get rid of that woman, because she instinctively knew that Luc was constantly irritated by his bossy secretary. And goodness knew what the woman was thinking, but Amy was not about to tell her the frightening tale of the watcher in black.

Anyway, the man hadn't come last night. Lucky for him because the police had been round every two hours, as promised. She was sure they would finally catch him. Thinking it over, she wasn't quite certain what she had wanted to say to Luc. It was just that she had this urge to talk to him and tell him how she had managed to sleep without fear the previous night.

She was grateful for everything Luc had done, and in spite of her worries she had enjoyed having dinner with him. When he wasn't being stiff and cold, he was easy to talk to. There was a lot of amusement in those dark eyes. He was an exciting man too. He made her tingle inside. She wondered if that was why she had been afraid of him before. She looked glumly at her computers.

'It's going to be a long day, boys,' she confided with a sigh, and, although she didn't mention it to either Jim or Alfie, she knew it would be a long day because Luc was not sitting next-door in his office.

Soon after Amy arrived home that evening, the patrol car came round and the police called in to see her.

'We've interviewed Mr Somerfield,' they told her, 'and if there's a man watching your house, it certainly isn't him.'

'There *is* a man watching the house and it must be him,' Amy insisted sharply. 'Obviously he's lying.'

'No, Miss Scott. Mr Somerfield's been away. He's been down to the south coast to inspect some properties. We checked up. He was definitely there.'

It had the awful ring of truth. Eric worked for a large property company and he often went away to look over the prospects of anything they were considering buying. It was nothing new. It was just part of his job.

'Well, there was one night when the man didn't come,' Amy reminded them rather desperately, but it was no use.

'He was away for a whole week, Miss Scott. We know where he was staying and pretty much everything about it. Bournemouth checked up for us. Mr Somerfield only just got back into town today. Whoever this man is, it definitely is not Mr Somerfield.'

They went off and Amy felt shaken. If it wasn't Eric then it was a stranger, somebody who had picked her out for reasons best known to himself. It meant that the watcher was mad, as far as she was concerned. She'd been living a low-profile life ever since she had parted company with Eric. Jill had been her only companion. Apart from the people in the office, there was nobody who saw her on a regular basis.

It was terrifying to think that some unknown man had singled her out with some sort of crazy determination and had been fixed enough in his ideas to stay either all night or part of the night, watching her house for over a week.

She desperately needed to talk this over with someone, but unless she got in touch with Peter and told him there was nobody at all. If Luc had been there she knew she would have rushed to him with the problem, but he was in Paris. He'd only been gone for one day and it seemed as if he'd been away for weeks.

Amy cheered herself up by telling herself that the police would catch the man, whoever he was, but once again she hadn't particularly liked their attitude. It had been polite and professional. They must get lots of calls from hysterical people who imagined things. They probably thought she was just the same. In fact, after one good night's sleep, Amy was beginning to wonder if it had all been imagination after all.

One look through the window at the tall light and the road around it reminded her that it was nothing of the sort. A man had been there watching the house. He had been dressed in dark clothes and he had stood for hours, staring up at her bedroom window. She also knew that unless the police caught him on one of their sweeps round the area, he would come back one night and stand there again.

Amy saw the patrol car come round several times before she went to bed. By this time she had managed to calm her nerves, and she went to sleep telling herself that nobody would be able to stand watching without being spotted by the police. There was a partial feeling of security, enough to allow her to sleep for most of the night, but she knew that the patrol car wouldn't be coming for very long. If nothing happened they would resume their normal duties.

When she went to work the next day she looked eagerly to see if Luc was back, but his office was empty. She would have been pleased to see him there even if he had been scowling at her, but he was still in Paris apparently. In any case, she didn't know where this feeling had come from that made her want to tell him all her latest, frightened thoughts. He was the boss and nothing more. It wasn't his business to follow her around protecting her.

She used her lunchtime to do a little shopping, and it made a change from watching out of windows and worrying. But she was glad to get back into the office later. She had almost felt as if the hairs on the back of her neck had been standing up with premonition. Somebody had been watching her in the supermarket, and later on in the street. Nobody had seemed to be paying any particular attention to her when she'd looked round carefully, but someone had been following her to each shop. She had been absolutely sure of it.

Paranoia, she told herself, but whatever she called it the feeling did not go until she was actually safely back in the building. When she got there, the news was not to her liking either. Gordon Sheen came in to see her.

'If you're working on anything particular with Luc at the moment, I'm taking it over,' he informed her.

'I'm not working with him,' Amy said. 'We finished the big project over a week ago.'

'That's fine, then.'

He started to leave and Amy asked quickly, 'Why are you taking over his jobs?'

'He's not going to be back for a week or more. He's had to go to Lyons and then he's off to

131

Germany. While they've got him over there, they're making the most of him. Maybe they'll keep him there permanently and send somebody else here in his place. I spent a lot of time at the Paris office when they were getting ready to combine with us. I know how much work Luc does. I was pretty astounded when they sent him over here. Now that things are working smoothly he could go back permanently to France. I wouldn't be surprised if he did.'

Gordon walked out and Amy sat and stared in a stunned manner at her computers. The thing that stunned her was the fact that the idea of Luc staying in France and never coming back gave her a peculiar empty feeling inside. It had nothing to do with the watcher outside her house either. It felt as if a little light had gone out inside her.

She never spoke a word to Jim and Alfie during the afternoon. She didn't feel like that any more. A certain ugliness had come into her life, and at the moment work was just work and nothing more. When the time came to leave she went quickly, wanting to get off the streets and lock herself into her house. The bijou residence was fast becoming a prison.

Luc slid into the fast traffic on the ring-road around Paris and picked up speed. It had been a hellish drive back from Lyons. The tourist traffic had been hectic and for once he had not felt like blaming the English, even though almost every other car seemed to have a British sticker on the back. To make matters worse, it had unexpectedly started to pour with rain.

He was later than he had intended to be too, because the last meeting had gone on endlessly, with everyone arguing in a pointless manner until he had been obliged to call them sharply to order. It had been his second trip to Lyons since he had come home. Sandwiched in between had been a trip to Germany. He felt tired, dirty and irritated.

Mostly he was irritated with himself, because he had told himself firmly that he was glad to be back home, speaking his own language, out of that boring town and back into the glitter of Paris. The truth was that even if he had been given the opportunity to enjoy the glitter he would not have wanted it. For a good deal of the time his mind had been on Amy and it annoyed him.

She was nothing to him. She was a peculiar computer person whose mind stopped working when she left her machines. She was trouble, and normally she was airily unaware of his presence. Unfortunately, he was *not* unaware of her presence. He had not been able to ignore her from the day he had arrived to take over the English side of the firm. Even when he was at his desk he could see her out of the corner of his eye, and lately he had taken to watching her intently when he should have been doing plenty of other things.

He left the ring-road and swooped down into the city fast, swearing fluently at a taxi that pulled across in front of him at the last minute, but his mind didn't even dwell on it. He was thinking about that little house, and wondering if the police car was still making a sweep past regularly. The two policemen who had called had not looked particularly convinced at Amy's story, but Luc was convinced. He had seen what a week of fear had done to her. He wondered if they had picked up that bastard Somerfield.

Once in his own apartment, Luc showered and then did what he had done every day for the past week. He sat at the telephone and considered calling Amy. Each time he had managed to stop himself. It was none of his business. She just happened to work for the firm and she must have friends. In any case, she had this uncle, and then there was the amorous solicitor.

He moved away from the phone before it could tempt him, but when it suddenly rang, he leapt back with an eagerness that disgusted him. It was Veronique, and his disappointment told him more than he wished to know. How could it have been Amy in any case? She had no idea where he lived, and even if she had known she would never have thought of ringing him. He was only the boss. He said, 'Jump' and she asked, 'How High?' Amy had pointed that out all by herself. The only reason he had been able to help her had been because he had forced his way into her affairs.

'*Luc, cheri*!' Veronique crooned in her usual sultry voice. 'I expected you back days ago.'

'I just arrived,' Luc told her. 'Not more than a few minutes ago as a matter of fact.'

'Oh, I'm sorry. I didn't give you time to ring me.'

Luc frowned at the phone. He hadn't actually considered ringing her, and that in itself was

134

disturbing. His mind had been back in England, in a boring town with an irritating woman who was delicately enchanting, odd in her behaviour and annoying beyond words. Besides, she was English.

'I haven't eaten,' he said quickly, before he could change his mind. 'Give me another half-hour to pull myself together and I'll collect you.'

'I'll be ready,' Veronique promised.

He put the phone down and frowned even more. Veronique expected him to be there when she called. Before he had left to work in England the whole thing had started to be a habit. In any case, he was too tired to go out, to face the traffic again.

He was going to go all the same, if only to see Veronique and have a good, long look at her, to allow another face to superimpose itself on the one that seemed to be haunting him lately. Veronique was a very beautiful blonde. She did not talk nonsense at the drop of a hat and she did not have violent former boyfriends hanging around at night. A few hours with Veronique would do him good.

Later he was not too sure. He was glad he had taken his car and not allowed her to collect him as he sometimes did. Veronique had wanted him to go back to her apartment with her, but the idea had struck him as midway between boring and alarming. He put it down to extreme tiredness. Fortunately, Veronique had put it down to exactly the same thing.

Her goodnight kiss had been lingering and possessive, and Luc had found that his enthusiasm had been sadly lacking. When he got back into his own apartment, he approached the telephone determinedly. A few words with Amy Scott and he would be in a fury with her as usual. His mind would right itself and he would be back to normal. Unfortunately when he glanced at his watch he realised that it was far too late to phone.

'Why didn't you tell me all this before?' Peter Jensen had met Amy for lunch that day, and looked absolutely appalled when she recounted her frightening tale of the man in black who watched her house.

'I knew you'd fuss,' Amy pronounced ruefully. 'I was right, wasn't I? You always fuss. You're going to fuss now.'

'Good God, Amy!' he muttered, trying to keep his voice low. 'This is serious. Let me remind you that you were the one who pointed out that there's nobody but you and I now. If I recall, you decided that we'd stand back to back against trouble. What do you call this but trouble?'

'Well, I've been frightened,' Amy admitted. 'I fully expected that the police would pick up Eric, though. It never occurred to me that it might be somebody else, a stranger.'

'They're sure?'

'Completely. Eric was miles away for the whole time that this was happening. In any case, it seems to be over now. There hasn't been a sight of the man for more than a week. I expect the police will stop coming round soon. More than likely it was some nutcase who finally decided to go elsewhere.'

She felt a little guilty that she was not mentioning the fact that Luc had taken a strong hand in this initially. She wasn't mentioning, either, that she felt as if she was being followed during the day. In point of fact, Amy had decided not to tell Peter anything, but when he'd invited her out to lunch she couldn't really sit there opposite him and keep quiet. It would have been tantamount to lying in some peculiar way.

'The moment this lunatic starts again you will let me know,' Peter ordered firmly.

'He probably won't start,' Amy murmured, but she had a deep-seated feeling that he would. 'I really don't see how the police can have frightened him off. If he'd seen them then it's equally true that they would have seen him, and that would have been the end of all this. Chances are, therefore, that he simply became tired of scaring me.'

'You're probably right,' Peter mused. 'But all the same, Amy, you should have told me, and the moment you start worrying again then you tell me at once. There's plenty of room at my house. You could stay there with me until they catch him.'

'I might just do that,' Amy promised. Not that she really intended to. Having another woman in the house, niece or not, would seriously cramp Peter's style. She didn't know who the latest female in his life was, but there would be somebody. There had always been somebody.

'Heard from Jill?' he asked as they drank coffee.

'Yes, a couple of postcards. She's enjoying it. I just wish she was here.'

'Well, she's not gone for good. How long does this exchange thing last did you say?'

'A year. It's going to seem longer.'

Everything seemed long to Amy at the moment. There was no Jill to tell her troubles to and Luc wasn't back. She couldn't understand why she was missing him when at one time she would have given anything just to see the back of him. She lived in dread of Gordon Sheen telling her that Luc would be staying in Paris permanently in future.

'I'm going to Bryan's office after work,' she mentioned to take her mind off Luc. 'This is the day I sign my will. It's a creepy proposition.'

'Leaving everything to the cats' home?' Peter enquired with a grin.

'I'm leaving everything to you,' Amy informed him adamantly. 'You threatened to do that with me so this is where I get my own back. Not that I have my hands on any money as yet. It's just that Bryan thinks I should set my affairs in order, in readiness for the time when I get run over by a bus.'

'Just the sort of thing to cheer you up,' Peter grunted. 'And I don't want your money, Amy. What about Jill?'

'Oh, I'll leave her something. In fact, according to Bryan, if anything happens to me, Jill will be very nicely taken care of.'

'This is pretty damned stupid,' Peter muttered. 'Nothing is going to happen to you. You're disgustingly young. Bryan Hetherington should never have brought this will business up.' He suddenly looked at her intently. 'How soon after he first mentioned it did you start to see this man watching the house?'

'What are you getting at?' Amy asked suspiciously. 'If you imagine that Bryan is trying to frighten me . . .'

'No, no. Of course not.' Peter muttered impatiently. 'I was just thinking, though, that the power of suggestion is very strong – not really understood. You were upset about Celia's death and then coming straight after that there is this rather depressing suggestion that you make a will.'

'What exactly are you saying?' Amy asked quietly.

'Well, Amy, have you ever given any thought to the possibility that the man . . .?'

'Is really a product of my imagination? That I imagined him watching the house? No, I have not!' Amy snapped. 'You know I'm not at all that sort of weak female, Uncle Peter. The man was there.'

'I was just wondering,' he explained rather sheepishly.

'Well, stop wondering. There was a man dressed in black, or at the least in dark clothes. He watched the house for a whole week. He frightened me to death.'

'OK, love. You saw him. I believe you. And don't call me Uncle Peter.'

'I did see him, whether you believe me or not,' Amy stated firmly. 'And I *shall* call you Uncle Peter. It's a punishment for doubting me.' She got up and collected her bag. 'I've got to get back to the office.' She felt so cross that she didn't really want to speak any more, in fact she bitterly regretted taking him into her confidence.

'Is the boss still bothering you?' Peter asked as they made their way to the street.

'He's in Paris,' Amy told him briefly. She suddenly didn't want to talk about Luc. Quite without warning, it was very private. If Jill had been there she wouldn't even have told her. Right out of the blue, Luc was important to her.

The will was all ready for her to sign, and after it had been witnessed Amy was free to go.

'How about dinner?' Bryan asked hopefully, and Amy could have cried with relief. She was just utterly sick of staying in at night and looking behind her during the day every time she ventured to the shops.

'Oh, thank you!' she exclaimed enthusiastically, and Bryan grinned all over his face. He hadn't really expected her to agree, not after last time's fiasco.

'We'll go out of town,' he promised. 'I'll pick you up a bit earlier and that will give us time to go further.'

Amy would have agreed to anything. Further meant that the likelihood of Eric spotting them was lessened. She might be able to shake off this feeling of impending doom that had settled on her too. She went home quite cheerfully, realizing as she did that being cheerful was getting to be a very rare event.

When she was almost ready to leave, the patrol car came round and stopped outside. Amy answered the door and her heart sank when she realized why they were there.

'This is going to be the last night, Miss Scott,' the policeman told her apologetically. 'We've done the circuit every night for a week. After tonight we're assigned to other duties, sorry.'

Amy knew they were not sorry, and she couldn't really blame them. Nothing had happened. It would happen after they were gone. Somehow the man had known the police were patrolling near the house. He would also know when they had been withdrawn. The pleasure of going out to dinner faded. All she wanted to do now was lock the door and barricade herself inside.

Still, the patrol car would come round this one last night. She might as well make the most of it. The telephone rang and she felt a great surge of excitement because she had the sudden idea that it would be Luc. It was Peter.

'Just checking to see that you're all right,' he told her.

'I'm fine. I'm just going out to dinner with Bryan.'

'Ah! Is it serious?' Peter asked.

'Serious? You mean am I about to become a solicitor's wife?' Amy asked. 'Do try to control your imagination, Uncle Peter. Bryan is taking me out to dinner and I'm looking forward to it because this will be my last night with the police round. My last night, therefore, to be able to come back with an easy mind.'

'What do you mean, "last night"?' Peter asked sharply.

'They're withdrawing the patrol car. I fully expected it. Anyway, the man's never been while they were here so he'll probably never come back. It will be an inexplicable interlude that's finally over.'

'I surely hope so,' Peter muttered. 'I don't like this, Amy. The moment you're worried or suspicious again, you ring me, do you hear?'

'Oh, I will,' Amy assured him. 'I'll be round at your house like a shot.' She didn't expect to have to but all the same it was nice to know he worried about her. She forgave him for doubting her.

When Bryan came she got into his car with a wide smile for him.

'The last supper,' she said cheerfully.

'What?'

'Never mind.' Amy decided to keep quiet. She was not about to tell Bryan about the man who watched her house. She even regretted telling Peter in a way. If she was imagining things then the fewer people who knew about it the better. It didn't seem to matter that Luc knew.

She let her mind reach out tentatively to consider Luc. Funny. She had no trouble at all in remembering every last thing about him minutely. He seemed to have became quite close to her. Imagination, no doubt, but even so it was thrilling in an odd sort of way she didn't exactly recognize. She just wished he was back.

Amy had a good night's sleep, well aware at the back of her mind that it might be the last for some time to come. It was a beautiful day next day and she had an upsurge of hope. Maybe it was all over? Maybe the man would never come back? She drove to work humming a little tune, and when she walked into the main office, the first person she saw was Luc.

Her heart leapt and she smiled brilliantly. She just couldn't help it, and Luc looked up at that moment and saw her. As usual he felt quite dazzled by the power of that smile, and in spite of all his useful lectures to himself his lips tilted in a slow smile of welcome.

Dieu! It was good to see her. She drifted in like a dream, her lips smiling, her eyes like blue stars again. He admitted that he'd missed her. It was no use fooling himself. He wanted to be near her.

Amy came straight up and popped her head round his door. Her heart was pounding with excitement. Even in the office, behind that desk, Luc managed to look dark and mysterious, as if he had some dangerous past that nobody would ever know about. She didn't care. He was back and it was all that mattered.

'Did you enjoy Paris?' she asked breathlessly.

'Of course,' he lied, unable to take his eyes off her.

'Was there anything tatty?'

'Definitely not. I never noticed one tawdry thing, nothing inferior or threadbare. As usual, the city sparkled.'

He was grinning, and she grinned back now. She could have danced with joy to see him here at last. It must have been premonition, that great upsurge of hope she'd felt this morning.

His eyes ran over her slowly, almost possessively, and her heartbeat quickened as a great shock of excitement flared through her.

'What about your problem?' Luc suddenly asked seriously, and the smile faded on her face.

'The man? He never came back while you were away. The police car came round each night but they didn't see anything. It wasn't Eric,' she added quietly. 'They checked up. He was on the south coast all the time on business. He only got back recently.'

Luc scowled. 'Are they sure?'

'Very sure. The local police where he was staying checked him out thoroughly.'

Luc looked thoughtful. Therefore the watcher was a stranger, which made matters even worse. If this continued there was real danger for her.

'It's more than likely that the man won't come back again,' Amy continued with an attempt at cheerfulness. 'Anyway, I'm not going to get worried about it. I've been getting on with my life as if he'd never been there at all. I even made my will.'

'You did *what*?' He realized she was talking to convince herself, but the subject matter startled him back to the present swiftly.

'Oh,' Amy gasped, blushing in confusion. 'I expect that sounds odd, telling you that right out of the blue. I had to do it in any case. I've got quite a lot of money coming to me and Bryan insisted that it would be wise to make a will.'

Luc quickly did a mental file-check and understood that she was speaking about her solicitor. It all sounded a bit depressing. Surely the damned will could have been left for now? He wondered if she would like to have dinner with him.

'If you're worried at all . . .' he began, but Amy cut in quickly.

'Not really. I've finally told Uncle Peter about the man watching the house. He insists that if the man comes back I'm to go to stay at his house – Uncle Peter's house, that is. He's got plenty of room, you see. I could easily move in with him for a while. After all, he's a relative – in a way.'

'Good,' Luc said quietly.

All right, so she was putting him back in his place. The smile was just natural and he supposed he should be pleased to have been on the receiving end of it. Before this had happened she hadn't even glanced in his direction. What did he want to go to dinner with her for anyway? It was bad for company discipline. He'd helped her and that was that. It had been his duty.

'Well, I'd better get on with my job,' Amy said uncomfortably when he just went on staring at her fixedly. 'I'm glad you're back,' she added shyly. Luc just nodded and gave her a faint smile as she left.

He really would have to get her out of his mind. And he would have to get a firm grip on his imagination. He was beginning to think of her in an altogether inappropriate way. She worked here. That was all. He would have to draw back, be more aloof, let her solve her own problems.

He even considered moving his office away from hers until he remembered how much he had to consult her. He wasn't prepared, either, to come each day and not be able to look up and see her. All he needed was self-control. And he'd never been short of self-control in his entire life.

He had good cause to doubt that later. He left the office just after Amy, and in his new frame of mind he hung back, so as not to encounter her in the lift or the parking area. All the same, as he was going down in the lift his mind wandered back to her problems.

If the police were sure that the watcher was not Somerfield then they were left with the problem of who? A total stranger? That really sounded alarming. Was someone stalking her? If so, why did he only come at night? Standing quite still and staring up at a window was not entirely the accepted idea of stalking.

Why wasn't this man following her everywhere? There was nothing to stop him watching the office. Luc stepped out of the lift into the underground parking area, his eyes narrowed thoughtfully, his mind pondering the problem. He was partly lost in thought, and he didn't immediately see what was happening. He noticed nothing untoward until he heard the voice.

'You've had the police checking up on me, you little bitch! When I got back here, I found the police had been swarming all over my street, the neighbours talking. Then they came to interview me. The neighbours are looking at me as if I'm a criminal now.'

'Don't be ridiculous!' Amy snapped. 'The police wanted to eliminate you, that's all.'

'Oh, I'll be eliminated all right, if they keep asking questions. I'll be eliminated right out of a job.'

'Look,' Amy said tightly, 'get out of my way and let me drive off. I'm going home and I don't want to see you. I don't want to speak to you either. And another thing, you've no right to be here in this private car park.'

'I'll be where I bloody well want to be!' Eric Somerfield raged. 'If I want to follow you around, I will. I'm going to haunt you from now on. You won't have to make up stories for the police because it will be all too real.'

He made a grab for her arm and flung her back to face him when she tried to walk off. He forced her back against a car and pushed his face close to hers in a threatening manner. 'It's no use telling anybody either. Don't imagine I'll be taken by surprise again, like I was at that restaurant.'

Luc appeared out of nowhere and touched his shoulder. As Somerfield turned, Luc hit him hard.

'You think not?' Luc asked with cold interest as Eric lay on the ground, looking up in a dazed manner. 'It seems to me that you will always be taken by surprise. Miss Scott now has grounds for a charge of assault against you if she wishes to pursue the matter.'

'I'm the one who's been assaulted,' Somerfield muttered, struggling to his feet and looking decidedly groggy.

'Merely a mild reprimand,' Luc corrected softly, smiling nastily and watching with clinical interest as a bruise began to form on Somerfield's chin.

'Miss Scott has already pointed out to you that you are trespassing. Get out of here in the same way that you came in. And keep away from her,' he added in a very quietly menacing tone.

'I expect you fancy her yourself,' Somerfield managed with sneering bravado when he was out of reach of Luc's lethal fists.

'Miss Scott works here, *m'sieur*,' Luc pointed out. Suddenly the amusement had gone and he was icily French, even though he was speaking his usual impeccable English. 'Just remember, however, that she has my protection.'

Somerfield lurched off. He was not entirely staggering, Amy noted, but he was definitely unsteady on his feet. She did wonder where an architect had learned to hit like that.

'I'm sorry,' she murmured, and Luc shot her a lightning glance at the uneasy sound of her voice.

'Sorry? Why are you sorry? Surely you can expect to go in safety on any part of Martell property. If you cannot, then I wish to know why. That *rustre* has no business to be here.'

'*Rustre?*' Amy queried faintly, and he frowned with annoyance at his own slip into French.

'It is a lout. *He* is a lout. You have no business to know him,' he finished, looking at her severely.

'Yes, well, hindsight is a wonderful thing,' Amy muttered.

'Providing that you have learned from it, then it can be excused,' Luc assured her in the same severe voice.

'Yes, sir,' Amy agreed meekly.

'*Idiote!*' Luc snapped, flashing her an irritated glance.

'I know what that means,' Amy told him quickly, not wanting to have her behaviour criticized in two languages.

Luc suddenly relaxed and grinned at her.

'I apologize,' he murmured. 'Are you all right? I rather think that I got here before things became too rough.'

'I'm fine,' Amy sighed, searching in her bag for her car keys.

'Then go home and forget about Somerfield.' She nodded and gave him a rather wan smile, but her eyes didn't shine and her face didn't light up in that almost magical manner. She was shocked and anxious and it showed.

Luc's thoughts dwelt on Eric Somerfield with a good deal of menace. She had enough problems without that creature pouncing on her every time he felt like it. Something would have to be done about him. On the subject of Somerfield, Luc realized that his thoughts were frequently violent.

And there was this watcher, Luc mused as he saw Amy drive off and then went to his own car. Would the man come back? Would he be there tonight? Theoretically, if the man merely came to stand by the lamppost and stare at the house, she was safe, but the whole thing sounded menacing – some madman watching her for no reason. How long would he be content to just stand there frightening her?

There must be a reason for this, even if it was not immediately apparent to the sane members of the population. A man like that would have some objective in view, and the obvious objective would be to attack her in some way at some time.

When Amy got home there was a card and a letter from Jill in America and she settled down to read both of them with a little sigh of relief. Jill represented normality; Jill was wholesome, sensible and good. If only she were here now.

America was a wonderful place, Jill wrote, and she was making the most of it. The letter was quite long, and after reading her way through it Amy felt restored to real life. Jill's response to the man who watched would have been to storm out and demand an explanation.

Amy would have done that herself except that instinct told her it would be a foolish and possibly dangerous thing to do. No, she would just hope that he did not come back again now that the police were not keeping an eye on the street.

It was beginning to get dark and Amy hurried to make her evening meal. Since the man had frightened her so much she had formed the habit of getting any jobs out of the way early in the evening. It seemed to have become an attitude of battening down the hatches and she felt like that again tonight, with no police car due.

She always felt safe when Luc was nearby, but as she carefully made sure that she had left no gaps in closing the kitchen curtains, Amy mused that right now Luc would be either eating out or sitting in his flat and dreaming of Paris. She made a wry little face. She was still sure there would be tatty places somewhere in such a big city, but he would never admit it. She was so glad he was back.

Luc was not dreaming of Paris. He was worrying about Amy. By now it was dark and he could just imagine her fear now that the patrol car was absent. He could visualize her looking carefully through the curtains, creeping about in the dark and trying not to draw attention to herself. He could imagine everything she had told him. His own imagination was also good enough for him to see the man watching her and feel the danger. He knew she had been telling the truth.

Luc decided to stop worrying about her and start acting. If the police had gone away then he would take a look for himself. He would do some patrolling on his own account. Besides, there was always that idiot Somerfield. He might have taken it into his head to go round to Amy's house tonight.

Men like that didn't take well to humiliation, and they could never take no for an answer. Men like that could never quite believe that any woman might want to see the back of them permanently. Luc put on a sweater and collected his car keys. One good, careful look at Amy's house and he would be more easy in his mind. Besides, he told himself, it was his duty.

Right at that moment, Amy was not easy in *her* mind. She was back to creeping around in the dark and it wasn't even particularly late yet. She was quite sure deep inside that the watcher had been

Eric, and if it had been he would surely not dare to try it again, not with all the recent police interest.

She tried not to think about how she would feel if she finally decided that it had not been Eric. For now, though, she was back to the beginning – peeping through cracks in the curtains and dreading the deep part of the night.

When she had one final look through the kitchen curtains before setting the alarm, Amy's heart leapt in fright because there was a man again, standing by the streetlight. It was only a momentary burst of fear, however, because she recognized the man almost instantly. It was Mr Phillips from a few doors further along the road. He was taking his dog out late tonight, apparently. He was usually earlier than this.

As she watched the dog ran off. That wasn't unusual either, although normally it ran off earlier, having been brought out as soon as the sky began to darken. It was a very untrained dog. It annoyed her every time she saw it behaving badly, because Mr Phillips was a nice, kind man and he didn't deserve to own a delinquent with a collar.

Mr Phillips did what he normally did under such trying circumstances – nothing. He stood under the light and whistled for the dog. It ignored him – another usual course of action. Amy relaxed. It was good to be able to contemplate normality, however foolish the normality was.

She smiled and was about to move away from the window and go up to bed when a dark shape suddenly bore down on Mr Phillips at speed. Amy stared in horror, her hand to her mouth. Somebody had come silently out of the shadows and he had come so quickly that she felt a flash of terror.

Only for a second, though. She recognized Luc, but by the time she was recovered from her shock and surprise, Luc had Mr Phillips in a firm necklock and looked as if he had every intention of savaging the poor man simply because he was waiting for his dog under the light.

CHAPTER 7

Amy raced for the door, hoping that nothing of a serious or permanent nature would occur before she got out into the street. Mr Phillips looked ready to collapse and Amy suspected that only Luc's strength was holding the poor man upright. She pulled the front door wide open and rushed outside.

'Luc!' she shouted as she leapt down her three front steps.

'I have him!' Luc assured her, swinging Phillips round so that she could see her tormentor. Luc looked ready to commit murder and Amy ran across to him.

'No, it's not him, Luc. That's Mr Phillips from just up the road. He's waiting for his dog.'

Mr Phillips nodded in frantic agreement, and it seemed to Amy that at any moment, his eyes would simply pop out of his head with fright.

'Please let him go, Luc,' Amy urged. 'This is the wrong man. I know this man.'

'*Merde*!' Luc snarled, and abruptly let go of his captive.

Mr Phillips sat precipitously on the pavement, gasping for air and quite unable to speak. The wretched dog came back and began to lick his face, an act that Amy was quite sure would be no help at all in this sort of emergency. She had a great desire to grasp the dog's collar and shake it hard.

'I'm so sorry, Mr Phillips.' She crouched down in front of him to make certain he was all right and to protect him from the dog's solicitous attention. 'It's so unfortunate that you were there, under the streetlight. It really was a question of you being in the wrong place at the wrong time.'

'I've often been here before,' Mr Phillips croaked plaintively.

'Yes, I know. But not recently, and not when it was so late. There have been things going on that you don't know anything about. A man's been watching me, following me. It's just unfortunate that you were mistaken for him, but it's all right now. I know you. It certainly wasn't you.'

'Wasn't me what?' Mr Phillips asked anxiously, his voice beginning to return but not his wits, apparently.

'It wasn't you watching me. This has all been a very sad mistake and I do hope you'll forgive and forget. I have enough trouble as it is, without gaining more.'

'It's OK.' Mr Phillips stood, albeit shakily, and cast a rather anxious glance in Luc's direction. 'Is this your bodyguard?'

'No. Actually,' Amy confessed, 'this is my boss.'

'He was swearing at me in French,' Mr Phillips told her with another suspicious glance at Luc.

'Yes, well, he does that,' Amy told him soothingly. 'He can't help it. He grew up in France and you know how they are there.'

'Hmm,' Mr Phillips agreed. He began to retreat in a sort of crab-like fashion and Amy looked at him worriedly.

'I could make you some tea,' she offered.

'No – er – thanks. I'll just go back home and lie down.'

'I hope you'll forgive this,' Amy persisted.

'Oh, yes. No harm done. Genuine mistake. Could have been the villain after all.'

'You're very understanding,' Amy crooned, and let him walk unsteadily away.

'Can see he's trained,' Mr Phillips pointed out as he moved off.

'Who?' Amy enquired in surprise, thinking of the dog, which certainly wasn't.

'This chap. Probably got trained in France. One of these special units.'

'Quite right,' Amy beamed. 'How very clever of you. Exactly right!'

'*Merde!*' Luc muttered under his breath. He took Amy's arm in a firm grip and led her across the road, pointing out irascibly that her front door was wide open.

'Anybody could have slipped inside as we stood talking,' he told her angrily. 'You just raced out and left the door wide open.'

'I was trying to save a man's life.'

'Think about yourself. Now you won't know who is in the house.'

'There's no need at all to frighten me more than

you have already,' Amy stated sharply. 'I saw you come out of the darkness like an assassin. If I hadn't got there in time, poor Mr Phillips would have collapsed completely.'

'He had no business to be standing all by himself under the streetlight,' Luc informed her irritably. 'And will you kindly stop allowing people to imagine that I'm a trained killer?'

'It's not my idea,' Amy muttered. 'They just see you and draw their own conclusions.'

'You confirmed his beliefs tonight. And stop introducing me as your boss.'

'You are.'

'I am in charge of the English section of the business. The word "boss" has unpleasant connotations. It suggests force.'

'Yes, well,' Amy agreed, 'Sometimes it fits. For example, my arm is going numb.'

'I apologize.' He let go of her arm and Amy gave it a good rub to get the circulation flowing. 'I have to search your house now,' Luc insisted as he urged her up the steps in a no-nonsense manner. 'Lock the door behind us and stay in the hall while I go through each room.'

'Yes, Commandant.'

He glared at her, and then went up the stairs as she stood by the locked door. Once again he was taking over everything, but on this occasion she was glad. Anybody could have slipped inside while she had been across the street. Left to herself she wouldn't have thought of that until she was in bed, and then she would have been terrified.

When he came back down she was still there like a good soldier, and Luc frowned at her suspiciously before he went to search the rest of the house.

'Nobody,' he told her. 'You're safe. I'll go, and in future . . .'

'I'll make some coffee,' Amy interrupted quickly. 'You can lecture me then.'

She didn't really want him to go yet. It was exciting to have him around, safe. She rushed into the kitchen before he could come and take over. She didn't really want any coffee. Since she had been in Luc's clutches she seemed to be constantly full of coffee.

She blushed at the thought of being in his clutches. It brought a mixture of excitement and panic bubbling up inside.

'Would you rather have tea?' she asked hopefully.

He had come into the kitchen and when she looked round he was staring at her thoughtfully, everything about him intent.

'If you like,' he murmured. 'I'm used to tea. My mother drinks it all the time.'

'Is she really English?' Amy asked, anxious to keep him there and willing to discuss absolutely anything for the whole night if necessary.

'Yes,' he murmured absently. He went on staring at her. 'Why did you tell that man there was somebody following you around?'

'Er – it was just something to say to calm him and explain things, so I . . .'

'Does it come naturally?' Luc intervened quietly.

'What?' Amy spun round and looked at him and was instantly trapped by his dark gaze.

'Lying,' he enlarged. 'Do you lie with ease or do you have to work out a detailed plan?'

'All right. So it was the truth,' Amy sighed, giving in and turning back to her tea-making. 'I've never actually seen anyone but I know that somebody has been following me around for days, even when the police were patrolling by the house at night. Whoever it is follows me from shop to shop. They follow me right back to the office. It's when I'm on foot, never when I'm driving – at least, I don't think so.' She gave another long sigh. 'Maybe it's imagination.'

Luc stepped forward and leaned against the draining board. He took her shoulders and brought her round to stand in front of him.

'Now,' he ordered firmly, keeping her shoulders under his strong hands, 'Let's have the whole story. Never mind imagination. Women have an instinct and I'm usually prepared to believe it.'

'Do you really think so?' Amy began eagerly. 'Not many men admit to the fact that women have this extra intuition, but I think it's because they're weaker physically and need an edge and – '

'Amy!' Luc warned sharply. He gazed down at her sternly and then his face relaxed into smiles as his hands tightened on her slender shoulders. 'If this watcher knew what you were really like, he would run away and go to watch a more reasonable person.'

'I'm not all that terrible,' Amy protested, going pink again.

'You are merely incredible. Now tell me about the feeling you have that you are being followed during the day. And Amy,' he added mildly, 'try not to leave anything out. Getting information from you is rather annoying. It comes in small, disconnected pieces.'

'Yes,' Amy said, looking up at him worriedly. 'I suppose I should have told you everything but I really don't want to impose on you.'

'Feel quite free to impose on me,' Luc invited with wry amusement. 'Do not hesitate to take advantage of my good nature. Now tell me about being followed.'

'It's just a feeling,' Amy confessed. 'At first I thought it was because I've been nervous, which is really a thing I'm not used to. But the feeling became so strong that I began to believe there was somebody not far behind me every time I was out – although I never actually saw anyone who seemed to be taking a lot of interest in me. I've done silly things, like going into a shop and then turning to come straight back out, hoping to catch them. Nobody even looked surprised, though. Everybody was going about their business normally. The only person who didn't appear to be normal was me. When I told you I only felt safe at work, I really meant it.'

Luc stood there looking thoughtful and Amy watched him anxiously, as if she was waiting to hang on to his every word.

'I'll have to give a good deal of thought to this,' he decided seriously. He suddenly gave a very self-disparaging laugh.

'What?' Amy asked quickly.

'You,' he informed her. 'It's the way you're looking at me, as if I have instant solutions. Even with my supposed specialist training it will take some thought.'

'Do you want your tea now?' Amy asked, still looking at him in an awe-stricken manner.

'Yes.'

He didn't let her go. Instead he did what he had been wanting to do for weeks. He bent his head quickly and covered her lips with his own. It was not a lingering kiss but it was stingingly sweet, possessive and strangely probing, as if he was questioning her without words. Amy gasped as excitement shot right down to her toes and heat flared inside her.

'Why did you do that?' she asked in a shaken voice when he slowly lifted his head.

'Impulse,' Luc assured her silkily, staring down into her eyes. His hands were still flexing on her shoulders, as if he was considering further action. 'I'm a very impulsive man, as you saw earlier. I'm frequently given to strange behaviour. I expect it's my special training.'

He let her go slowly and sat down at the kitchen table, waiting for his tea. Almost immediately he was frowning, back to business as if nothing had happened. He was sitting there like some casual visitor, like the gas man who couldn't find the meter and had to give it some deep consideration.

Amy, on the other hand, was distracted, utterly shaken. He didn't know what he'd done to her. Her legs were trembling. She didn't know what to say or do. She seemed to be going hot and cold with sharp bursts of feeling. She wasn't even sure if she remembered how to make tea now.

The telephone rang and Amy almost jumped out of her skin. It was Peter.

'Just checking again,' he told her. 'Are you all right, Amy?'

'I'm fine!' she snapped, and then realized how she must sound. 'Oh, I'm sorry, Uncle Peter,' she said in a more reasonable voice. 'I'm a bit on edge. It's just that it's late and I didn't expect to hear from you at this hour.'

'Why don't you let me fetch you over here now?' Peter said. 'It's ridiculous staying there and being frightened.'

'I'm not really frightened,' Amy assured him quickly. 'Being on edge is not actually fright, you know. Anyway, if this man who was watching the house has seen the police patrol car he's probably been scared off for good. It's merely a question of settling down again. I'm sure it's all over.'

When she put the phone down, Luc was watching her intently again.

'Are you sure it's all over?' he asked quietly.

'I'm not sure, but it probably is. He never came when the police were round every night so I'm assuming that he saw them and took the hint. For all he knows, they may be back again. They might just be staggering the times after all. He won't know anything different from that, will he?'

'It's logical to assume that he will consider the possibility of staggered patrol times,' Luc agreed.

He got up to leave and then turned back to look at her. 'Will you be able to sleep?'

'Yes,' Amy said with a quick grin. 'I'll be too busy remembering how you scared Mr Phillips to think about the man in black.'

Luc gave her a wry glance.

'I'm glad I was able to amuse you. Goodnight, Amy.'

'Thank you,' she said softly.

'My pleasure. It has been, after all, an entertaining evening. I get very bored in this town. A little detective work will lessen the monotony. I imagine I will improve my skills, given time.'

'You won't have to,' Amy said quickly, hoping he didn't improve his skills at kissing her. She would faint. 'It's all over.'

'I'm sure you're right,' Luc agreed as he left, but Amy could tell by the look on his face that he didn't really think so – and, deep inside, neither did she. The watcher would be back.

At the weekend, Bryan called her and asked her to go out to dinner again. Amy gave the thought some quick consideration and agreed. She was a bit uneasy, though, because of the idea that Peter had had. She didn't want Bryan to start imagining that she would be happy to have him as a boyfriend. It was something that had never occurred to her until Peter had mentioned it.

'What did you decide to do about your aunt's house?' Bryan asked as they ate.

'I still don't know,' Amy said thoughtfully. 'To tell you the truth I've been putting it off.'

She did not add that the man watching her had pushed most other thoughts to the back of her mind, with the possible exception of Luc. She thought about him almost constantly.

'Just send an agent in to give a valuation of the things in the house and then send another one to value the property,' Bryan suggested.

'I couldn't do that,' Amy decided. 'There are some beautiful things in that house and I would want to keep them, even if they were going to be stored until I have a bigger house.'

'You're thinking of moving house when you get your money?'

'Not at all. I was meaning at some time in the future.'

'I see. Like when you get married,' Bryan mused aloud.

'Should that day ever come, I'll consider the treasures stored from Aunt Celia's house, but it isn't even that. I suppose it's simply because I couldn't bear to see them go. I grew up with most of those things around me. In any case,' she added quietly, 'there are a few things there that belonged to my mother and father.'

'So when are you going?'

'Maybe tomorrow. It's Sunday. I'll have the whole day and nothing to do with it. I might as well get this over and done with.'

'Want me to come with you?' Bryan asked, and she detected a sort of hopefulness in his voice that alerted her to Peter's words.

'No. I'd rather go alone.' She was not about to encourage anything other than either friendship or a good client-solicitor relationship. Besides, she never stopped thinking of Luc, foolish though it was. Right at this moment she was waiting for Monday, when she would be back at work.

Luc rang that night, when she was almost ready for bed.

'I wanted to see if you were all right,' he told her as she answered the phone.

'So far, so good,' Amy managed cheerfully, thinking how thrilling it was to hear his dark voice with that oddly sensuous accent.

'Then I will not patrol the street tonight.'

'Please don't,' Amy laughed. 'Mr Phillips will not be so forgiving if you attack him again.'

'Have you been hiding inside all day?' Luc asked quietly, and Amy felt another burst of excitement that he was interested enough to ask.

'I've been out to dinner with Bryan,' she told him brightly, suddenly feeling that she must hide behind somebody in case he picked up her vibes as she had said she picked up his. 'I haven't been in long.'

There was a decided pause and then Luc asked, 'What will you do to pass your time tomorrow?'

'I'm going to have a look round my aunt's house. I have to decide what to do with it and I haven't been up there since she died. Bryan offered to go with me but I wanted to go alone,' she added quickly, still filled with the need to hold him off in case he knew how she was beginning to feel.

'Would you like me to go with you?' Luc asked softly.

'I wouldn't want to – ' Amy began breathlessly, but he cut in immediately, finishing her sentence for her.

'Impose on me? I told you to feel free. In any case, it would be a kindness to me. I am invariably bored at the weekend and also I have never been round an English country house. I would like to go. I would be interested. Give me the address and I will join you there.'

Amy felt as if she was glowing all over. She gave him the address and the time she would be going and when she put the phone down she was trembling. She was getting close to him and she didn't know how it had happened. She did know that she was glad, though, glad and excited. She had been dreading the idea of going into the empty house with all its memories, but now it was like a thrilling adventure because Luc would be there.

Just before bed Peter rang to check on her, and she told him, too, that she was going up to Celia's house. He offered to go with her but she declined his offer very firmly.

'You would feel uncomfortable,' she reminded him. 'You know how things were between you and Aunt Celia. I don't need a chaperon. Besides, I'm going to the church too. I'm taking flowers for the grave.'

'It will make you miserable, Amy.'

'No, Uncle Peter. I've got over that. I suppose the wretched man watching the house helped me to get over it in some obscure way.'

'Well, if you're perfectly sure,' Peter agreed reluctantly.

'I am. Don't worry.'

As Amy put the phone down she realized that she had in fact lied. She had told him that she didn't need a chaperon and she didn't, but she had not said one word about Luc going with her. Luc was her thrilling secret. She wasn't about to tell anyone, and in any case there was nothing to tell. He was just being kind, being concerned for her because she worked for him.

He made her feel safe, anyhow. Maybe Luc wanted to get the chance to use his specialist training again? She had thought of him as a lethal weapon and he was. She went to bed without even one thought about a man watching the house, and as far as she knew he never came, because she slept peacefully all night.

On Sunday, Amy decided to go early. For one thing she wanted to go to the church and leave some flowers on her aunt's grave, and for another she was too restless to simply wait. She had been in a frenzy of sorting clothes since breakfast time because she couldn't decide what to wear when she met Luc.

She told herself that it was very stupid, but all the same it did not prevent her from spending a long time trying things on and then discarding them. She was obsessed with the thought of sophisticated women from Paris, even though she was not quite sure what they would wear and this was Sunday, not a working day, so she had to look different.

In the end she wore what she felt comfortable in, and that was another dress the colour of ripe corn with flat shoes that were a near perfect match. Aunt Celia had dragged her over half of London to find the shoes and Amy decided that if her aunt had thought the outfit suitable then it must be suitable. In any case, she told herself in a fit of despondency, in all probability Luc would not notice. He might not even arrive.

She knew where there was a florist who stayed open until lunchtime and she wanted to call in there. So at ten o'clock, a good hour before she had arranged to meet Luc at the house, she set off, feeling excited and greatly unsettled. It was the very first time in her life that she had been both eager and scared about meeting a man.

There was still a mist about the morning but the sun was trying to break through strongly and Amy felt as if this was some sort of adventure. The worry about the dark watcher had held her in its grip for too long and now she felt free, as if she had taken a wild spring into the air. There was a slightly guilty feeling that this was the first time she had been to visit her aunt's grave since the funeral but it did not worry her overmuch. Aunt Celia had been a very 'no-nonsense' person and she would not have wanted any foolish sentimentality. Besides, the watcher had put almost everything else out of Amy's mind.

She stopped her car in almost the same place it had been parked on the day of the funeral and was surprised that the same despondency did not descend on her. It was even more quiet this time because there were no other visitors, and by the look of it there was no Sunday service in the church today. Amy knew that the vicar ran three other churches, as was the usual way in these country parishes. Apparently it was the turn of another section of his widespread flock to receive him today.

She found Aunt Celia's grave with no trouble and was annoyed with herself that it looked a little neglected. As yet there was no possibility of putting up a headstone but there were weeds already, and Amy spent a few minutes pulling them out and clearing everything away.

It was wonderfully peaceful. The birds were singing in the trees around the edge of the churchyard. Everything was bathed in a soft tranquillity.

'It's not such a bad place, Aunt Celia,' Amy said quietly. 'I know you're watching from somewhere and I do hope you're behaving yourself, because I'm certain you won't be allowed to have fits of bad temper up there.'

She crouched down and put the small stone vase she had brought with her at the head of the grave, congratulating herself that she had even remembered to bring a small bottle with water in it to fill the vase up. The flowers looked very nice when she finally had them arranged. They were bright, cheerful and, again, tranquil.

Amy decided that later in the year she would plant something here, perhaps a Christmas rose? It would make things more normal for her aunt. Celia had loved gardening. Maybe when the headstone was fixed in place she could get some decorative ivy to train around it.

She sat back on her heels to survey her work, her dress tucked around her legs to keep it from the soil. Amy congratulated herself on the job and it was then, when she was absolutely still, that she became aware that she was under observation.

It was not some fanciful thought that Celia was watching over her either. It was real, immediate, and she was instantly wary. Without turning, she let her eyes wander over the churchyard, amongst the trees and low bushes, around the front of the church, everywhere that was in her vision. And she saw nobody at all.

Even so, every instinct in her told her that she was not mistaken, and Amy's heart began to pound painfully when she felt again the rising of the hair on the back of her neck that had warned her in town in the past that she was being followed.

She spun round quickly, standing and looking intently to the places behind her that she had not yet observed and there was nothing. At least she saw nothing at first and then, as she stood staring, she imagined she saw a slight movement in the shadows beyond the trees by the wall.

It was nothing much, just a darker shadow, a more definite image, a movement that was more than the breeze in the foliage. She stared hard into these deep shadows by the church wall and then came to her senses. She was alone here; the place was deserted and silent. That it was daytime, a bright Sunday morning, meant nothing. The bare fact was that she was alone and she felt with everything in her that the watcher was back and right here with her.

Amy moved carefully, trying to appear nonchalant, then she swept up the empty plastic bottle she had brought water in and raced for the gate as if the devil pursued her. Indeed, she felt for a few seconds that he did.

Even out in the church lane there was nobody around. This was a village miles from the outskirts of the town where she lived. Today there was no church service and so today there was nothing to bring anyone other than a casual stroller up the lane to the church. Amy didn't feel safe until she was in her car with the doors locked. Even then she was shaking, wild-eyed.

She drove off fast but she kept her wits about her. Aunt Celia's house was not too far from here but she was not about to lead the person watching her to the house; she had no intention of being trapped in there if Luc decided not to come after all. She drove off in another direction. She had lived here for most of her life and she could come at the house from an entirely different route.

About fifteen minutes later, after going through two more villages and skirting the main road, she turned into Aunt Celia's drive and parked the car by the front steps. She had no intention of inspecting the garden either, to see if the man who had looked after it was still keeping things tidy. She walked quickly up the steps and into the house, feeling that she had made it to base with some skill and a good deal of luck.

She needed a cup of tea, but although things had been left exactly as they had been when her aunt had died, there was no fresh milk. She found a bottle of brandy, her aunt's favourite soother, and poured herself a carefully measured portion. Even with the aid of this liquid courage, it was quite a few minutes before Amy stopped trembling and told herself that she was safe.

She knew it had been the man, the same one. Every instinct told her. But how had he known? How had he got there? He seemed almost to be able to read her mind, know her intentions. She stood in the kitchen and sipped her brandy until she felt better.

Finally she began to look round the house, and the enormity of the task ahead of her slowly sank into her mind. Not only had *she* lived here for most of her life, so had Aunt Celia, and her aunt had been here for a good deal longer. This was more than a house that was beautifully and tastefully furnished, it was filled with treasures her aunt had collected and it contained a lifetime of living.

Every shelf, every cupboard was packed, every drawer was filled to capacity. Even if Amy had not had a job to go to each day, there was months of work in this house, sorting, deciding, looking through old, much loved possessions. The responsibility was overwhelming and she walked slowly through the downstairs rooms, looking at the pictures, the ornaments, the vast array of possessions and knowing that she would never be able to face this duty.

Upstairs it was the same, but much more painfully intimate. There were her aunt's clothes, even her expensive make-up still on the shining top of the dressing table. How could she send a firm in here and say, 'Clear this up'? This was her own responsibility. Amy knew she would have felt better if she had never come here today. And, apart from anything else, there had been that watching shadow in the churchyard.

She walked to the window of her old room and looked down on to the garden, because this was a good, safe place to get a view of the part-time gardener's work. She was pleased to see that he had been working quite hard, even though totally unsupervised. Celia would have been harassing him daily.

Amy smiled at the thought, seeing in her mind's eye the tall, stately figure of her aunt sailing across the lawn to bear down on the man unfortunate enough to work for her.

The smile died on her face and she drew back quickly behind the curtain when she saw the same dark shadow in the trees that edged the lawn at the bottom of the long garden. Somehow he had known she was coming here; somehow he had followed.

She flattened herself against the wall, almost too afraid to breathe even though she was inside and he was out there. The thought of her car close to the house didn't help at all. At this moment the steps that led from the door seemed to be endless, the distance to the car many dangerous miles. She was trapped. She would be here all night. She was alone.

She risked a careful glance and the dark shadow was still there. The watcher was pursuing her, hunting her down for reasons she could not begin to imagine. Her heart was beating like a hammer, almost deafening her, and she was almost too paralyzed with fear to hear the sound of another car approaching.

It was only as Luc's black Porsche swept into the drive and came up to the house that she remembered he had promised to meet her here. And he had come!

Any pulled herself away from the wall and ran on trembling legs to the wide corridor that led to the stairs. She almost fell down the stairs in her anxiety to get to the front door. It was locked; he might not wait. If he left she would be alone. She fell upon the door, her fingers shaking so much that for seconds turning the key defeated it. He was just coming up the steps when she pulled the door open and she flew to meet him, her face pale, her legs shaking and wild fear in her eyes.

'Luc!'

Amy flung herself at him with no other thought than to feel the astonishing air of power he gave off whenever he was near. She launched herself against his wide chest, almost knocking him over. Luc braced himself against the attack and she felt blissful relief when his arms came round her, holding her fast.

He was clearly astounded but she didn't care at all. The fact was that he was *here*. She buried her face against him, wound her arms round his neck in what amounted to a stranglehold and held on to him with a good deal of frightened urgency.

'Evidently you are pleased to see me,' he murmured against her hair. He finally managed to untangle himself from her ferocious grip and look down into her face. 'It would be very gratifying under normal circumstances, but I have a suspicious mind. What happened?'

'He's here,' Amy whispered, still hanging on to his arms and showing no tendency to let him move more than an inch away from her. 'The man in black, the watcher. He's here in the garden.'

'Where?' Instantly alert, Luc put her firmly from him and spun round to scan the garden with narrowed dark eyes.

'Round the side of the house, under the trees by the wall. He's in the deep shadows, watching.'

'Stay here!' Luc ordered, and made to move away, but Amy protested instantly and grabbed his arm again.

'No! I'm not standing here by myself. He might come round the other way while you're round that side.'

'Then come,' Luc said harshly. 'If he is there. I will get him.'

Amy hoped he would, in fact she knew he would, and she didn't care how much of his special training he used on the man who was turning her life into a nightmare. She hoped that Luc would beat him up and shake him silly. Luc held out his hand and she put her own hand into his very willingly.

There was nobody. Amy recovered enough to do her own searching as she went along with Luc. Her blue eyes looked as intently as his own dark, intense gaze did but there was nobody at all. The breeze tossed the leaves in the tops of the trees. It gently bent the flowers and scattered their sweet perfume over the garden. But there was no sign at all of any intruder, not even one glimpse of the man in the black clothes.

They went round the whole garden and then arrived back at the front steps. Amy withdrew her hand from Luc's strong grasp and looked at him forlornly.

'He *was* here, Luc. I swear it.'

Luc said nothing. He merely stood, still and tall, looking at her pale, anxious face, and she was embarrassed as well as scared. He probably thought she was mad.

'Would you like to look round the house now?' she asked shakily.

'No.' He spoke abruptly, almost angrily, and Amy's face flushed with colour. He thought she had been making a small but dramatic scene.

He looked at her steadily and then said, 'Do you have anything in the house that you need to collect?'

'My bag,' Amy confessed in a defeated voice.

'Then get it, lock the door and drive away behind me.'

'But . . .' Amy began and he looked down at her, his dark brows raised in frustration and a rather alarming frown growing deeper by the second. He looked a bit like a devil with his darkness and that expression on his face.

'You have never been very good at obeying orders,' he pointed out severely. 'You will now do exactly as you are told. Collect your bag, lock the door and follow me.'

Amy did not say, Yes, sir, although it seemed natural to say it at that moment. He would have probably exploded with rage, though. He had been searching the garden for a non-existent man and obviously he was going home and just making her go with him because he felt responsible for her. She wondered if he was going to drive to the nearest hospital and ask them to test her mental faculties.

Amy decided that to obey would be wise and said nothing else. She got her bag, locked the door and he stood and opened her car door for her, and saw her into the driving seat with a darkly annoyed look on his face that was clearly directed at her.

'Follow closely,' he ordered severely.

'Yes,' Amy agreed, rather like a timid mouse who was trying, without much hope, to placate the cat.

He drove off and Amy followed immediately behind him. She would rather have been in front because she would have felt safer. Even as they left her eyes were worriedly searching the bushes for any likely assassin. And she knew she had seen the same watcher. He had not been so clearly visible in the churchyard or in her aunt's garden as he had been under the street light opposite her house, but all the same he had been there and it had been the same man.

Nothing would convince her otherwise but she knew what Luc must be thinking. He would be asking himself if she had ever suffered from any form of persecution mania. He would be pondering on whether or not she was in the middle of a nervous breakdown. At this rate she would be, very soon.

Luc drove to Amy's house and she felt very downcast. He was delivering her home and washing his hands of the whole procedure and she couldn't blame him at all. She had behaved in a quite bizarre manner since she had first known him and to him this must be just about the last straw.

He left his car at the same time that she got out of hers and he still had that severe look on his face.

'Is the alarm system switched on in your house?' he asked shortly.

'Yes,' Amy assured him with an earnest look that was clearly trying to please while at the same time being efficient.

'Good. Then lock your car and get into mine.'

That really shook Amy. She was quite taken aback.

'If you want to talk to me we could talk inside the house,' she began, but he gave her another of his impatient looks.

'I do not want to talk at the moment,' he told her crisply. 'I want to eat. So do you. It is almost lunchtime. We will drive away from the town and eat in a more country atmosphere. We will talk there when we have eaten.'

'Oh, right,' Amy murmured, as if she had realized his intentions ages ago. She got into his car and gave a great sigh before he had the chance to get in himself and hear it. If he was going to accuse her of anything, at least he was going to do it in pleasant surroundings. It couldn't be all that bad.

Maybe it *would* be bad, though, she thought a little while later when they had left the town behind. Luc just drove silently. He wasn't about to make small talk. He sat there frowning at the road and quite obviously he was thinking deeply. The relief she had felt when he had insisted on lunch had now faded away. She decided that if he began to be nasty she would simply shout at him, boss or not.

He stopped the car at a very quiet country inn by the river that skirted the town. The river widened and deepened as it flowed out into the country and at this point it was fast-flowing, sparkling in the sun. There were willows by the bank, dipping towards the stream, and Amy would have been very glad to be here with Luc – had the circumstances been different.

'I have eaten here before,' Luc told her quietly. 'The food is good and it's a very quiet and comfortable place. We're a little early, so perhaps it will not be too full.'

Amy was glad of that. If she had to raise her voice at him, she didn't particularly want to do it in front of a fascinated audience.

CHAPTER 8

As it turned out, there was no audience. The only other customers were a couple in late middle age who sat at a corner table and read guidebooks. They were both clad in walking boots and stout clothes. They were very intent on the guidebooks and their own conversation.

Amy relaxed a little but she could not relax completely, because she knew that in spite of being so far out of town, so far away from her aunt's house, she was still frightened. Wherever she went, the man in the dark clothes would follow her. At the moment it felt as if he would follow her for the rest of her life.

While they ate Luc was very thoughtful, and as Amy had no idea how his thoughts were running, or what he would eventually say, she was silent too and very uptight.

'This man,' Luc asked finally, 'Did you get a better look at him today than you did when he was outside your house?'

'No.' Amy shook her head gloomily. 'A worse look. Both times today he was standing in shadows, under trees. It seemed as if he was trying to keep as far away from me as possible. Maybe he thought I would recognize him.'

'Both times today?' Luc queried sharply, fixing her with a dark frown.

'I came early because I wanted to go to the church and take flowers for my aunt,' Amy told him. 'It was all right at first – at least, I think it was. I talked to her a minute and did some weeding, then I arranged the flowers. That was when I felt scared – just like I feel when I'm walking through town, I looked around without moving but I couldn't see anything, then I jumped up quickly and stared behind me. I think I caught him off guard because I saw him standing under the trees a good way off. He was well hidden but I saw him.'

'What did you do?' Luc asked in a tight voice, his eyes unswervingly on her face.

'I ran. There was no service at the church today so there was nobody there. The lane to the church is a bit lonely too. I raced to my car, locked myself in and drove off.'

'So he followed you to your aunt's house,' Luc concluded.

'No, he didn't. I thought of that. I didn't go straight to Aunt Celia's house. I drove there by a roundabout way. It took me about fifteen to twenty minutes and nobody was following me. Anyway,' she added as a new thought occurred to her, 'there was no other car in the church lane. So how did he get there in the first place and how did he get to Aunt Celia's afterwards?'

'If he didn't follow you, then he already knew exactly where you were going and he had a car hidden – unless he could have walked there in twenty minutes?'

'He couldn't,' Amy stated emphatically. 'It's too far.' She looked down at her hands in a burst of embarrassment. 'I suppose I should have challenged him.'

'*Dieu!*' Luc exclaimed sharply. 'You should have done no such thing. Do not ever challenge this man and do not ever be alone like that again. Do you hear me?'

'Yes.' Amy nodded frantically.

It was just what she had thought herself. But how long could she go on making sure that she was with someone else? What sort of a life was that?

'I volunteered to go with you to your aunt's house today so that you would not be alone,' Luc began angrily.

'You wanted to see round an English country house,' Amy reminded him, giving him a startled look.

'I lied,' he informed her blandly. 'You are so peculiar. With you it is sometimes necessary to be circumspect.'

'Circumspect?' Amy questioned crossly. 'Don't feel obliged to use a big word. "Lie" will do quite nicely. You've just informed me that you think nothing of lying to me because I'm peculiar. Do you imagine I'm an idiot?'

'Frequently,' he murmured sardonically, finishing his coffee and walking off to the bar to pay the bill.

182

Amy stared after him in annoyance. She didn't know this man really, not when you came to look at things sensibly. And, when you looked at things sensibly, he had forced his way into her life and seemed to be taking over, just as he took over the coffee-making, the kitchen and just about everything else.

She was glaring at him when he came back to the table. He was stuffing notes into his back pocket with an attitude of carelessness that shocked her.

'You'll get your pocket picked,' she assured him fiercely, hoping he would and imagining it with a good deal of pleasure.

'You think so?' he drawled, giving her an ironic look.

No, she didn't. Not unless the thief wanted to end up halfway up a tree, hanging over the branch and looking down in a pained manner. Who would dare to even approach Luc? She sniffed irritably and to her surprise he grinned down at her and came to help her to her feet.

'Come along,' he ordered in that imperious manner of his. 'We will now walk and talk.'

'I believe I would rather go straight back home,' Amy informed him stiffly, still very much annoyed and on her dignity. He merely grinned again.

'You would not,' he assured her. 'You would rather walk and talk. It is Sunday, early afternoon, the sun is shining. People walk and talk. Even in Paris they do that.'

'Even in the tatty places?' Amy enquired in a superior voice as they stepped outside into the sunshine.

'There are no tatty places in my city,' Luc assured her calmly, ignoring her irritation. 'It glitters. It is famous all over the world. It is a city for lovers.'

That shut her up. Amy blushed and looked away, her superiority fading fast. Luc glanced at her sideways, with a quick flash of amusement that she didn't notice. She was peculiar, this little pest, but it was easy enough to silence her.

His amusement vanished when he thought of someone following her. To think that it was yet another man in dark clothes stalking her was stretching the imagination too far. Then how the hell had he known where she would be today? Luc frowned and looked down at her.

'Did you tell Somerfield that you were going to the house today?' he asked sharply, and Amy's head shot up, her embarrassment vanishing at once.

'I did not!' she snapped. 'I can quite clearly see why you think I'm an idiot. You know damned well that I avoid Eric. Why, you even had to hit him in our own car park.'

'Do not swear,' Luc ordered mildly, his temper restored miraculously.

'Why not? You do. You uttered a nasty little French word when you attacked poor Mr Phillips for nothing.'

'It is not the same. Besides, I was annoyed.'

'Well, so am I,' Amy informed him angrily. 'If you think I would see Eric and tell him anything at all then you have a very low opinion of me. You have no right to judge me. Therefore, I'm annoyed

– damned annoyed,' she added for good measure. 'And I don't know why I'm here with you, listening to all this abuse.'

'I want to walk,' Luc reminded her in the same mild voice.

'Buy a dog!' Amy snapped, and turned on her heel to leave him and walk off.

He caught her hand, enclosing it in his powerful fingers, and when she looked up he was laughing down at her.

'I would rather see you angry than frightened,' he said quietly. 'Walk with me, Amy. It will be better to walk beside me than to have me throw you over my shoulder and proceed in that manner.'

She suddenly smiled, her annoyance waning when she imagined the picture he painted. He was quite likely to do it too.

'Don't try to dictate to me then,' she advised a little huffily. 'And just remember this: I could sabotage your whole office network if I wanted to.'

'I know,' he laughed. 'I have even seen you when you were considering it. What stopped you?'

'You would have been furious,' Amy pointed out. 'At that time, I was a bit scared of you. I'm not now.'

'I will have to give that some thought,' Luc mused with a quick grin. 'I cannot afford to become lax with my staff.'

He kept her hand in his and Amy suddenly realized it. A few minutes before it had been restrictive, now it was warm and she wanted to curl her fingers round his, but she wasn't sure if she dared do it.

The impulse was so strong, though, that she tentatively moved her fingers just a little bit and Luc simply adjusted his grip, his own fingers lacing with hers. The palm of his hand was warm against her own and the intimacy sent a shock of awareness right through to her toes, just as it had done when he had kissed her so quickly in the kitchen of her house. She felt as if she wasn't actually breathing.

'We must do something about this man,' Luc told her a minute later, his frown coming back. 'We have a stalker here, Amy. He must be stopped.'

'Nobody has seen him but me,' Amy reminded him quietly. 'I feel as if the police didn't believe me. They just did their duty and went.'

'I will speak to them,' Luc decided firmly.

'How can you? You haven't seen the man. It would be just like before. What will you say? All you can do is tell them that I see a man watching me. They won't believe you either.'

He was silent for a while and Amy asked worriedly, 'Do you believe me, Luc?'

'Of course I believe you.' He turned quickly to look down at her anxious face. 'I have seen you sleepless, afraid, and, in any case, you are not the sort of woman who would create a fantasy about such a thing.'

'Thank you,' Amy whispered.

'There is no necessity to thank me,' Luc told her. 'You are strange but you are exceedingly clever. Your strangeness has something to do with your unruly tongue. I have not yet fathomed it out adequately.'

Amy giggled and his hand tightened on hers.

They were a good way from the inn and Luc's car by now, and he stopped at a low wall that edged the river. Here, the water raced over quite large rocks. There was a wonderful murmur of cool sound, a brilliant glitter on the water, and Luc released her hand and leaned against the wall, looking down into the racing, splashing water.

Amy put her hands on the wall and started to climb up to sit on top of it, and Luc instantly lifted her up. His hands spanned her slender waist and she could feel their strength, their warmth. This time her breath really did stop for a second, but he let her go at once. He was thoughtful, his eyes again on the water.

'I really think you should not stay at your house alone,' he said quietly. 'The fact that the man knew where you were today and followed you shows that he is back. In fact it shows that he has never given up at all. This means he was well aware that the police were coming round regularly. He also knew when they stopped the patrolling. He is therefore either watching from hiding all the time or he is getting information from someone.'

'Who?' Amy asked, giving him a frightened look.

'If I knew that we would be able to put a stop to it smartly,' Luc grunted.

'If they would tell you,' Amy pointed out glumly.

'I would squeeze it from them somehow,' Luc assured her quietly, and Amy didn't doubt it for one moment.

'It's not really your problem,' she muttered, almost to herself. 'This is all my own problem.'

'So who will deal with it if I do not?' Luc asked arrogantly, and she shook her head. There was no one. There was only Bryan now, and her Uncle Peter. Neither of them could compare to Luc in any way. Luc was what might be called a civilized savage – if there could possibly be such a thing.

'You would like your solicitor friend to see to your welfare?' Luc suddenly asked in a stiff voice.

'Bryan's not capable. At least I don't think so. He could go to the police and maybe make them listen because he is, after all, a solicitor and he's quite impressive. But I don't think he could grab people by the neck and squeeze the truth out of them.'

'In other words he is a little more civilized than I am?' Luc enquired in the same stiff manner. And Amy answered quite guilelessly because she was still musing away at things in her head.

'Oh, yes,' she murmured almost vaguely. 'He's a lot more civilized than you. Although I was thinking a while ago that you're quite civilized, really, for who you are.'

'Thank you.' Luc glared at her, turning his head to glare more potently. 'I assume you are once again dwelling on my special training?'

She ignored that, merely because she was still thinking.

'Uncle Peter would make a very big fuss, interfere with my life and not do anything much really. He wouldn't have a lot of competence in catching criminals as far as I can see. He doesn't have that kind of expertise. What he is, *really*, is a rich playboy. He's fifty. I wonder how old you have to be before you can stop being called a playboy?'

'Let's go,' Luc ordered suddenly, giving her a wry look as she mused aloud and he detected a glimpse of the pink cloud approaching again. 'I will deal with you. You work for me. I am responsible for you.'

He lifted her down in the same manner he had lifted her up, and even though she was still musing away in her head. Amy caught her breath because of the sudden shaft of excitement that raced through her. She blushed again.

'You're not really responsible,' she pointed out shakily.

'I have decided to be responsible,' he informed her imperiously. 'If I wait for you to make your mind up, this man in black clothes will have aged a great deal and will no longer be a threat because of his advanced years. I wish to catch him while he is still living.'

'You're very sarcastic,' Amy complained, but he just nodded his head, took her hand in his and urged her along briskly.

'*D'accord*,' he agreed.

Amy couldn't sleep. There was nobody watching her now but her thoughts would not let the fright of the morning go. In her mind she could see the terrifying stillness and the uncanny silence of the watching figure under the trees in the churchyard. She tried to pinpoint him more closely, tried to magnify him and imagine his face, tried to give

189

some substance to the figure, but it was too alarming and made her more frightened still.

Luc had called in with her when they had come back from their lunchtime walk and his presence had calmed her, as it had been calming her all afternoon. He had checked everything, even things that didn't need to be checked, and then he'd asked her if she had a telephone by the bed.

'Yes, I have,' she'd told him.

'Then write down this number. It's the telephone number at my flat here in town. If you see the man, ring me at once whatever the time is. Sooner or later I am going to catch him. Let us hope it will be sooner, but be certain he is going to pay dearly for this.'

When he left he had ordered her to lock the door and not to answer it unless she could see clearly who was there. He'd looked down at her sternly as he gave the order, with Amy nodding in obedience.

'It's useless to tell you not to worry,' he'd said quietly, 'but finally we will get him and he will know then what worry is like.' Then, unexpectedly, he'd kissed the tip of her nose. She was still standing there stunned and glowing when he drove away.

Now she was wasting good sleeping time, simply mulling things over, frightening herself with the man who was not even there tonight and exciting herself with thoughts of Luc. She didn't really know how she felt about Luc. Surely it wasn't possible to feel as she had done before, scared, annoyed and defiant, and then to suddenly want to see him all the time.

It was because he was protecting her. Surely it had to be that. This terrible man who watched her had in reality brought her and Luc close, but it would all settle to normality when the man finally went.

It suddenly occurred to her as she turned restlessly in bed that before Aunt Celia had died everything had been perfectly splendid, no worries, no fear, no problems. Things had all fallen apart after her aunt's funeral. But what had really changed except for the one fact that Aunt Celia was dead?

As far as Amy could see, nothing. All the other people in her life were behaving as she would have expected. Even Eric's behaviour was normal – for him. There was the one big difference of her feelings for Luc, and, of course, Jill had left for America. Apart from that, things were just the same. Amy went to sleep still puzzled and anxious.

The man came in the middle of the night, and once again Amy had a sort of premonition that made her wake up and go to look through the window. He was there, staring up at her room, even though the room was in darkness. He was completely still, a darker shadow in the shadows made by the light above him. And even though he made no movement he was as intent as if he was gathering himself to strike.

After seeing him during the day, and having him follow her so stealthily and so cleverly, Amy was more frightened than ever at the sight of him. She had encountered him in daylight and he had followed her to her aunt's house almost uncannily. He was more real than ever, more sinister, and the thought that he was much more determined to harm her was uppermost in her mind.

She sat on the bed and tried to think straight. Luc had told her to ring him, but in all probability the man would be gone before Luc could get here. It would just be so much more a waste of time. Amy was also very much aware that nobody had seen this man except herself.

Sooner or later Luc would begin to doubt her. She knew that Peter doubted her already, otherwise he would never have made that suggestion about the making of her will triggering this off in her mind.

She tried to go back to sleep but she couldn't, and as soon as it was light Amy got up and went downstairs. By now, of course, the man had gone. He never showed his face to the bright light of day. Even outside in the churchyard and at her aunt's house he had hidden in shadows. Maybe he wasn't real? Maybe her mind had conjured him up when her aunt had died? She had no idea how real things were to people when they were imagining it. For the first time she gave that thought some credence.

When she arrived at the office, Amy was tired and dispirited. Once more she had no idea how she was going to get through the day, do her work and keep on her feet. Everything had started again, as if it had never stopped. Nothing had improved except that for now Luc believed her, and she was not scared of Luc any more.

She was more scared of the thrilling feelings that rushed through her when he was near. And that was pretty silly after all. He undoubtedly had a woman in Paris who was smoothly groomed and completely sure of herself, a woman who would have confronted the watcher in the dark and laughed in his face.

Luc saw her come in and he knew instantly that the man was back. She hadn't rung him either. He wondered how far she trusted him. Today her trust in him was going to be really put to the test and he had no idea how she would react. He reminded himself rather grimly that in fact he never had any idea how she would react.

He had been here early this morning, long before anyone else had arrived. He had been making plans after he had left her the night before and now he signalled Amy to come to his office as soon as she looked up and saw him.

'I am going to Paris for a few days,' he announced, watching her face intently to look for reaction. What he saw was disappointment. In fact, she went quite pale.

'Oh,' she murmured despondently. 'I expect they need you there a lot.'

'They do.' He stood watching her, seeing far more than she realized. She tightened her hands together, a sure sign that she was distressed, and the fact that he knew such small things about her came as quite a shock to Luc.

'I see. Well, things being what they are, I have to admit that I'll miss you.' Amy sighed and turned away, ready to leave his office and sink into the depths of gloom without him.

'I don't think so,' Luc informed her quietly. 'You will not miss me at all because I'm taking you to Paris.'

He had been waiting to see how she would take the announcement and he was not in any way disappointed. She turned back to look at him and myriad expressions flashed over her startled face. She looked shocked, scared, bewildered, and then wonderfully, astonishingly happy.

She looked so beautiful, even though she was tired, and once again he got that flashing, brilliant smile that lit up her beauty further. It was like a light coming on inside her.

'Oh, thank you,' she gasped. 'I do hope you won't get into trouble for taking me with you. People will wonder about it. Do you have a good plan?'

Luc knew right at that moment how very much he wanted her, how very much he had wanted her for a long time. It explained a lot of things. Succumbing to the inevitable, he gave her a long, slow smile.

'I'm sure I'll think of something,' he said softly.

He seemed to have thought of everything Amy realized. She was to go home, pack for a few days in Paris, and she was to prepare herself to meet his father who thought her work was excellent. His father might wish her to demonstrate her talents to other people. There would be a temporary replacement here to take her place.

'Oh,' Amy muttered, casting an anxious look at Jim, Alfie and the boys, but Luc was very forceful.

'They will survive without you for a while,' he assured her. 'And,' he added sternly, 'you will leave any necessary computer passwords for the new person who will take your place. The office must run smoothly while we're away. I do not want things grinding to a halt because you have stone-walled the system.'

'Firewalled,' Amy corrected with a quick grin.

'Exactly,' he agreed, giving her a severe glance. 'Whatever it is you do in your little empire to control all of us, you will undo it for now. Gordon Sheen will take over. You will tell him your secrets.'

'All right,' Amy agreed cheerfully. 'It's no big deal. When we come back I can change all the passwords again.'

'I feared as much,' Luc murmured with a resigned sigh. 'Now, accomplish all that and then go home. I'll pick you up at your house in about two hours, starting from this minute.'

Amy rushed off and he watched her go, his eyes thoughtful. Was she glad to be going with him for his own sake or was she simply vastly relieved to get away from the lunatic who was watching her? It was something he might never know. All the same, his father had demanded his presence and he had not been able to contemplate leaving Amy behind to face danger alone. Perhaps this trip would put off the man who waited outside her house and followed her wherever she went.

After a moment's thought he rang the local police and told them that Amy would be away for a few days. He pointed out that in view of her problems with a stalker it would perhaps be wise for them to look at her house from time to time. It would not be good, he told them, for Miss Scott to return and find her home wrecked. It would be serious, in view of the fact that her problems had been thoroughly reported previously.

They took the point, as he had expected. It satisfied him to some extent. Luc believed in tying off loose ends as far as possible. He also believed in using any force necessary. In this case, his firm was an important part of the economy of the district and he was the managing director.

Oddly enough, Amy was thinking about that too. She was dealing with her computers and carrying out Luc's orders to release their innermost secrets and at the same time she had butterflies in her stomach about the trip to Paris.

Some of the things she had said to Luc recently seemed to be highlighted in her mind. It had become easy enough to forget his position lately. She had shouted at him on several occasions. In the normal course of events she had no difficulty in answering back when under pressure, and the fact that Luc had stormed into her private life made her forget quite frequently who he was. She only remembered nowadays when she actually saw him in his glass-walled tower. He was *the boss*.

All the same, he had kissed her, held her hand, teased her – when he wasn't being chauvinistic. She wasn't entirely sure how to cope with him. She admitted that she had never been entirely sure how to cope with a man anyway, not unless it concerned computers.

His father wanted to see her and she would probably have to give a few tips to other designers.

That would be possible, providing that they understood English. She had a sudden terrible thought. Suppose his father wanted her to stay in Paris and act as some sort of adviser to these other designers? Suppose she had to stay there while Luc came back to England? Her heart sank. She didn't want to be away from Luc. The thought was utterly depressing.

He was nowhere to be seen when she had finished but she just went on obeying orders. If Luc said something he always meant it. Amy went rushing home to get ready, her mind full of unimportant things, like how would she compete with the glamour of the women in Paris, and where would she stay when she got there, and suppose she wasn't as good at her job as his father thought?

Her self-confidence was reaching a frightening low. It was probably because of another sleepless night, she told herself hopefully. Anyway, things would be all right; Luc would see to it – unless he decided to turn on her and call her an idiot in front of everybody. He was quite capable of doing that.

By the time he arrived to collect her she was in a dither, trembling with nerves and asking herself who she thought she was, to be going to Paris to tell other people how to do better. She couldn't even cope with a man who did nothing more than watch her. The last thought brought a real shiver, not some imagined lack of ability. She would be away from here. The man would never know where she was. It was possible that by the time she returned he would have given up his obsessive campaign.

At the last minute she rang Peter to let him know what was happening, and by a stroke of good fortune he was at home. He could have been at some race meeting, watching one of his horses, but he was there in the house.

'Thank goodness I caught you in,' Amy said rather breathlessly. 'I haven't more than a minute but I'd better tell you that I'm going to Paris. I thought I'd ring and let you know in case you got worried when you couldn't get in touch with me.'

'Paris!' Peter exclaimed. 'What the devil are you going there for?'

'It's for the firm,' Amy told him, trying for an important stance. 'Martell Industries want me to go for a few days to improve their computer design team.'

'My word, Amy! I really had no idea you were so good. This is a feather in your cap and no mistake. You're really important.'

'Oh, it's nothing, really,' Amy assured him quickly, thinking that boasting might bring about disaster and seeing herself sitting with a small crowd round her and making an utter fool of herself. 'I'll just be in Paris for a few days and I expect I'll be in and out of the main office there. Not much time really to enjoy the city. Look, I have to go; I'm being collected. I'll ring you when I get back.'

Amy also gave Bryan a quick ring at his office in case he thought she had died in her sleep, worrying over Eric. After all, she had no real idea of how long she would be in Paris. The last time Luc had gone he had been there for a week and Bryan was sure to get in touch with her before then, even if only to let her know how the processing of her aunt's money was getting along.

She had just put the phone down when she saw Luc's car arrive outside and she felt her heart fluttering all over again. She was so nervous that she didn't know what to say to him. All she could do was go to the door with her suitcase and stare at him anxiously.

He came up the steps to collect her things and he assessed her state of mind with one swift glance. She was in a panic. Was it because of going to Paris or was it because of being with him? He had no way of knowing.

All he did know was that in a soft green dress with a matching jacket she looked fit to eat, and lately he'd had a great desire to devour her. The irritating Miss Scott was a fluttering whirl of feminine anxieties, beautiful, silky-soft and not an annoying Computer Person at all. He would settle for that any day. He hoped she had brought her pink cloud with her. He was longing to be swept up on to it. Restraining himself from searching for it would be his greatest problem.

As they pulled away from her house Luc gave the streetlight a quick, ferocious glance. It was a pity that he couldn't be in two places at once. It would have been very interesting to stay in her house while she was away. Going outside in the night to lay his hands on the man who watched her would have been very satisfying.

He looked thoughtful. The idea had a lot going for it. But it would have to wait. For now he was taking her to Paris. He wondered what his father would make of her? She might be a trembling, vulnerable female at the moment, but he knew her well enough to realize that once in front of a computer she would display a remarkable change of character.

They were to travel on *Le Shuttle*, and it was getting late when they finally arrived at the terminal.

'Do you always come this way?' Amy asked in an awe-stricken voice.

'Usually, unless I'm flying. It's quick and I can have my own car with me. You are afraid?' he asked with a lightning glance at her.

'I think I'm excited but I'm not sure yet,' Amy murmured. 'I might be both, actually. I'm not really looking forward to showing anybody how to do things better. I'll feel pompous and – and silly.'

Luc gave a quick, dark laugh.

'You are the best. Your sudden lack of faith in yourself is astonishing. I have always been quite sure that you would be very capable of sabotaging the firm and walking out if I took you to task on anything.'

'I decided against that,' Amy reminded him. 'I told you, if you recall.'

'Yes, you did, but I have always feared that you would simply leave in any case.'

'Feared?'

'Certainly,' he assured her, not looking at her but moving forward smoothly to embark on the train. 'Your dislike of me has always been apparent.'

'I was overwhelmed,' Amy confessed quietly. 'I used to think you were icy cold, and only with me too.'

'And now I am not?' Luc enquired softly.

She shook her head and stifled a yawn.

'I feel safe with you,' she murmured sleepily.

While he was mulling that over, and trying to see where that left him in the confusion of her pink cloud, she closed her eyes, and the next time he looked at her she was asleep. He smiled to himself. At least she didn't hate him, and there were all manner of possibilities and rewards attached to the position of being her guardian angel.

He let her sleep. He knew she had been awake for most of the night even though she had not said one word about the return of the man who watched her. He wondered what his mother would make of his Computer Person? More importantly, what would his father make of her? He had initially told his father in a very irritated manner that she might be the best but she was an infuriating employee who was only allowed to continue with the English side of the firm because of her great skills.

His lips twisted with amusement when he imagined his father's first sight of her. His father would pronounce him mad to be irritated by this entrancing little creature. There was something wonderfully endearing about Amy. She was enticing, fascinating and tempting. The fact that she was so skilled at her job and then so utterly ingenuous in her daily life brought out the protective nature in a man. And his father was a Frenchman.

He sat quietly beside her when the train moved off into the tunnel and admitted ruefully that in this little enclosed capsule he wanted to turn her into his arms and kiss her until she was dizzy. Maybe in Paris he would do that. She would be dazed by his city and he was bringing her home.

He grinned wryly to himself when he thought of his mother. She would raise her elegant eyebrows and swoop down protectively on Amy at once. He intended to take her home immediately. She would not be in some hotel by herself, and his own apartment was, unfortunately, out of the question.

He suddenly realized that he hadn't told her about any arrangements for her welfare in Paris. She had come with him all the same. She trusted him, felt safe with him. That could prove to be a burden, because he wanted her. His body had never seemed to recover from the view of her behind that flimsy curtain with the light behind her. So far, however, his mind had curbed him strictly and reminded him of duty. He wondered how long his mind would have control, because he was definitely not on its side at all.

Amy thought she would never recover from the sight of Luc's home. Set outside Paris, it was what could only be described as a modern mansion. The lovely things in her aunt's house now moved into perspective, because the house where Luc had grown up seemed to be filled with treasures. It spoke of an elegant, wealthy way of life, and clearly Luc had always been used to it.

From the moment when the door was opened by a dark-clad servant who was classified in Amy's mind immediately as the butler, whether he was or not, Amy felt in a state of open-mouthed astonishment.

'You will meet my mother first of all,' Luc told her, after the man had taken her suitcase and disappeared and Luc had led her into a room off the hall, 'and then she will show you to your room. I expect you'll want to freshen up and get settled before we have the evening meal.'

Amy was, frankly, scared.

'But – but I thought . . . Surely you'll want me in some hotel?' she asked anxiously.

Luc felt a wave of heat inside and his muscles tensed as a flare of sexual anticipation flooded over him. At the moment he wanted her wherever he could get her, hotel or small wooden hut.

'Naturally my mother will wish you to stay here.' He spoke firmly, rather austerely, and Amy felt subdued.

'She may change her mind,' she murmured, looking round rather anxiously. 'I'll be an intruder.'

'You will not,' Luc corrected. 'You will be made welcome. We are extremely civilized.'

'But she doesn't know what I'm like,' Amy persisted, leaning closer to whisper her warning. 'You know how often I irritate you.'

They were standing in a room that would have taken up the entire floor space, top and bottom, of Amy's townhouse. She assumed it was the drawing room. Luc reached out and tilted her chin, looking into her eyes in a way that almost hypnotized her.

'You no longer irritate me,' he assured her quietly. 'I have learned to cope with you. I know your strange little ways. I even wink at Jim and Alfie as I pass your office. They know me very well. I believe they like me.'

'Luc?' Amy enquired in a startled voice, wondering if he was going to introduce her to his mother as a maniac from England who had to be humoured if she was to remain in a quiet state.

He smiled down at her, quite taking her breath away; and his hand smoothed her hair back in such a gentle manner that she felt shaky inside.

'Stop worrying,' he ordered softly. 'My mother will like you. My father is quite prepared to listen to any lecture you may wish to give on the subject of computers. You are safe here and a long way from the lunatic who stares at your house. You are here to relax.'

'I thought I was here to work?' Amy reminded him, and he gave one of his lazy, masculine shrugs.

'We will see if we can fit any work in – although, to be strictly truthful, I have simply spirited you away. I did not wish to come to Paris and leave you alone and vulnerable. When we go back, I intend to catch that man. He will be glad to be handed over to the police,' he finished darkly.

CHAPTER 9

'So I'm not going to do any work? Not going to give any special tips to the people who work here and . . .'

'That will depend on how my father reacts to you.' Luc's dark eyes flashed over her, noting every small worry on her face. 'He may question you very seriously about your work and ask you to help. On the other hand, he may decide that you look far too delicate to work at all. If that is the case, he will probably tell me to fire you immediately.'

'Oh!' Amy gasped, stunned by this seriously revealed agenda.

Luc burst into laughter and she realized he was merely teasing her. She glared at him and moved two steps away.

'Look! I'm anxious enough without you saying things like that. If I knew where the butler had taken my suitcase I would leave.'

'The *butler*?' Luc threw his head back and laughed louder, thoroughly enjoying himself. 'Do not mention it to him. He will become full of his own importance and my mother will have to speak sharply to him.' He grinned wickedly at her. 'He is merely the husband of the housekeeper. He does odd jobs and answers the door if he happens to be close to it when someone knocks. In the normal course of events, he does not *buttle*.'

'Please, Luc,' Amy begged as she became almost disorientated by his teasing. He softened immediately and smiled down at her.

'You have had some bad days and bad nights recently,' he reminded her quietly. 'Relax, Amy. You will be safe here and you will be very welcome. My mother is English, so what is there to worry about?'

'I think you worry me more than anyone else,' Amy muttered. 'I rarely know where I am with you.'

Luc was greatly tempted to show her exactly where she was with him, to make the situation quite clear by lifting her up and carrying her to the deep sofa at the side of the room, but before he could succumb to the temptation, his mother appeared and he greeted her with a good deal of relief.

'This is Amy,' he said in English. 'She is in a state of complete anxiety at the moment.'

'As you're in the same room with her, I'm not at all surprised,' his mother assured him, glancing from one to the other. 'How do you do, Amy?' she continued. 'I'm Ann Martell. I'm so glad you're here. It will be wonderful to speak only English and you can bring me up to date on all the news. I do miss things, even after all these years. Silly things, really, like the plays on television. Luc brings me books and videos. I have quite a collection.'

Amy relaxed. She wasn't even worried that his mother did look a little like the duchess she had imagined. She was superbly dressed and her hair was definitely grey, but not at all in the way Amy had thought. Amy decided that if the fashion did catch on after all it wouldn't be as bad as she had expected.

Ann Martell looked superb, like a mature film star. She was wearing the brooch too, and Amy's eyes fastened on it.

'Ah, the brooch.' Ann Martell smiled as she noticed Amy's interest. 'Luc told me that you were the one who chose it and had it wrapped. Does he send you out to do his shopping, Amy?'

'No. Actually I was taking time off without permission and he caught me,' Amy said frankly, and then blushed like a wild rose.

'I twisted her arm behind her back, and when she was screaming sufficiently I made her choose the brooch and the scarf,' Luc told his mother with a grin.

'He's quite dreadful,' his mother confided to Amy. 'He's exactly like his father.'

'Madame, you are undermining my authority,' Luc stated with mock severity. 'Amy is already almost too much to handle because of her skills.'

'Oh, yes,' Ann Martell murmured, completely ignoring Luc. 'You're the girl who can do anything with a computer. It astonishes me. My husband is dying to meet you.'

'But later,' Luc ordered firmly as Amy looked as if she was about to sink to the floor in terror. 'Where is she to sleep? I will escort her upstairs.'

'I'll take her,' his mother said, smiling at Amy and heading for the door. 'You get yourself settled in, Luc, and have a rest before dinner. I imagine that when your father gets home he'll want you to talk about work as usual.'

She took Amy upstairs and Amy didn't know where Luc went. She dared not look round to see if he was following because he would notice how much she wanted to cling to him for safety, and that was quite ridiculous. Aunt Celia had drilled into her all the necessary things to survive this situation smoothly after all. What she was doing here was paying a visit to some wealthy people who just happened to be Luc's parents.

She was a bit worried, though, as to how he intended to explain her. On second thoughts he had probably explained her already, because his mother had obviously been expecting her. All this confusion was because she was tired and worried about the man outside her house.

She brightened considerably when she realized that he could do exactly as he liked for a few days because she wouldn't be there. It was a pity that it wasn't winter. If it had been, he would probably have frozen into an interesting statue before they got back home. She hoped Luc would not agree to leave her here if his father asked to borrow her for a while. She didn't want to be separated from Luc. She even wished he was here now to show her to her room.

Ann Martell showed her into a lovely room facing the back of the house.

'Make yourself quite at home, Amy,' she said, patting Amy's hand and smiling at her.

Amy did. As soon as Luc's mother had left the room, Amy lay back on the bed for a minute and promptly fell asleep. There was no watching man here to frighten her and she relaxed. She was still asleep when Luc came half an hour later to find out where she was. He had thought that she might just be hiding in her room, too shy to come down and meet anyone at all.

He knocked on the door softly, but when he got no reply, he opened the door and put his head round it to look into the bedroom. He saw her at once, curled up on the bed and sleeping soundly.

'Sleeping Beauty,' he murmured, smiling at the picture she made lying there. He came in to wake her up. It was getting dangerously close to dinner time and if she was late down she would be embarrassed. He touched her arm and spoke to her.

'Time to get up, Amy,' he whispered, and this time her eyes came straight open and looked into his. She didn't grumble at him as she had done at her own house, instead she just went on looking at him with those incredible eyes.

'Have you forgotten who I am?' he asked softly, and she shook her head and smiled, still saying nothing. She looked enchanting, as usual, languid, soft, waiting to be touched. His manhood grew heavy and hot.

'Do you intend to stay here all the time and refuse to come downstairs?' he asked huskily, his gaze locked with hers.

'No. I'll make an effort,' she promised sleepily. 'I didn't intend to go to sleep.'

'You're very tired,' Luc reminded her.

'I know. It will take ages to get back to normal. They say you never really catch up on lost sleep.'

'Do they?' Luc enquired in the same husky voice.

At the moment he felt that he would never be back to normal. He drew away when she stood up, his hands flexing by his sides, his whole being aching to reach for her. Her cheeks flushed softly and he wondered if she knew how he was feeling.

'I'll hurry down,' she told him tremulously. 'I have to take a quick shower.'

Luc's mind instantly pictured that and completely lost the battle to restrain him.

'Don't tempt me,' he said thickly, and reached for her, enclosing her in his arms and searching urgently for her lips.

He could feel the immediate shock in her. It trembled through her whole body. She stiffened and his mind pointed out that this was not fair, that he had surprised her when she was only half awake. He was taking advantage of her, it said sternly. But he thrust the thought away and raised his hands to cup her face gently, softening the kiss to tender persuasion.

The effect it had on her was instantaneous. She gave a little sigh against his mouth and leaned towards him as if she was wanting more. Her response astonished him, left him nonplussed. He was certain, now that his initial demanding action had calmed him, that her first response had contained fear. But she had been living with Somerfield. She wasn't exactly a girl. Maybe Somerfield had been rough with her?

Luc softened his demands even more, threading his fingers through her hair, planting teasing kisses along the length of her lips, and he felt her fingers clench against his shoulders as she began to press closer to him.

Dieu! She was like warm honey, sweet and clinging, and her soft body was pressed against his aroused manhood. His hands became more demanding, and this time he felt no shiver of fear in her.

'Luc!' She breathed his name into his mouth and Luc's arms tightened on her, his mind on the very close proximity of the bed.

There was a soft knocking at the door and his mother's voice.

'Amy? It's almost time for dinner.'

Luc lifted his head and looked down ruefully into Amy's flushed face, his expression changing to amusement when she instantly stepped into the fray.

'I'm just about to have a quick shower,' she called, in a definitely fluttery voice. Then she fled into the bathroom without even glancing at Luc again.

His mind berated him as soon as he gave it the opportunity. It told him that he should never have kissed her like that. She was a guest in this house.

But he wasn't listening to his mind very much. He was still hearing his own needs, and he walked to the door, taking a deep breath and facing his mother when she was just about to leave and go back down the stairs.

'I went to wake her up,' he explained in a very casual voice as his mother simply stopped and looked at him with the maternal glance he had known from childhood. He had never succeeded in fooling her yet.

'She's – different, Luc,' Ann Martell said quietly. 'She needs careful treatment. She's not like the women you're used to.'

'How do you know?' he asked, with a faint smile of admiration at her astute assessment of his state of mind.

'I've met her now. She's rather delicate in a way, and very vulnerable.'

'Because she's English?' Luc enquired wryly.

'Certainly not. I'm English and there's nothing vulnerable about me. Amy is different, and I'm not at all sure if she's capable of coping with you.'

'Stop worrying,' Luc murmured, tucking her hand in his arm and proceeding to the stairs with her. 'I know all Amy's problems.'

'Then I hope she understands yours,' his mother said with the quiet sarcasm she was capable of.

'I expect you do?' Luc grinned.

'I've been married to your father for nearly forty years. I'm well acquainted with "problems". Amy needs careful handling.'

'I was just handling her extremely carefully,' Luc said with a rueful grin.

'You're abominable,' his mother told him, giving him a fond smile.

Downstairs Luc poured a drink for them both as they waited for Amy, and also one for his father, who usually arrived at the last minute with flowers for his wife.

'Are you going to tell Veronique?' Ann Martell asked quietly, her eyes on his dark face.

'Tell her what?'

'Don't fence with me, Luc. I know you too well. Are you going to tell her about Amy?'

'There's nothing to tell, Maman. Let it rest.'

'There will be something to tell,' his mother assured him in the same quiet voice. 'You're different with this girl. You will not be able to forget her as easily as you have forgotten the others.'

'*Dieu!* You make me sound like Lothario,' Luc protested, scowling at her.

'I know you.' She gave a shrug that would have done credit to his father and Luc relaxed.

'She's different, as you pointed out. I don't know how she feels. I know that she's grateful to me and relies on me. And don't ask,' he insisted when his mother looked intrigued. 'Don't be fooled by Amy either. She's a lot tougher than she looks. If she feels like it she shouts at me, even though she calls me "the boss".'

'Does she really?' Ann Martell burst into laughter and Luc glanced at her wryly.

'It's not so funny. She also allows people to think that I'm trained in martial arts. Some special army

213

unit here in France has trained me, apparently. She's a cunning little witch. She never actually announces these things but she implies it.'

His mother sat smiling, filled with amusement, and after a while Luc glanced at her and grinned.

'Don't be altogether on her side,' he warned ruefully. 'I might very well need you on my side.

'You'll survive,' his mother assured him. 'You're just like your father. Here he is now,' she added, getting to her feet. 'If he has brought me more flowers I'll not know where to put them.'

'Romantic,' Luc stated firmly.

'Probably habit,' his mother assured him drily. 'In fact, if it were not your father, I would begin to imagine that it was even suspicious.'

'You think so? Another woman?'

His mother gave him an amused look and went to meet his father, and Luc smiled too. He knew them both too well. There would never be another woman. For his parents, romance had never died. He wondered what it was like.

He glanced at his watch and wondered where Amy was. He wondered if she had slipped in the shower and actually began to get to his feet to go and see. It was ridiculous. He was always worrying about her. If romance was like that then he didn't want to know.

He wanted her, though. It was an ache inside. Maybe bringing her to Paris had been a bad idea but all the same he could not have left her behind. Deep in his mind he knew she was in real danger. There was a plan behind the watching. It was not just some idiotic man who had taken a fancy to her.

It always seemed to Luc that peril was close behind Amy every day. He had instinctively known that for some time.

When she came down almost at once and walked into the room, Luc's physical reaction to her told its own story. He wished the house was empty, wished they were alone. She looked lovely in a pale blue dress he had never seen before. For once it was not a flowing creation; it was straight-cut, with a slit at the hem for easy walking. It showed a length of slender leg and his eyes were drawn to that silken length and couldn't seem to look away. Everything inside him tightened.

He took a deep breath and met her anxious gaze.

'You look beautiful,' he told her quietly.

He couldn't smile, though, his own desires were too raw. He could only stare into her eyes and try to control his feelings by sheer willpower. Amy stared back, her cheeks faintly flushed, and Luc knew that they were both thinking about the time in her bedroom.

He prayed his mother would come back quickly, because right at this moment he could think of absolutely nothing to say to her except, I want you. I want you this minute. That would be enough to frighten his Computer Person into instant flight and his mother would probably try to kill him.

At least the thought of that made him smile, and right at that moment his mother and father walked into the room.

'Mademoiselle Scott. *Enchanté.*' Henri Martell bowed over her hand while his mother looked on with a good deal of satisfaction.

Amy gave him a startled, wide-eyed glance and then said, very carefully and slowly, '*Je regrette, m'sieur. Je ne parle pas Français*,' in very schoolgirl French.

'*C'est incroyable*,' Luc drawled mockingly. 'My strange Computer Person is bilingual.'

'Luc!' his mother protested sharply as Amy blushed. 'You're quite abominable!'

'She knows that already,' Luc murmured, his eyes gleaming and moving over Amy's smooth, flushed cheeks. 'But after all, I am the boss. She knows that too – *n'est-ce-pas, ma petite?*'

'We all speak English,' Luc's father said smoothly, his eyes flashing from one to the other and twinkling in amusement. 'We are very pleased to have you stay with us, Miss Scott. I will call you Amy, if you will permit.'

'Thank you,' Amy said quietly, her reproving glance on Luc.

Luc grinned at her and took her arm.

'Come along. We will now eat,' he stated firmly. 'The butler is probably tired of waiting for us.'

His mother and father both looked intrigued now, but Amy glared at Luc and surreptitiously punched him in the arm. She couldn't understand why everyone looked delighted at that

When Amy finally recovered from her embarrassment she began to enjoy herself. This was a tight little family unit and she had never really known one herself, because there had only ever been Aunt Celia as she grew up. This warm, teasing family group was something she had only ever speculated about. Now she was in the middle of it, and Luc's mother and father were drawing her in more closely all the time. This warmth was something she had missed for many years of her life.

'Do you have any brothers and sisters, Amy?' Ann Martell suddenly asked, and Amy shook her head.

'No, I was an only child. There was just my father, really, and he died when I was thirteen. That's why I lived with Aunt Celia.'

'Oh, I'm sorry,' Ann Martell said. 'So your aunt Celia has been both a mother and father to you?'

'Yes, and she died a little while ago so there's really nobody else now. Well, there's my uncle Peter. He was my father's stepbrother — Aunt Celia's stepbrother too. But I've always called him Uncle. There's just the two of us left.'

'I expect you're very close,' Ann said soothingly.

Luc noticed that his mother was looking a bit confused. She was worried that she had upset Amy, although Amy didn't look particularly upset. She looked bright and cheerful. Luc could see that she was enjoying herself and he was glad. He wanted to reach out and close his hand over hers, but of course he wouldn't do that, couldn't do that.

'I suppose,' Amy said in a vaguely assessing sort of voice, 'that I've always been — well — lonely, in a way. Not particularly lonely — that's a bad way of putting it. You see, I'm totally engrossed in my computers.'

She cast a little glance in Luc's direction and he raised one sardonic eyebrow. They seemed to be on good ground here. She was going to tell his parents about Jim and Alfie. He wondered if she would name them.

'I've always worked with computers,' Amy continued, 'and I suppose when I was at university they engrossed me so much that I didn't gather a lot of friends around me. So, when you come to think of it, there's just Jill Davis and she's in America now.'

'How dreadful for you,' Luc's mother said.

'She has me,' Luc pointed out in his normally sardonic voice. 'I'm usually around.'

His father carried on eating and smiled, and after a while, when there was a gap in the conversation, he said, 'The job I've got for you is going to take some time, Luc.'

Luc's head shot up.

'Is it outside Paris?'

'No. It's in our own part of the city. We've got some problems with the new tower. It's proving to be a nuisance. I want somebody on it who knows what they're doing.'

'*You* know what you're doing,' Luc said, eyeing his father suspiciously.

'I've got too much to do in the office. I can't deal with everything.

'There's Didier. He's as good as I am.'

'No, he's not,' Henri Martell murmured. He glanced at Amy. 'I am assuming that you've got a replacement in for Amy at the moment?'

'Yes.' Luc stiffened, alert. If his father was going to suggest that Amy went back without him there was going to be a very big quarrel.

'Well, then, in that case there's no reason why she shouldn't stay here, is there?'

His father had that suspiciously innocent look about him that Luc had known all his life. His mother looked very pleased too and he knew how their minds were running. They liked Amy. It was time he got married and they were helping things along.

It was a bit tricky. He wanted her with him but he wanted to be alone with her. Besides, he knew what his father was going to say next. She could come into the Paris office and assist. Luc's mind ran round all the men who were in the Paris office. Good-looking men. Frenchmen!

'We'll see,' he muttered, the tone of his voice making his mother and father glance at each other. Amy glanced at him. Certainly Luc seemed annoyed and she didn't quite know why.

He was pretty much subdued for the rest of the evening, but they were both tired. Bedtime soon came around and Amy settled into the room that Ann Martell had allotted to her. It was comfortable, even more beautiful than her own little room at home, even more beautiful than the room she had lived in at her aunt's, and it had one thing going for it that neither of the other rooms had. She was in Paris, safe in Luc's home. The man could not get to her here.

The next morning Amy came downstairs bright and cheerful. She had slept beautifully and she was looking forward to meeting Luc at breakfast. In fact, her heart was hammering with anticipation.

He was in the dining room when she walked in and he didn't say anything at all. He just looked at her intently. Ann and Henri were there, and greeted her with warm smiles. Luc helped her to her chair and still said nothing.

'Did you sleep well, Amy?' Ann asked.

'Oh, yes, very well. It was so peaceful and I didn't have to worry about – ' She suddenly stopped and Luc waited, watching her. 'Anything,' she finished with deliberate vagueness.

His mother and father didn't seem to notice the gap but Luc noticed. So she had decided not to tell them. He wasn't sure how it reflected on him. It seemed so right for him to be with her that he had expected her to lean forward in her usual conspiratorial manner and tell them everything. But she hadn't done and he wondered why.

He didn't speak to her but he couldn't take his eyes from her. This was the girl he wanted, but in many ways, apart from the fact that he had befriended her, he was as far away from her as ever. She was with him now because she was afraid, and no amount of fooling himself would alter that fact.

'Are you driving into work with me or do you want to take your own car?' his father asked suddenly.

It shook Luc out of his obsessive staring at Amy. He looked away abruptly. He was embarrassing her; her face was going pink.

'I'll take my own car,' he said. 'If I have to go anywhere I don't like to rely on anyone else driving me around.'

'Then you'll be going with Luc, I expect, Amy?'

'Me?' She looked up, startled, and then her face fell a little. 'Oh, dear, yes. Today's the day when I have to tell people what to do.'

Henri Martell burst into laughter.

'Not precisely, Amy. I thought you might like to have a look around the place, and if there are any problems we can ask for your guidance. You are our expert after all.'

'I'm sure there are other people who are just as good as I am,' Amy murmured uneasily. 'I do tend to boast about my computers. But it's only a job after all.'

'I think you make it into a little more than just a job,' Henri said smoothly. 'People in the English office who have seen your work are most impressed.'

Ann was looking from one to the other and Luc could tell that his mother was very pleased about how things were going. It reminded him of Veronique. He was going to have to see Veronique. Suddenly he only wanted to be with this strange creature, who had irritated him until quite recently, and in all fairness he had to break off contact with Veronique. Even if nothing came of his obsession with Amy, he couldn't allow Veronique to go on thinking that he was interested.

When he thought back, he had not been interested for a very long time. He wondered if it had been habit and nothing more. Veronique was just like him and he had thought it good to have someone like himself. It *wasn't* good.

Knowing Amy had changed him. Amy brought out everything in him that had been hidden for such a long time; his protectiveness, his amusement, and, he admitted ruefully, his possessiveness.

When breakfast was over, Amy disappeared upstairs. She came back down very quickly and Luc was waiting for her in the hall, wondering how long she would be and why she had gone up there in the first place. When he saw her coming down the stairs, everything inside him tightened up again and it was a very strange mixture of feelings that flooded through him.

Again here was the fierce sexual anticipation, but clouding over that was very great annoyance, a sort of bleak, wretched disturbance to his mind. She had changed her clothes. The silky enchanting image had gone. Amy had acquired sophistication and she had acquired it in about ten minutes.

Her hair was fastened back, pulled up behind her head, with strands of it curling round her ears. She was wearing earrings, but more than anything else she was wearing a suit, an expensive-looking suit with a silk finish. It was dark red. It fitted beautifully. And the skirt was well above her knees. Luc felt a possessive fury growing inside him. She was not going out wearing that!

She had teamed it with a little top and obviously they had been bought together. The top was red and white stripes, exactly the same red that was in the suit. A very expensive outfit altogether. She had told him how she had done a lot of shopping with her aunt Celia and his idea of Aunt Celia did an about-face. If Aunt Celia approved of this short skirt, this sexy little jacket, then Aunt Celia had not been the lady he had thought she was.

He went on staring at Amy furiously, and she

stopped on the bottom step and looked quite nonplussed.

'Is something wrong?' she asked, wondering what she had done this time.

'I did not expect that you would go to get changed,' Luc said, trying to keep the harshness out of his voice but failing utterly.

'But I'm going to work.'

'You are not going to work. You are going to look round the office. You are going to poke your nose into other people's business and thoroughly enjoy it. It is not necessary to go dressed as if you were going to some sort of magnificent conference.'

Amy looked hurt but, as usual, she faced him head on.

'I'm in Paris. I can't go round looking a mess.'

'You never look a mess,' Luc said tautly. 'You always look delightful, beautiful. You looked delightful and beautiful when you came down to breakfast this morning, so why did you go back and change into that?'

'It's none of your business!' Amy informed him, her annoyance flaring.

'You are merely going into an office.'

'I'm in *Paris*!' she said loudly. 'I want to look like a Parisienne.'

Luc was a completely taken aback. He couldn't understand why she wanted to look like a Parisienne. His idea of how a woman should look had changed very swiftly. A woman should look as Amy usually looked. A woman should look softly feminine, ready to be touched, ready to be kissed and possessed. He glared at her.

'It is not suitable,' he said coldly.

'What's wrong with it?' Amy asked wildly, looking down at her clothes and then back at him with complete exasperation on her face. Eric had always told her she didn't look perfect. Now Luc was doing it. She felt thoroughly miserable but extremely annoyed.

'Nothing.'

Luc turned away and walked to the front door, standing with it open, waiting for her. 'My father has already left,' he said impatiently.

Amy walked across the hall as he watched her. She still had that small, delicate look about her in actual fact. She was wearing flat-heeled shoes, carrying a matching bag. She looked extremely provocative in Luc's opinion. He closed the front door behind her and walked down the steps, opened the car door for her and glared at the length of her legs as she slid smoothly into the seat.

He didn't say anything for a few minutes as he drove along, and then he almost exploded.

'There are men in the office!' he said with near violence.

Amy looked round at him in a startled way.

'I expect there are. What of it? There are men in our office too.'

'These men.' Luc grated through clenched teeth, 'are Frenchmen!'

Amy mulled that over.

'I see,' she murmured finally. 'You think I've dressed up to provoke attention from *Frenchmen*.'

'No, I do not,' Luc snarled, casting her a furious

glance. 'I am merely pointing out that you are putting yourself at risk.'

'Do you mean they'll attack me? Are these the sort of people your father allows in his offices?'

'You know perfectly well I mean nothing of the sort. They will be all around you like flies around honey.'

'You're being insulting,' Amy told him in a cold voice, her whole body stiff and annoyed. 'I object to your remarks. And even if they were round me "like flies round honey", it has absolutely nothing to do with you. Your father asked me to go to the office today, and let me remind you that *you* asked me to come to Paris.'

Luc was silent and Amy felt terribly miserable. Luc had done everything for her and here they were, her first day in Paris, and they were quarrelling like enemies. She bit at her lower lip, wondering how to set things right.

'If you want to take me back, it's all right,' she said quietly.

Luc stared through the windscreen and his hands tightened on the wheel. He had hurt her, shouted at her – again.

'I'm sorry,' he muttered. 'I do not want to take you back. And you look delightful. Whatever you wear you look delightful.'

He knew what was wrong with him. He was jealous.

In fact it was worse, it was anticipated jealousy. Nobody had seen her yet except him.

'Forgive me, Amy?' he asked quietly. 'Sometimes I am a brute.'

'Yes, you are,' she told him, in full agreement. His lips quirked. She was not subdued for long, this Computer Person of his.

'You must just become very English,' he advised, relaxing and beginning to enjoy being with her. 'Take that aloof attitude that English people can take.'

'Does your mother take that attitude?' Amy asked, very interested.

'Of course. I think that is what attracted my father to her in the first place. Apparently she ignored him for months and months. Now he brings her flowers every day, more than she requires.'

'That's wonderful,' Amy said with a little laugh. 'How romantic. I noticed the house was filled with flowers.'

'Pretty soon it will look like a funeral parlour, according to my mother.'

Now that Luc was relaxed, Amy could relax too, and she was looking out of the windows. They were not going into the middle of Paris. Martell Industries had their offices well on the outskirts.

Luc flashed on to the ring road and began to skirt the city. He noticed with some amusement that Amy was gripping the seat, and he had to admit that when his countrymen were in a hurry to get to work, they really moved.

'It's all right,' he assured her. 'We will be out of this soon. This is a necessary evil because we would not wish to go meandering through Paris to get to where we are going.'

'I suppose not,' she said in a quiet little voice, but she was very glad when they were finally on the road to work. She had no idea where they were. She had no idea where they were going, but she did know that the traffic was not so frighteningly fast. She looked out of the car window with interest and Luc shot her an amused glance.

'You are looking for tatty places?' he asked, and Amy laughed.

'I forgot all about that. You shouldn't have reminded me – but you have to admit there are some high-rise flats.'

'A lot of people live in or around Paris. They have to live somewhere.'

'I suppose so,' Amy agreed. 'It's a pity, though. If there were just places like the Arc de Triomphe and Notre Dame, things like that, it would be lovely.'

'There would be no people. Don't you like people?'

'Some people,' Amy confessed quietly, and after a moment's thought added, 'I haven't had a great deal to do with people. There was university, of course, but by then, I suppose, my attitude had become set.'

'Set?' Luc asked with amusement at the back of his question. She was talking as if she was an old maid.

'Well, I don't suppose I had what you might call a normal childhood. My father was ill for a long time – in fact, he was dying. So really, from the age of about eight, there was always a sort of gloom over the place, and then when he died I went to Aunt Celia's. It took me long time to recover and

Aunt Celia was not a motherly sort of woman. She wasn't like your mother, you know.'

'Nobody is quite like my mother,' Luc said with a smile. He reached across and took her hand. 'You are going to make me very sorry for you,' he said.

'I didn't mean to,' Amy laughed. She was glad he had taken her hand, even if he was feeling sorry for her. A great tingle shot up her arm. It was such a thrill just being with Luc. It brightened life. It was wonderful.

'Were you lonely at your aunt Celia's house?' he asked quietly.

'If I was, I didn't notice it. She had visitors from time to time but she was very arrogant, you know, very autocratic. She liked to rule everything. She *did* rule everything. It was like being in a sort of eighteenth-century atmosphere. She never married. Her attitude to life was scornful.'

'You're very good at describing things,' Luc said. He let her hand go as they came to a tricky part of the road and she was disappointed that he still kept his hands on the wheel after that.

'Tell me some more about Aunt Celia.'

'There's not much more to tell. She was very fond of my father but she didn't get on well with Uncle Peter. In fact, finally, she never spoke to him that I can think of, and she never spoke *about* him either. She pretended he didn't exist.'

'Why?' Luc asked.

'I don't know. Uncle Peter used to say things about her, and he still does, but even so, he's wary about mentioning her. He used to visit when I was small but he didn't come very often, and then suddenly he didn't come at all. I once heard them having a terrible argument but I couldn't tell what they were quarrelling about. After that they never got in touch with each other again and Peter never came back. It's funny. They all grew up together after all.'

Luc murmured vaguely. He was thinking about the life she had led – a strange life, and yet she had come out of it relatively unscathed. He thought about the warmth of his own family. Amy had never known anything like that. He had a far-flung family and, in the manner of French families, they often gathered together, laughed, drank wine, talked endlessly.

He had an aunt who had a vineyard further south and his memories of childhood were of them all descending upon her. They would eat out under the trees by the house. There was always a very long table with an enormous white cloth. Friends of his aunt, other relatives who would come at the same time would all be talking and laughing in the sunshine.

Warmth. Amy had missed out on that. His mother had no relatives now – well, nobody that he was in touch with. Somewhere there was an English cousin who used to come over. Luc had been quite close to him at one time. He hadn't been in touch with him for ages. He must look him up when he got back to England. Suddenly things like that seemed important.

Amy had thought he hated the English, disliked being in England. That wasn't true. What he had hated was leaving Paris, but now he didn't care. It wasn't important and didn't matter. What mattered to him was the strange girl at his side.

'What about university?' he asked. 'Surely you had friends there?'

'Oh, yes.'

'What about boyfriends there?' he persisted, driving himself on, not liking it at all but wanting to know.

'Not really,' she said slowly. 'Of course there were plenty of men at university that I was friendly with, but not anyone who could be called a boyfriend.'

'You mean they never asked you out in the evenings?'

'Rarely,' Amy said, still in that vague manner.

'Why?'

'I don't know.' She turned round and glanced at him and then gave a sigh. 'I always imagined it was because they thought I was mechanical.'

Luc grinned to himself.

'Now why would they think that?'

'I only seemed to be interested in computers. Until recently that's all I *was* interested in,' she confessed, flushing and looking away quickly when his eyes turned on her intently.

Luc felt a great burst of pleasure. They had thought she was mechanical. He felt as if he had discovered a hidden princess that nobody else had found. Somebody who had been waiting for him to find her. The Sleeping Beauty. He thought of Somerfield.

'What about Somerfield?' he asked, before he could stop himself.

'What about him?' Amy stiffened up and Luc knew his worst forebodings.

'Somerfield was a boyfriend,' he pointed out.

'Yes. But more than anything else he was a mistake.'

CHAPTER 10

'Then why did you keep on going out with him?' Luc asked in a taut voice.

'Stupidity,' Amy said, as she had said so often before to herself. She had told herself that frequently, but she didn't want to talk about it to Luc. Her own foolishness with Eric had embarrassed her. It embarrassed her now. She didn't want to spoil her time with Luc by talking about Eric Somerfield.

Luc glanced at her and saw the expression on her face. He dropped the subject at once. So she had lived with Somerfield, actually lived with him. The idea cut through him unexpectedly. He felt something well up from a deep core inside. It was like grief. He had to shake himself out of it.

She was not an enchanted princess. He was not a knight. That was the last thing he was and he was by no means innocent himself. Who was, nowadays?

They were driving along a wide boulevard and he suddenly turned left and pulled in front of huge gates. There was a uniformed guard who gave Luc a little salute as he opened the gates for them. They rolled back electronically and Luc pulled into courtyard at the front of the building.

Amy felt quite trapped. Everything would be computerized. She swallowed uneasily. She hoped that Luc's father didn't really mean her to go around telling people what to do.

Luc glanced at her and mistook the look on her face. He thought he had really upset her about Somerfield. Damn! When would he learn to keep his mouth shut? When would he learn to treat her carefully and not roar at her or push her beyond where she was prepared to go?

He got out of the car and went round to help her out, and once again his eyes slid to those long, sleek legs and he had to work at making himself relax. She was not flirtatious in any way. In fact, in most ways she was shy, unless she was having a little burst of temper. But he wasn't sure how she would cope with several Frenchmen ogling her and trying to get close.

He tried to shake himself out of the feeling. He knew these men. They were nice, pleasant, many of them happily married and none of them Lotharios. But, in the way of his countrymen, show them a woman and they would react. He led Amy inside the building.

They hadn't got beyond the foyer before Luc became aware of eyes on her – male eyes. A scowl began on his face and he knew it wouldn't leave until they'd gone from the building and arrived back home. He had to get control of it, and of himself.

Luc's father came up, and from the speed with which he appeared Luc surmised that he had been hanging around waiting to capture Amy. He frowned more blackly still. It seemed to him that everybody was wanting to capture Amy. He wondered why they hadn't wanted to capture her in the office in England. Everybody treated her with a great deal of respect back there. Of course, they knew her. They knew his Computer Person. Maybe if his father had her here permanently he would change his mind, once he discovered that Amy was quite capable of locking the computers so that they all looked glumly at anyone else who tried to touch them.

'The work I need you for is on your desk in your office,' Henri said to Luc. 'I'll take Amy round.'

Luc glared at him, his dark brows drawn together angrily.

'You've got an office here?' Amy enquired in great wonder.

'Luc has an office everywhere,' his father told her in a comforting voice, only just restraining himself from patting Amy on her hand. She was such a delightful little creature. 'Luc has an office here, one in England and one in several other places,' Henri said.

'I do all the work and my father collects the profits,' Luc growled. He gave his father another grim look and walked off.

'He's annoyed,' Amy confided, leaning closer to Henri in her usual, secret little way, as if she was giving out privileged information. 'I think he's annoyed with me.'

234

'That's most unlikely,' Henri said, beaming down at her. 'Luc is very quick-tempered. He has always been quick-tempered.'

'Yes,' Amy mused in a considering voice, 'that's true.' She shrugged her shoulders in a manner that would have done credit to Luc. 'But then again, so am I.'

Henri smiled to himself. 'Come, I will show you around,' he offered. 'They talk about you here, you know, and I'm sure everyone wants to see you. They've seen some of your work.'

Over an hour later, when Luc came to look for her, he saw exactly what he had expected to see; Amy in the middle of a small crowd of men who all looked to him as if they wanted to put their arms round her. They were not doing so, of course – their manners were impeccable – but Amy was looking very bright-eyed and not at all flustered.

It seemed to him that she was talking away fifty to the dozen and he wanted to walk across, grab her and give her a good shaking. There were one or two noses he would have liked to punch too.

He walked forward. He had had more than enough of this. Before he got there, however, he saw one of the girls turn round and speak to Amy. This was a new girl to the office, at least new in that she'd been there for only about a year. She always irritated Luc, as people frequently did.

Henri came up and at least that was one thing – some of the men walked away and got on with the business they should have been doing all the time. Luc was surprised his father hadn't sent them packing before now. But his father looked like a dog with two tails. He was showing Amy off as if he had invented her.

Luc kept on striding forward, his dark face furious. When he got there, Amy was bending over, looking at the computer.

'It looks wrong,' the girl said uneasily, and his father became professional at once.

'It is wrong,' he agreed flatly, eyeing the screen with no enthusiasm.

Amy bent further. 'No building could stand if it was like that,' she pointed out in a very professional voice. 'It's the back elevation.'

Luc slowed down, a little smile coming to his face. His Computer Person was in action.

'Are you working from the plans?' she asked.

'They're here.' The girl looked very worried. She brought them forward. There was a little quaver in her voice. She's stupid, Luc thought with what amounted to great glee, looking with pride at Amy. Amy was not stupid.

'If you could let me sit down?' Amy suggested.

'Oh, of course.' The girl jumped up, looking relieved to give up this difficult project to somebody else. She watched Amy in fascination and so did Luc's father. Luc didn't need to. He knew what those flying, delicate fingers could do.

'Now, *here*,' Amy said in a very firm, teaching voice, 'this is where you made the mistake originally.' Very slowly, showing the girl each stage, she put the building together as it should have been.

Luc saw a slow smile come to his father's face. He looked up and caught Luc's eye and nodded. Amy knew what she was doing.

'She is good,' he murmured in a low voice as Luc came up to him.

'She is the best,' Luc stated emphatically.

'We could do with her here.'

'Believe me, you could not!' Luc rasped, glaring at his father ferociously.

After a few minutes, Amy stood up, and the girl was beaming at her.

'I'm taking you to lunch,' Luc stated firmly, before anyone could speak, and his father looked surprised but said nothing. It seemed to Luc that when Amy was there it was very easy to please his father. He decided to make the best use of it.

'Well done,' he murmured to Amy as they walked away. 'That girl is stupid.'

Amy stopped and stared at him.

'She is not stupid. She's frightened.'

'You are never frightened,' Luc pointed out in a satisfied voice.

'How do you know?' Amy demanded.

'I can tell. When you are in front of your computers you are efficient, you are bossy, you are . . .'

'A nuisance?' Amy queried frostily.

'Sometimes.' Luc grinned at her. 'I suppose it's just that that particular girl gets on my nerves. She irritates me.'

'And I'm sure she knows that,' Amy said reprovingly. 'She's young.'

'So are you.'

'I'm not as young as that.'

'She's university-trained. She should know what she's doing.'

'Oh, Luc!' Amy said crossly. 'Don't take that chauvinistic attitude. It's not acceptable. You get more out of people if you coax them along.'

'I never have to coax you along,' Luc muttered, still looking around him suspiciously.

'Well, I'm different,' Amy told him smoothly. 'She's very shy. She cares about people. I really don't care about anything but my computers. So you see, I'm immune to certain things.'

Luc glared down at her and then smiled. She was not exactly speaking the truth. He remembered how she had reacted when he had kissed her. He would have to see to it that he changed her attitude. He took her arm and headed to the door.

Immediately heads turned, all of them male. That certain look was on their faces as they watched Amy leave and Luc stared coldly at all of them as he clamped Amy closer to his side. He hoped his father had no thoughts of keeping Amy here and sending him back alone to England. This was *his* Computer Person. In the past, duels had been fought over less.

For the rest of the week Amy thoroughly enjoyed herself, and Luc relaxed. She was being very subtly integrated into his family by his mother and father. Luc approved – besides, he was with her every day.

It was true that he didn't have time to be beside her when she was going round the office, but she was getting into her stride, helping people, and a lot of the rather irritating attention that the men had been giving her was now over. They recognized her for what she was – an expert.

Luc was satisfied. At night she just fitted in with his family cosily. On two or three occasions they went out, but Luc thought it would be a good idea for the four of them to go together. His desire to be alone with Amy was too strong to be denied and there was safety in numbers.

Amy loved everything. She loved going to work each day with Luc. She loved the drive home with him and she was really relaxed with his mother and father. She was part of a family, a new and wonderful feeling.

On the Saturday Luc decided that she deserved a treat. At lunchtime he told his father that he was leaving for the day, going back to the city and taking Amy with him.

'I don't know how long we're going to be here but Amy has not actually seen Paris yet. This is her chance.'

His father nodded and merely smiled. As far as he was concerned things were going exactly as he wanted them to go. He just wished that Amy was working for him instead of Luc, but he knew better than to raise the matter. He had seen how his son looked at Amy. He also saw how comfortable she was in Luc's presence. It was the biggest feeling of satisfaction he had had for a very long time.

Luc and Amy had lunch at the place where they usually ate and then they drove back into the city. This time, Amy was so excited that it brought a smile to Luc's lips. She was as pleased as a child and he was delighted at the sheer pleasure she was getting out of this.

He was glad to be able to show her his city. Of course there was no way he could show her all of it, but sooner or later she would know it as well as he did. He was certain of that. He was determined about it. He could not now imagine the time when he would be willing to put Amy out of his life.

His conscience pricked a little when he realized that he had not yet spoken to Veronique. He would have to get around to it, but for now all he could think about was that he was in Paris and Amy was with him. He knew he had thought of this for a long time but had never actually admitted it to himself. Amy brought a certain magic into his days. She would have done that even if he had not wanted her physically – and he did want her physically. It was a daily torture, a very sweet torture.

They were walking along when somebody he knew stopped to speak to him. Amy could not follow the swift French and she whispered to Luc that she was going to go across the road to look in a particularly interesting boutique. They were in a pedestrian area with no traffic for her to worry about so Luc just nodded and watched her walk across the road. He was back to his conversation almost at once and even for a moment forgot Amy. She was with him and he was content.

Meanwhile, Amy was looking at the lovely clothes in the shop window. She was pleased when she realized that now she could buy things if she wanted to without any problem at all. She wondered how Bryan was getting on with her aunt's will and she felt a bit guilty when she remembered that she had not even sent a postcard to either Bryan or her uncle Peter.

Jill had written to her many times, and so far all *she* had done was send one postcard. It would really surprise Jill to get a card from Paris. She would have to get around to doing that, although she didn't know how long she would be staying. At the moment she could have stayed for ever. She was so happy being with Luc.

She turned her head and looked back at him, smiling to herself. He was talking in that swift way he had, his hands moving to emphasize a point as he spoke. To Amy he was so much more handsome than any of the men in the office here. He was tall and dark, perfect as far as she could see.

There was a small arcade near the boutique, and as Luc was still occupied she decided to wander down the arcade. Everything was so glamorous, so glittering, the displays in the shop windows so beautifully arranged, with that certain touch to them that was French. There was probably an extra touch that was Parisian.

It was when she was coming out of the arcade that she suddenly stiffened. It was a feeling she had not had for more than a week. Someone was following her. She shrugged it off impatiently. Of course no one was following her. She was nowhere near her home town. She was in another country, another city. She was with Luc in Paris.

All the same, Amy quickened her steps, and as she came back to the corner she could see Luc across the road. He was still facing the man he had met and they were both laughing. Her heart gave a little skip of excitement and gladness when she saw him. He was beginning to mean far too much to her. It was foolish, but at the moment she was luxuriating in it, loving every minute of her time with him.

She gave one more admiring glance at the window of the boutique, and as she turned to look she also glanced back down the small arcade. It was only a casual glance, sheer chance, because she had been thinking only of Luc. Her eyes had merely strayed in that direction.

He was there – the man! Everything inside her came to frightened attention. She couldn't believe it. She stood perfectly still but once again he was too far away. There was bright sunlight in Amy's face and the watcher was positioned strategically in the shadows at the end of the narrow arcade. Even so she had no doubts. She knew the outline, the shape, the height, the bulkiness. He had followed her here to Paris. He would never stop following her.

As he disappeared from sight, Amy spun round and raced across the road. Had it not been a pedestrian precinct, if there had been traffic coming, she would have run straight out under some car. Luckily there was nothing. The danger was not in the road – it was right behind her.

Just moving away from his acquaintance, who was walking off, Luc turned to look for her and saw her flying across the road towards him. Her face was pale. She had her eyes fixed on him, staring wildly.

'*Dieu!*'

He sprang into life, every protective instinct alert. She had seen something to alarm her. Something or somebody had upset her badly. He took a pace forward but he never managed to approach Amy. She rushed at him, flung herself against his chest as she had done at her aunt's house, tightening her arms round his neck, pushing her face against him as his arms came tightly round her.

'What is it, *ma petite*?' he asked quickly. 'What happened to you?'

'Luc, I've seen him. He's here!'

To his horror she began to cry, not loud, sobbing cries but small, unhappy tears that streamed down her face.

'Luc, I can't get away from him. He's going to be watching me for the rest of my life.'

Luc felt the shock hit him too, and he tightened her against him for a second before he pulled her arms from around his neck and held them at her sides. He kept a close hold on her and looked deeply into her eyes.

'Amy, it's impossible,' he told her quietly. 'We are in Paris, miles away from him.'

'I know,' she whispered, 'but, Luc, he was there. I swear it.'

'He cannot have been here. You imagined it, *ma petite*, because of all the fear you have had at home.'

'I didn't imagine it, Luc,' she sighed wearily, with tears still streaming down her face. 'He was there.'

She seemed so forlorn, as if she stood all by herself to face the world, and Luc experienced the same rush of feeling he had first known when she had originally told him about the man. He would do anything to protect her. He looked across the road and then took her hand firmly in his.

'Come. Show me,' he ordered quietly.

They went back across to the boutique and Amy pointed to the place where she had last seen the man.

'He was there. He really was, Luc. He dived out of the way as soon as he knew I'd seen him.'

Luc's eyes narrowed. She was so certain, so frightened.

'You will stay here, at this corner, and you will watch,' he ordered, looking down at her. 'Nobody can hurt you, Amy. There are too many people around. Wait right here for me. I am going to search. I know this area very well.'

Luc went quickly down the arcade and Amy's eyes followed him until he disappeared in the same direction as the man who had been following her. Deep inside she knew he would find nothing. Nobody ever saw the watcher except her.

People glanced at her curiously as they passed and she wiped the tears from her face with the back of her hand, but really she didn't care. Everything, every fear was back again.

She seemed to wait for a long time, but eventually Luc came. He looked puzzled and angry. He looked hot.

'Well?' Amy asked urgently, and he stared down at her with a frown.

'There's not a sight of anyone at all who could possibly be the man you have been describing to me. Nobody who could even remotely resemble him. I know every turn, every nook and cranny in this area. How could he have simply disappeared?'

Amy looked away from him, her face frozen in numb acceptance. Luc didn't believe her. He had never doubted her since this had begun but now she had put her own credibility with him to a great test, the final test. She could understand why he thought she was imagining all this. The idea had come often enough into her own mind lately.

'All right, Luc,' she sighed.

She turned away, looking defeated, and when Luc glanced down at her face he could see fresh tears welling up in her eyes. He had to get her out of here, off the street. She needed privacy. She needed to sit down with a drink. His eyes scanned the buildings and rested on a café, but he knew it would not do. If Amy wanted to cry with this shock then she would not need people looking at her curiously.

'Let's go,' he murmured, taking her arm and starting off towards the main road.

'Are we going back to the office?'

She only asked vaguely, and he could tell that she was too desolate to care where they went.

'I have my apartment in this area. We will go there until you recover.'

To take her to his apartment would have been dangerous earlier, but now his desire was tempered with other things and the greatest thing was his anxiety for her. He could tell by the way she simply came along with him that she had no real idea of where they were going and didn't care in any case.

She looked worn out, beaten, all her bright personality crushed.

They turned into a wide avenue lined with chestnut trees but Luc suspected that Amy saw nothing other than the fear in her own mind. He held her hand but her fingers were limp in his own, and finally he put his arm round her and hugged her close as they walked.

Amy seemed to be without feeling. There was no thrill that Luc had his arm tightly round her, no singing pleasure that she was so close to him. She only faintly remembered what he had told her and she couldn't even remember where they were going.

They turned into a large, old building. Once through the main doors a great curved staircase faced them and to the side a gleaming lift that looked like a cage, something from the Paris of long ago. Luc led her into it and closed the doors, but even as they went slowly upwards Amy stood like stone, seeing nothing.

When he finally unlocked a door on a small top corridor and ushered her inside a spacious entrance hall she simply gazed around blankly.

'Where are we?'

'My apartment. It was close and you're shocked. I'll get you a brandy.'

He took her into a large, bright room that overlooked the quiet avenue and all she could think of saying was, 'We've abandoned your car.' She spoke in the same dull voice, and Luc glanced at her worriedly.

'I'll get it soon,' he assured her as he went to find her a drink.

She didn't sit down, she walked about, her eyes dazed-looking, and he had to remind her several times to sip the brandy. She finally put it down almost untasted and went to stare out of the window.

'He's sure to have followed us, you know,' she told him in a dull voice. 'We made no attempt to shake him off. He'll be there soon, under those lovely trees, looking up here and waiting.'

Luc strode over to her and stood close, searching carefully for something to say that would neither alarm her nor subdue her further.

'You're safe with me,' he finally said tautly. 'Nobody can hurt you.'

His arms came round her waist as he pulled her back against him, and although she came softly and sweetly he could tell she did it almost automatically. Her mind was out there, anxiously considering the road, the area, even the whole city.

'He couldn't have been there, Amy,' Luc murmured, his face against her hair. 'We're miles away from England.'

'It's all right. He frightened me, but then again, it's not unusual. He's frightened me before. But that's not why I'm so devastated.'

'Then why, *ma petite*?' Luc asked, raising his head and looking puzzled.

Her shoulders fell in the same defeated way.

'I think it's because I've lost you,' she confessed in little more than a whisper.

Luc turned her slowly to face him, keeping his arms in a loose circle around her waist.

247

'You have not lost me, Amy,' he assured her urgently. 'I am here, as you see.'

She gave him a wan little smile. 'I'm not a child, Luc. Physically you're here, but mentally you've stepped away. You're taking care of me just like a guardian angel but you don't believe me any more. Nobody has ever seen this man but me and they don't believe me. The police didn't, Uncle Peter didn't, but you did. Now I've pushed you too far, expected you to believe that this lunatic has followed me to Paris. You're logical and it doesn't make sense. I can see that. But he *was* there, Luc. He was right there, watching me.'

It seemed to Luc that she was delicately stepping away, looking at him sadly and leaving him even though his arms were round her.

'I believe you!' he told her compellingly, but she gave him that same little smile and shook her head.

'It doesn't matter.'

'It does! It matters to me!' In his frustration he tightened her against him and she slowly wound her arms around his neck, looking up into his dark face, but he knew her mind was not with him. He threaded his fingers through her hair and tilted her face closer to his.

'If you leave me, if you slip away from me, I will make you come back,' he threatened fiercely. 'You belong to me and so does this *imbécile* who follows you. I will kill him!'

Amy smiled at his ferocity, but she was away from him in her head and he knew it. He was relegated to another place, a distant place. He looked into her blue eyes and saw that he had become just another sadness.

'Come back to me!' he ordered forcefully, and brought his mouth down roughly on hers, pulling her closer, his fingers tightening in her shining hair.

He felt her startled response to his almost savage demand and he thought for one second that he had merely frightened her more. But her arms tightened around his neck, and as he softened at her instant reaction her body moved closer, warming against him, her delicate fingers stroking against his neck and face, and Luc gave a low groan of pleasure as he held her more gently and deepened the kiss.

His finger probed lightly against her lips and Amy opened her mouth to the urgent invasion of his tongue, her warm sigh drifting into him, fuelling his desire. He could feel the soft pressure of her breasts against the hardness of his chest and his hands began to move over her, searching her spine and the rounded contours of her hips, sensuously drawing her into his desire.

Amy seemed to burst into flames. She moaned against his mouth and pressed closer into the hard cradle of his hips, the fervency of her actions bringing Luc more speedily to his senses than anything else could have done. He knew he should not be making love to her, however much he wanted to. She had been shocked, frightened, and for all he knew she was responding so ardently because she wanted comfort. Besides, she was at his mercy at the moment.

'We must stop, *chérie*,' he whispered, lifting his head and burying his face in her shining hair. 'You are in danger.'

'I'm safe,' she moaned. 'You're here.'

Luc gave a wry laugh and tightened his arms.

'At the moment, I *am* the danger,' he warned her in a shaken voice. He lifted her head, cupping her flushed face in his hands and looking deeply into her eyes. 'I want you. You surely know that. But I brought you here to make you feel safe, to give you time to recover from your fright. I thought I could cope with being alone here with you, but obviously I cannot. We will go home now, back to my mother's house. My mother does not stand for any nonsense.'

'Is that what it was?' Amy asked tremulously. 'Was it nonsense?'

'It was heaven,' Luc murmured, dropping a lingering kiss on her lips. 'I floated with you on your small pink cloud and you did not take it away from me this time. Unfortunately, I had to leap off it myself.'

He put her from him and smoothed her hair.

'I can bring the car or you can come with me to get it.'

'I'll come with you,' Amy decided with a quick, anxious look at the window.

'He is not there, *ma petite*,' Luc assured her quietly. 'And even if he is there, hiding up a tree, we are leaving. By the time he succeeds in finding us again we will be in England, and this time, I will have him.'

'Do you believe me, Luc?' Amy asked with an almost piteous look at him.

He stared into her eyes, holding her gaze, willing her to trust him.

'I believe you, Amy,' he assured her deeply. 'For a moment earlier I could not, but I know you well. Somehow he has followed. We have been in Paris long enough for him to have managed it. I am beginning to get the hang of this whole affair.'

'Oh, Luc!' She smiled radiantly, her whole face lighting up. 'I was thinking that perhaps I've gone mad.'

'You have not,' Luc assured her wryly. 'That distinction is mine. Now let's get out of here before my insanity surfaces again. You will be safe with my mother.'

'I'm safe with you,' Amy said rather dreamily, and he slanted her a quick glance with dark, glittering eyes.

'Not unless I'm unconscious,' he murmured drily, moving her to the door with a certain amount of speed. 'Come, I have plans. Tomorrow we will put them into action. I mean to catch myself a scoundrel.'

'I hope you use your special skills on him,' Amy muttered angrily, standing waiting as he locked the door of his apartment.

Luc's lips quirked in amusement. 'Every one of them,' he promised. 'I shall resume my training the moment we arrive in England.'

Luc did not drive immediately back home. As far as he was concerned Amy had had quite enough stress for one day and taking her on the ring road around Paris had frightened her before. Instead he went through the city, and although the traffic was bad it was nothing to compare with the alarming speed of the traffic on the ring road.

She didn't question the different route. He took her past the Arc de Triomphe, Notre Dame, but when he glanced at her she was not gazing at them with the wide-eyed excitement that she normally showed, she was sitting in a sort of daze, thinking . . .

Luc knew this had been a great shock to her, whatever she had seen. He had to admit that deep inside he was not entirely convinced that she had seen the man when she was shopping. It seemed to him almost impossible and, while he was still open-minded about the entire affair, he was beginning to wonder if Amy was perhaps not in a state of depression about the whole thing. So depressed that this afternoon she had been seeing things. It was true that nobody but Amy had ever seen the watcher.

He shook himself out of doubts. She was not the sort of person who would become hysterical and get herself into such a state because she had imagined things. She had certainly seen something. He wasn't sure if she would be willing to tell his mother and father when they reached home, and he wasn't sure if he had the right to tell them, although he would have dearly loved to talk it over with someone else.

When they got back, Ann Martell saw immediately that there was something wrong with Amy and in her usual manner she glanced at Luc – a look of disapproval and suspicion. He frowned at her and shook his head as he led

Amy into one of the more comfortable sitting rooms. He ordered tea for her and then excused himself for a moment to slip out and speak to his mother,

'Luc, what is it? What has been happening? Your father told me you'd left work early to take Amy around Paris. What happened?'

'I don't know if Amy will want to tell you,' Luc muttered. 'And I'm not sure if I have the right to tell you myself.'

'At least tell me it's nothing to do with you.'

'Of course it's nothing to do with me!' he snarled, and then shook his head in exasperation. 'I'm sorry, Maman. We have had somewhat of a trial this afternoon and we ended up at my flat. I had to take Amy there to recover.'

'You didn't . . .?'

'No, I did not,' Luc snapped, glaring at her.

Ann relaxed, but she was still looking very worried and Luc sincerely hoped that Amy would be prepared to tell his mother and father about the man who was following her, otherwise he would never hear the end of this.

At dinner Amy was still very silent. She made an effort but obviously she was not capable of pulling herself completely out of this just yet.

It was evident to Luc that his mother had said something to his father because Henri Martell did not push the matter at all. He kept up a flow of conversation about nothing in particular just to bring some sort of relaxation around the table. Amy hardly spoke at all, and finally Luc reached across and covered her hand with his.

'It is entirely up to you, of course,' he murmured, 'But surely as many people who know about this the better?'

Amy seemed to bring herself back from a long way off; she looked round with almost dazed eyes, 'I suppose so,' she agreed quietly.

'Luc has told us nothing, Amy,' Ann assured her. 'But if you wish to tell us about whatever it is that's troubling you, you know that we will be very happy to help.'

Amy gave a wan little smile, 'I'm not sure that anyone can help. I'm not sure it isn't all in my head.'

'Of course it is not!' Luc snapped, even though he had some doubts about this afternoon himself. 'We both know that someone is following you.'

Ann and Henri Martell immediately came to attention.

'Following you?' Henri asked furiously. 'Who is following you?'

Amy gave a long sigh and made her mind up. She had to tell them. If she was mad, then at least they had the right to know that too. They had been very good to her, and in this short time she'd grown fond of Luc's mother and father.

'I'd better tell you from the beginning,' she said. 'A few weeks after my aunt died, a man came and stood outside the house – my house. He spent the night there, just staring up at the window. It was quite frightening.'

'Was it someone you knew?' Ann asked quickly.

'At first I thought it was someone I used to go out with. I thought it was Eric because it's just the

254

sort of stupid, frightening thing he would do. But then I wasn't too sure. He was the same shape, in a way, but it was impossible to see the man's face. I assumed that it would be just one night of worry because I know Eric; he couldn't keep anything up for long. But when the man kept coming, for over a week, I got into quite a state, I'm afraid – '

'She told me,' Luc interrupted.

'He made me tell him,' Amy corrected with a quick glance at Luc, which, to his relief, contained some of her old amusement.

'And then what happened?' Henri asked carefully.

'Luc came around to the house and then he called the police. They patrolled the area every couple of hours during the night for a week but they didn't see anything. Finally they had to withdraw the patrol. There were other jobs for them to do. During that time Luc was in Paris.'

'Oh, yes, then Lyons and Germany,' Henri murmured, remembering the time because of Luc's bad temper throughout his visit.

'When I came back the police patrol had been removed,' Luc continued. 'Amy was of the opinion that it had probably scared the man off. I thought so too. What I did not know then,' he added, casting a reproving glance at Amy, 'was that she was, in fact, being followed in the town too, right back to the office.'

'And in the daylight! Did you see him?' Ann asked eagerly.

'No. I just knew there was someone following me. I began to think I was imagining everything.

Even now I am not sure that I haven't been imagining it!'

'It is not imagination,' Luc pronounced, glancing at her sternly. 'We know that.'

'But we don't! It's wonderful that you believe me but you've never seen the man, Luc. Nobody has ever seen the man and you know what Peter thinks – '

'This is your Uncle Peter?' Henri interrupted.

'Yes, my Uncle Peter. He thinks it's because my aunt died and I was upset and then Bryan Hetherington, my solicitor, immediately told me I had to make a will of my own because I'm going to be quite well off. Peter was of the opinion that it had depressed me. He thinks I'm beginning to imagine things.'

Everyone was silent and Amy wished she had never mentioned that particular point.

'Anyway,' she continued quickly, 'Luc thought he'd caught the man one evening but it wasn't him. It was somebody from up the road.' Amy bit her lip nervously. 'And then I went to put some flowers on my aunt's grave and the man was there, watching me from the end of the churchyard, under the trees. I managed to get to my car and went to my aunt's house but I didn't lead him there. I went by another route. I went into the house and locked the door and later on, when I looked out of the window, he was there again.' Her voice was beginning to rise a little hysterically as she relived the time and Luc patted her hand.

'It's all right. It is all right, *ma petite*,' he assured her.

CHAPTER 11

'Well, afterwards,' Amy continued, 'Luc came, and straight away we searched the garden. It was only a few minutes after I'd seen the man and we looked all over but there was nobody. The next day we came here, and I've been so happy. Then, today, he was watching me again – right in Paris, miles away from England, and I know when I think about it seriously that it's absolutely impossible. He couldn't possibly follow me here and how would he find out where I was? It must be imagination.'

Luc was silent. That was exactly what he had thought himself, but the more he looked at Amy's strained face, and the more he heard the terror in her voice, the more he doubted his instant judgement when she had told him about the man in Paris.

Henri leaned forward in a very businesslike way, folded his arms on the table and looked from one to the other.

'Obviously this must stop at once. So what are we going to do about it?' he enquired, and Luc smiled to himself. This was his father – no words, take action. His mother was also looking quite grim; she didn't like to see Amy in this state. They were doing what his family always did, closing ranks.

Amy was silent, but she could feel the atmosphere and it felt good. She was not alone. Everything about their expressions told her that.

'Let us take it for a proven fact that the man has followed you to Paris,' Henri Martell said. 'We must ask ourselves how he has managed it.' He looked seriously at Amy. 'How many people knew that you were coming here with Luc?'

'My odious secretary,' Luc cut in before Amy could speak. 'Also, Gordon Sheen.' Luc's father shook his head.

'Too unlikely to consider. People do things for a reason. What possible reason could there be for either of them to pursue Amy?'

'None,' Luc agreed quietly.

'Did you tell anyone, Amy?' Henri asked.

'I told my solicitor, because he'll be wanting to get in touch with me and I didn't know how long I would be away.'

Luc held back a quick frown. Much as he disliked the idea of another man, the solicitor was unlikely to have any reason to persecute Amy. He looked more likely to be an inadequate rival for her affections.

'Of course,' Amy added, 'I had to let Uncle Peter know, because he's worried about me and if he couldn't get in touch with me he would panic.'

Luc's father looked thoughtful and Ann Martell said quietly, 'Paris is a huge city. It would be impossible to track someone down here, especially in such a short time.'

'Naturally the people at the office knew that both of us would be in and out of the Martell offices here,' Luc pointed out. 'It would be reasonably easy for someone to ring up and ask for me and be told that I was at the Paris office.'

'And Amy?' his mother enquired.

Luc shrugged. 'We left together, left from Amy's house. I picked her up from there and we drove off in my car. If the house is being watched then to conclude that we were both bound for the same destination would be a reasonable assumption.'

'I told Uncle Peter where I was going,' Amy pointed out. 'Anybody looking for me could have asked him. He's not always sensible.'

'As he knows about your problem, any enquiries would have possibly alerted him,' Luc said quickly. 'I doubt if anyone would have asked your uncle.'

His father gave him an odd glance but let that go, and Ann Martell drummed her polished nails on the edge of the table.

'As far as I can see, we are no further forward,' she pronounced. 'All this is far too mysterious for my liking. What does anyone have to gain by persecuting Amy?'

'Perhaps they're only doing it for wicked pleasure,' Amy mused gloomily. 'Or perhaps it's someone slightly mad who has just decided to pick on me. Or perhaps I'm simply letting my imagination run away with me.'

'Nonsense!' Luc's father stated emphatically, before Luc could open his mouth. 'You are very clever. If you say that this man is watching you then be assured that he is. Our problem is not to question your sanity. Our problem is to trap him. Luc and I will think of a way. You can be sure of that.'

Amy smiled. She felt surrounded by warmth. Luc and his father disappeared to talk things over in private and Ann suggested that Amy went to bed. She sat with Amy for a while in the sitting room while they drank coffee, and Luc and his father went into Henri's study.

'You should get some rest, Amy. You've had a great shock today,' Ann said. 'You're quite safe here. Nobody could possibly get into the house, and even if anyone knew where you were, which is unlikely, they can come and stand in the garden for as long as they like. I hope it pours with rain and drowns them. Don't worry. Luc and Henri will come up with a plan. They work smoothly together and they are both very quick.'

Later, when Amy went to bed, she passed the study where Luc and his father were speaking. She couldn't follow the rapid flow of French. Even if she had been able to speak the language she could not have kept up with two Frenchmen in earnest discussion.

She did hear her own name mentioned several times, however, and the depressing thought came sneaking into her head that perhaps Luc was telling his father that she was imagining the whole thing. By now she wasn't sure herself. She just didn't know what to do. For now, the warmth of this family was around her, but it would all end soon and then she would be alone once more.

A long time later, Amy was still pacing about her room. She had undressed and was wearing her dressing gown but she was still too agitated to sleep and she had to admit that one of the things that was agitating her most was her own doubt about herself.

She went through everything minutely, from ever since this had started, and asked herself, could it be imagination? Could it be some sort of an illusion created by a mind that was distressed?

She thought back to her aunt's funeral and the things that had happened quite recently afterwards. Jill had gone to America. Eric had appeared so precipitately in the restaurant and caused that scene. She asked herself just how distressed had she been by everything, and the answer was not too much, and then only at the time.

Distress had never stopped her arguing with Luc. It had not stopped her defiantly deciding to take a half-day off and it had not stopped her being almost insolent to him when they were working.

She thought of the other things that had distressed her during her life before – her father's death for one thing. That had been a deep, deep hurt that had never quite gone, but she hadn't imagined anyone following her then; she hadn't imagined anything at all.

She couldn't believe her aunt's death and the things that had happened afterwards could have brought her to the stage where she could see someone and actually believe that they were there if they were not.

The more Amy thought about it, the more she was sure. She hadn't imagined anything and she was back to the conclusion she had come to in the first place; somebody was following her, watching her, going everywhere she went, even to the extent of following her to Paris.

How they had followed her, how they had found her in such a huge city, she had no idea, but she was convinced that the man had been there. She was also convinced that he was probably in the grounds of the house right now, staring up, trying to find the window where she would be.

She walked over and pulled the curtains back, looking out into the night with a feeling of anger that this man should be disturbing her life. There was no chance of seeing anything; it was pitch-black. She could see the outline of the huge trees against the night sky and for a moment she let her imagination run free. He would be out there, standing under one of those trees, standing as he always did, absolutely still, a silent watcher in the dark.

Amy let the curtains fall into place with a shudder. This was no good. She was frightening herself even more. She continued pacing, thinking, and after a while there was a slight knock on her door,

'Come in,' she called.

She thought it would be Ann, come to see if she was all right, but in fact it was Luc. He popped his head around the door, and when he saw she was in her dressing gown he came into the room and closed the door behind him.

'I heard you talking about me,' Amy told him straight out, and he could tell by the look on her face just exactly what she thought.

'My father and I were trying to come up with some sort of a plan,' he said.

'How best to make sure that I don't go quite utterly mad?' Amy asked in a very brittle voice.

He walked across the room and took her by the shoulders.

'You are not even slightly mad,' he assured her firmly. 'You are bright, clever, highly intelligent. Somebody *is* following you. The plan was how to trap him.'

'I'm sorry.' Amy sighed. 'It's just that I've been walking about here doubting myself.'

'Do not doubt yourself,' Luc ordered. 'There is nothing to be gained by that. If doubting yourself would make you any less afraid, then I would say, doubt yourself a little, but it would simply give you two fears. There would be the fear that the man is possibly following you and the fear that you are going mad. I cannot see much point in giving yourself two fears when one is more than sufficient.'

Amy smiled. Luc certainly had a way of bringing

her back into the present with a rush. She sat down on one of the chairs in the bedroom,

'So what did you decide?' she asked.

'I think we have come up with a plan to catch him. I thought of it myself this afternoon, and my father agrees. He has tweaked it a little, to refine it.'

He grinned at her and Amy smiled widely. She could just imagine Henri Martell refining somebody's plans.

'Tomorrow we go back to England,' Luc told her. 'We will put the plan into action immediately. I see no reason why this *rustre* should be allowed to linger about any further than necessary. We will catch him.'

Amy remembered what '*rustre*' was – another French word she'd learned.

'Lout,' she translated quietly.

'Precisely,' Luc agreed. 'We will catch this lout. This is two louts, you know, if you count Somerfield as the first one.'

'How lucky I am,' Amy murmured drily.

Luc stopped pacing and came across to her, taking her hands and pulling her to her feet.

'We have a long drive ahead of us tomorrow and at the end of it we have work to do. Go to sleep now, Amy. Everything will be all right.'

Amy gave him a doubtful little smile and he leaned down and kissed her forehead. Immediately her hands tightened on his sleeves and he felt the swift rush of desire. He cupped her face in his hands and kissed her urgently, and then just as swiftly he drew back, shaking his head.

'No, *chérie*,' he said ruefully. 'My insanity of this afternoon was quite enough for one day. Until this is over we will concentrate all our efforts on the man who is watching you.'

'And after that?' Amy asked breathlessly.

He looked deeply into her eyes.

'After that, we will see,' he told her sensuously.

Amy gave a little smile, merely a quirk of the lips, but he saw it.

'Do not imagine you have me wrapped around your little finger,' he advised with a frown, but the look in his eyes told her that in a way she *did* have him wrapped around her little finger. But if he was trapped, she was equally trapped, and the thought of that wiped out a lot of the depression she had been feeling before he came up to speak to her.

'Bed!' Luc ordered firmly as he went to the door. 'No more pacing about. You can sleep in absolute certainty that you are safe. No one can get into the house. We are locked up tightly and in any case,' he added, with a sardonic glance at her as he got to the door, 'there is always the butler.'

Amy giggled, astonished that she could. Luc had this strange effect on her. He wiped out most other thoughts from her mind. She suddenly did feel safe. And why not? Nobody could get in, and if they did Luc would get them.

Next morning she was called quite early. In spite of her fears she had had a very good night's sleep. They were all assembled at breakfast and Ann was particularly charming and gentle with her. Amy liked Luc's mother very much. She wished she could see her more often.

'Everything will be all right, Amy,' Ann Martell said to her when the time came to say goodbye.

She kissed Amy on both cheeks in the French manner and gave her a very warm hug.

'You'll see, it will be all right and soon you will be coming back to us.'

It gave Amy a little glow inside to know that somebody liked her so much, and then Luc's father took her hand and smiled down at her.

'Luc will catch him, Amy, have no doubt about that.'

She didn't really have any doubts. Luc would catch the watcher – if he was real.

On the journey back to England, and as they travelled north, Amy's depression began to descend again. It had been all right in that huge house outside Paris, with three other people there, but now she would be back in her own little house. She wondered if the man was still in Paris. She wondered if they had managed to give him the slip, if he would think she was still there and spend some days watching for her.

She knew he would finally come back, but at least if he was fooled for a couple of days it would give her some small respite. She shook her head. Somehow he would know, and of course if she was imagining him then she was bringing him back home in her own head, a phantom she had invented out of her nightmares.

Luc glanced at her from time to time but said nothing. There was nothing he could do to reassure her. The only thing he could do for Amy was to catch this man and he was determined to do that. He had talked his plan over with his father and he was sure it was a good plan. He'd also told his father his suspicions, and his father, after some thought, had been inclined to agree.

It was late by the time they arrived back at Amy's house. Luc took her in and carried her suitcase, but before they could get the door closed Mr Phillips came rushing across to speak to them.

Both Luc and Amy had noticed him with his dog as they drew up outside but by a mutual, unspoken agreement they had ignored his presence. Luc had not been too pleased with that little episode, and as Mr Phillips appeared breathlessly before them Luc's dark eyes narrowed alarmingly.

'I've been keeping watch,' Mr Phillips announced proudly. Amy noticed the way he kept his distance from Luc after giving him one wary glance.

'I've been in Paris,' Amy told him, with a little touch of pride that brought a softening to Luc's expression.

'Knew you were away,' Mr Phillips said importantly. 'Kept watch in the evening. After I took the dog out I came back and spent an hour each night at the bedroom window. Watched in the dark – and I *saw* him!'

Her neighbour pulled himself up as if he was waiting for a round of applause, but Amy was not happy. If Mr Phillips had seen the man here then she could not have seen the man in Paris.

'When did you see him?' she asked in a dejected voice.

'Twice,' he informed her. 'Last night and the night before that.'

Amy's shoulders fell in defeat. So she had not seen the man in Paris. It had all been in her mind. Luc shot a quick glance at her and decided it was time to intervene.

'Exactly who did you see, *m'sieur*?'

Mr Phillips cast an anxious glance in Luc's direction and edged closer to Amy.

'*You* know,' he explained, nodding his head vigorously and giving her a knowing but warning look. She just stared at him blankly. It seemed to alarm him even more, because he drew further away from Luc and leaned across to whisper in her ear before she could stop him. '*You* know,' he insisted in a stage whisper. 'It's the feller you used to go out with. The one before this one.'

Amy's mouth fell open.

'Impossible!' she said shakily.

'Same one,' Phillips assured her. He stood back proudly, carefully not looking at Luc. 'Feller came twice and he was hanging around. He came and looked in your window, although it was too dark for him to see anything. I watched him both times until he left. It was him, all right. Plain as day.'

Amy gave him a slight smile. It was all she could manage and he walked off quite pleased with himself when she finally managed to thank him.

'That's what good neighbours are for,' he reminded her. He gave Luc a wide berth as he left and Luc took Amy's arm and urged her inside.

'He says it was Eric,' she told Luc.

'Mmm, I heard,' he assured her grimly.

'But if it was Eric, and if he was here, then I must have imagined the man in Paris.'

She felt more devastated than ever, even if it meant that she had not been followed to France. She was doubting herself again instantly.

'I think we have what the English call crossed wires here,' Luc growled. 'The fact that Somerfield has been hanging around alters nothing. What it means is that he has not yet got the message clearly enough. I will deal with Somerfield. You may forget him.'

'Oh, Luc, I don't want you to attack Eric,' Amy pleaded urgently.

'You still care about this uncouth creature?' Luc glared at her and she gave a big sigh and shook her head.

'No, I don't. I care about you getting into trouble if you beat him up.'

'I do not beat people up,' Luc snapped. He looked at her anxious face and suddenly leaned forward and kissed her fiercely, although the kiss lasted only a second. 'I will simply speak to him. I will get his address from the police.'

'I have his address,' Amy volunteered warily.

'It will be better if I get it from the police,' Luc assured her. He glanced at her in amusement. 'At the same time I will point out to them that you are already being watched by some unknown man and that they have assured us the man is not Somerfield. No doubt they will want to warn him officially.'

Amy stared at him and saw the laughter dancing at the back of his dark eyes.

'You're quite wicked,' she said shakily. 'You're pulling rank, aren't you? You're using your position as one of the top employers round here to get the police to come down on Eric like a ton of bricks.'

'The English have a very colourful way of speaking,' Luc mused, 'but it usually conveys the message clearly. I am beginning to really appreciate my mother's language.'

Amy knew it was useless to argue. Luc would do what he thought best. The fact that he thoroughly disliked Eric would have no bearing on his actions – she hoped.

Once again he looked around the house, checking every room, checking the windows, checking the back door.

It was a strangely built house, as were many modern townhouses. It was in a row and therefore anyone who wished to get round the back had to go to the end of the street and come at it from another way. It had also been built with a kitchen at the front, and this was where she had been standing when she had originally seen the man.

In many ways the whole house was back to front. The whole row was the same, but she had always thought it a good idea. There was nothing particular to see when you looked out of the kitchen window except other houses across the road. But at the back of the house there was a garden.

Amy had never had to do very much to it. There was a paved patio, a small area of lawn which she cut from time to time, bulbs and flowers. Mowing the tiny area of lawn and weeding was all she ever

had to do to maintain it. Her aunt had disapproved, having great gardens of her own, but
again Amy had pointed out that she was a working
person, a businesswoman. She had rapidly discovered that the expression impressed Aunt Celia, and
Amy truly didn't have time for the maintenance of
gardens.

The way into the house from the back was
through patio doors. Amy had never had much
fear about anyone getting in there, oddly enough.
There was a service road that ran down at the end of
her garden. It was shared by all the other houses in
the road. But the danger had always seemed to Amy
to come from the front, from the area she could see
from her kitchen window. The large glass patio
door at the back was double-glazed, well locked,
and the room was protected by the usual one-eyed
Cyclops that was the sensor for the alarm system.

Before Luc went, he opened the patio door and
walked outside. It was already getting dark and
there was nothing to see. He looked up at the wall.

'You have no security lights?' he asked.

'No, I never got around to that. Uncle Peter
suggested it, but to tell you the honest truth by the
time he'd finished fussing about the alarm system I
couldn't be bothered with him fussing about anything else.'

'Your uncle dealt with the alarm system?' Luc
asked, turning to watch her.

'Well, I was at work so Peter came and saw to
everything. He was here to keep an eye on things
when the men were putting the system in. He
locked the house, unlocked the house and so on.'

'He has a key to your house, then?' Luc queried.

'Not now. He gave it back to me.'

'I see. So, you decided you didn't want him fussing with security lights after he'd finished fussing with the alarm system?'

'That's it,' Amy said with a quick grin. 'Uncle Peter is capable of a great deal of fuss, as you would know if you met him.'

Luc said nothing. He walked round the perimeter of the garden and looked at the gate, looked up and down the little road at the back. There were no lights there.

'You don't get traffic here?' he called back to Amy.

'Not much. If anything is to be delivered, sometimes it comes down the back, but not often because it's much more convenient to come down the main road and park outside the house. The men who empty the refuse bins always bring their lorry down here, and in any case you couldn't park out there as it would block the road.'

'Hmm,' Luc murmured.

Amy couldn't quite understand why Luc was interested in this particular area, seeing that the man had always been round the front.

'The man is never there,' she reminded him.

'So far, no.'

'He won't ever stand there,' Amy said quietly.

'You think not?'

'In a way I'm sure. I don't know exactly why I'm so sure, but I am.'

'Why is that?' Luc asked, coming closer to look at her.

'Because he wants me to see him. He wants me to be afraid. If he was at the back I wouldn't see him because there are no lights. I could imagine him there, of course, but it wouldn't be the same. I'm sure that in spite of the risk of being caught he has to stand where I can see him. He has to stand under the light so that I'll know he's watching me, so I'll know he means me harm.'

Luc looked at her silently, once again reminding himself how very astute she was, his Computer Person.

'Yes,' he murmured in agreement. 'And when he was watching from under the trees in the church-yard and your aunt's house?'

'I've been thinking about that too,' Amy murmured reflectively as they went back into the house and Luc very carefully locked the patio doors and drew the curtains. 'He could quite easily have hidden so that I wouldn't have been aware of him at all. For example, he could have been on the other side of the wall, just peeping over. But he came on the inside of the wall and he stood under the trees, well concealed so that I couldn't see who it was but knowing that if I turned round I would realize he was there.'

Yes, Luc thought. He could understand that. It would frighten her. It was intended to frighten her. He wondered if any actual physical harm was intended or if this was merely to put mental stress on Amy, bring her to a breakdown. It was one of the things he had been talking over with his father the night before.

'And of course you saw him in Paris,' Luc mused thoughtfully.

'Again, just enough for me to see him but no more,' Amy agreed quietly.

He walked across and pulled her into his arms and looked down at her,

'You are a very clever person,' he congratulated in a soft voice, and Amy smiled wryly.

'I'm beginning to think I'm a very mad person.'

'You are not, *ma petite*. But we are up against someone who is also very clever. We must find out who he is and make sure he is stopped.'

Luc continued to look into her eyes, his arms only loosely round her, and Amy gazed back, mesmerized. His eyes were so deep, dark as a moonless night. She had never felt the sort of awareness with anyone that she felt with him.

'Will you kiss me, please, Luc?' she whispered almost without thought.

'If I do, will you stop me from going crazy?' he asked in a thrillingly husky voice.

'No.' She shook her head almost wildly and Luc's hand came up to capture it, his fingers tightening in her hair as his mouth crushed hers possessively.

'The sight of you is a wonderful torture to me,' he groaned against her lips. 'I want you, *chérie*. I want you very badly.'

He began to kiss her urgently and Amy wound her arms tightly round his neck, returning his kisses with all the hidden sweetness in her. And, once again, Luc's desire grew. He had never known a feeling quite like it, this raw need that seemed to fill him when he touched Amy. He didn't even have to touch her, it was there as soon as he saw her, an order from his body as if he must feed an addiction.

He drew her closer with a rough urgency and she came softly against the hard, sexual demand of his body. The feel of her against him only aroused him further and he swept her off her feet, moving with her to the wide settee. He almost fell on it, tumbling Amy down on top of him and capturing her face in his hands.

He murmured to her in a voice thick with passion, but Amy could not understand the huskily whispered French. She knew she should be afraid, though. Pictures of Eric's violence filled her head for a second and, although she knew this was Luc, she stiffened momentarily.

'What is it, *ma belle*? I am frightening you?' Luc asked in a hoarse whisper. His lips went to her throat, heated and urgent, and she could feel the hard, muscular length of his body beneath her own.

'No,' she lied shakily, and Luc went still, looking up at her with dark, intense eyes.

'You're lying, *ma petite*,' he said softly. 'You want me but you are afraid. You think I will hurt you?'

'No,' Amy said quickly, shaking her head. 'Not you. I know you would never hurt me.'

'But I am following in the steps of someone who did, *n'est-ce pas*? Somerfield!'

The dark eyes narrowed and he moved, lifting her from him and sitting up abruptly. Amy collapsed to the floor, kneeling in front of him, her head bowed in a sort of subdued manner that stopped Luc's anger at once. The flare of furious jealousy died.

She looked crushed, her shining hair hiding her face, and Luc's expression softened. He leaned forward and drew her between his thighs, capturing her face in warm palms, forcing her to look up at him. The purple-blue eyes were unhappy. They were not shining like stars.

'I want to take you to bed,' he told her quietly. 'I want to make love to you slowly and gently because it is what we both need. Unfortunately, I cannot promise either slowness or gentleness at this moment. All I can promise is that I would never hurt you as Somerfield obviously did.'

'I want to be with you, Luc,' Amy confessed, her lips trembling.

'I know that, *chérie*,' Luc muttered ruefully. 'I am not exactly a callow youth. But I will be fighting the ghost of Somerfield, a particularly uncouth ghost. Now is not the time. Already you are afraid of this man who follows and watches you. I am certainly not about to subject you to more fear.'

To his amusement, Amy looked bitterly disappointed. She gazed up at him with wide eyes.

'Perhaps if you – if you made me . . . Later I might have got over all the things that . . .'

Luc's dark brows shot up in astonishment and then he gave a great shout of laughter. He got to his feet and pulled her upwards, gently into his arms.

'You are suggesting kill or cure?' he laughed as he buried his face in her clouds of fragrant hair. '*Chérie*, I am not qualified for such a task. My special training did not cover sex therapy.'

Amy could feel him laughing. She could feel it rippling through him and she felt annoyed and very silly. She went extremely quiet.

Luc lifted his head and looked down at her, his face still amused but the laughter gone.

'What is between us will not go away,' he promised softly. 'It has been there for a long time and I think we both know it.'

Amy nodded and he captured her mouth gently, making no demands on her. It was a long, slow kiss that soothed and thrilled, and Amy sighed blissfully against his mouth.

'If I am very careful and use all my self-control,' Luc murmured tautly, 'I will be able to kiss you. We will make do with that.'

'For always?' Amy asked in a horrified voice.

'I am not made of stone,' Luc muttered in a pained voice. 'I have been waiting for you since I first saw you.'

Amy smiled her brilliant smile and he put her away from him with a low groan.

'You must help me and do exactly as you are told,' he said firmly. 'I am the boss and I will give the orders. First, we will catch the man who is making your life a misery.'

'And then?' Amy asked breathlessly.

'Then we will see,' Luc promised. 'Right now, I intend to escape. You are a siren and I must save myself.'

When Luc had gone, Amy realized that she was as frightened now as she had ever been, and with Luc out of the house everywhere seemed cold and lonely. She knew there were more interludes in her life now when she had bursts of happiness, but she was always thrown back into fear. Once again she couldn't help remembering that all this had happened since Aunt Celia had died.

She went to bed, setting the alarms on her way up, but her mind wouldn't stop running round in circles trying to find a solution, and asking herself, why me?

She'd heard about people being troubled by stalkers but she had never imagined anything like this. She had always thought of the victims being important people, celebrities, film stars, and the stalkers unbalanced people who were trying to get close to them. People who sent them letters, people who attended every function just to see them but who did it quite openly. A sort of great nuisance, only bringing fear because of their persistence.

This was different and, as Luc had remarked to her in the past, it was a strange way to go about stalking her. This was somebody who was making quite sure that she did not know his identity. Somebody who, for the most part, stood absolutely still and simply watched.

Perhaps if she had been a different sort of person she could have shrugged off the idea that it was frightening. She could have glanced at him in scorn and gone to bed. But instinct told her there was more to it than that. Instinct told her she was in danger.

She wasn't quite sure where the danger would come from, though. Would he break in one night? Would she suddenly wake up to find him hovering over the bed? Would he be there to kill her? To assault her?

Amy just didn't know. She had searched every corner of her mind and she couldn't come up with any idea as to who this could be, why it was happening or what he would finally do. But she did know instinctively, deep-down, that one night he would certainly do something. He obviously knew every move she made.

Amy felt weary. She got into bed and as she did so she decided that in a way she had something to thank the watcher for. He had brought Luc close to her. Without this trouble Luc would perhaps never have admitted how he felt. He might have just gone back to Paris one day and never seen her again. All the same, she could have done without the watcher's dark presence. She fell asleep, blissfully aware of the memory of Luc's arms around her.

When she got to work next morning, Luc was already there. He didn't call her into his office. He just looked across at her questioningly and she shook her head. The man had not come in the night. Luc smiled when he saw her cheeks flood with colour, a reaction brought on by memories, and Amy hurried into her office and settled herself in front of Jim, Alfie and their brothers. She tried not to think about how it would have been this morning if Luc had stayed with her.

The person who had been working in her place was not here today and Amy was glad; she was very possessive about her machines and she didn't want anyone explaining what had been done while she was away. She was quite capable of finding out for herself. She quickly scanned the computers, moving from one to the other rather anxiously. As far as she could see everything was still in order.

When she glanced up Luc was just passing her office, and although he wasn't looking at her he was grinning to himself. No doubt he had seen her muttering to her computers and looking to see if anybody had damaged them. On this occasion she didn't mind. It gave her a wonderful feeling to have Luc close by.

Her mind kept trying to turn to the coming night but she refused to think of anything but her job. She told herself that everything was back to normal. It wasn't, of course, unless normal was being awake at night and having a stranger staring at her. She sighed aloud. Maybe that was what 'normal' would be for ever.

Luc came in at lunchtime, just as she was thinking of going down to the canteen,

'We'll go out to lunch,' he ordered, giving her no opportunity to question him. He even went so far as to pick up her bag and stand waiting, and Amy could not suppress a giggle.

'What?' Luc asked in a repressive manner.

'It's you. It's the way you order me about.'

'It is my job to order you about.' Luc looked at her with some severity. 'I am the boss, if you recall.'

'When I called you that, you didn't like it,' Amy reminded him in amusement.

He motioned her to go to the door and followed her, his lips suddenly quirking. At least so far she had a grip on herself. He wondered how she would take it when he explained his plan to her.

'Last night we were both tired after the journey,' he reminded her later, as they ate lunch. 'I left things. Did the man come around?'

'Not that I saw; I slept.'

'Good.' Luc looked at her approvingly. 'Tonight I'm going to come and stay all night.'

'With me?'

She looked hopeful, her face lit up, and Luc decided to play it safe – in spite of the quick burst of arousal her eagerness brought.

'I intend to sit up in your kitchen. I intend to see what this man is about.'

'If he sees you arrive he won't come,' Amy pointed out, dashed into gloom.

'I intend to come early and park my car up the road. I shall walk down to your house. We will have a meal. You may cook it,' Luc allowed condescendingly.

'You're very generous.'

Luc frowned at her.

'After the meal you will go to bed and I will sit up and watch.' He leaned back, quite smugly pleased with himself, or so it seemed to Amy.

'You can't sit and watch all night. You'll be half-dead in the morning.'

'Why do the English use ridiculous expressions?' Luc enquired irritably. 'One is either dead or not dead. One cannot be half-dead.'

'I'm not too sure about that,' Amy mused, 'but

I'll let it go for now. If you sit up all night you'll be too tired to go to work. And if you fall asleep, you won't wake up when the man comes. I'm the only one with the instinct for that.'

She looked at him triumphantly and Luc glowered at her for a second. She could never let even one thing go. She always grasped things and shook them like a terrier. She could be very irritating.

'If your instinct wakes you and the man is there, you will creep downstairs and tell me.'

CHAPTER 12

Luc looked smugly pleased with himself again, as if this was a match of some sort and he had scored the final point.

'All right,' Amy conceded, 'but you'd better not let anyone see you come in because it will be bad for your reputation.'

Luc wanted to shout with laughter. Only the fact that they were in a crowded restaurant stopped him.

'What about your own reputation?' he asked, his dark eyes dancing with amusement.

'I'm not much bothered about that. It seems to me that after the upset with Eric in that restaurant my reputation is already shot to pieces.'

The amusement died and Luc frowned blackly. Even at this stage he did not like to hear Somerfield's name on her lips.

'I assure you I can take care of my own reputation. Besides, there are certain things that people expect of me,' he muttered crossly.

'Like what?' Amy gave him a puzzled look.

'I am a Frenchman. Naturally they expect a certain amount of romantic dalliance.'

Amy grinned wryly.

'It's very strange how you've done this about-face. Not long ago you seemed to think that everything reprehensible was English.' She put her head on one side and thought for a second. 'I wonder if the man watching me is English?'

'Of course he is,' Luc snapped. 'No Frenchman would do anything so stupid.' He glared at her. 'You are suggesting that it is me?'

'I didn't suggest it was a Frenchman at all. Anyway, I wouldn't be frightened if it was you,' Amy muttered, going back to her lunch gloomily. 'I'd just stare right back every minute.'

She was too busy deliberating inside her head to notice that Luc's face softened as his eyes scanned her thoughtful expression.

When Luc arrived later it was still quite light. Amy had rushed home after work and started preparations for a meal. Tonight, because Luc was here, she would not have to creep about the house in the darkness; she would not have to go to bed early and she knew she would sleep soundly because Luc was in the house.

Instead of the usual fear and worry she was filled with a bubbling excitement. Soon Luc would be here. He could stay all night and guard her, and, more than that, he would be here, close to her.

He knocked on the door and she let in him. A careful look outside assured her that his car was not there. Her own car was the only one standing at the front of the house. Unless someone had actually seen him arrive they would not know he was with her, and as soon as lights had to be put on they would draw the curtains. To all intents and purposes she would be alone.

'I parked two streets away,' Luc said when he saw her peering around him to look. 'Unless someone is actually watching the house they will have no idea I'm here. Providing, of course, that we do not stand here staring at the street for any length of time,' he finished mockingly.

Amy stepped back quickly and closed the door and Luc immediately pulled her into his arms and kissed her fiercely.

'I have been waiting all day to do that,' he whispered, looking down into her bemused eyes. 'I could not work for thinking about it. It is definitely rationed, however,' he warned her, stepping clear and smiling at her flustered appearance.

He wandered around the house while Amy made the meal and he came into the kitchen frequently to watch her. There was an elegance about everything she did. He realized he could watch her for the rest of his life. He realized too that being here alone with her was dangerous, but his desire for her was more than tempered by his desire to catch this man who was making her life a misery.

He would control his own emotions and if anything would build up an even greater anger. He was looking forward to laying his hands on the man who silently watched in the night.

After the the meal, Amy decided to read. Luc watched television and he was almost lulled into a comfortable feeling that this was normal, just Amy and himself.

He resisted the temptation to look through the window. He knew the man would not come until it was very late. When finally it became a strain to just sit there waiting with Luc, Amy decided that it was time to go to bed.

Of course there could be no alarm put on tonight – Luc's presence downstairs would activate it. But she wasn't bothered about that. Luc was better than any alarm. She went to bed, contriving to sidle her way through the door, and Luc did some contriving of his own for the same reason. He merely nodded to her. If he got up to kiss her goodnight she would never get up the stairs, not unless he went with her.

When she had gone, Luc made himself comfortable in the chair, put his feet on a stool and prepared to wait. It was eleven o'clock. He would give the man a couple of hours, then he would get up to see if the watcher was there. After that it was merely a question of speed, because tonight he was determined to catch whoever was watching Amy.

But, even so, especially after his talk with his father, he had an uneasiness at the back of his mind that it would not be quite so straightforward as that. There was a great deal of cunning behind whoever was watching. The man would not be quite as easy to catch as he had at first thought when he had pounced on Amy's neighbour. Things were much more complicated than he had at first realized.

Some restless dream woke Amy in the middle of the night. For a moment she switched on the bedside light and glanced at her watch, and then quickly switched the light off again. It was four-thirty. She got out of bed to look through the window, wondering if her dream had not been the only thing that had awakened her, wondering if her instincts were once more in action. But the man was not there.

She crept downstairs to have a look at Luc and smiled to herself. As she had expected, he was fast asleep in the chair. He looked very uncomfortable.

Amy wondered whether or not she should wake him and then decided against it. Spending an uncomfortable night sitting in a chair was a decision he had made all by himself. Besides, he might feel a bit foolish if she woke him up. She smiled to herself and crept back upstairs.

There was another good reason for not waking him too. She knew the danger with Luc and herself alone in the same house. The feeling between them had grown too strong to be ignored. Amy got back into bed and to her great surprise fell asleep almost immediately.

When she came down in the morning to make breakfast Luc was already awake. He had made himself some coffee and was sitting in a chair at the kitchen table. He was massaging the back of his neck and Amy tried to hide a little smile but Luc noticed.

'I fell asleep,' he growled.

'I know. I crept downstairs about four o'clock and there you were, out to the world. You looked uncomfortable but I decided to leave you.'

'Thank you very much!' Luc snapped irascibly. 'That was good of you.'

'Well, you made your own decision, and that's what you decided you were going to do. Besides, I thought you might feel a bit foolish if I woke you up.'

'Not as foolish as I feel now. My head refuses to move. And let us not pretend, *ma petite*. I know why you did not wake me.'

Even in his present piteous condition he was still the most sensuous man Amy had ever seen, but when she looked confused and blushed he took pity on her.

'What woke you?' he asked. 'Did the man come?'

'Of course not. If he'd come I would certainly have had you up at once and running across the road to get him.'

She made breakfast and Luc looked very pleased.

'An English breakfast,' he murmured. 'It is one of the things that the English do very well.'

'One of the *few* things, I expect you mean,' Amy countered. By this time he had recovered sufficiently to smile.

They ate their breakfast almost in silence, but it was a very companionable silence, it seemed right to be with Luc. After a while he said, 'This is not going to work.' He looked deeply thoughtful.

'Well, sometimes he doesn't come,' Amy pointed out. She was a bit anxious that Luc would give up the whole thing.

'I have been wondering if the man is watching the house throughout the whole day,' Luc murmured.

He looked towards the kitchen curtains, jabbing his fork in the general direction of the other side of the street. 'There is a row of identical houses across there and it occurs to me that the man might be in one of those houses, watching.'

'There's a slight drawback to that,' Amy pointed out. 'I thought of it myself and it occurred to me that if he's watching during the day to check on my activities, like when he follows me into town and trails me round the shops, it means he has to keep awake watching the house all the time during the day – unless he knows for sure that I'm at work. Take, for example, when I went to Aunt Celia's grave and up to her house. That was a Sunday. If we conclude that he's watching the house all the time then he would have to be awake all day in order to follow me because it wasn't a work day.'

Luc nodded.

'Agreed.'

'But if, after doing that, he wanted to stand and watch the house at night, it would mean he was awake all day and all night. He couldn't keep that up.'

'Also agreed,' Luc muttered, looking very grim. 'I have considered this.'

Amy looked at him expectantly. She'd assumed he would have thought of it.

'So where does that leave us?'

'Possibly with two people,' Luc suggested quietly.

He looked up and Amy's eyes widened; she had never thought of that. He wondered if he was frightening her even more and shook his head at once.

'It's merely speculation. But I feel, even though we have only tried this experiment once, that somehow the man knows I am here with you.'

'So what are we going to do?'

Amy began to collect the dishes and put them into the dishwasher and Luc stood up and stretched.

'I'd been thinking of another plan before you came down,' he told her slowly. 'You have an invitation to stay with your uncle Peter?'

'Yes.' Amy spun round and looked at him. 'I didn't want to, though. He's always got a girl or someone hanging around – well, a woman, but quite young. It would rather cramp his style.'

'All the same,' Luc insisted, 'I think his style is going to be cramped. We have to contrive to have me in the house but we have to make the man think you are here and alone.'

'I don't see how we can manage it, Luc.'

'I've thought about it,' Luc told her. 'If you drive up to the house in the evening from work and park your car and come inside you are alone.'

'Of course!' Amy stared at him, wondering what he was going to say next.

'I then come and run my car down the service road at the back. I come in through the patio door, you pick up your bag for the night and you go out through the patio door. You take my car and you go to your uncle Peter's.'

Amy leaned against the sink, looking thoughtful.

'So the person will think that I'm in the house,

and even if they are in a house across the street, they can't watch the back. They won't know I've left and they won't know you've arrived.'

'Precisely,' Luc stated.

'It's worth a try,' Amy agreed. 'When do we do it?'

'Tonight, I think.'

'There's another problem,' Amy mused. She began to clear up. She glanced at the clock; it was getting time to go to work. 'We'll be back where we were last night.'

'How is that?'

'You'll fall asleep in the chair,' Amy reminded him with a little smile of triumph. 'And I won't be here to wake you. Wouldn't it be better if – ?'

'It would not,' Luc interrupted quickly before she had a chance to finish. 'I want you to go to your uncle's house.'

'Then how are you going to stay awake?'

'If it becomes necessary, I will take the day off and sleep during the day,' Luc stated with some triumph. He wasn't at all sure he could spend another night with her and retain his sanity. 'In fact,' he continued, 'I could do that now. I feel absolutely wretched.' Amy gave a little smile and he frowned at her.

'I am being wretched on your behalf.'

'I know, Luc.' She came across and put her hands on his shoulders. 'You're very good to me.'

Luc's face went taught. In spite of his stiff neck and pounding headache, he wanted to be close to her.

'Pretty soon, *chérie*, I am going to be more than good to you,' he promised softly. 'Trying to be merely good to you is killing me slowly. Now, let's go and you can do me a great favour. You can drive me two streets away to collect my car. I really do not have the strength to walk that far.'

Amy left her house, grinning to herself, and Luc sat in her car, scowling at the road. He looked like a bear with a sore head. He felt like a bear with a sore head. He *did* have a sore head. He grumbled under his breath all the way to his car.

'Shall I tell them you're not coming into the office today?'

'Certainly,' Luc snapped, 'if you want them all looking at you out of their eye corners.'

'Why should they?'

'They will wonder how you know my plans,' he pointed out with a smooth, knowing smile that made her blush. 'They will wonder how you could possibly know that the boss is too tired to come to work. They will also wonder why I am so tired. I will ring my efficient secretary.'

'Your bossy secretary,' Amy corrected with a frown.

'My bossy secretary,' Luc admitted. 'Do not forget to make arrangements to stay with your uncle tonight. Drive home as if nothing had happened and I will arrive later as we planned.'

They reached his car and Amy finally plucked up the courage to ask about Eric.

'Did you get Eric's address from the police?'

He slanted a peculiar glance at her and merely smiled to himself.

'Luc! What have you done?' Amy gasped.

'Why, nothing, *ma petite*. Why do you insist on thinking I am uncivilized? I merely complained to the police on your behalf. I then called on Somerfield before the police could forbid me to do so. He has agreed not to call on you again at any time.'

'You threatened him,' Amy accused.

'Certainly not. I explained life as it is now or as it could be. It was a most amicable discussion. He was friendly. He explained that he is seriously thinking of moving to another town.'

Luc got out and Amy was still staring after him when he drove off, smiling to himself. Amy drove on to work. She smiled too, and shook her head. Luc was just this side of civilized, but only just.

She suddenly felt a great upsurge of joy, her spirits flying, Luc was doing all this for her. Not all that long ago he had merely been an irascible boss, now he was very close to her, very dear to her. She went into work with a smile on her face and just stopped herself in time before she told his bossy secretary that Luc would not be in.

She knew the moment that Luc had rung because the woman assumed a very important look. She was going to take charge for the day. Amy sat herself in front of her computers and winked at Jim.

'She doesn't know what we know, Jim,' she whispered, and started work with more vigour than she had felt for a long time.

During lunchtime she rang Peter, and once again was quite surprised to find he was at home.

'Oh, I feel terrible, Uncle Peter,' she said mournfully.

'You'll feel worse if you keep calling me Uncle.' The laughter died out of his voice and he sounded concerned. 'What is it Amy? Is that man still watching you, love?'

'Yes, he is. I really feel dreadful. I'm just not getting a decent night's sleep.'

'Then come to me,' Peter ordered instantly.

'Can I come tonight, Uncle Peter?' Amy asked in a pitiful voice.

'You certainly can. I'll collect you.'

'No. It's all right, I'll come by myself after dinner.'

She didn't tell him a word about the plan. As usual she didn't want to share Luc with anyone, but also she was learning a great deal of caution. The less people knew about this the better, and then again Peter would fuss – he always fussed. She rather suspected, too, that he would be a gossip if the opportunity arose.

It was only when Amy got home that night that she realized she would have some explaining to do when she arrived at Peter's house driving a black Porsche. It was something she hadn't thought of, and neither, apparently, had Luc. She would have to wait until he came and then discuss the matter with him.

Luc came about seven, and while they ate their meal Amy told him what she thought about the cars.

'It's a problem.'

'Not really.' Amy assured him. 'When I arrive at Uncle Peter's house it will be fairly dark. He won't notice what sort of car I'm in so I won't have any explanations to make. Of course, I could tell him everything.'

294

'We will keep this strictly between ourselves,' Luc ordered. He reached across the table and took her hand. 'Soon all this will be over. Then you can tell him.'

'I hope it *is* soon,' Amy said quietly.

'So do I. This man is ruining my personal life.'

Amy knew what he meant. She kept it warmly inside her, and when Luc suddenly looked up at her, her eyes were glowing. He stared at her. He would be very glad when he had caught this damn nuisance who was outside the house so that he could settle to some sort of normal relationship with Amy, because he wanted her very badly. With a little luck he could get rid of the man, but he would never be rid of this burning desire he had for Amy.

As soon as it was getting dark, and when it was fast approaching half past eight, Luc escorted Amy to the back service road. He had parked his car by her gate, regardless of who might have wished to get down the lane.

'It's perfectly easy to manage,' he told her. 'I don't know what direction your uncle lives in but do not turn in this direction at all, even if you have to make a wide sweep around. Don't let anyone in this street see where you are going.' He suddenly pulled her into his arms and kissed her hungrily. 'And take care, Amy.'

'I will,' she said breathlessly. She got into the car, fumbling with the keys for a moment, and then felt the power of the car's ignition. It was totally different from her own car, but she was a good driver and Luc didn't seem to have any doubt whatsoever that she could handle the Porsche.

It was dark when she arrived at Peter's house. He lived in a very large house at the opposite side of the town from her aunt's place. It had always seemed to Amy that the two of them had lived as far away from each other as they possibly could.

She came quietly into the drive and pulled to the side, well out of the way of the lighted windows. She just did not want to explain to Peter how it was that she was driving Luc's car. She didn't want the questions that would come – the endless questions. Peter never left anything alone. He always wanted to go on and on about it. She felt a little guilty that she was not telling him about the plan, after all he was the only sort of family she had left, but she had more or less promised Luc.

She rang the bell and Peter welcomed her with a huge hug and took her case.

'There's nothing to worry about now, Amy. You're safe here. You should have been here weeks ago.'

'You're probably right,' Amy sighed, a feeling of guilt washing over again that this was all a trick and Peter was not part of it. 'I'm really tired.'

'We'll have a quick drink and then you can get off to bed. Before the housekeeper left she prepared a room for you.'

Amy knew that her uncle had no live-in servants of any description – that, as she had told Luc, would also have cramped his style. But as far as she could make out there was no woman in the house now, whoever his latest lady-love was.

'Are we alone?' she asked, as he handed her a drink.

'Just you and me and the bogeyman,' Peter assured her with a grin. He clinked his glass with hers. 'Here to us, love. Destruction to the bogeyman.'

It did not make Amy feel any better to have the watcher called the bogeyman, but she joined the toast. Her mind was on Luc, his lethal fists, his speed and the way he could come like a tiger out of the night. She would have loved to see him catch that man and probably tonight he would.

She went to bed and slept very peacefully, and she had her breakfast with Peter in the morning.

'All right?' he asked, when she came down.

'Perfectly all right.'

She had forgotten all about Luc's car, but while she was speaking to Peter he glanced out of the window. From his immediate attitude, Amy realized he could see the Porsche.

'Spending some of your money?' he asked in peculiarly quiet voice.

'Haven't got it yet,' Amy pointed out cheerfully.

'So where did you get the new Porsche?'

'Oh, that! Somebody lent it to me. My car is a bit unreliable at the moment. Breaking down at night with that imbecile around wouldn't be very amusing.'

'I see.'

Peter didn't say anything else. Amy waited for the usual questions but, to her surprise, none were forthcoming. She decided that he was being diplomatic. After all, she was always diplomatic with him and never enquired about his latest girlfriend. The fact that there was not one of them in the house at the moment surprised her, but it was none of her business.

Amy went to work quite cheerfully, but when she got there she was very startled to find Luc in his office, in spite of his sleepless night. He glanced up at her as she came in but he was back to the black frowns. Amy almost rushed into his office, quite forgetting that at work he was the boss.

'What happened?' she asked quickly.

'Nothing happened,' Luc snapped. 'Not one damned thing! *Dieu!* I sat up all night. I stared until my eyes were popping from my head and all I saw was an empty street and one streetlamp. Not even a cat walked down the road. Nobody came at all.'

'Oh!' Amy leaned against the door and looked downcast. 'So I'm imagining it, aren't I?

'I don't think so,' Luc said more quietly. 'Sometimes he does not come. You said that yourself. But we will see; I will be there again tonight.'

'So why have you come to work today?'

'Because I am supposed to be running this damn place,' Luc reminded her testily. 'I have to put in an appearance sometimes. I can't spend all my time guarding you. Things will grind to a halt here.'

'You don't *have* to spend any time guarding me.'

Luc looked up and saw how the thoughtless words had hit Amy very hard. Her purple-blue eyes looked almost bruised.

'I want to guard you, Amy,' he assured her quickly. 'Ignore my bad temper. It's just that I was all geared up to catch the man, to beat him senseless, and he didn't come. We will try again tonight. Besides,' he added softly, 'I'm physically frustrated. I expected to have all this finished by now. Our lives back to normal.'

'What's normal?' Amy asked gloomily when she had stopped blushing brightly and her breath was even again. 'How did you get to work?'

'I used your car.'

'We're getting ourselves into deep water here,' Amy pronounced

'Why?' He looked up at her seriously. 'What is the deep water?'

'Uncle Peter noticed your car parked outside this morning. I'd just forgotten all about it. He went a bit stiff.'

'How do you mean, "stiff"?' Luc asked, with an intense look at her.

'He asked me if I'd been spending the money from the will on a Porsche.'

'And what did you say to him?'

'I told him my car was a bit unreliable and a friend had lent it to me.'

Luc thought for a moment and then shrugged.

'We will keep things as they are. I will come round, just as I did last night, and you will take my car. It is essential that your own car stays in front of your house.'

'And what do I tell Peter?'

'You could tell him to mind his own damn business,' Luc rasped. 'But, failing that, tell him the Porsche is mine. Tell him we are lovers.'

'Luc!' Amy blushed brightly and he grinned.

'Seriously, *ma petite*, he's a long way from us; he doesn't know what's happening at all. You've not told him?'

'No, I haven't. But I felt as if I was lying.'

'You did not tell him a lie.'

'It's lying by omission, Luc.'

'Very well, continue to lie by omission,' Luc ordered.

Amy didn't see that she had a lot of choice. She looked up and Luc's secretary was coming towards them. She was bearing down on them like a sergeant major and Luc swore under his breath.

'I will have to get rid of that woman.'

'I second that,' said Amy as she made a quick getaway.

'Tonight,' Luc called after her. 'I'm going home to sleep this afternoon.'

'Oh, right,' Amy agreed, escaping fast. 'Good.'

When she was back in front of her computers she had time to think. She suspected that this car business was going to trap them, but then she shook off the uneasiness. Only Peter knew what was happening about the cars, and he didn't know the whole truth.

Amy settled down to work and put the whole thing out of her mind. One thing was for sure; she had a lot to look forward to. She would be having dinner again with Luc and then she would be sleeping peacefully and safely at her uncle's house.

They repeated the whole procedure that night and everything was the same. Peter greeted her, they had a drink, they talked and later she went to bed.

This time, to her surprise, Peter began to talk about Aunt Celia, and Amy realized, rather guiltily, that she hardly ever thought about Aunt Celia now. She made this point to Peter.

'Are you surprised at that?' he asked. 'After all, since Celia died lots of things have happened to you.'

'They have,' Amy murmured gloomily. 'Unpleasant things, like this man watching me all the time.'

'You had a trip to Paris,' Peter reminded her, trying to cheer her up.

'I really enjoyed that,' Amy smiled.

'Did anything momentous happen?'

Amy was just about to tell him about the man, who had even managed to follow her to Paris, but she decided to keep quiet. Once again, with Peter, it would involve a long, detailed explanation. She would have to bring in Luc's mother and father, she would have to bring in Luc, and she just didn't want to do it.

He had no idea she was close to Luc. All he knew was that the firm had asked her to go to Paris and it had been, as he'd put it, a feather in her cap. She left it without enlightening him further.

In the middle of the night, Amy had her premonition again. She had been sleeping very deeply but, she imagined, not as deeply as normal because she was in a strange room. She had never stayed in Peter's house before until the previous night, and she was so nervous nowadays that she had felt a tendency to lock the door – until she found out that there was no key, not even a keyhole.

But even so she had managed to go to sleep.

She had told herself not to be stupid, that she was quite safe here, but when she woke in the night with her usual burst of anxiety she knew without being told that the man was close by.

Unlike her own house, Peter's house had security lights and he kept them on all night. It made the garden bright, floodlit. They had talked it over in the past because Amy had always thought it best to crouch in the dark with any lights to come on quickly and startle intruders. But Peter had disagreed. He said that a lighted area would put them off entirely. She didn't know if he had thought of this himself or if it had come from the police, but that has what he did and she still thought he was wrong.

She did not think that now, though, because when she looked at the curtains it was bright as day with the powerful lights.

There was a long gravelled drive that led from the road and, like at her aunt's house, there was a stone wall round the whole perimeter of the property, with trees and bushes. Mostly there were ornamental bushes, but there were some quite large trees too.

The security lighting flooded the driveway and much of the lawn on all sides of the house. There were, of course, a few dark patches but mostly it was brilliantly lit.

Amy got up and went across to look through the curtains, but because she was always very cautious she did not draw them wide open; she merely peeped through the crack at the side.

There was a feeling of relief to see the whole area was brightly lit and Amy smiled to herself. So much for intuition. She was getting far too nervous.

She stood for a second, admiring the garden in the lights. There were some beautiful flowering bushes here and it made her wonder if she should have a big garden of her own. It made her wonder if she should take over her aunt's house and move out of town. She wasn't sure now, though, that she dared do that – not since she had seen the man up there.

Amy was just going back to bed when a movement in the shadows caught her eye. Immediately she went cold all over, shivers running down her spine, and then she saw the familiar figure. The inevitability of it shocked her into stillness.

This time he was not taking too much care; she seemed to have caught him off guard. He stepped partly into the light, but his head was down, as if he was searching for something. Once again she could not see his face, but she could see him just as clearly as she had done under the lamp outside her own house.

She let the curtain drop and flattened herself against the wall, her heart pounding. He had followed her here.

The thought came to her mind, as it had done in Paris, that he would follow her wherever she went, follow her for ever.

Amy suddenly realized that as the man was in the light, and as Peter was in the house with her, they might catch him. She was fairly familiar with the house. There was a curved wrought-iron balustrade on the staircase that came round the side of the wall and along to the top landing. The top landing also had a wrought-iron balustrade that made a gallery, looking down on the large parquet-floored hall.

Amy flew along this gallery. Peter's room was at the end of it and she hammered on his door.

'Uncle Peter! Uncle Peter!' she shouted.

He was awake very quickly, and he came to the door shrugging into his dressing gown.

'What's wrong Amy? What happened?'

'The man! He's in the garden!'

'What? It's impossible,' Peter said, staring at her in amazement. 'Nobody knows you're here.'

'It's true, Uncle Peter! He's in the garden now. Come to my room and you'll see him under the trees.'

Peter went along to her room but she stopped him as he was about to switch on the light.

'Don't!' Amy ordered quickly. 'Don't let him know you're awake.'

Peter gave her a strange glance, but he came over to the window with her and looked through the side of the curtains. Amy peered through the other side and to her great relief the man was still there. She wished Luc was here, Luc was fast; Luc would catch him.

'Where is he?' Peter asked.

'Right there!' Amy told him in an exasperated voice. 'Surely you can see him?'

'I can't, but I'll get him all the same,' Peter told her furiously. 'Bloody cheek, coming here!' He dived out of the room, and when Amy grabbed her robe and followed him on to the landing she saw him go down the stairs and search inside a tall, deep cupboard. When he came out, he was carrying a shotgun.

'You can't shoot him!' Amy yelled, hastily fastening herself into her robe. 'You can't just kill him!'

'I'll shoot the bastard in his backside.'

Peter flung open the front door violently, and Amy was so worried about the situation she seemed to have created that she raced down the stairs after him. But by the time she got to the front door Peter was heading across the lawn looking like a wild bull.

She could see the man; she could see him even more clearly from here. If he would just lift his head she would be able to see his face, she would be able to tell if he was anyone she knew. As she watched, the man turned away.

'He's going, Uncle Peter! He's going to get away,' she shouted.

Peter marched forward and to Amy's astonishment he seemed to be searching. The man was there as plain as day, but Peter was searching for him.

'He's there, right in front of you!' she yelled.

The man slowly withdrew to the edge of the lawn, up to the wall, and Amy couldn't understand why Peter hadn't kept up his mad bull attitude, raised the gun and fired, because he couldn't have been more than a hundred yards from the man at this point. He *must* see him! It was so light that it was impossible to miss him.

But Peter just kept charging on. He passed the man as close as he would pass someone in the street. The man didn't move and Peter didn't look at him. If Peter had lifted his hand he could have touched the man, but he didn't even glance in that direction.

Amy could hear Peter swearing under his breath, stomping around in his slippers, poking the gun into bushes. She was watching his progress, almost open-mouthed, and when she looked back to where the man had been there was nobody at all.

He had gone, disappeared. She had never felt so shocked before in her life. She couldn't understand why Peter hadn't seen him.

Peter came back in eventually, slammed the door and locked it.

'Blast!' he grated angrily. 'He got away.'

Amy didn't know what to say to him. She didn't know whether to confess or keep things to herself. She wanted Luc very badly. She wanted to fling herself into his arms and cry.

'He was right there, Uncle Peter,' she managed tremulously.

'Well, he'd gone when I got out there,' Peter muttered furiously. 'You've got to admit that, Amy.'

'No. You were as close to him as you are to me at this moment. I don't know why you didn't see him.'

'Now look, love,' Peter said in an exasperated manner. 'There's nothing wrong with my eyesight. I don't wear spectacles or anything. I'm in good shape. I came when you called and I chased the damned man, but I might just as well have been chasing a shadow.'

Amy nodded glumly. He was in good shape and she knew it. It wasn't long since she'd been thinking to herself that he looked younger than plenty of men half his age. She knew there was nothing wrong with his eyes either; that was what frightened her so much.

He should have seen the man and he'd been angry enough to carry out his threat and shoot. But he had not seen anyone at all. Maybe he hadn't seen anyone because nobody had been there? She had just been seeing things, inventing her own nightmares.

Deep inside, her mind protested at the thought, but Peter hadn't seen anyone. Peter was the only one who had ever come close to the man, the only one besides herself who could have seen him.

Her mind was flying around inside like a wild bird, trying to explain it, but there was really nothing to explain. Peter had been close enough to touch the man but Peter hadn't seen him. And even while he'd been there, standing almost next to him, Amy had seen the man herself.

'I'm sorry, Uncle Peter,' Amy murmured unsteadily. 'I agree. He got away.'

'He won't get away next time,' Peter growled.

He carefully checked the door again.

'I'm putting the alarm on,' he told her. 'Don't usually bother with it, but this time I think we need it.'

He went to the neat little box on the wall and fixed the alarm and then they both went upstairs. By the time the alarm buzzer had finished sounding Amy was in her room and alone again.

She sat down on the edge of the bed and now she didn't know what to think. She went to look through the window again but the man wasn't there. Her mind wasn't conjuring him up at this particular time. Her mind had already done its damage. Amy felt tears welling up in her eyes.

She wanted Luc; she wanted him very badly. She wanted to tell him about this but what would she say?

CHAPTER 13

Amy left as soon as it was light. She didn't feel like staying to have breakfast with Uncle Peter. She was too agitated and the only thing she could think of was seeing Luc as quickly as possible, even though she dreaded what he would think.

Peter was downstairs drinking coffee and looking very much the worse for wear after his disturbed night. As soon as he saw her he jumped up.

'I'll get you some coffee.'

'No, thanks.' Amy was very firm. She was pale and shaken but she knew she had to get out of the house. 'I'm going back home. I have to get changed for work in any case.'

'You don't exactly look fit for work,' Peter pointed out, eyeing her worriedly.

Amy shook her head and pressed her lips together. Any more words and she would burst into tears.

'I can't just stay away from work because I had a fright.'

'I couldn't see the damned man,' Peter snapped as he sat back at the table and put his head in his hands. 'I feel as if I've been up all night.'

Amy didn't mention that in fact she *had* been up all night. She had not been able to go back to sleep.

'Sooner or later somebody is going to get him, Amy,' Peter assured her.

If he exists, Amy thought to herself, and although Peter was saying these words the way he was glancing at her belied all he said. He had been in the garden, under the light. He had even taken a gun with him and there had been nobody at all.

With her own eyes she had seen Peter as close to the man as she was close to Peter now, and he had seen nothing. It proved everything she had been worrying about for ages. She was imagining this man.

She drove off as quickly as she could and this time she didn't glance into the hedge as she passed. She knew there was going to be nobody there. She didn't care either if anyone was watching her when she pulled up outside her own house in Luc's car.

She took her keys out and unlocked the door and then dived inside as if a devil pursued her. Luc was sitting in the kitchen. He had obviously been up all night and when she went in he jumped to his feet.

'What happened?' he asked quickly. 'Why are you here at this time in the morning.'

'Because we're wasting our time,' Amy assured him in a quiet, final voice. She put her bag and keys down and stood with her hands clenched at her sides. She was tense enough to snap in two and he could see it.

'Sit down and tell me,' he ordered.

'Last night the man came,' Amy said, making herself speak very slowly and carefully. 'Uncle

Peter's house has floodlights all round it, lights he keeps on all night. It's a very large garden, just as large as Aunt Celia's, and like in Aunt Celia's garden there's a wall round the property. There are a lot of ornamental bushes, trees – plenty of cover. I felt he was there. It woke me as usual. I saw him by the wall, but this time he actually stepped forward.'

'To look up at your window?' Luc asked.

'No, he wasn't looking up. He was scanning the ground as if he'd dropped something.'

Luc said nothing but he nodded his head. 'Carry on,' he ordered.

'I couldn't believe how bold he was being but obviously he wanted me to know he was there. Somehow he knows that his presence wakes me.' Amy looked down at her clenched hands, feeling incapable of continuing, but she pulled herself together rapidly. 'This time I wasn't alone. Peter was there and I suddenly realized it. I ran along and woke him up.'

'What happened then?' Luc asked.

'He was furious. He's got a shotgun. He went tearing downstairs in his dressing gown, pulled the shotgun out of the cupboard and went rushing outside to shoot the man.'

'And?' Luc enquired softly.

'I didn't want him to kill the man so I ran after him down the stairs, calling to him, but he didn't take any notice. He was just saying he would get the man this time. He raced across the lawn in the direction of the man and he couldn't see him at all.'

Amy stopped and stared up at Luc, who was watching her intently, his dark eyes holding hers.

'Your uncle couldn't see him?'

'That's why I told you we're wasting our time,' Amy explained tremulously. 'The man wasn't there.'

'He had gone?'

'No. I could still see him. He was still there but he didn't even bother to lift his head. It was as if Uncle Peter didn't exist and Uncle Peter went past him, still searching, as if the man wasn't there either. That's understandable, of course, because he wasn't there at all. I imagined it.'

'Don't jump to conclusions,' Luc ordered tersely. 'Tell me exactly what happened next.'

'Peter ended up about as close to the man as I am to you,' Amy explained, taking a deep breath. 'I shouted to him that the man was there. I couldn't believe why Peter couldn't see him in the bright lights. I could have seen his face clearly if he hadn't had that damned hat on.'

'Shh,' Luc murmured soothingly. 'Don't get upset. Just tell me everything.'

'Peter walked right past the man to go and search in the bushes. He was stamping about, swearing and furious. I turned to shout to him again and when I turned back the man had disappeared. Peter came back later and said the man had obviously got away. But, Luc! He could have reached out and touched him.' Amy turned away miserably and stared out of the window. 'The man doesn't exist. He's merely in my imagination.'

'We will have breakfast,' Luc ordered quietly, and Amy snapped at him, turning further away.

'I don't want any breakfast.'

'After breakfast we will discuss the next part of the plan,' he continued, acting as if she had never spoken at all.

'What's the point of having a plan? Haven't you been listening, Luc? The man does not exist!'

'You've brought my car round to the front,' Luc noticed, frowning out of the window.'

'What the hell does it matter?' Amy raged, taking her shock and misery out on Luc. 'Nobody's going to see it because nobody is there!'

'Possibly,' Luc murmured in a manner that irritated her even more.

'What do you mean – possibly?'

'I'm not prepared to tell you yet. My plan isn't finished and I intend to work it through to the end.'

'It's a waste of time,' Amy muttered in exasperation. 'Maybe I ought to be going for psychiatric treatment instead of following your plan.'

'We will cross that bridge *if* we come to it,' Luc informed her, and Amy was dumbfounded.

'After all I've just told you, do you still believe that I actually see the man?'

Luc was making coffee and he turned to stare at her over his shoulder, the dark eyes glittering with intelligence. 'Yes, I do,' he said firmly.

'Then what's the matter with Uncle Peter?' Amy was almost open-mouthed.

Luc's lips quirked coldly and he turned away.

'Perhaps it was a trick of the light,' he murmured sardonically.

Amy didn't know what to say. The whole situation was mad as far as she was concerned. Failing that, *she* was mad.

Luc made toast, with no attempt to try for the English breakfast, and they ate in silence, Amy's eyes never leaving her plate. From time to time Luc glanced up at her but he said nothing. He was thinking. She looked very shaken, almost as bad as she had done during the week before she had told him her problems. She looked almost as tired too. It was partly shock. He realized that the biggest shock was that now she doubted herself.

They both went to work, and when it was getting round to lunchtime, Luc went home to sleep. He called in to tell her but she didn't even take her eyes from her computer, and he walked across to her, swinging her around in her chair and leaning over her.

'Look, *ma petite*,' he said. 'Don't think about it. Work with your computers. Tonight we will think about it.'

'There's nothing to think about,' she said in a dull voice, but Luc's hand tilted her downcast face.

'Don't doubt me so much,'

'I'm not doubting you, Luc,' Amy said quietly. 'I'm doubting myself.'

'You think I am unintelligent?' he enquired with a definite look of arrogance.

'No. It's just that I think I'm probably mad and I'm wondering what caused the madness.'

His hand came up and lightly touched her cheek. 'I would have spotted your madness right from the beginning. Tonight I think you may go to your uncle Peter's in your own car.'

But later, when the time came for her to leave and spend the night at Peter's house, Amy felt on the edge of panic. She was safe in her own house with Luc, and he believed in her. The night she had spent at Peter's had been too traumatic. It had been shocking enough to see the man and know that once again he had followed her, known every move she made, but the fact that Peter hadn't been able to see him had hit Amy badly. Her self-confidence was gone completely.

When Luc urged her to set off to her uncle Peter's house, Amy suddenly burst into tears. She just couldn't hold them back and Luc was horrified.

'Don't, Amy! Don't cry, *chérie*,' he begged urgently, coming to her and taking her tightly into his arms. 'Tonight I will get him. I promise you.'

'I can't, Luc,' Amy sobbed. 'I can't face it again, not so soon. Just let me have this one night off.'

Luc rocked her in his arms, burying his face in her hair.

'Oh, Amy,' he sighed. 'I don't want you to go anywhere. I want to be here with you. But we have to catch this man who stalks you. You must be allowed to return to a normal life.'

'I'm normal when I'm with you,' Amy wept, looking up with mournful tear-filled eyes. 'I feel normal and safe with you.'

'Nothing is normal at the moment,' Luc assured her in a driven voice. 'I do not want to go away from you or to send you away for the night. But when this is over, you will probably feel differently about me.'

That stopped Amy's tears, and she looked up into the dark eyes that watched her with a burning intensity.

'I'll never feel differently about you,' she whispered shakily. 'If you think that when this is over I'll stop wanting to be with you . . .'

'I *do* think that, *ma petite*,' Luc assured her unevenly. 'I would not take advantage of you at a time like this.'

'The man might kill me,' Amy reminded him seriously. 'If he does then I'll never have known what it would be like with you.'

'Don't say that!' Luc ordered savagely. 'He will not kill you.'

'Just give me this one night away from the fear,' Amy whispered, winding her arms slowly round his neck. 'Stay with me, Luc. Stay with me all night.'

'*Dieu!* If you knew how much I want to.'

Luc looked down at her, his whole body aroused by her pleading. She was making no attempt to disguise what she meant. It was all there on her face. Amy slowly closed her eyes and leaned closer, her lips parted, begging to be kissed, and everything inside Luc snapped as he brought her tightly against him and claimed her beseeching lips with his own.

Once again she seemed to burst into flame, tightening her arms around his neck, kissing him back in a wild, abandoned way as his hands began to move over her possessively. Everywhere he touched her seemed to burn, and Amy moaned into his mouth as her legs went weak. She almost collapsed against him and Luc buried his face in her neck, kissing the tender spot near her shoulder, his action sending a shuddering thrill through her that reached her toes.

He stroked his hand over her breast and felt the swelling ripeness, and although he knew that it was partly fear of the night that held her to him, he also knew he could not let her go this time.

'Not here,' he said thickly, sweeping her into his arms and making for the door and the stairs. 'We will go to bed while I am still able to move.'

He had felt the fear in her before, known it for what it was when he had kissed her, but if she feared anything now it was not the thought of making love with him. When he placed her on the bed she gave a small, incoherent cry, trying to hold him close to her, and Luc moved her arms from around his neck, his breathing uneven as he began to undress her.

If she was going to remember Somerfield he knew it would be now, and he half expected it, but she knelt up and began to frantically unbutton his shirt as he pulled his light sweater off and let it drop to the floor. He allowed her to continue, his hands stroking her, his lips dropping light, teasing kisses on her face and neck.

When they were both undressed he pulled her close to him, letting her feel the magic of her skin against his. Once again Amy's arms were wound tightly around his neck and he was free to press her body close, to allow his hands to roam over her. He waited until she was almost sobbing with pleasure and excitement and then he lowered her to the bed and came down with her, his strong thigh over her legs, holding her captive.

'Luc!' Amy tossed beneath him and his hand cupped her breast, taking it into the warmth of his mouth. He could tell by her reaction that this was new to her. She threw her head back and gave a small feminine cry that seemed to flash through Luc like electricity through a wire, arousing his whole body into heated impatience.

He tried to contain raw desire. He had never before in his life felt on the very edge of losing control. His hand stroked her legs, moving higher until he could feel the heat radiating from her feminine centre. It was more than enough to drive him on. His fingers covered her warmth and then slid carefully inside her.

Amy gasped at the unexpected intimate contact. She tensed for a second and then moved against his hand, begging for more, and Luc's lips captured her own fiercely as he hung on to his own control by sheer will power.

He stroked her more urgently, feeling the honeyed moisture on his hand, and Amy tossed frantically, her head moving wildly on the pillows.

'Luc!' she ordered in a trembling voice, and he knew it had to be now. She was ready for him and he was so aroused it was deeply painful, a growing torment.

He felt her body begin to ripple in excited spasms and he came into her with an almost desperate need. He groaned as he felt her silken warmth close tightly around him and for a second he felt only satisfaction.

Amy felt pain, brief but very real, and unexpectedly her pleasure seemed to be suspended in time, her body tensed for rejection. But not for long. The feelings were too great – so great that she shrieked with the joy of it.

Luc's reaction was very different. With him, too, there was a heartbeat of time when everything stopped, but he was too committed to leave her. The rhythm continued and it was only later, when his breathing had returned to normal and he was able to look down into her flushed, enchanted face, that Luc got out the words that seemed to be burning into his brain.

'You were a *virgin*!'

Amy looked up at him shyly, her eyes half hidden by thick lashes, her flushed cheeks tinted with even more colour.

'Does it matter?' she asked anxiously.

Luc's dark eyes seemed to be piercing her soul. She couldn't tell whether he was angry or not. He just stared down at her and Amy wriggled uneasily.

'Keep still!' Luc ordered sharply as her surreptitious movements tightened his body. In a very little while he would want her all over again, and he knew it was highly unlikely that she would enjoy it a second time so soon after this unexpected initiation.

Amy went as still as a mouse would be when watching him from a very unsafe corner, and the sight of her guilty, timid look made Luc suddenly want to shout with laughter. This had been a trip on the pink cloud beyond all his expectations. As far as he could tell she had not given one thought to the consequences when she had begged to stay with him all night.

He slowly relaxed, but his eyes never left hers as he gently stroked her hair back from her face.

'If I had known,' he told her quietly. 'I would have been more careful with you, more tender.'

'I thought you were,' Amy informed him, with such a look of innocent puzzlement that Luc smiled and covered her mouth warmly with his lips. He was relieved to feel her relax too. He felt as if he had been given the earth.

'Did I hurt you very much?' he asked huskily as he moved from her and folded her in his arms, holding her tightly against him.

'Only for about half a second,' Amy decided after a small time of consideration. 'It was more of a surprise than anything else.'

'I know what you mean,' Luc agreed ruefully. He drew his head back and looked down at her. 'I thought . . . Amy, you were involved with Somerfield.'

'Oh, not like that,' she said, looking up at him with shocked eyes. 'I just went out with him, that's all.'

Luc knew without doubt that that *was* all. He had found out in the most amazing way possible.

'I imagined that you – lived with him,' he told

her, with a slight feeling of apprehension as to how she would take this piece of speculation. Amy was quite capable of unusual reactions.

'Of course I didn't *live* with him,' she told him firmly. 'He thought it would be a good idea but I didn't. In fact,' she added in her normal conspiratorial manner, her voice lowered, 'by that time I'd come to my senses and just wanted to see the back of him really. But he was difficult to get rid of, a bit frightening. He could be quite rough.'

'How *did* you get rid of him?' Luc enquired. It almost hurt him to hear that someone had treated her roughly. He also had the suspicion that he was being drawn into a very unreal world. He didn't actually want to talk about Somerfield at this particular time. He was still stunned at the way Amy had given herself to him so willingly, so completely. He wanted to think about that. But apparently Amy was deeply into her subject at the moment.

She didn't answer his question and he looked down at her and repeated it.

'How did you manage to get rid of him, *ma petite*?'

Amy blushed.

'Well,' she murmured, 'he tried to do – *that*.'

'What?' Luc asked, dumbfounded.

'That,' she explained with uneasy embarrassment.

'Ah! He tried to make love to you.'

'It wasn't love,' Amy stated emphatically. 'I didn't like the idea at all.'

'I am amazed he was willing to stop,' Luc muttered, glaring ferociously at the ceiling when he thought of it.

'Oh, he wasn't,' Amy explained in a scandalized voice. 'It was very unpleasant. I had to hit him with a lamp. Then I pushed him outside and locked the door.'

Luc could just imagine it. He grinned like an idiot.

'That would undoubtably have dampened his ardour.'

'Well, he had his car there,' Amy pointed out huffily. 'It wasn't as if he had to walk anywhere, was it?'

'No. You are quite right,' Luc agreed, still grinning.

'I needed a new lampshade, though,' Amy mused in a grieved voice. 'It took ages to find another one to match. Aunt Celia had given me that lamp and she didn't believe my explanation about the way it had been squashed up.'

'What did you tell her? Did you tell her about Somerfield?'

'Heavens, no!' Amy exclaimed, quite shocked. 'Aunt Celia never knew about Eric. She would never have approved. I just told her that I sat on the lamp by accident.'

Luc tried to suppress his laughter but it was difficult. When he had made love to women in the past there had either been awkwardness or very unreal romantic drama afterwards. Amy was profoundly engrossed in the dire tale of the squashed lampshade.

She was lying naked in his arms, she had just lost her virginity, somewhere outside in the night a man was stalking her, and yet, she was peaceful, comfortable and almost unreal.

But she was happiness, Luc realized, softly feminine and trusting. He turned to her, pulling her tightly against him. He felt protective, possessive, and she came softly and willingly at once. It suddenly occurred to him that he couldn't imagine being without her. When he started to kiss her again she was instantly back to excited pleasure. So warm and giving, his Computer Person.

'Amy,' he said achingly into her mouth. 'Amy, *chérie*.'

She wound her arms around his neck again. He could feel her breasts against the hardness of his chest. His knee moved between her legs and all she did was press herself closer.

'I want you again, *ma petite*,' he murmured thickly, afraid now to hurt her. But she burrowed into his warmth, her fingers moving in the thick darkness of his hair.

'Oh, Luc!' she whispered. 'Yes, please.'

When he moved over her she was yielding, silken, warm, innocently sensuous.

'You will kill me,' Luc gasped as he came into her. 'I will die of desire. But I will die happily with you in my arms.'

To his great joy she was just the same again, sweetly demanding, going wild in his arms, behaving as if she was part of him. And even when they fell into a satisfied, exhausted sleep, Luc kept her wrapped tightly against him.

The man came in the night. Even though Amy was exhausted and content, the awareness of the dark, menacing presence brought her to wakefulness.

She was still in Luc's arms, and the temptation to stay there and not move was almost overwhelming. She was safe. A whole crowd of stalkers could be outside but she was safe with Luc. The man had to be caught, though, and what better time than now, when Luc was with her?

Amy moved carefully from Luc's possessive embrace, slid from the bed and picked up her robe, slipping it on as she made her way quietly to the window. When she looked through the curtains she could see the man clearly. He was as he had been from the first, very visible but unrecognizable.

For a few seconds, Amy watched him. She was not afraid. She only had to turn her head and she could also see Luc. It was safe enough to study the unknown watcher but she was no nearer than ever to knowing who he really was.

Amy decided to risk going across to wake Luc. She was faintly scared that when Luc got up and came to look there would be nobody for him to see, but she didn't want to call to him. She was, she realized, becoming obsessed with stealth.

Luc stirred before she had even left the window. '*Chérie?*' he murmured sleepily. '*Viens, ma belle.* What are you doing away from me?'

'He's here, Luc!' Amy hissed urgently. 'The man came. He's outside now, watching.'

Amy wondered if Luc would be awake enough to take in what she was saying, but she should have known better. He surged straight out of bed, naked and furious, and the words had barely left her mouth before he was beside her, peering into the street.

For a second he stared down and Amy stood anxiously by.

'Can you see him, Luc?' she asked worriedly, half expecting another episode like the one she had endured at Uncle Peter's house.

'Oh, yes. I can see him,' Luc assured her through furiously clenched teeth. 'Tall, dark and bulky. *Alors!* I will have him!'

He began to pull on his clothes, searching in the dim light for the things he had discarded wildly when they came to bed, and Amy started to help.

'No!' he ordered. 'Watch him. If he's going to disappear I want to know where he goes.'

'Be careful. He might have a knife,' Amy warned as Luc made for the bedroom door.

'He might have a broken nose,' Luc snarled. 'And with any luck it will be my privilege to present it to him.'

Amy turned back to watch. The man was still there. She actually found herself smiling. Bulky or not, the man didn't stand a chance against Luc. Luc was her lethal weapon. Luc was fast and silent.

But Luc was anything but silent. As he raced into the kitchen towards the door, the alarm went off. It almost made Amy jump out of her skin, and she bit into her lip guiltily as she ran to turn it off. Even in her sensually confused state when they had come to bed, she had reached out and switched on the alarm as she was carried past it. The action was programmed into her brain by now.

The din was stilled at once as she reached the control box, but for a few seconds there had been enough noise to warn anyone listening.

She heard Luc wrench the door open and then his normal, furious exclamation.

'*Merde!*'

Amy knew why. The man would have gone and it was her fault.

She went downstairs to look for herself and stood at the open door as Luc searched the street. He was prowling along the opposite side of the road, hunting, and Amy gave a quick shiver that was nothing to do with the cooler night air. Luc was going to be livid. He was going to shout at her and really she couldn't blame him. She was dreading what he would say. She almost felt like locking him out.

By the time he came back she was really cold, her bare feet feeling icy on the step, and as Luc came up to her she couldn't think of one thing to say to excuse herself. An apology seemed to be the only way out of this and she apologized immediately, before he could roar at her.

'I'm sorry, Luc,' she murmured, thoroughly subdued.

He just took her arm and led her back into the warmth of the house, closing and locking the door behind them.

'I forgot about the alarm,' she ventured when he said nothing. There was still no reply and Amy began to feel panic-stricken. 'I'll make you some tea,' she offered shakily.

Luc just swung her up into his arms and marched off up the stairs, and Amy dared not even think about putting the alarm on this time. He dropped her down in the middle of the bed and stood watching her as he stripped off his clothes.

It frightened her to death. He was fully aroused and she knew it was something to do with anger. Amy didn't have much idea of what made a man get like that but she assumed that anger could do it just as well as desire. She watched with terrified eyes, and all Luc did was stare down at her grimly until the last of his clothes hit the floor. She tried to shrink away as he came down to her, but he reached out one strong hand and fastened it around her wrist before she could consider any good method of escape.

He lay half over her, staring into her wide, anxious eyes, and then he leaned over and kissed her so tenderly that she felt like crying.

'*Idiote*,' he said softly. 'Only you would arrange to warn the enemy with bells and sirens. You are a delicious madwoman.'

'I did it automatically, Luc,' Amy told him worriedly. 'It's something I do all the time, and in the excitement I forgot.'

He grinned down at her as he proceeded to get the robe free of her body and drop it over the side of the bed.

'I will now show you something else you can do all the time,' he promised. 'But not automatically, please.'

Luc pulled her gently towards him and Amy gave a shuddering sigh of pleasure and relief.

'I thought you would be furious.'

'I was, but then I realized that it was only to be expected from a Computer Person such as yourself.'

'My feet are cold,' Amy complained as his arms closed around her.

'I will kiss them better.' He slid lower in the bed and lifted one foot at a time to his lips, kissing her toes and nibbling at them until she forgot anything but excitement. By the time he had reached her knees, Amy had also forgotten about the man outside.

'Now,' he said thickly as he moved over her, 'You can reward me for my useless efforts out in the cold night air.'

Amy wrapped her arms round his neck and opened like a flower to his demands. Once again she was warm and giving, and Luc groaned against her lips.

'Nothing about you is automatic, *ma petite*,' he murmured huskily. 'You are like the sunshine.'

Later, as they lay in each other's arms, Luc stroked back her hair and said aloud the thing that was on both their minds.

'He was there, Amy. I saw him. Exactly as you have always described him.'

'So it isn't imagination,' Amy whispered. 'Oh, Luc, I'm so glad you saw him at last. I can't think why Uncle Peter didn't.'

Luc was silent for a few minutes, and then he said, 'Sometimes a man will not admit to any faults in his masculine make-up. It is pride. Perhaps when he is alone he needs to wear spectacles but refuses to allow anyone else to know. It would not be unusual.'

'He's quite vain,' Amy mused. 'He likes younger women around him.'

'Then we probably have the explanation,' Luc told her. 'He is grimly hanging on to his youth.'

'How sad,' Amy said, yawning sleepily.

Luc folded her more closely against him, lulling her to sleep. His eyes were still wide open, narrowed and thoughtful. He was not thinking sad thoughts. He was working out the final stages of his plan and wondering how far he could allow Amy to take the risk that would most certainly be there. The thing was inevitable, and sooner rather than later. He wondered if a night in his arms would have given her courage.

During the next day, Amy felt as if she was walking on air. She hardly saw work. The computers sat there as usual, but all she could think of was Luc. There was this tremendous desire to keep turning her head to look at him, but, apart from a few times when the need to see him got the better of her good sense, she sat at her machines and tried to be normal.

Nothing was really normal at all. She knew she loved Luc and the thought had been singing through her head since she had got up and made breakfast. It had been wonderful to talk to him, to sit opposite him at the table, to look up and see the dark eyes on her, smiling, warm, no longer icily cold.

She knew he would be there tonight too, and she planned to cook an elaborate meal with candles on the table. She told herself dreamily that she was living with Luc. She had a lover, a French lover, and beyond that she dared not think. She would not allow the thought that he would one day leave her and go back to Paris to even take shape in her mind. She would live for now. She would live happily.

Amy decided to go out for lunch and do some shopping at the same time. Luc had disappeared and she could not wait for him in any case. In spite of what had happened she was always overwhelmed by the knowledge that he was the boss. He ruled the place and he was sometimes so superior that she didn't quite know how to speak to him.

She put the thought of anyone following her right out of her head. She wanted to shop for dinner tonight and she wanted to make the whole thing magical. She would buy some silver candles. She was too happy to bother about any man following her.

And, oddly enough, she did not get the feeling of being observed. She did her shopping and put the things in her car and then went to eat. It seemed only natural to have lunch where she had first talked to Luc and, after taking the escalator to the top floor restaurant, Amy ordered her meal and then chose a very secluded corner where a large potted palm kept her almost completely hidden from view.

If the man was following her at the moment, she would spot him if he came in. She very much doubted that he would follow her into this place, but it was impossible to tell what he would do next and she wanted to know who it was.

Her meal was served and Amy glanced up from time to time to scan the restaurant for any sign that she was under observation. Nobody had followed her. There was no man dogging her footsteps.

The man who came in a few minutes later was Luc. He didn't look round. He knew exactly where he was going and Amy, who had started to rise with a smile of welcome on her face, sank back to her seat in her little hiding place when Luc walked forward to the woman he had obviously arranged to meet here.

Amy felt as if the bottom had dropped out of the world. She knew that Luc would never have expected her to be here. Normally she ate in the canteen at work, and Luc did too. It was only today, when she had been planning a romantic meal for two, that she had decided to eat out. Otherwise she would never have known that Luc was meeting this woman.

One look at her told Amy all she needed to know. The woman was French and beautiful. Amy shrank back behind her potted palm. It was impossible to escape, impossible not to be in the position of spying on them. As Luc walked forward the woman leapt up, smiling and happy to see him. She cupped his face in her hands and kissed him lingeringly on the mouth. Amy left her lunch and fled while Luc was still occupied.

'I know this is unusual,' Veronique said huskily, 'but I had to see you, Luc, *chéri*.'

It was all Luc could do to stop his normal black frown surfacing. He had wanted to take Amy out to lunch, but the call from Veronique had stopped him in his tracks. She had been phoning from the station and he had been hard pressed not to snap at her. Guilt had kept him silent. He should have spoken to Veronique ages ago, because he had known deep down how he felt about Amy for a long time.

Before he had the chance to speak, Veronique was explaining her lightning visit to England.

'I'm getting married, Luc,' she said a trifle theatrically. 'I'm sorry I didn't tell you,' she continued, when Luc just stared at her in stunned silence, 'and I know this is going to hurt you, but I've been seeing somebody for quite a while now.'

'Why shouldn't you?' Luc asked in a dazed voice. 'We didn't have any real – arrangement.'

'Oh, Luc! You're so generous. *I* never felt that we had any arrangement, but I know you did. It's so like you to be noble.'

'I am not noble,' Luc corrected. He couldn't help comparing her to Amy. Veronique was so dramatic. Amy was so wonderfully, gloriously mad.

He thought about her tale of the squashed lampshade and he knew that if Somerfield walked in here right now he would not be able to stop himself from roaring with laughter at just the sight of the vanquished Eric. His lips quirked and his eyes gleamed with amusement.

'Oh, Luc, *chéri*. Don't smile that little sad smile. I know this is hurting you.'

'Not at all,' Luc managed in a slightly choked voice. Holding in a grin was something of a problem but he managed it. 'I'm not at all hurt, Veronique,' he said. 'Don't let thoughts of my distress worry you. Marry your hero and do it with my blessing.'

'You don't mind, Luc?' Veronique asked suspiciously.

'I am seeing someone myself,' he confessed. 'I had intended to tell you before now, so you see there is no cause for regret.'

Her face froze over for a second.

'Seeing someone?' She looked as if she couldn't believe it.

'She is English,' Luc said quietly.

Veronique made a great effort to pull herself together and Luc could see that she felt somewhat out-manoeuvred. Her dramatic visit had rather fallen flat. Veronique wanted one husband and one ex-lover fighting over her. Amy did not have an ex-lover. She was his very own.

'So all is well,' Veronique murmured, with a very suspicious glance at him in case he was quietly nursing a broken heart.

'Very well,' Luc assured her. 'I feel rather guilty that you were able to tell me your news before I had acquainted you with mine. I had every intention of calling on you when we were in Paris, but I'm afraid a crisis arose that needed us both back in England quickly.'

'You took her to Paris?'

'A little while ago. I would have told you then. I intended to tell you then. But as it turned out, I could not. The noble behaviour is all yours, Veronique. I hope you will be happy.'

They had lunch and then Veronique insisted on flying off at great speed. She intended to do some shopping in London for her wedding.

Luc was glad. He didn't want to subject Amy to Veronique's forceful personality. He didn't quite know how Amy would take to it. Amy was utterly unpredictable.

If she met Veronique it would mean that he would have to alter his plans, because he didn't want Amy to be upset. He suspected that she would be facing enough upset as it was, and she would be facing it very soon – perhaps this coming night.

Amy tried not to look when Luc came back into the office. She had been dreading the thought of him bringing the woman back with him, dreading that she would have to look once again at the beautiful blonde. The happiness of a night spent with Luc was shattered.

He didn't bring the woman with him, though, and he didn't come in to speak to her. Amy felt devastated, utterly forlorn and alone. He seemed to be frantically busy, and soon after he came back there were lengthy telephone calls. She could faintly hear him speaking rapidly, sometimes in French and sometimes in English. Luc's world had not changed. Only her own world was different.

CHAPTER 14

It was not until well into the afternoon that Luc came in to speak to her. He carefully closed her door behind him and, instead of coming over to her, sat on the edge of the desk that held Jim in his position of authority. Amy tensed up, wondering what he was going to say.

'I have to go to Paris immediately after work.'

Amy had been expecting that perhaps he would speak of the previous night, or even that he would tell her about the woman. She had not expected any mention of his leaving so abruptly.

'I see.' Amy looked away and tried to take it lightly but it was hard.

'Only for this one night,' Luc assured her. 'During tomorrow I will come back. I promise.' He watched her with narrowed eyes. Something was wrong. Amy had distanced herself. The warm, willing person of last night was gone and he had no idea why. He gave some swift consideration to changing his plans but decided against it. 'I'm sorry, Amy. I know this is rather sudden – ' he began.

'It's all right,' Amy interrupted quickly, making herself meet his intense eyes. 'I have the alarm, after all. Maybe we frightened him off last night.'

'I want you to go to your uncle Peter's house tonight,' Luc ordered. 'Your uncle may be hiding bad eyesight but he is there all the same. I do not want to think that you will be alone when I'm away.'

Amy nodded. Right at this moment the man in black didn't seem important. The future seemed empty. Of course Luc would be going to Paris with the woman.

'You will promise me,' Luc insisted. 'You will stay with your uncle tonight.'

'All right,' Amy agreed. 'I can't say I'm looking forward to it, but it's better than being alone.'

'Go before it gets too dark. Have dinner with him,' Luc suggested.

'I'll ring him now.'

'Good. I will leave as soon as I can.' Luc went to the door and he didn't kiss her goodbye. Of course, he wouldn't want to now. There was the glamorous woman from Paris here. Amy wondered if she was staying in Luc's flat to wait for him.

After a while she phoned Peter and had to pretend great joy when he insisted that she come earlier and have dinner with him. He simply volunteered to take her out for a meal. Amy didn't need to mention it and she felt like an ungrateful wretch.

She felt that she was using Peter, putting on his good nature, tricking him. She only wanted to go out with Luc. She only wanted to be anywhere

336

with Luc. But she knew that the brief happiness was over. So far she hadn't even thought beyond that.

Later she knew she would be angry, but, even so, she also knew that she had encouraged the lovemaking, almost pleaded for it, and Luc was a man. What had she expected? That he would declare undying love? Aunt Celia had been right. She knew nothing about men; she knew nothing about anything except her computers.

Later in the afternoon she had to consult Luc, but when she went to his office to ask where he was, the irritating secretary informed her that Mr Martell had already left for Paris. He hadn't even said goodbye. Amy walked out blindly. She felt as if he had never given her one thought. He was probably contemptuous about her willing surrender. She had never felt so bleakly unhappy in her whole life.

Amy arrived at Peter's early. She was dressed up for going out but she had little interest in it. She had been only too glad to get out of her own house. In her mind, the bijou residence was finished, over and done with. She would never be able to stay there and not think of Luc.

Her mind wouldn't stop searching for him, imagining him in Paris. She painted pictures of him in her head, pictures that included his mother and father, but she couldn't paint in the woman, the glamorous woman who had kissed Luc so openly and so possessively.

When she arrived at Peter's house he seemed to be quite stunned, and stared at her almost vaguely for a minute. He was acting just like somebody who had been hiding something and she watched him wryly, wondering if he had just been dispatching one of his women friends.

It only added to her feeling of guilt. She would have to spend the evening pretending. No good would come of it because even if she was safe here she could not go on messing up Peter's life, and as soon as she went back to her own house to sleep the man would come back. And now she didn't even have Luc. She would never again let Luc help her. He didn't belong to her. He belonged to another woman.

'Remember me?' she asked with unwilling amusement when Peter kept her standing on the step and stared at her in silence.

It brought him rapidly to his senses.

'Oh! Amy! I don't know what came over me.'

To her astonishment he went a dull red and looked extremely upset. He stepped aside and Amy walked into the hall, but even then he seemed distracted, uneasy.

'I hadn't forgotten you were coming,' he assured her hastily when she looked at him with some surprise.

'Are you all right?' Amy asked. He certainly didn't look all right. He looked as if he had been shocked by something and she felt uneasy. Maybe it was her fault. Maybe her problems were upsetting his easy, casual life to such an extent that he was feeling ill.

'I could go back and stay at home tonight,' she volunteered, and that suggestion seemed to pull

338

him back to his right mind because he took her arm firmly, marching her into the drawing room.

'What rubbish!' he said briskly. 'We're going out for dinner and then you'll stay here. You've brought your things, I hope?'

'Everything I need,' Amy assured him.

'Right. We'll get off in a minute, then. I'll just have a quick drink.'

Amy frowned as he walked off. Peter never needed a quick drink. He wasn't that sort of man. There was definitely something wrong. Perhaps he would tell her later. She mused about it and realized that for a while now Peter had not exactly been himself. A lot of his easygoing *bonhomie* had vanished. It had actually vanished even before Aunt Celia's funeral.

Perhaps he was ill and saying nothing. It was possible, taking into consideration his inability to see the man who had been outside the house. Maybe Luc had been wrong when he had surmised that Peter was hiding his need for spectacles. Maybe there was something much more serious?

'I'll drive,' she stated firmly when Peter was finally ready to leave. If he needed spectacles she would not risk having him drive, and in any case the chance to sit quietly while she did the driving would help him to relax because he was certainly on edge.

Amy frowned at the road. If that man came tonight the idea of having Peter tackle him did not now seem too good. Suppose he had heart trouble, like Aunt Celia? A shock might kill him. She needed Luc.

Tears came into her eyes immediately. She couldn't have Luc. He didn't belong to her at all. She would never be able to be close to Luc ever again.

During the meal Peter relaxed, but not before he had behaved in a clumsy, bizarre way that was utterly alien to his usual suave ways. He knocked Amy's drink over and the tablecloth had to be changed even before the meal was served. He was hot with embarrassment, another first for him.

'God!' he muttered. 'I don't know what's wrong with me tonight. Here, have my drink, Amy.' He was so shaken by his own clumsiness that Amy took his drink without protest and made light of the whole situation. It took a while to get him settled and she was glad when the meal duly arrived and quiet reigned again.

'Seen any more of your stalker?' he asked as they ate.

'From time to time,' Amy told him cagily. She didn't want to talk about it for two reasons. One, she didn't want him upset any further, and two, she didn't want to think about Luc.

'It's a funny business,' Peter mused. 'I could have caught the damned chap that other time, if I'd seen him.'

'It was a pity he got away,' Amy agreed.

'You were sure you'd seen him,' Peter reminded her. 'Can't think why I didn't.'

Amy knew what he was suggesting. He still thought it was her imagination. She could have told him triumphantly that Luc had seen the man but she kept silent. Luc was still her secret and he had warned her to say nothing to anyone. She knew it would have been all right to tell Peter but she hesitated. Peter was behaving oddly.

To have it confirmed that the man existed would scare him, perhaps, and already he looked as if he was having difficulty in keeping himself in one secure piece. She sighed and got on with her meal. Things were getting more complicated by the day – and more miserable. The police should be dealing with her problem, but nobody believed her except Luc.

She missed him. She missed him terribly. And there was the rest of her life to remember how much she loved him and how little he cared.

'Hetherington should never have bothered you with that will business so soon after Celia's funeral,' Peter suddenly muttered. 'Damned upsetting. It could have waited.'

'Probably,' Amy agreed quietly, knowing exactly where his mind was taking him. 'Anyway, it doesn't matter. The whole thing is over now. I signed the will ages ago.'

Peter glanced up at her gloomily.

'Too late to change anything now.'

'What's to change?' Amy enquired drily. 'I only have you.' She had thought that she might have Luc, but that dream was ended.

Peter reached over and patted her hand in a kindly way.

'Never mind, love,' he said quietly. 'I expect it will all be over soon. I'm sorry, you know.'

'It's not your fault that a lunatic is watching me,' Amy assured him glumly.

He seemed to make an effort to cheer up but it was a strange meal, not at all like her usual outings with Peter. Amy felt she would be glad when they got back to his house and he could go to bed. Maybe he would feel better tomorrow.

Peter insisted on coffee when they got back but Amy was suddenly feeling very tired. The previous night she seemed to have been awake for hours and now, with Luc in Paris and feeling relatively safe with Uncle Peter, she just wanted to go to bed. She didn't want to talk. She didn't even want to think. All she wanted to do was put her head on a pillow and sleep.

Once in bed, she seemed to be falling asleep immediately and she gave little thought to the man who followed her. She had actually seen Peter put the night alarm on, and in any case she was not alone. Whatever happened, she had to sleep. She found herself yawning deeply.

Going out for a meal hadn't been really enjoyable but it had helped to pass the time – because she was already fretting for Luc. He had promised to be back tomorrow, although it didn't matter, really. He didn't care about her and she loved him.

She drifted into sleep, surprised even as she sank deeply into it that she was so tired, so light-headed. She would have thought that her misery about Luc would have kept her awake, but it didn't seem to be doing that. When she opened her eyes just a little, the room appeared to be hazy and the effort to look at it was too much. Everything had worn her out lately. Amy felt strange, uneasy, and she slept, her breathing deep and steady.

When the sounds woke her later, she was disorientated, confused, and only by getting a firm grip on her mind did she realize where she was — safe at Peter's house, sleeping in his spare room. She lay half awake, trying to wake completely and finding it very difficult. She seemed to be still on the edge of a dream, a deep, heavy dream.

Somehow she knew she had been awakened and that she should get up to look outside, but the desire to move was very dulled. Even the effort needed to keep her eyes open seemed to be too much. She felt almost semi-conscious.

When the sound came again, she suddenly knew that this time she had not awakened by instinct. The sound was very close. It was in the room!

Amy made her eyes open and stay open. She felt more than tired. The room was still hazy, dream-like, undefined — as if she was seeing it through swaying silken curtains. Everything seemed like an illusion, but deep inside her instinct for survival probed at her brain. She could feel danger all around her. Immediate danger.

She managed to sit up and began to reach out for the bedside lamp. It was frightening to feel as she did, almost anaesthetized. She couldn't reach the switch of the lamp. She knocked against it and the lamp rocked on its base, almost falling.

'Oh, damn!' Amy whispered, and even her tongue had difficulty getting round the words. She felt heavy and only slightly in control. She reached out again and this time the lamp fell to the floor. The crash it made shocked her into holding a little more grip on reality and she swung her legs to the edge of the bed, wondering if she would be able to walk.

That was when she saw the door more clearly. It was slowly opening and a tall, bulky figure moved like a shadow against the light from the corridor outside. The nightmare had actually been in the room with her, and now he was stealthily leaving.

Amy opened her mouth to scream but no sound came. Her vocal cords seemed to be frozen, her legs and arms useless. The man slipped silently through the door into the passage and Amy stood, swaying dizzily and then falling to her knees as her legs gave way under her.

She had to warn Peter. She had to tell him that this time the man was actually in the house, moving about unhindered. He could have killed her while she slept. He could even now kill Peter. Perhaps he had done that already? Amy was gripped with real terror as she imagined the man creeping about the house with them both asleep and defenceless.

She could only get to the door by crawling along, and even that was such a great effort that she felt perspiration on her face. The man was now out of sight, somewhere upstairs in the corridor, but she had to follow and find out.

Oh, Luc, she thought desperately. I need you, Luc. I need you so badly.

She got to the door and pulled herself upright by the frame. She tried to shout again and this time sound came, but only faintly. The light in the corridor seemed to be very bright. It penetrated the shadows in her mind and it helped. The hazy, dreamlike feeling sharpened, and even though she could not yet see very clearly, she knew that this was all real and not some dreadful nightmare.

She could see the man going down the stairs. He was moving slowly, as if it didn't matter, as if he knew he would never be caught. Amy stared, and deep inside she felt a burst of anger that penetrated the cloudiness of her mind even more. How dared he do this to her? He couldn't get away. She would not allow it!

'Peter! Peter!' she shouted, and this time the words came out clearly, loudly. She hung on to the door, keeping herself upright by sheer will power as she called again and again.

The man was now almost at the bottom of the stairs, walking slowly by the wrought-iron balustrades, taking his time. He didn't even look round when she shouted, and the awful thought came to Amy that the shouting was only in her own head. The idea took hold of her, almost convincing her that none of this was real.

She refused to acknowledge the thought and kept on screaming for Peter, and as he finally shot out of his room at the end of the corridor Amy pointed shakily to the stairs.

'There!' she gasped. 'He's there. He's in the house. Look!'

Peter rushed up to her and grasped her arm.

'Amy?' he said uneasily.

'Look,' she whispered. 'Look at him. He's actually in the house. He was in my room. Oh, look at his hat, Uncle Peter, it's got such a big brim. It's frightening. He looks strange.'

'Amy!' Peter gave her a shake and made her turn her eyes to his. She seemed dazed, drugged. He stared at her and frowned.

'You've had a dream,' he told her firmly. 'What did you take? Sleeping pills?'

'No!' Amy tried to shake her head, tried to drive away the feeling of unreality. 'The man was here. He just went into the dining room.'

'Amy!' he warned quietly.

'He's there now. I know he can't get out because you set the alarm.' She turned to look at him in horror. 'How has he got in anyway?'

'He hasn't got in, love,' Peter told her patiently. 'You dreamed it, imagined it.'

'I didn't,' Amy whispered. 'I saw him in my room and he went down the stairs. You must have seen him. He was right there when you came out of your room. He's in the dining room now. You can get him, Uncle Peter. There's no way out of that room except into the hall.'

'I'll go and look,' Peter said with a resigned sigh. 'You stay here. I don't want you falling down the stairs.'

The stairs were swimming in front of Amy's eyes, spinning, moving, twisting. Even now she was not absolutely sure that she was awake. Some small voice inside her told her that she *was* possibly dreaming, but if she was dreaming then it was very real to her. She dared not step forward and attempt the stairs.

She saw Peter go down and then saw him turn to the dining room. He seemed to be such a long time in there that Amy risked her balance and went down two steps. She hung on to the wrought-iron balustrade and shouted again.

'Peter! Uncle Peter!' Her voice seemed to be louder now, and the thought came into her mind that if she was still asleep, still dreaming this frightening dream, then surely the sound of her own shouting would wake her.

There was something bothering her at the back of her mind, something she should have noted, but she couldn't bring it forward, couldn't remember what it was. It was something wrong, something that didn't fit into all this.

Amy went down a few more steps, clinging on to the balustrade, and just then Peter came out of the dining room and looked up at her.

'Amy!' he said worriedly. 'You'll fall. Stay there.'

He started up the stairs and, looking beyond him, Amy saw the man come out of the dining room.

'There! He's there!' she shouted, and Peter shook his head and stood looking up at her.

'Oh, Amy. You'll have to see somebody about this. It's gone on long enough. You've got everything mixed up, love. You're constantly seeing things.'

Amy heard him but she could also see the man. He was walking with his head down, making for the door. He was deliberately keeping his face hidden.

'He's getting away,' she whispered.

'He's not there, Amy.' Peter turned to look and then turned back to her. 'There's nobody. Get back into bed, love. I'll call the doctor. This has got to be sorted out.'

But she could still see the man clearly. Amy pushed past Peter and went down a few more steps.

'Switch the hall light on.' she said shakily. 'I'll be able to see better. Hurry! He's going to get away through the front door.'

'There's nobody there, Amy,' Peter said, exasperated now. 'Nobody ever sees this man but you. Surely that's some reflection on how disturbed your mind is? Nobody could have got either in or out through the door or any window. The alarm would have gone off.'

Amy stopped and thought. She turned to look at him. She remembered seeing him set the alarm before they went to bed. If she could remember that, then this was no dream.

'My mind isn't disturbed,' she said quietly, clinging to the cold wrought iron. 'I can see the man now. He's almost at the door. He's going slowly to frighten me.'

'Amy, I can't see him,' Peter insisted, looking down at her seriously. 'You're the only one who ever sees this man.'

'Oh, no, I'm not,' Amy told him with soft triumph. 'Luc has seen him. You might think that I'm going mad but Luc doesn't. The man is right there, Uncle Peter. He's actually in your house. Either you know he's there or you're blind.'

Amy turned swiftly, too swiftly, and as she turned she saw the man open the front door. No alarm sounded and her eyes flashed to the neat box on the wall. The red light was not steady. It was pulsing away quietly. The alarm was not set at all, even though she had seen Peter set it as they went to bed.

Somebody had switched off the alarm and somebody had unlocked the front door.

The man slid out into the night, and at that moment Amy slipped and fell down the last few steps. Her head hit the hard parquet floor of the hall and for a minute she lay helpless.

Peter didn't move to help her; he simply stood on the stairs above and looked down into her white face.

'Oh, poor Amy,' he said quietly. 'My poor little Amy.' And then Amy blacked out completely.

It was only for a minute, and when she came round the hall seemed to be full of people, full of noise. As she lay dazed, Luc burst in and rushed across to her.

'Don't move, *chérie!*' he ordered urgently when she tried to sit up. '*Oh, mon Dieu!* What have I done, letting you face this? You will be all right. Tell me you will be all right.'

He turned and snapped to the other men in the hall, and at that moment Amy noticed that they were policemen.

'Get an ambulance,' he ordered. 'She's hurt.'

'I'm not hurt, Luc,' Amy murmured shakily. 'I only fell a few steps. I banged my head a bit, but it's nothing much.'

'You can't possibly know,' Luc insisted.

'Luc, it's *my* head,' Amy reminded him. 'I know what hurts. I'm just a bit dazed, but I was dazed from the moment I woke up.'

Luc looked into her eyes and saw the slightly dilated pupils. His expression became even more grim and he glared at Peter Jensen, who was still standing shocked and bewildered on the stairs.

'What have you done to her?' Luc snarled furiously. He leapt to his feet to start upstairs but the voice of the police sergeant hit him at once.

'*Mr Martell!*'

The warning was clear and Luc stopped, containing his rage with difficulty. He came back to Amy, crouching down beside her.

'*Oh, chérie,*' he murmured, 'I have put you at such a risk. I swear I did not know how far they were prepared to go at this stage.'

Amy couldn't understand what he was talking about. She just wanted to get up, to feel better. She raised her head and began to struggle.

'Help me to get up, Luc,' she said weakly.

'You may be badly hurt,' he warned her, and she somehow found the strength to glare at him.

'If I am, it's not from falling down three steps,' she told him. 'Help me up or I'll do it myself.'

Luc helped her and she was soon standing unsteadily. He kept his arm round her waist, but Amy was too shaken and too bewildered to take much notice of the fact. Luc turned his menacing gaze back on Peter Jensen and it dawned on Amy that in all this time Peter had not moved one inch.

350

'What did you give her to get her into this state?' Luc asked violently.

'It was nothing much,' Peter protested. 'It was only a bit of something I slipped into her coffee, last thing before bed.'

'*Shut up, you fool!*'

Amy turned her head at the sound of the familiar voice, and she saw the man who had followed her and frightened her for such a long time. The large hat was gone and the disguise seemed to have faded with it. The clothes were the same, the darkness, the bulkiness, but now Amy knew why it had been so necessary for the man to keep his face hidden. Because it wasn't a man at all. It was Jill.

Amy just stared, and Luc tightened his arm around her. Jill didn't look at either of them. Her eyes were on Peter and her face was twisted in anger.

'Don't say anything at all,' she ordered coldly.

'I knew it wouldn't work,' Peter said, ignoring her command. 'I told you it wouldn't work once Martell was involved.'

'Keep your mouth shut, you stupid fool!' Jill shouted. 'It was all your fault in the first place.'

'It wasn't. You had the idea years ago. I had nothing to do with Celia dying.'

Jill Davis began to struggle, but whether she was trying to escape or whether she was trying to get her hands on Peter nobody knew. The sergeant took charge and signalled to the men with him.

'Take both of them out to the cars,' he ordered, and Amy looked up into Luc's face with dazed eyes.

'Why?' she whispered, and then she fainted and he swept her up into his arms.

'I'm taking her home,' he said with a steely-eyed look at the sergeant. 'You know her address. I want a doctor there by the time I arrive with her.'

He received a rather subdued nod and the words he had quite come to expect.

'A doctor will be there, Mr Martell. Don't worry.'

Don't worry! Luc glowered at him. Everyone drew back as Luc stalked to the door, carrying Amy in his arms.

'I really love her, you know. She was almost like a daughter to me,' Peter Jensen said pitifully, staring at Amy's pale face as Luc strode past him.

He was being held securely by one of the policemen, but as Luc paused in his stride, and turned violent dark eyes on him, Peter drew back anxiously. Luc cast the same sort of glance on Jill Davis, but she met his dark-eyed loathing with no expression on her face at all.

Luc put Amy gently into his car and drove away. He was suffering the torments of hell. Nothing had gone as he had planned. He had never thought that they would drug her. He had not expected that they would be prepared to go to this final stage so soon.

He had alerted the police as soon as he'd had the last information from his father, but he had imagined that there would be more time left. He had simply been intent on catching the watcher and confronting Jensen. He could easily have lost Amy in the process.

Amy came round before they reached her house, but she lay back in the seat keeping utterly silent and Luc glanced at her every few seconds, his dark eyes anxious. They drew up outside her house and to his great relief the doctor drew up behind them.

'Get her on her bed,' the doctor said quietly. 'I'll have a look at her.'

'More than a look,' Luc snapped, glancing at him, and the doctor held up his hand in acknowledgement.

'Figure of speech,' he murmured. 'I know what happened. The police briefed me. Don't worry.'

'If anyone says that to me ever again,' Luc muttered through clenched teeth, 'I will bang some heads together.'

'No sign of concussion or any injury from her fall,' the doctor said as he examined Amy and Luc hovered close by. 'She's been given some sort of sedative by the look of it, but the pupils are not too dilated now. I think the silence and the pallor are due to shock. She needs quiet and sleep. I hesitate to give her anything else until we know exactly what was slipped into her drink.'

'I'll see that she sleeps,' Luc assured him, his eyes never leaving Amy's face. 'Are you sure it's safe for her to sleep after that fall?'

'Three steps,' Amy muttered, trying to focus on them both. 'The headache is nothing to do with that.'

'You have a headache, *chérie*?' Luc began anxiously, but the doctor caught the slightly exasperated look on Amy's face and smiled.

'Result of not sleeping off the drug,' he said firmly. 'Let her sleep.'

'Thank you,' Amy muttered, and turned on her side, closing her eyes and ignoring them both.

'I'll see myself out,' the doctor said. 'I'll call round in the morning. Meanwhile, if anything happens call this number.' He held out a card but Luc was already carefully getting Amy out of her dressing gown and under the sheets. She was grumbling in her sleepy state and Luc was muttering endearments in French.

'Card on the dressing table,' the doctor said with a grin. 'Did you hear me?'

'Naturally. I am not deaf!' Luc snapped, and then looked round a trifle sheepishly. 'I beg your pardon. I am angry at the moment. Thank you for coming.'

'That's all right.' The doctor paused in the doorway and glanced back. 'Don't leave her alone. When she finally wakes up she may have problems facing this affair.'

'I will be right beside her,' Luc vowed. 'My mother will be here tomorrow. She is a strong woman and Amy likes her. My mother is English.'

The doctor gave him a wry glance and left. He looked at his watch. It was four in the morning. In his opinion the girl would sleep for quite a few hours. He wasn't worried about her. He had never seen such a ferocious guard dog as Martell. He would be interested in hearing the whole story but he was not a full-time police doctor. He imagined that the sergeant would clam up now that the main excitement was over.

354

Luc sat by Amy for a long time. He felt that he should not take his eyes from her. He had nearly lost her. The thought went round and round in his mind, tormenting him. He wanted to get into bed beside her and hold her terribly tight, but it would disturb her and she must sleep.

Her sleep seemed to be normal and quiet, and after a while he looked through the window and saw that it was daylight. He was hungry, tired, but he could not allow himself any rest yet. He went down to make coffee, and when the daylight strengthened he phoned Paris.

Amy slept until late in the afternoon. She awakened slowly, peacefully, stretching and turning as she opened her eyes. She thought she was still dreaming when she saw Luc's mother sitting in a chair by the window, reading a book.

Ann Martell glanced up and then came across to sit on the edge of the bed and smiled down at Amy. 'How do you feel now?'

'Better, I think.' Amy looked at her with puzzled eyes. 'I feel disorientated. What are you doing here? How did you get here?'

'Luc telephoned early this morning. We came over at once. Henri is with Luc at the moment but I expect they'll be here soon enough.'

'I can't understand why he asked you to come,' Amy murmured, and Ann leaned across to stroke her hair back in such a motherly way that Amy could have cried.

'I told you that if you needed us we would be with you. Luc thought you needed us now. In any

355

case, he would not consider leaving you alone. When we arrived he was able to sleep for a while, but now he has to see to quite a lot of things. The more people here the better.'

'I'm fine now,' Amy said quietly. 'My uncle Peter . . .'

'Don't, dear,' Ann advised softly. 'This has all been a terrible shock for you. Luc will talk it over with you and then everything will be all right.'

'Luc doesn't owe me anything,' Amy said faintly, looking away.

'That is something you will work out between you. But you will work it out, Amy. At this moment Luc is torturing himself with the thought that he put you at risk. That will have to be talked out too. It's all something that you must face together.' She stood up briskly. 'Now, I'm going to make you some tea and then you can tell me what you wish to eat.'

'Almost anything,' Amy muttered. 'I'm starving.'

'That's a good sign,' Ann said as she left the room to go down to Amy's small kitchen.

Amy watched her till the last minute. The fact that Luc's mother was here only served to make her more anxious. Everything was changed. She refused to think about it but at the back of her mind she knew that now she had nobody at all.

Both Peter and Jill had tried to harm her. She didn't understand how at the moment, but she remembered the police and she remembered some of the things Peter had said. They were permanently out of her life. So was Luc.

There was the woman from Paris, and somehow Amy found that she remembered the woman much more clearly than her terrible fright at her uncle's house and all the subsequent happenings. Luc was trying to look after her but he didn't belong to her. He never would.

Ann brought her tea and while she was drinking it Amy could hear the sound of cooking. It reminded her of Luc's way of taking charge of the kitchen. It brought a sad smile to her face and she knew she had to shake herself out of this melancholy. Nothing was about to change, no matter how she yearned for things to be different.

Amy got up to go downstairs. She still did not feel up to dressing, but she changed into a white frilly nightie and got out her very best white dressing gown. It was silky and luxurious, an extravagance she had allowed herself before Aunt Celia's death.

When Ann looked round, Amy was in the kitchen right behind her, and after one close look Luc's mother let the matter rest.

'Sit down, Amy,' she suggested. 'You still look a little shaken. In a few minutes I'll have a delicious mushroom omelette ready for you.'

'Thank you,' Amy muttered. 'I'm hungry enough to eat the pan.'

'Then we progress,' Luc's mother declared in a satisfied voice.

She glanced at Amy from the corner of her eye and wondered what the effect would be on Luc of this dreamy apparition in white. She knew Luc well enough to realize how he felt about Amy, even though he did refer to her as a Computer Person. At this moment Amy looked like a fairy tale princess.

Ann frowned worriedly when she realized that Amy had not shown any desire to be told about Luc. She rather suspected that her son was frantic about this delicate-looking girl. Ann chewed at her lip and kept quiet. She never interfered, however great the temptation. Luc did not encourage any sort of meddling in his private affairs.

By the time Luc and his father arrived Amy had eaten and was sitting with her feet up on the settee in her small but charming sitting room. Luc's mother was trying to get some sort of conversation going but it was difficult when she was determined not to either interfere or bring up the subject of Amy's uncle. She was greatly pleased to hear Luc's voice in the hall, but quite alarmed to see that Amy stiffened visibly.

'How are you feeling now, Amy?' Luc's father came in first and bent over to kiss her hand, an action which Amy thought was rather courtly. Luc just stood in the doorway, and she could tell nothing from his impassive face. He was so wonderfully familiar and yet so distant.

'I feel all right,' she assured Henri, smiling up at him and avoiding any eye contact with Luc.

'The doctor will be round soon,' Luc said quietly, and Amy looked up with a sharp glance in his direction.

'I don't need the doctor!'

'Nevertheless,' Luc stated coldly, 'he will be here, and you have no alternative but to see him. You are now part of a court case, the victim of a conspiracy and possible murder attempt.'

'*Luc!*' Ann gasped, giving him a horrified look, but Luc's father intervened swiftly.

'Luc is right,' he said, sitting down and facing Amy. 'We have been with the police for quite a while. Amy's uncle has confessed.'

'Oh, dear,' Ann breathed, looking anxiously at Amy. 'This is so terrible. I really do not know what to say.'

'You could say, Thank God they are caught and Amy is safe,' Luc snarled, turning away to go into the kitchen and make coffee for himself and his father.

Amy bit down hard on her lip to stop the tears that welled in her eyes. These people were not strangers who had attacked her. This was her uncle Peter and Jill, her friend for years. She had never felt so lost and lonely. Ann and Henri were being kind, but they didn't know that Luc would just walk out of her life too.

He came back in and silently handed his father a cup of coffee, and Amy realized they were all feeling embarrassed, too embarrassed to talk. There was a tight, awkward atmosphere in the room and Luc did not lighten it at all. He stood in his usual manner, silent and dark, with one broad shoulder propped against the wall. He was drinking his coffee, but even without looking up Amy knew that the dark eyes were on her. She could almost feel the anger radiating from him.

'You have no alternative but to be involved in this, Amy,' Henri Martell said quietly. 'I expect that finally you will have to appear in court.'

Amy's head shot up, her eyes open wide.

'I couldn't!' she whispered.

Her distress went through Luc like a knife. His rage at the two people who were supposed to have cared about her knew no bounds at that moment. She looked down, clenching her hands in her lap, and Luc's eyes skimmed over her. He felt as he had felt when he had just walked into the house with his father and seen her – shattered.

She looked utterly desirable in the white robe and nightie. She looked like a bride. The robe had fallen open below her knees and the frills at the bottom of the nightie frothed round her slim ankles. Even her toes were beautiful.

He wanted to gather her close, to protect her, cherish her. There was nothing computer-efficient about her now, and he longed to hear her speaking in the old way, her feet firmly on her fluffy pink cloud. But she was distant, holding herself together, hurting.

'I'll gather all the cups together before the doctor comes,' Ann said uneasily. She jumped up to take action and Luc walked slowly across to take her place in the chair facing Amy.

'Eventually you will have to know everything,' he told her quietly. 'Sooner or later the police will be here to take your statement. They are bound to tell you things, things that perhaps you will not want to know. Would you prefer it if I told you?'

Amy bit her lips together and looked at him, her eyes swimming with tears.

360

'Oh, Luc,' she whispered, and it was too much for him to bear. He didn't care whether his father was there or not. He moved over on to the settee with her and folded her gently in his arms.

'It is all right, *chérie*,' he said softly. 'You have suffered for a long time and there is more to come, but I am here, *ma pauvre petite. Viens, ma belle.* We will face everything and we will defeat them all.'

Amy curled up in his arms and allowed herself to cry, and Luc rested his face against the shining nut-brown hair that fell to her shoulders. His hands moved soothingly over her back and he was so warm, so strong, that Amy could have stayed there for the rest of her life. But she knew she could not, and the knowledge made her cry even more.

In the doorway from the kitchen Ann Martell stopped, her own eyes filling with tears, and Henri took one look at the overall scene and got to his feet.

'We will go and settle our things in at your flat,' he said quietly to Luc.

Luc glanced up at him gratefully.

'Take my car,' he said. 'The keys are on the hall table.'

It only occurred to him at that moment how much he belonged with Amy. It was natural to drop his keys down on her table, to make coffee in her kitchen, to take her into his arms.

'I'll come back to make dinner,' Ann promised, sniffing her tears away. She opened her mouth again to speak to Amy but Henri shook his head and motioned her to the door. At this moment Amy did not need any goodbyes. She did not need any words of sympathy. She needed Luc, and Henri was content to leave them alone.

CHAPTER 15

After a while, Amy sat up and moved from Luc. She moved carefully, but to Luc it seemed that she was tearing herself out of his arms. He needed to hold her. He felt empty when she was away from him, and his guilt at what she had suffered and was about to suffer seemed to know no limit.

'You're very good to me, Luc,' Amy said quietly.

'Why should I not be good to you?' he asked almost roughly.

He sat up and got to his feet abruptly, pacing about because he could not stay near her and stop himself from holding her. He had always been afraid that when this was over she would come to feel differently about him, not want him any more. Was that what was happening now?

He knew she was distressed, shaken by her ordeal, but even before it had happened he had noticed the way she had distanced herself. When he had come back into the office after his lunch with Veronique Amy had been different, and he feared that it was because she was coming to her senses about him.

Nothing about them was alike, and he had always recognized that fact. Now she was avoiding his eyes. She had seemed to be more relaxed with his mother and father than she was with him. And yet, not too long ago she had been delirious in his arms, begging to be loved. He had been inside her, closer to her than anyone else had ever been. He couldn't contemplate being without her.

'It's no use, Luc, and it doesn't matter. Really it doesn't.'

'What are you talking about?' He swung round to stare down at her but she was still avoiding his eyes.

'I – I don't blame you,' Amy whispered. 'It was all my fault.'

'It was not,' he muttered in exasperation. 'I placed you at risk. I was so sure of how they were going that I gave no thought to the fact that their plans might have been rushed along with more speed. I merely expected to catch them. I did not expect them to attack you so soon.'

Amy looked up at him in wide-eyed astonishment.

'I'm not taking about that.'

Luc stared down at her, the normal frown on his dark face. She did not appear to be on that pink cloud at the moment so what did she mean? He gave a deep, heartfelt sigh, wondering if he would ever really understand her.

'Perhaps you had better explain what we are talking about, then. It is fairly clear that I do not know.'

Before Amy could speak the doorbell rang, and Luc glanced at his watch.

'The doctor, no doubt,' he muttered.

'I don't need to see him,' Amy protested quickly, but it was too late for that. Luc was already striding to the door and she sat back in defeat.

He was determined to look after her, even though his feelings had never been as deep as hers, even though he was committed to another woman. She wondered if she should go upstairs. She would feel embarrassed now if Luc insisted on staying in the room.

There was no need to go, however. The doctor was the same one. She remembered him vaguely from the night before, and at the sight of him all the previous evening's terror flooded back for a minute.

'Amy?' Luc said quickly, seeing her face.

'Nothing to worry about,' the doctor said. 'Only to be expected. Mine was the last unwelcome face she saw.'

'This is Dr Chalmers,' Luc said, his words spaced out with great care, so as not to alarm her further. His caution earned him an indignant glance from Amy.

'We've proved I'm not mad,' she snapped. 'There's no need whatsoever to treat me like a halfwit who needs special precautions.'

Luc glowered at her, his brows drawn together in a deep black frown. Dr Chalmers made a small choked noise that might have been a groan, a sound of stifled embarrassment, or a well-controlled desire to laugh. It looked suspiciously like the latter to Amy. He got a glare too.

'I can see without any investigation that you're well on the way to recovery,' he said. He took her wrist to feel for a pulse and Luc turned away, one black brow raised caustically. The doctor would probably discover that her heart was racing due to rage. She could be quite infuriating.

The pupils of her eyes were inspected and then the doctor sat back and regarded her steadily.

'Any headache, nausea, dizziness?' he asked in a very professional voice.

'No.' Amy shook her head, feeling quite subdued suddenly. She wanted to jump up and throw her arms round Luc, and now she had made him angry. She hadn't meant to do that. 'I just feel very tired,' she finished quietly.

'Not surprising. You were drugged last night.'

'Drugged? With what?' Amy asked, looking at him in amazement.

'Chloral hydrate. It used to be called a Mickey Finn in the old gangster movies of the thirties. To be technical, it's a central nervous system depressant.'

Amy just stared at him in silence, and it was more than Luc could bear. He came and sat beside her, his eyes on the doctor.

'What happens with this drug?' he asked in a tense voice.

'Sleepiness, mental confusion, unsteadiness. It can be followed by a coma, depending on the amount taken.'

'*Mon Dieu!*' Luc breathed. He felt shaken, horrified in fact. He could have lost her.

Amy was white-faced. She moved closer to him and he collected her in an almost automatic gesture, lifting her slender legs across his thighs and soothingly stroking her foot. Dr Chalmers ignored them. He was into his medical stride.

'How – how do you know it was that particular drug?' Amy asked in a trembling voice.

'Peter Jensen confessed. In fact, according to the police, he's not stopped talking since they picked him up. The woman refuses to speak. She's the hard one. Clearly, though, she was the one who obtained the chloral hydrate. She's a nurse.'

'Jill!' Amy covered her face with her hands and Luc put his arm tightly around her. 'But Jill was in America,' Amy whispered.

'No, she was not, *chérie*,' Luc said quietly. 'She never went there at all. Somebody else posted those cards and letters to you. I will tell you all about it later.' He looked back at Dr Chalmers. 'How did they get Amy to take this drug?'

'A cup of coffee at bedtime, apparently, according to Jensen. He was supposed to give it to her during dinner. It's more effective with wine or any alcohol. He lost his nerve.'

'He knocked my drink over,' Amy whispered, remembering Peter's clumsiness. 'They had to change the tablecloth and reset the table. He was embarrassed and gave me his drink.'

Chalmers nodded. 'That fits in with what he told the police. When it got right down to it, he couldn't do it.' He gave Amy a wry glance. 'Don't let that soften your heart, however. He would have been quite happy if Jill Davis had been able to administer the dose. It was Jensen who put the dose in your bedtime drink.'

'If he spilled the first lot, where did the second amount come from?' Luc asked in a taut voice.

'The leftovers,' Dr Chalmers said quietly. 'If Miss Scott had been given the original amount we would not be sitting hear now, considering events. As it turned out, however, the result might have been the same. Miss Scott was drugged, unable to react normally, seeing things through a haze and unsteady on her feet. Once on the stairs she could have fallen from the top to the bottom.'

'So they made quite sure that I would wake up and follow the man I'd been seeing,' Amy said in a low voice. 'Jill woke me up and then let me see her going through the door. They knew I would get up and call to Uncle Peter.'

'If you hadn't done it the first time,' Chalmers informed her, 'they were going to try again until you did. But you got up. You pulled yourself together.'

'I'm good at that,' Amy told him sadly. 'I expect I always will be.'

Luc's face seemed to contract in pain, and the doctor looked from one to the other.

'I can safely leave you now, anyway,' he said, getting to his feet. 'You only have to call if you need me, but I think you'll be fine later, and by tomorrow this should all be out of your system. All you are now is tired.'

'I know,' Amy murmured. 'I think I'll go back to bed.'

'Good idea.' Dr Chalmers nodded and Luc saw him to the door.

Luc did not think it was a good idea at all. Amy needed to talk this out and she needed him, whether she knew it or not. If she went upstairs she would be lying awake, grieving for her swine of an uncle, grieving for her hard-faced, hard-hearted friend.

When he came back in she was on her feet and Luc reacted completely in character.

'Sit down,' he ordered. 'You and I have some unfinished business. First of all we will sort ourselves out and then we will talk all the horror away.'

'You're not a psychiatrist,' Amy reminded him shakily, and he glared at her in the usual manner.

'I am your private detective, your boss and your lover,' he snapped. 'Sit down. It can either be on that settee or on my lap, but whichever you choose you will sit.'

Amy sat down abruptly and stared at him with such a look of melancholy that he relented.

'What is it, *mon amour*?' he asked softly. 'I know there is more than this particular nightmare. You promised that you would always feel the same about me. What has made you change your mind.'

'I saw you, Luc,' she whispered. 'I saw you with that glamorous Frenchwoman. She kissed you and you had lunch with her.'

'Ah!' Luc was so relieved that his legs felt shaky. 'Is that why you are so distant from me? Is that all?'

'All?' Amy asked indignantly. 'How many women do you have? How many women do you sleep with?'

369

He smiled down at her, delighted by her obvious jealousy.

'Only you, *ma petite*. Only you since I first saw you. It is difficult for a Frenchman but, like you, I am capable of pulling myself together. I can wait years for you if necessary, but I hope you will not insist on that to punish me.'

'I don't understand you,' Amy said fretfully.

'Then I will explain myself.' He went to crouch down in front of her, looking up into her face, and for a second he was silent. His dark eyes lanced over her possessively and finally rested on her foot. It had escaped the white, frothy frills of her nightie and it tempted him beyond reason. He took it in his hand and began to kiss her toes.

'Stop that!' Amy ordered sharply. 'You're not sliding out of this.'

Luc laughed softly, his breath warm and exciting against her toes.

'It is a such beautiful little foot,' he murmured seductively. 'I am perfectly happy making love to your toes.'

'It's not love,' Amy said tightly. 'There's that other woman.'

Luc sat beside her and pulled her on to his lap, ignoring her struggles, but she sat upright, straight as a rod and stiff with disapproval.

'It was Veronique,' he explained, hiding his laughter.

'Well, I don't care,' Amy informed him coldly.

'I see. Then you will not wish to know that I have known her for years, have even, in my most bored moments, considered marrying her just to get the whole business of marriage over and done with.'

'That,' Amy said, 'is absolutely disgraceful!'

'I know, *chérie*,' Luc murmured contritely. 'My character is not too good. You recognized that from the first. Fortunately, I met you and discovered that there was more to a woman than the sheer necessity of a marriage to please my mother and obtain an heir to carry on the Martell tradition. I discovered an electronic witch who sometimes sat on a fluffy pink cloud and sometimes let me ride on it too while she talked all manner of nonsense.'

'I do not!' Amy snapped. 'I'm clever – and you told me that yourself,' she added triumphantly.

'You have a dual personality,' Luc told her seriously, his eyes dancing with laughter. 'I am very lucky. I have two women in one beautiful body.'

'It won't work, Luc,' Amy said sharply, turning to glare at him. 'You can keep me here on your knee until the cows come home but it still won't work. I saw you with that woman.'

'I have never heard about the cows coming home before,' Luc confessed. 'My mother will explain it, no doubt.' He pulled her tightly against him, taking her completely by surprise. 'I do not and never have loved Veronique,' he said quietly. 'She came to England quite unexpectedly, and she came to inform me that she is getting married soon – and not to me, I am happy to say. I told her about you. She was not amused. Veronique likes to be indispensable.'

371

'Greedy,' Amy pointed out, allowing herself to settle against him.

'But nothing to do with me,' Luc said firmly.

Amy turned to look at him and saw the truth in his eyes.

'I was unhappy,' she murmured in her usual honest way. 'I thought . . .'

'You thought I was behaving like a Lothario? I have never had either the time or the inclination. I like to work. The idea of marriage was, as I said, a necessity.'

'I see,' Amy said quietly.

'You do not,' Luc corrected. 'My parents came like a thunderbolt from Paris while you slept. I needed help and they arrived immediately. My mother stayed to watch over you for me and my father and I went to the police. But it was not his first effort on your behalf. He has been gathering information since we were in Paris, and last night the police were there with me to catch the man in black who followed you because my father had rung them,'

'Really?' Amy asked wide-eyed. 'What did he say to convince them?'

'He said, "Somebody is trying to harm my future daughter-in-law." They paid strict attention when he told them all he had learned through his investigations.'

Amy just sat very still and looked into Luc's dark eyes, and in a second she got that long, slow smile that made her heart leap.

'We cannot disappoint him, *mon amour*,' Luc said softly. 'I think you had better marry me soon.

For myself I would not care but, as you can understand, my father has already chosen his daughter-in-law and I am afraid that nobody else will do.'

His smile grew until happiness was spread across his face, and all Amy could do was be still and look at him.

'It's an odd way to propose,' she muttered finally.

'It is all because of my special training. I have learned to cover my tracks, to take no chances. When you confess to loving me, I will ask you again, and this time I will kneel and kiss your beautiful foot.'

'It won't be necessary,' Amy said as she flung herself into his arms.

A long time later, Amy lifted her head from Luc's shoulder and asked the question he had really been dreading. He was treating her like an invalid, holding her very carefully, refusing to allow his desire for her to surface. And Amy had shown no inclination at all to get up and move away from him. They could both have stayed like that for ever, but then Amy asked the dark question that hung between them.

'Why, Luc? Why did they do this to me?'

'The oldest reason in the world, *chérie*. Money.'

'But Uncle Peter has plenty of money of his own, and I haven't even got any money yet.'

'You will have, Amy. That's what all this is about. Because Peter Jensen has next to nothing as far as money goes. My father discovered this.

Very soon now, his creditors are going to be swarming all over him. He is living on credit and has been for some time. He has been keeping up appearances and waiting for you to have control of your aunt Celia's wealth. His wealth was gambled away over the years and he gambled more to try to get it back. It is usually the same and the idea never works.'

'Luc, I can't understand any of this,' Amy protested. 'It sounds to me as if everything has been sheer chance. How, for example, did they know that I would get all Aunt Celia's money?'

'Who else would she leave it to, *chérie?*' Luc asked.

'But they had no idea she would just die suddenly.'

Luc was silent for a moment, and then he said quietly, 'They knew, Amy. Your aunt did not just suddenly die. Jill Davis killed her.'

Amy stared at him in horror and then buried her face against his shoulder.

'How do you know, Luc?' she whispered.

'As I told you, your uncle is talking, confessing to everything. He is not exactly cut out for cold-blooded murder. Desperation drove him on, desperation and Jill Davis. That woman is capable of anything.'

'It's so difficult to believe. She's been a friend to me since my father died.'

'My sweet,' Luc said softly, 'she has been biding her time, and she was prepared to wait for twelve years to get what she wanted. She wanted Peter Jensen but, more than anything else, she wanted your money.'

'I was leaving her a lot,' Amy murmured.

'You are only twenty-five, and she could not wait for such a long time on the off-chance of anything happening to you – neither could Jensen. He needed money now, not later.'

'So they wanted to kill me too?'

'Initially no, according to your uncle. You were to be frightened into a complete breakdown so that he could control everything you had. He was sure that in time he could resurrect his own fortunes. He insists that until that last night he had no idea that Jill Davis planned to kill you. At the restaurant he lost his nerve, could not go through with it. They had intended to say that you had been imagining a man following you, and the police would have confirmed that. The idea was to make it look as if you took the drug to kill yourself because you could not go on with so much mental fear. Some of the chloral hydrate would have been found in your house because your uncle still had a key. When he locked up after the workmen who installed your alarm system, he had a duplicate made. He could have got in here at any time.'

'Why didn't he give me a bigger dose later, then?'

'He did not have any more, except the small leftover amount, and he could not bring himself to kill you. He was prepared, however, to stand by while you fell to your death on the stairs. But you did not. You are my clever, brave Computer Person.'

Luc rocked her close, willing her to face the unpalatable facts, and in a short while there was another ring on the doorbell. He felt relieved. It would be his mother and father, and at the moment Amy needed a lot of people around her. She needed to know that there were more people who cared about her than the two who had pretended affection for so long.

'We will talk if Amy feels up to it,' Ann Martell stated as she sat down and looked a trifle anxiously at Amy's pale face. 'In a little while I will prepare a meal.'

'I'm up to talking,' Amy assured her quietly. 'Luc has already told me some of the things. I have to face this and put it behind me.'

'We will all be with you,' Luc's father said firmly. 'You have a family, Amy.'

'Luc told me,' Amy said with one of her sudden brilliant smiles.

'And?' Luc's mother asked with a thread of dread in her voice.

'She is not opposed to the idea,' Luc murmured, handing out drinks and then sitting next to Amy. 'I have planned a second proposal later, when the idea has firmly settled in.' He pulled Amy close and she came softly and willingly. Luc's mother smiled in satisfaction and rested back comfortably in the chair.

'What really happened to Aunt Celia?' Amy asked in a few seconds.

It was Luc's father who answered that.

'You aunt had a bad heart,' he said quietly. 'She never told you because she did not want you to worry. She was on medication and could have lived out her life with no trouble. Unfortunately, Jill

Davis knew about the condition and planned accordingly. Apparently she often did small things for your aunt?'

'Yes. She collected medicine for her and came to give her any injections that she needed, like flu jabs. I don't know where she got the things from but it pleased Aunt Celia. She liked to think she was above other people. The fact that she had an experienced hospital sister at her beck and call was quite a boost for her ego.'

'Miss Davis took the drugs from the hospital a little at a time,' Luc's father said. 'She was just waiting for an opportunity. When she was due to go to America, the chance came. Your aunt was quite annoyed about being left without this unimportant but necessary medical servant. She knew she would need her flu jab later in the year. She would need lots of small things and now she would have to either call the doctor or, more unpleasantly, go to see him.'

'So how did Jill Davis take advantage of that?' Ann asked.

'She persuaded Amy's aunt that it was perfectly feasible to have her injection early. It was already almost the end of summer. She told her it would make no difference and by the time another one was needed, why, she would be back in England and able to administer it.'

'She did not inject her against influenza,' Luc's father said grimly. 'Instead, she injected Amy's aunt with an air bubble.'

'Air?' Amy repeated, looking at him in a puzzled way.

'Injected air can stop the heart by blocking off blood vessels. Air in the heart compresses it and blocks the vascular system, stopping blood supply and oxygen. It will cause death.'

'But wouldn't somebody know?' Ann asked with a shudder.

'It is detectable because it froths, but it is only detectable in an autopsy. Amy's aunt Celia was already having treatment for heart problems. To all intents and purposes she simply had a heart attack. Unfortunate, but not entirely unexpected.'

'So they got away with it?' Amy whispered.

'Completely,' Henri Martell said quietly. 'Peter Jensen had few qualms. He hated your aunt and *she* hated him very soundly. He had tricked your father out of most of his money before he died. Jill Davis nursed your father in his last days and she was able to get him to sign almost anything in his condition. He was in great pain, constantly sedated. She was one witness, the doctor was the other. They were both above reproach and the doctor was completely unaware of the subterfuge.'

'Somehow,' Luc said, 'according to your uncle, your aunt Celia either knew everything, or suspected. She whisked you away and refused to allow him anywhere near you. She did not, however, know of Jill Davis's part in the affair, and so she allowed the contact to continue and eventually it led to her own death.'

Ann stood and glanced warningly at Luc.

'I am about to prepare dinner,' she stated. 'I think Amy has had quite enough of this for now.'

378

'I have some more questions,' Amy protested, but Luc looked down at her pale face and shook his head.

'Later, *chérie*. I will bring you a coffee for now and then we will talk about this after dinner, if you feel up to it.'

Amy wrinkled her nose.

'I make much better coffee than you do,' she muttered. 'I'll go and do my own, if you don't mind.'

Luc didn't mind. It was a good idea to take her thoughts off this for a while. All the same, he moved with her to the kitchen like a sheepdog with a very delicate lamb in his charge.

Henri Martell watched them go and smiled his satisfaction. There was not much doubt about Luc's feelings for Amy and, as she had willingly sat with his arms around her, right in front of her future parents-in-law, he assumed she felt the same.

As to this dreadful business, Amy would get over it eventually. Henri had a great deal of respect for the intelligence of Luc's future wife. He thought she looked beautiful in white. He hoped they would marry in Paris. He also hoped that he would be allowed to give the bride away because she had no relatives. He frowned and sat back comfortably, pondering on whether it would be permitted as he would be the bridegroom's father.

It was only after dinner that the subject of Amy's problems was mentioned again. Amy brought it up herself.

'How did Jill manage to be here?' she asked.

'Apparently, when she went to America last year – supposedly to get this exchange visit,' Luc explained, 'she set up an arrangement for cards and letters to be sent to you. She told her employers here that she was going, but later she declined the offer from America and simply stayed here. A house opposite you was rented in another name and she was ready for action.'

'So she watched me and followed me and stood there at night,' Amy mused. 'How could she, though? When did she sleep, eat?'

'Sometimes the man watching you was Peter Jensen,' Luc's father told her. 'Miss Davis is tall, and well made for a woman. With men's clothes, a little packing and her face hidden she was a man to the casual observer, and she never let you see her clearly.'

'No,' Amy mused, 'she didn't. But what about Paris? How did they manage that?'

'In Paris it was your uncle, and they managed it because you told him where you were going. It needed little effort to find the Martell offices, wait and then follow you.'

Amy nodded and sat in silence for a while. She had told Peter too much and he had used it all against her.

'Why did they bring their plans forward so suddenly?' Ann wanted to know.

'Because I very nearly caught the watcher,' Luc said quietly. 'I was staying here and Amy went to stay at her uncle's. We arranged a quite elaborate plan for her to leave and me to get in without being seen. I came down the back service road. It was

380

very good for them, or so they thought, because Amy saw the man at her uncle's place and Jensen pretended that he saw nobody there, convincing her it was imagination.'

'So how did you come to nearly get him?' Ann asked in a puzzled voice.

'I stayed one night when Amy was too upset to go to her uncle's house. In the night she saw him and alerted me.' He gave Amy a wry glance. 'I would have had him then, whichever one was playing the part at that time, but unfortunately my worried little companion had set the alarm. It warned him off.'

Amy blushed and Luc's parents looked at her indulgently. She was hoping that Luc would not go on to explain that he had jumped naked out of her bed to try to catch the man. He might just do it. He was French after all.

'That was the night they decided to speed things up,' Luc continued, to Amy's vast relief. 'In the first place the watcher saw me, and in the second place we had been careless with the cars. They knew I had seen too much and they knew that there was little chance of convincing Amy that she was steadily going mad. They had to act swiftly and they did.'

'Too swiftly,' Henri muttered with a frown.

'Yes,' Luc said regretfully. 'I underestimated them and Amy was in great danger. Already her uncle had seen my Porsche and become a little suspicious. When I chased out to get the man they had to act fast, because now *I* knew it was not Amy's imagination.'

'It could all have worked,' Amy said with a shudder. 'Seeing the man put me under a lot of stress. At one time I didn't know where to turn.'

'You turned to me, *ma petite*,' Luc said, holding her closely. 'It was natural.'

'I didn't even like you!' Amy protested.

'You were obviously confused about your feelings. The moment your feelings became clear you fell in love with me.'

'What,' Amy asked haughtily, 'gave you that peculiar idea?'

'I was allowed to ride on your pink cloud. I know that the privilege is not given to others. It was all the proof I needed.'

'That seems to be a reasonable assumption,' Amy said, managing to stifle a giggle. Her face suddenly fell and she looked sad.

'What is it, Amy?' Luc's mother asked quickly.

'I shouldn't be happy,' Amy pointed out quietly. 'There are two people in prison and Aunt Celia died.'

'None of this was your fault, Amy,' Henri Martell said firmly. 'You could have been a victim and in many ways you were. This has changed your life a good deal.'

Amy nodded, and after a few seconds she looked up and smiled.

'Something good came out of it,' she reminded them.

'What was that, *ma petite*?' Luc asked.

'You,' Amy told him, looking into his dark eyes and smiling her brilliant smile. It took his breath away.

Ann stood and signalled to Henri.

'It is time to leave,' she stated firmly. 'Amy needs sleep and I am rather tired myself.'

She glanced at her son with Amy, and Henri took the point at once.

'I will take your car again,' he told Luc. 'When you are ready to come back to the flat perhaps you can borrow Amy's car?'

'Fine,' Luc assured him with an amused grin. 'I will borrow Amy's car – if I come back to the flat. Do not, however, expect me. She should not be left.'

'Of course,' Henri agreed solemnly, containing his amusement with difficulty.

When they had gone, Luc looked at Amy and then stood, pulling her to her feet and into his arms.

'I will not make love to you tonight,' he said resolutely.

'Nobody asked you,' Amy pointed out, her cheeks flushing softly.

'It is just as well,' Luc murmured, sweeping her into his arms and carrying her up the stairs. 'You are not yet recovered and I am inflexible in my resolve.'

'I admire your strength of character,' Amy murmured with a little grin on her face.

Luc looked at her sternly.

'In my special unit in France I was coached in self-discipline,' he assured her. 'Such things became firmly fixed in the subconscious.'

Amy put her head on his shoulder and giggled, but when he put her down carefully on the bed and began to help her off with her robe her smile died, and she looked so saddened that his own happiness choked inside him.

'Oh, Luc,' she said softly. 'I thought they cared about me.'

'I know, *mon amour*,' he whispered, tucking her up in bed and sitting beside her to stroke her hair. 'It is very bad for you but it will pass. You have my mother and father to take their place and you have me. I love you, *chérie*.'

'I love you too, Luc,' Amy sighed, closing her eyes and snuggling down to sleep.

'Then we will be happy,' he promised, 'and all this will one day seem like a dream, far from you. There will be your own family to love you too.'

He sat watching her but she was already asleep, his Computer Person. Luc smiled and after a while he undressed and slid carefully into bed beside her. She was safe at last. She could sleep through the night with no fear. He drew her gently into his arms and soon he slept too. There would be no watcher in the night ever again.

By the time morning came, Amy was feeling much stronger. She awoke in Luc's arms and although he merely smiled at her, kissed her and then got up to make breakfast, he was there. He had been there beside her all night. He loved her. He had said it and Luc always meant what he said. Besides, she could see it in his eyes.

She was dreading the day, but not with the deep sadness she had expected. Breakfast with Luc would be a time of persistent lecturing as he tried to bring her mind round to facing this, but she already knew that she must face it. There was a terrible feeling of betrayal but also there was love, Luc's love, and the affection of his mother and father.

When she went to make her statement they all went with her – a tight family group and she was at the centre of it. As to Peter and Jill, Amy never wanted to face them again. It was all over.

They didn't go straight back to Amy's house. Luc's parents wanted to see the house Aunt Celia had left her and now she could face it without fear or sadness.

'I think we will keep it,' Luc murmured as his parents walked round the house and left them for a while in the hall. 'It will be our English country house.'

'Aunt Celia would have liked that,' Amy told him with a smile. 'She was quite a snob. It would please her to know that we had something you call an English country house.'

'We will live in Paris, of course,' Luc informed her imperiously.

'Oh, but . . .' Amy began, and Luc sighed in resignation.

'You may take your computer friends with you. The firm will buy others for the English office.'

'That's all right, then,' Amy said, pleased and showing it. Luc grinned down at her.

'My parents will want us to be close to them, *chérie*. They are very fond of their English daughter-in-law.'

'I'm not that yet,' Amy pointed out.

'You will be,' Luc murmured, kissing her deeply. 'And it had better be soon. I am suffering.' He looked down into her eyes. 'No more sadness, Amy. We will leave all this fear behind. You will have your own family to love you.'

Amy nodded and leaned against his shoulder. She did not want to see either Peter or Jill. They were the past. They had to be. Luc was the future and after a while all the sadness would go.

Four months later, Luc stood in the bedroom of their house just outside Paris and watched Amy getting dressed for an evening out with his parents. His mind was skimming over the day, remembering how his mother had breezed into the Paris office of Martell International and collected Amy.

'Amy and I have planned a shopping trip,' she'd told Luc and his father imperiously. 'She needs some glamorous clothes for – maternity purposes.'

'Nobody could possibly tell yet,' Luc had stated a trifle irritatedly, his eyes travelling possessively over Amy's still slender figure. 'We need her here. She is extremely busy.'

'We are not about to wait until the last minute,' Ann Martell had insisted. 'All will be normal for a while, and then one day without warning – *poof*! Nothing will fit.'

Luc and his father had glanced at each other and acknowledged defeat. Amy was in the middle of a difficult project and they had both been hovering over her intently, waiting for the finished framework to come up on screen.

Now she was methodically closing down, and apart from the fact that nobody else could do the work, nobody else would be able to open up the machines. Jim, Alfie and the 'boys' had been brought from England when Luc and Amy moved to Paris, and she still kept all their secrets protected.

'I have not yet seen these garments for – maternity purposes,' Luc murmured now, as he stood in their bedroom and watched her intently. He was dressed already and Amy glanced at him through the mirror as she finished off her preparations.

Although she was still in her satin slip, Luc looked extremely handsome in dinner jacket and black tie.

'I put them away,' she said. 'There'll be time enough to see them when they're needed.'

'When things suddenly go *poof*?' Luc enquired with a grin.

Amy frowned through the mirror.

'It's early days yet,' she pointed out.

She reached to get her dress and Luc's eyes fell on her shadow against the wall. It reminded him of the night long ago when he had first seen that erotic shadow dance, and his body felt the same reaction. He walked to the phone and dialled his parents' house.

'What are you doing?' Amy asked, her hands stilled on her dress.

'I am telling my mother that we will be late.'

'But we won't be!'

'Believe me, *chérie*, we will be very late,' Luc assured her, with a searing glance at her that almost made her heart stop.

'Amy needs a little rest,' he told his mother. 'We will join you at the restaurant. No, she is perfectly well,' he added before he put the phone down.

'This is too much, Luc,' Amy said breathlessly as he walked towards her, his dark eyes gleaming.

'Not yet, *mon amour*,' he told her thickly as he swept her off her feet and into his arms. 'But I have great confidence in you.'

THE EXCITING NEW NAME
IN WOMEN'S FICTION!

PLEASE HELP ME TO HELP YOU!

Dear *Scarlet* Reader,

As Editor of *Scarlet* Books I want to make sure that the books I offer you every month are up to the high standards *Scarlet* readers expect. And to do that I need to know a little more about you and your reading likes and dislikes. So please spare a few minutes to fill in the short questionnaire on the following pages and send it to me.

Looking forward to hearing from you,

Sally Cooper

Editor-in-Chief, *Scarlet*

QUESTIONNAIRE

Please tick the appropriate boxes to indicate your answers

1 Where did you get this Scarlet title?
Bought in supermarket ☐
Bought at my local bookstore ☐ Bought at chain bookstore ☐
Bought at book exchange or used bookstore ☐
Borrowed from a friend ☐
Other (please indicate) _____

2 Did you enjoy reading it?
A lot ☐   A little ☐   Not at all ☐

3 What did you particularly like about this book?
Believable characters ☐   Easy to read ☐
Good value for money ☐   Enjoyable locations ☐
Interesting story ☐   Modern setting ☐
Other _____

4 What did you particularly dislike about this book?
_____

5 Would you buy another Scarlet book?
Yes ☐   No ☐

6 What other kinds of book do you enjoy reading?
Horror ☐   Puzzle books ☐   Historical fiction ☐
General fiction ☐   Crime/Detective ☐   Cookery ☐
Other (please indicate) _____

7 Which magazines do you enjoy reading?
1. _____
2. _____
3. _____

And now a little about you –
8 How old are you?
Under 25 ☐   25–34 ☐   35–44 ☐
45–54 ☐   55–64 ☐   over 65 ☐

cont.

9 What is your marital status?

Single ☐   Married/living with partner ☐
Widowed ☐   Separated/divorced ☐

10 What is your current occupation?

Employed full-time ☐   Employed part-time ☐
Student ☐   Housewife full-time ☐
Unemployed ☐   Retired ☐

11 Do you have children? If so, how many and how old are they?

_____

_____

12 What is your annual household income?

under $15,000	☐	or	£10,000	☐
$15–25,000	☐	or	£10–20,000	☐
$25–35,000	☐	or	£20–30,000	☐
$35–50,000	☐	or	£30–40,000	☐
over $50,000	☐	or	£40,000	☐

Miss/Mrs/Ms _____

Address _____

_____

_____ Postcode: _____

Thank you for completing this questionnaire. Now tear it out – put it in an envelope and send it, before 31 July 1998, to:

Sally Cooper, Editor-in-Chief

USA/Can. address
SCARLET c/o London Bridge
85 River Rock Drive
Suite 202
Buffalo
NY 14207
USA

UK address/No stamp required
SCARLET
FREEPOST LON 3335
LONDON W8 4BR
Please use block capitals for address

ADARK/1/98

Scarlet titles coming next month:

THE MOST DANGEROUS GAME Mary Wibberley

Scarlet is delighted to announce the return to writing of this very popular author! 'Devlin' comes into Catherine's life when she is in need of protection and finds herself in that most clichéd of all situations – she's fallen in love with her bodyguard! The problem is that Devlin will leave when the job's over . . . won't he?

DANGEROUS DECEPTION Lisa Andrews

Luis Quevedo needs a fiancée in a hurry to please his grandfather. Emma fits the bill and desperately needs the money. Then she makes the mistake of falling in love with her 'fiancé' . . .

CRAVEN'S BRIDE Danielle Shaw

For ten years, Max Craven has blamed Alison for the death of his daughter. Now he returns home and finds his feelings for Alison have undergone a transformation. Surely he can't be in love with her?

BLUE SILK PROMISE Julia Wild

When Nick recovers consciousness after a serious accident, he finds himself married within days. Nick can't believe he's forgotten the woman he loves so passionately. Then little by little, he begins to realize that his beloved Kayanne thinks he's his own brother!